A NOVEL

CHRONICLES OF NICKY SPADE

BOOK 3: ADMIT ONE

CHRONICLES OF NICKY SPADE

BOOK 3: ADMIT ONE

JANICE WILLIAMS
AND TRACEY SCHUMANN

Primix Publishing
11620 Wilshire Blvd
Suite 900, West Wilshire Center, Los Angeles, CA, 90025
www.primixpublishing.com
Phone: 1-800-538-5788

Published by Primix Publishing   04/12/2022

ISBN: 978-1-957676-14-2(sc)
ISBN: 978-1-957676-15-9(e)

Library of Congress Control Number: 2022905569

CONTENTS

"Music on a cloudy day can bring sunshine to the soul."
Janice Williams

PROLOGUE

It seemed the old saying, *time heals all wounds*, held no truth for Nicole Hampton. She had lost too much. Her father, famous rock icon Nicky Spade, had been laid to rest without her knowing him. Leaving behind his music, memorabilia, and legendary stories, it had to carry her for a lifetime. Later his beautiful wife, Jenna, would be buried beside him.

Even though Nicole had endured more than her share of tragedies, life still held a few beautiful moments. First, she discovered her brother, Cameron, with whom she shared many similarities. Then, she met Drew, the love of her life. Soon afterward, Nicole and Drew welcomed their first child, Nicholas. Given his grandfather's name, Nicholas mirrored his image. However, Nicole still felt restless. The urgency to do something different, something outside of the box, consumed her. It would only take one phone call, one more tragic turn of events, for her to finally know her real purpose.

Her date with destiny set her on a path to stardom, not much unlike that of her famous father. There were only two questions she asked herself. First, "Was there room at the top for a female?" Second, "Would she ever be considered a viable member of the elitists' men's club?" Nicole Hampton would stop at nothing until she reached the pinnacle of success.

CHAPTER ONE

The Call

Screams resonated from the living room. Drew immediately rushed in, finding Nicole huddled on the floor. He panicked, fearing the worst.

"Babe, for heaven's sake, what's wrong?"

"Oh, Drew, Jerry just called. It's Bruce. He passed away last night."

Kneeling beside Nicole, he held her in his arms. She was inconsolable. Bruce had managed the band Black Tie Affair for many years. Upon discovering her talented father, Nicky Spade, Bruce had been credited for putting him on a path to stardom. Having no family of his own, Bruce had always considered the band members of his extended family and treated them as such. Nicole, never having known her biological father thought of Bruce as a dad. Drew realized his loss would be devastating. Bruce had supported Nicole and her mother, Kate, through many hardships.

"Sweetheart, Bruce was very sick. Considering that he was living in a care facility for people with Alzheimer's, don't you think it was probably for the best? His quality of life had greatly diminished. I couldn't imagine living one day under those difficult circumstances,"

Drew explained sympathetically. Picking Nicole up, his muscular arms flexed, causing a ripple across his tattoos as he carried her to the sofa.

"I know how much you loved him. We all did. He was one hell of a guy," Drew said softly as he gently laid her down. "I'm going to warm a washcloth and bring you a glass of water." He pulled back strands of her long black hair away from her blue eyes and wiped her forehead.

"Babe, please don't cry. Sit up and drink a few sips of water. Finally, Bruce is reunited with Nicky and Jenna. You know how much he loved those two. Did Jerry mention how your Mom was taking the news?"

"Not very good. I could hear Mom crying in the background."

"Well, if it will make you feel any better, why don't we take Nicholas and go up to their suite."

Continuing to wipe her face, Drew looked down at her attentively with his piercing green eyes. His heart ached for her. "Your mom's suite is only a few floors up. I'll get Nicholas ready." Kate, Nicole's mother, and her husband, Jerry, stayed in the same hotel.

"Okay," Nicole said, wiping her eyes as she got up from the sofa.

A few moments later, Jerry, Nicole's stepfather, heard a knock at the door. Standing in the forefront outside the door was Drew sporting a black Mohawk and Nicole, who was weeping as she held Nicholas, their two-year-old son.

"Hey Jerry, Nicole wanted to come over and check on Kate. How's she taking the news?"

"Come in. Kate's taking it pretty hard. She's in the bedroom." Opening the door wider, he stepped back, allowing them to enter. As Nicole walked past, Jerry put an arm around her shoulders, giving it a gentle squeeze. Then, leaning down to kiss her forehead, he whispered, "I'm so sorry I had to break this to you over the phone, but I was afraid to leave your mom."

"Sweetheart, do you want me to take Nicholas so you can go in and sit with Kate?" Drew suggested quietly.

"No. I'll keep him with me."

Nicole unconsciously tightened her grip on her small son. He was a source of strength, and she would need him to help her through the difficult moment. Then, making her way down the dim hallway, she followed the muffled cries from one of the bedrooms. Nicole opened the door quietly, finding Kate weeping with her head buried in a pillow.

"Hey, Mom," Nicole whispered. "I can't believe Bruce is gone."

Sitting at the edge of the bed, she laid Nicholas next to his grandmother and leaned over to hug her mom.

Kate peeked out from her pillow, her tousled black curls sticking to her wet cheeks. With a ragged breath, she slowly smiled, "Oh honey, he was in bad health. It's just so hard to lose someone like Bruce. He loved you. You do know that right?" she asked, giving her daughter a gentle kiss on the forehead.

"Mom, I know. Where's Cameron? Does he know?"

"Yes. He's on his way over with the guys." Kate sat up and propped herself against the head of the bed, admiring her grandson, who was crawling toward her.

Nicole had recently discovered she had a half-brother from her biological father's first and only marriage. However, she had only been made aware of this fact by her mother after his death. Cameron, her half-brother, was the lead singer in his band, House of Cards. They were all currently on tour promoting the band and trying to help Cameron build his legend apart from his father. It certainly helped that he had inherited his father's handsome Italian features. His olive complexion, dark hair, and tall, muscular build made him very popular with the girls. The only attribute he inherited from his mother was his azure blue eyes.

As fate would have it, Nicole had fallen in love with Drew, the lead guitarist in House of Cards. Drew was a little older than the other band members. However, he was the best guitarist Bruce had ever come across since discovering Nicky Spade. Nicholas, their son, was born shortly afterward. He was undeniably another genetic twin of his grandfather.

On tour now with House of Cards, it had truly become a family affair with the addition of Jerry and Kate. Jerry, Nicky's cousin, was also a former band member of Black Tie Affair. Having worked as the band's stylist, Kate had fallen madly in love with Nicky Spade. After a twist of fate, Nicky had been catapulted to the status of a world-renowned rock icon. Their steamy love affair had resulted in Nicole's conception.

After the untimely death of the legendary Nicky Spade, it brought life to a new generation of ambitious and talented artists.

Jerry walked over to the bar to make a drink as Drew lounged back on the sofa.

"What are your thoughts as far as a funeral goes?" Drew questioned.

"Well, I wanted to wait until everyone was together to discuss my ideas. We were the only family Bruce had except for his nephew, Jeff, and I haven't heard from him in years." Stopping to reminisce, Jerry ran his hand through his clean-cut, salt and pepper hair. "Unfortunately, I have no way to contact him." After pouring himself a glass of Jack Daniels, he walked over and sat across from Drew. Pulling the coffee table closer, he put his short legs on top and pulled out his cigarettes, careful not to spill his drink.

"That's too bad. Bruce was one of a kind. He defined the word *gentleman*. It's so hard to believe he's gone. As our manager, Bruce was a huge part of this band and the world we live in," Drew replied, staring at the ceiling as he contemplated their loss. After discovering Nicky Spade, Bruce had changed the lives of so many people while pushing him to the top. In a real sense, none of them would be where they were today had it not been for Bruce Weber.

"Believe me, I know. My thoughts are to have Bruce cremated. I want to take his ashes and scatter them as he would have wanted. But, I don't want to make another trip to Michigan. He deserves so much more. Middleton was fine for Nicky and Jenna, but I don't see him wanting to be there." Jerry wiped tears away from his eyes with the back of his hand. "I loved that man."

"I know," Drew smiled compassionately, getting up to answer the knock at the door. Standing outside was a small gang of handsome young men, with Cameron standing tall at the forefront. Covered in bizarre tattoos and sporting Mohawks, their appearance made it easy to know they were members of a punk rock band.

"Hey guys, come in. I guess you've all heard the unfortunate news regarding Bruce." Drew opened the door wide to let all the boys inside. They strutted in and immediately parted in different directions while each gave Drew a sad ceremonious nod of their heads. Some headed straight for the bar. No surprise there. However, Cameron and Harry headed toward Jerry, their manager, sitting in the living room.

"Yes, we've heard. That's why we're here. So how's everyone coping with his sudden loss?" Cameron asked while combing his fingers through the length of his brightly colored Mohawk.

"Well, as good as can be expected." Drew shrugged, waving them over to the white leather sofas.

"Hey Jerry, I hated to hear about Bruce. What are your plans? Do you have the plane ready to take us back to Vancouver?" Harry asked, plopping down on the matching leather chair, hands on each armrest as he crossed his legs. Harry was the drummer for House of Cards and the most boisterous.

Jerry scanned the dim hallway to ensure Kate and Nicole were still in the back bedroom, "Why don't you guys follow me outside to the balcony? If they walk out, I don't want to discuss this in front of the girls. Harry, grab a few bottles of beer before you come out."

Jerry walked outside and leaned against the balcony's railing as he lit another cigarette. Pausing for a brief moment, he gazed at the incredible views of the harbor while taking a slow sip of his drink, savoring the taste. Inwardly, the news was killing him. However, he had to remain strong. He could never allow himself to be vulnerable in front of the guys. Bruce had been a legend in the music industry, and Jerry knew he wouldn't be where he was today without him.

"Hey Harry, throw me a bottle of beer. Jerry, can I bum one of those smokes from you?" Drew asked. Jerry continued to stare off into the distance contemplating the loss of Bruce. Finally, moments later, he was brought back from his deep thoughts.

"Sure, need a lighter?" he offered, searching his pocket as he took a long drag.

"Yes, thanks, man," Drew answered, scarcely catching the beer Harry tossed before it slipped through his hands.

Jerry turned around to ensure the boys were nearby and the girls were still absent. "Well, guys, we will finish our commitment in New Zealand," he paused briefly. "Odd, isn't it? Bruce was here in Auckland when he received his diagnosis of Alzheimer's. Now here we are again, two years later, and we get the news that he's gone. We made our way through those difficult days. We'll do it again," Jerry continued searching his pocket for the lighter. He handed it to Drew along with his pack of cigarettes.

"Jerry, however, you want to handle this, we're all behind you," Cameron said softly, cupping his hand to buffer the wind as he lit his cigarette.

"Yeah, man, Cameron's right," Doug agreed while leaning an elbow against the rail. He was the other bass guitarist for the band.

"Thanks, guys. I knew I could count on you. As soon as our gig is finished, we'll fly back to Vancouver. We'll take Bruce's remains and make one stop before our next venue to scatter his ashes. I'm thinking Hawaii. Bruce sure loved those islands. It was one of his favorite places, so we'll say our final good-byes on Oahu. What are your thoughts?"

"That sounds nice. I think Bruce would approve," Cameron mentioned flipping his wind-swept hair away from his eyes.

Jerry extinguished his cigarette on the railing tossing the butt over the side.

"Okay. I'm going inside to check on Kate and Nicole now. There are plenty of drinks in the fridge. Cameron, why don't you call room service and order a few pizzas for everybody. I would suggest we all go out to eat in honor of Bruce, but I don't think the girls feel up to it at the moment."

"Okay, man, that sounds good. We don't have to be on stage until 8:00 tonight, so there's plenty of time to enjoy a few pizzas," Cameron mentioned, following Jerry back into the warmth of the room.

Jerry approached the bedroom door cautiously and was surprised to hear laughter coming from inside.

"Hey, Babe, how are you feeling? I'm so glad that you've both stopped crying," Jerry smiled, sitting down on the bed next to Nicholas. "Bruce wouldn't want either of you to be sad. He loved life and lived it to the fullest. You both know that. Cameron has ordered pizza. It should be here soon. I'll take this handsome guy into the living room," Jerry grinned, picking Nicholas up. "Grandpa is going to get his little man some apple juice."

"Thanks, Jerry, there's a juice bottle in the diaper bag. Mom, I love you. No more crying. Let's go eat pizza with the guys."

"Okay, Sweetheart. Pizza sounds good." Kate answered, trying to force a smile as she got out of bed.

Making their way into the living room, Nicole caught sight of Cameron. Rushing over, she wrapped her arms around him. "Hey Sis, how are you holding up?" Cameron asked as he leaned back, staring into her eyes.

Nicole hesitated for a second, thinking of all the good things Bruce had done for her. She knew this was not something you get over. She would always miss him and think of him throughout her life. But, she also knew that her tears would upset her mother even more. Bruce was such a huge part of their life, and they would miss him terribly.

"I'll be all right. It's just hard losing Bruce, but mom and I will be okay," Nicole replied, keeping her tears at bay.

After room service had delivered their order, everyone sat in the living room enjoying pizza and beer. Jerry had a few more glasses of Jack Daniels while everyone took turns reminiscing about Bruce.

"Okay. Does everyone have a drink? I want to make a toast to Bruce," Jerry announced.

"Here's to Bruce. He'll never be forgotten. We're only here because of him. He loved everyone in this room, and his dedication, hard work, and abilities were legendary. Bruce could sell out arenas before our names went on the marquee. So, Bruce, here's to you. We love you."

CHAPTER TWO

Contemplating a Dream

Taking a deep breath, Nicole sat back in her leather seat as their private jet lifted off the runway of the Honolulu International Airport. The past two days had been difficult. It had not been easy for them to say their final goodbyes to Bruce. For her especially, the grieving process had somehow resurrected extraordinary memories. Memories that now haunted her and which she hadn't shared with Drew. If he knew, certainly he would think she had gone mad. However, it seemed the perfect time to test the waters. Nicole glanced around the cabin. The guys were all zoned out, wearing headphones while listening to their favorite tunes. Nicholas had fallen asleep in between Kate and Jerry. They had chosen to sit with him in the back of the aircraft. Nicole needed to talk with someone regarding her plans, and Drew seemed the perfect candidate.

Reaching over, she took his hand. "Babe, something has been weighing heavily on my mind. I don't know how to explain it or where to start."

"Well, the beginning would be a good place," he smiled teasingly.

"Please don't make light of what I'm about to tell you. Losing

Bruce hasn't been easy. However, it's given me a reason to reflect on my time with him. Also, the many long talks we shared when I was younger," Nicole paused, unsure how he would react to what she was about to say. "What would you think if I told you I wanted to follow in his footsteps?"

Drew shifted in his seat, staring intently at Nicole. "What do you mean?"

Nicole hesitated, "I think I would love to do Bruce's old job. Before we met, he was grooming me as a band manager for years. I chose modeling at the time because it was so easy to fall into."

Drew sat back in his seat, utterly confused. Where was this coming from, he wondered?

"What are you talking about?" he asked, feeling hurt. "Are you wanting to search for other bands to manage? Where would you even start to do something like that?" he questioned again, completely confused.

Nicole hesitated. "Jerry has mentioned to me confidentially that this will be his last tour." She waited to hear his thoughts suspecting this conversation wasn't going her way by the expression on his face.

Drew took a long pause to process what she had just said. After a moment, he could feel his anger bubbling up to the surface. He turned to her look at her closely.

"Are you telling me you want to become the band's new manager? Look, Doll, that's a mighty demanding business. I love you, but female managers are practically unheard of in this business. Seriously, do you know what you're saying?" Drew quizzed with a profound stare. What was she thinking? Certainly, she didn't think she could be his boss and manage him at home and work.

"Well, that's just what I expected. I knew you wouldn't understand," Nicole snapped back, letting go of his hand. Suddenly feeling the sting of tears fill her eyes, she turned to look out the window. She wouldn't give him the satisfaction of seeing her cry.

"Sweetheart, Bruce was talented," Drew said delicately, tempering his words as he leaned over. "That man not only knew how to sell tickets and fill seats, he knew this business better than anyone I've ever known."

"So you think I'm not smart enough. You think being a woman is a handicap," Nicole scoffed, reaching into her purse for a tissue to catch the tears welling within her eyes.

"No. Doll, it isn't that at all. Listen to me. The music industry is brutal," Drew remarked, trying to pull her close to him. "The guys and I have the easy part. We walk out on stage each night and perform, something we love to do. Bruce and Jerry, well, Jerry, now that Bruce has passed, have always had the hard part. Jerry has always worked tirelessly to keep us at the top of the charts and booked every week. Do you even know the effort it takes to plan and schedule a world tour?" Curiously, he searched her face. He wondered how she would do this with their child. What was she thinking? He slowly realized they had never discussed precisely how their roles would work. He had assumed she wanted to be with their son and simply be a mom. Obviously, she had not thought it through. He needed to try and nip this in the bud, so he decided to plow ahead.

"Babe, I'm not saying you don't have what it takes, but what about Nicholas, he's so young, and I know we haven't talked. But I want more children," he pressed gently. "I want him to have brothers and sisters. You were an only child. You know what that's like. Babe, I love you. Honestly, I do. Please, just take some time and think about everything. Now stop being silly, and come over here. Let me kiss those tears away," he winked.

Nicole turned to look at him intently as she pushed him back with her manicured nails. What the hell? They had never discussed having more kids. She had assumed he wouldn't want any more children, especially living on the road and everything that entailed. She had not considered how she would feel about having another child, particularly this soon. She had easily given up so much of her career to follow Drew and support him. When she needed his support, he would deny her what she felt was due to her. Feeling an inner rage, she did her best to calm her voice.

"Drew, you're going to eat those words one day. Babe, you have no idea how serious I am. I gave up a career in modeling to be with you. I love Nicholas, and if it's more babies you want, that's not a problem,"

Nicole smirked. "Babe, believe me, I can chew gum and walk at the same time. You'll see," she fumed, quickly getting out of her seat to check on Nicholas.

For the rest of their flight into Singapore, it seemed relatively quiet. Drew was sure she had just suffered a moment of temporary insanity due to her grief. But, on the other hand, Nicole was sure he would soon regret every chauvinist remark he had just made.

Nicole was anxious to settle into their hotel upon arrival at the Singapore Changi Airport. Jerry had reserved suites at the luxurious Imperial Hotel. Watching out her window as the limo parked next to the jet, she walked to the back of the plane.

"Mom, I'll take Nicholas. Drew is getting our carry-on bags," she mentioned, gently reaching to take the sleeping child from his grandmother.

"Oh, he's fine, we've got him," Kate said, quickly pushing her away with her hands. "He slept most of the way, but I'm afraid he will be wide awake and full of energy when we arrive at the hotel."

"That's okay. Drew will stay up with him while I get a few hours of sleep." That'll teach him. He needs to learn to take care of Nicholas. She thought, laughing to herself.

Once inside the limo and on their way downtown, Drew took Nicole's hand and kissed it lovingly. He felt terrible about their earlier fight. However, he was confident that she would rethink the consequences of such a job and change her mind given enough time. So he decided he would make it easier for her to admit she was wrong and help her save face.

"Babe, I'm sorry for what I said earlier," he whispered. "Trust me. If you're serious, I'll support your dreams. I love you. I don't want to see you get hurt. This industry can be vicious," Drew added, giving her a gentle kiss.

Nicole knew better than to think he would support her at this point. However, she was jet-lagged and tired and had no desire to continue the argument.

"Thanks. That means a lot to me. I love you too," she answered quietly, reaching inside the diaper bag for a Sippy cup. The rest of the drive was quiet.

After getting settled into their new temporary residence, Nicole got some much-needed rest while Drew entertained the little man in his life. The band had three more concerts scheduled before their next venue, Hong Kong.

"Good morning, Sunshine," Drew winked, pulling back the drapes.

"Wow. You seem to be in a great mood," Nicole smiled, stretching her arms as she pulled herself out of bed. She put on her silk robe and walked into the adjoining room to check on Nicholas.

"Why shouldn't I be?" he answered, relieved things were finally going back to normal. "Oh, I forgot to mention, your Mom called while you were sleeping last night."

Nicholas looked like an angel asleep in his bed. He's going to be such a little heartbreaker, Nicole thought. Nicholas was the mirror image of his late grandfather, Nicky Spade, with his wavy black hair and sparkling blue eyes.

"Oh yeah. What did she want?" Nicole softly whispered, closing the sleeping child's door.

"She's going downtown to get in a little shopping this morning and wanted to know if you wanted to tag along. So she said she would stop by around 9:00 a.m.," Drew said, sauntering into the kitchen shirtless and barefoot. His blue jeans barely hung on his hips, exposing his ripped abdominal muscles. He was pouring a cup of coffee for her when she walked in with her tousled dark hair. Nicole was a rare breed of woman who looked stunning first thing in the morning with no makeup.

"Sure. What time is it? Would you mind watching Nicholas?" she yawned, reaching for her coffee cup.

"Of course, I'll watch Nicholas," Drew winked. "I think rehearsals start at 5:00 p.m. this evening. So you'll have plenty of time to shop. Do you want me to arrange a limo for you girls, or are you brave enough to wing it on your own?" he asked, leaning back against the counter, eyeing her seductively.

"Drew, it's Singapore. It wouldn't be as exciting if we took the limo.

I'm jumping in the shower. Why don't you call room service and order breakfast? Oh, and please listen for Nicholas. He's still sleeping," Nicole answered, oblivious to Drew's intentions.

"Oh, so our little guy is asleep, is he?" Drew teased. Quickly scooping Nicole into his arms, he playfully tossed her over his shoulder and carried her back toward the bedroom.

"Babe, it's almost 8:00 a.m. What are you thinking?" she giggled, his intentions dawning on her.

"Well, not about the time, that's for sure," Drew winked.

Later that morning, Kate and Nicole made their way through the busy downtown streets. Singapore appeared a perfect dichotomy, a mixture of old and new buildings. It incorporated small shops scattered along the narrow streets. Juggling their shopping bags precariously on both arms, Kate suggested stopping for lunch. The aromas coming from a nearby noodle stall were overwhelmingly delicious. The stalls were the equivalent of an open-air café. Walking in, they ordered the perfect Singapore snack. It consisted of curry laksa, spicy noodle soup with bean curd puffs, fish sticks, and hot milk tea. Sitting outside, they leisurely enjoyed the exotic ambiance of the local area and its cuisine with their bags snuggled and secured underneath their table.

Nicole thought it would be an excellent time to approach Kate about her ideas for managing the band. She probably should have approached her first, she thought. Her mother had always been bold and independent. If anyone supported her and her endeavors, it would be her mom. However, Nicole needed to be very careful as Kate did not know about Jerry's looming retirement. Jerry had not discussed it with her yet as he knew there were only two things Kate loved most. First, being with her daughter and grandson, and the second was, traveling. Kate had been all over the world. He was still worried about how she would adapt to his retirement.

"Mom, after losing Bruce, I've thought about what I want to do with my life," Nicole said, sipping her tea as she carefully watched for her mother's expression.

"Well, that sounds serious. So what is it you want to do? Are you thinking of returning to your career in modeling?" Kate asked, not bothering to look up as she continued eating.

"No. I want to work with the band," Nicole answered, taking another sip of tea.

"Oh, you would make a great stylist. I've always loved my job," Kate squealed with delight, looking at Nicole. She had always dreamed her daughter one day would work side-by-side with her.

"No, Mom, not as a stylist. I want to work in management. Bruce always suggested that I would make a great manager one day," Nicole replied, staring intently at her mom.

"Wow. I never expected you to be interested in management or the desire to follow Bruce's career path. Have you talked to Jerry yet? Would you like to work with him?" Kate knew Jerry would be a great mentor. Next to Bruce, Jerry was considered to be an exceptional manager. He was able to step up after Bruce's diagnosis of Alzheimer's disease.

"Yes, I know. Trust me. I've given this a lot of thought. I discussed it with Drew yesterday during our flight coming into Singapore," Nicole grimaced, looking down as she stirred her hot tea.

"What did he think?" Kate inquired. Now she was paying attention to Nicole's expressions, trying to see where her daughter was going with this conversation.

"Well, to begin with, I think he was a bit shocked."

Nicole hesitated. She knew her mother would have no problem giving Drew a piece of her mind if she discovered he was anything less than supportive of her daughter. The last thing Nicole needed was for Drew and Kate to get into it when she needed both of their support. So she continued cautiously.

"Drew knows the music industry can be brutal. He also mentioned that there aren't many women in management. He was being chauvinistic. Then out of nowhere, he throws a bombshell at me. Apparently, he now wants more children."

"And you don't?" Kate questioned, looking confused and disappointed.

She had wondered when or if Nicole would give her another grandchild. However, she had decided early on to leave it to them to decide. She never saw herself as the nagging mother demanding grandkids.

"Mom, this isn't about how many children I want, for heaven's sakes. Sure I would love to give Nicholas a brother or sister or both. But this is what I want. Do you understand? Can't I do something for myself?" Nicole explained, feeling exasperated. "You know I love Nicholas. I would never do anything to hurt him. However, I've been restless since giving up modeling. I love being a mom. But I feel there's more to life. That's just one part of who I am," Nicole added, searching for her mother's approval.

"Nicole, if you're serious about this and it seems that you are, I will support you. I'm sure Drew will, too," Kate reassured her.

"Thanks, Mom. I was wondering how Jerry would take the news. Do you think he would be willing to show me the ropes, help me get my feet wet, so to speak? Jerry's done a great job with the band. It wasn't easy for him to take over from Bruce on such short notice. I've got a few ideas that I would like to discuss with him. I overheard the guys talking, and Drew told me that Doug is planning to leave the band," Nicole felt winded as she excitedly spilled out her plans. Finally, someone who would listen to her. She had so many great ideas about how to manage the band.

"Wait. Slow down. What did you say about Doug? Isn't he happy with his position?" Kate looked confused and was becoming agitated. It was apparent to Kate that Jerry had no idea Doug was leaving the band. Had Jerry known about Doug going, he would have told her. She knew managers had to stay on top of all of the information regarding band members. She knew from experience that if managers lose control of even one band member, you risk hurting the entire band. Hearing this was very troubling to hear.

"Oh, Mom, here you go again. There's life outside of belonging to a band. Doug is in love with Alondra. They're getting married. He's already given her an engagement ring," Nicole exclaimed. How was it even possible Kate hadn't seen this coming? Usually, her mom was good at reading people. Plus, she was missing the bigger picture here.

"What? Does Jerry know about this?" Kate asked, obviously frustrated as she leaned forward, resting both elbows on the table.

"No. That's Doug's personal life. He doesn't owe Jerry an explanation for everything he does. In fact, they're planning to be married when the band goes on hiatus at the end of the year. He's not coming back. His parents have just moved to Oahu, opened their own business, and his Dad is putting pressure on him to quit the band and move to Oahu permanently."

"Wow. I'm shocked. I can't believe Jerry doesn't know about this. Even worse, I can't believe Doug wouldn't tell him. Does he even understand the significance of him leaving?" Kate stated in disbelief.

She was beyond pissed at this point. Rubbing her forehead, she continued with her rant.

"This puts Jerry in a tight bind and a very stressful situation. You know your step-father is not getting any younger, and it's a lot of work to find a talented replacement in such a short period. But, honestly, what's wrong with young people these days? You need to talk to Doug. Better yet, Jerry and I will talk to Doug. That boy is going to get a serious piece of my mind."

"Well, maybe this is where I can help. Unfortunately, I don't have time to explain my ideas to you right now, but I have a plan," Nicole answered, glancing down at her watch, trying to calm Kate.

"Mom, you cannot say a word about this to Jerry. Do you understand? If this gets out before Doug is ready to make Jerry aware of his engagement or his plans to leave the band, it could get ugly. I don't want to be the one that causes hurt feelings between Doug and Jerry. But, please, you have to promise me," Nicole pleaded.

Their conversation had not gone quite the way she expected or was hoping. She had not realized her mom would be this upset. She had hoped she would have time to explain more of her plan in order to keep Kate from blowing her top.

"I'll think about it," Kate said grudgingly. "Do the rest of the guys know about this?" Her voice was stern, and it was apparent she was trying to keep her temper in check at this point.

"Yes," Nicole replied with a look that begged her mom to say nothing.

"Wow. I'm stunned. I cannot believe that Jerry doesn't know," Kate whispered frantically.

"Mom, we have to go. It's getting late. I need to get back in time to bathe Nicholas before leaving for the auditorium. We'll discuss this later, I promise. Please don't worry. I have a plan."

"Okay," Kate replied, grabbing her shopping bags. "But this isn't the end of this conversation. Jerry needs to know, and the sooner, the better."

Arriving back at the hotel, Nicole was exhausted.

Nichole walked in laden with shopping bags. Then, dumping them on the floor in the living room, she collapsed on the couch.

"So, did you and your Mom have fun shopping?" Drew asked, catching sight of Nicole from the balcony as he finished a cigarette.

"Yes. We did. You should see the shoes I found today. They're gorgeous." Nicole smiled, reaching down to pick up Nicholas. He squealed with delight at seeing his mom and snuggled in her lap. "What did you and Daddy do today while Mommy was away?" she asked, smothering him with hugs and kisses.

Drew came in, sliding the balcony door closed. The smell of fresh smoke permeated his clothes. "Oh, I read a few books to him. Then I decided to take him out in his stroller to get some fresh air. After that, I fed him lunch, and then, we took a short nap." Drew sat across from Nicole, propping his feet on the coffee table.

"Seems like you both had a full day. I'll watch him if you want to get dressed," Nicole mentioned letting the squirming baby down to play.

"That sounds good. I need to get a shower. Did you happen to tell your mom about your new career?" Drew inquired. He thought for sure Kate would be on his side. He knew deep down she wanted more grandkids. Undoubtedly, the idea of her daughter running around and leaving their son behind wouldn't sit well with her either. But, now, he felt confident that he wouldn't have to be the bad guy. Let her mother talk to her, he thought.

"Yes, but there's no time to discuss it now. Maybe after the concert tonight, we can go to dinner with them. What are the boys planning to do after the show?" Nicole asked, slipping off her sandals and curling her feet under her. She leaned back into the armrest, running her fingers through her long hair.

"Oh, I've reserved a small entertainment complex. It offers go-cart racing, pinball machines, and even bowling. Do you want to go?"

"Well, if Mom and Jerry will watch Nicholas. Maybe afterward, we can come back and have a late dinner. It would be a great time to continue our conversation with Mom and Jerry and discuss future possibilities. I've got an idea that I would like to discuss with him. What do you think? Are you up for a late dinner?" Nicole inquired, her eyes narrowing as she dared him to contradict her.

"Okay, Babe sounds good," Drew said, getting off the couch and walking into the bathroom. Damn, he thought Kate would have more consideration for her grandson's wellbeing. Maybe Grandma figured she would be raising him? Well, if he was going to have to be the bad guy, so be it. As he started a hot shower, he simply shook his head.

Nicole grabbed the remote and turned on the television while sitting on the couch. She flipped to a channel that caught her attention. A documentary of Nicky Spade was on detailing the rise and fall of his career. She thought of Cameron. He was extremely talented and already making a name for himself despite being in their father's shadow. She realized at that moment she wanted to have her own legacy. It now more than ever confirmed her desire to be part of this industry. Finally, she knew her decision was right.

CHAPTER THREE

Plan of Action

There was only one thing on Nicole's mind as she got out of bed the following day. Last night had not afforded her the chance to discuss her ideas with Jerry. Kate and Jerry had gone to bed early, leaving Nicole disappointed and anxious about discussing her plans with everyone. She needed to talk to Jerry about her ideas this morning before their schedules became hectic. She was determined to finally run her plan of action past him and get his thoughts.

She could hear Drew making noise in the kitchen as he made coffee. "Babe, have you ordered breakfast?" Nicole called out while dressing Nicholas in blue denim overalls.

"No. Not yet," Drew yelled back.

"I think I'll call Mom and ask if they would like to come over and eat breakfast with us," she loudly stated while trying to get Nicholas's cooperation as he bounced on the bed.

"Okay. Is there any particular reason?"

He knew what was coming. He began to pray hard it wouldn't be a repeat of their earlier discussion. He didn't relish an argument so early in the morning. However, he could become heated just thinking about Nicole's unrealistic expectations.

"To be brutally honest, I do have an agenda," Nicole said, walking into the living room. "You know I discussed the idea of becoming involved in management yesterday with Mom. But because it was late, we didn't have time to finish our discussion. I also made her aware that Doug is leaving the band at the end of this year."

"You did what?" Drew yelled, slamming his coffee cup on the counter. "Nicole, I don't freaking believe this."

"Oh, Drew, don't be so dramatic. I think you're overreacting."

"Babe, I only told you because I thought I could trust you," he vented, looking at her in complete disgust. "I didn't think you would tell anyone, especially discuss it with your mother. You do know that Jerry doesn't know. What were you thinking?"

"Geez. We're all family. What affects one of us sooner or later affects everyone. So I don't see the big deal at this point."

"Well, you might be right. However, I'm not sure Jerry is ready to face losing Doug, and shouldn't he be the one to tell him?" Drew continued as the volume of his voice began to rise.

"Maybe, but I've got a plan."

"A plan?" Drew shouted. "Babe, this better be good. You realize that you're not exactly working in management yet, right?" he asked, staring at her as if she had gone entirely crazy.

"Have a little faith. I've got a great idea. It will work for everyone except Doug because he wants out," Nicole continued, quickly becoming tired of his temper tantrum.

"Well, Babe, I can't wait to hear this," Drew sarcastically remarked, throwing his hands in the air. "I just hope Jerry likes this so-called plan of yours. I think your career could be in jeopardy before it gets off the ground, especially if he doesn't like what you have to say." Just then, a soft knock was heard at the door.

"Okay. Batter up. But, Doll, you better hit this out of the ballpark," Drew demanded angrily, walking back into the kitchen.

Nicole hesitated for just a brief moment before answering the door.

Then, she quickly gathered her thoughts, knowing the battle was beginning.

"Hey Mom, come in. Hey Jerry," Nicole smiled, giving them both a quick hug. "Drew, why don't you bring coffee out for everyone while I put Nicholas in his playpen? Mom, would you like to order room service for everyone?"

"Sure, what would you like? How about fruit and waffles?

"Oh, that sounds delicious," Nicole agreed. "Could you please add a carafe of orange juice and some extra coffee?"

"No problem. I'll call room service."

"Hey Nicholas, how's Grandpa's favorite little boy this morning?" Jerry smiled, walking over to the playpen for a quick hug. After putting the little man down, Jerry and Drew walked outside to the balcony to have a cigarette.

"So, what's this all about?" Jerry inquired, reaching into his pocket for a lighter.

"Well, I think I will let Nicole fill you in on all the details," Drew suggested lighting a Cuban cigar. Jerry looked inquisitively at the cigar and raised an eyebrow?

"When did you start smoking cigars?"

"Well, it just seemed appropriate this morning," Drew grinned. He was feeling feisty after the heated discussion between him and Nicole. Bruce was notorious for always smoking Cuban cigars. It seemed to be the one accessory he was never without.

"You want a drink? Perhaps something a little stronger than caffeine?" Drew asked, raising his brows once more. Now Jerry knew something was up. But, whatever it was wouldn't bode well.

"Okay, guys, breakfast has arrived. Come inside, and let's eat before it gets cold," Kate announced, sliding open the patio door.

Drew and Jerry walked back inside. The odor from the cigar permeated the room, and the smell produced a knee-jerk reaction from Nicole. Walking up, she punched Drew hard in his upper arm. He simply looked at her with a nonchalant attitude. Her little outburst didn't bother him. On the contrary, he inwardly smiled, knowing his joke had got her attention.

"So, Babe," she whispered. "You think that's funny? Are you deliberately trying to sabotage my talk with Jerry?" Nicole fumed.

"No, honestly, I swear I'm not. I thought it would be an amusing way to bring Bruce into the conversation without you girls becoming emotional. You want to join me?" Drew laughed, holding the cigar butt out to Nicole.

"Put that nasty thing out right now," Nicole demanded. "Oh, you just wait, this isn't over," Nicole insisted, grabbing the cigar butt and putting it in his coffee cup.

"Wow. Doll, you promise," Drew winked seductively. He was starting to think this fight might come with some benefits later. He had forgotten how sexy she was when she was mad. He walked into the kitchen and put the coffee cup in the sink.

"Is everything okay?" Kate questioned, overhearing bits of their conversation while noticing the menacing look on her daughter's face.

"Oh yes. I was reminding Drew that we don't smoke around Nicholas," Nicole answered, pasting a pleasant smile on her face.

As everyone enjoyed breakfast, she fed Nicholas and laid him in his crib for a morning nap.

"Okay, Sweetheart, Kate said you wanted to talk to me," Jerry mentioned pouring himself another cup of coffee. "I don't have long. I've got an appointment at the radio station later this morning. We're doing a promotional. I'm giving away some free tickets to a few lucky fans. I've got to keep those seats filled," Jerry grinned.

"Well, Jerry, that's kind of what I wanted to talk to you about." Nicole leaned forward, putting her elbows on the table.

"Oh, what's on your mind?" Then, staring at her inquisitively, Jerry sat back in his chair.

"I don't know where to start," Nicole paused, gathering her thoughts. "I guess it all started when I heard the tragic news about losing Bruce. You know how much he meant to Mom and me."

"Sure, Kate has told me. There'll never be another man like Bruce. He was such a gentleman in every sense of the word," Jerry answered, sitting forward as he placed his hand over hers.

"Well, Jerry, I think you're right about that. However, the keyword here is, *man*," she hinted.

"What? I don't think I'm following you?" Jerry squinted his eyes, becoming totally confused by her statement.

Hearing what she had to say, Drew began to feel bad about how he had reacted earlier. It was times like this that made him admire her tenacity. He was starting to see just how much this whole idea meant to her. He realized at that moment just how much like her father Nicole was. The stories of Nicky Spade's drive and ambition were downright legendary. He decided then he would do anything to support her.

"Jerry, I guess what I'm trying to say is," Nicole paused again, looking down as she pulled some of her loose hair behind her ear.

"Honey, I love you," Jerry spoke up. "What's on that sweet mind of yours?" he asked impatiently. "Remember, I don't have all day," he quickly reminded her.

"Okay, Jerry, I want to work with you in management. I want to become a manager, just like you and Bruce. I've thought about this a lot. I want this more than anything. Well, almost anything," she winked, looking over at Drew.

"Wow. I'll have to say you've caught me off guard. Are you saying that you're not going to continue pursuing your modeling career? I always figured you would be a famous model or stylist like your mom."

"You're right. I'm not interested in modeling anymore. Listen, Jerry, I love modeling, but I don't see it in my future. I crave the excitement and energy of being involved behind the scenes of our band, especially on a world tour. I know the hard work and commitment to schedule the venues, promote them, and sell tickets. I've watched you and Bruce over the years. He was a genius as well as a legend. We shared many long talks when I was younger. Bruce always told me he hoped I might decide to join him one day. He said he would love to help me get started in the industry. Just ask Mom. She knows," Nicole continued glancing at Kate.

"Yes. I'll have to admit Nicole is right. Bruce always encouraged her and reminded her that she could do anything. Perhaps she would want to follow him into the business one day," Kate smiled encouragingly.

"Jerry, you have no idea my passion for making this happen. In fact, I've got an idea or plan I wanted to discuss with you. So I'm going to climb out on a limb here. I hope I don't live to regret it," Nicole paused again, quickly weighing how he might react. "Doug plans to leave the band at the end of this tour." It only took a moment for the news to sink in as everyone sat around the breakfast table waiting for his reaction.

"What! How come I didn't know about this?" Jerry furiously demanded, scooting his chair back.

"Quiet Jerry, you'll wake Nicholas," Kate quickly reminded him, placing her hand gently on his knee.

"Drew, is she right? Is Doug planning to quit?" Jerry looked at Drew, hoping somehow he would contradict what Nicole had just said. Instead, Drew nodded with a sad look in his eyes. Jerry stood up and quickly grabbed his cigarettes. He steamed off in a fit of rage as he walked outside to the balcony.

"Yes. Jerry, calm down. Doug was going to tell you," Drew answered, following close behind him. "It has nothing to do with you or the band. He's simply in love with Alondra. They're going to get married, and the real reason he's quitting is that his parents recently moved to Oahu. They've opened a small rental business for tourists. His Dad wants him to move to Oahu and help get their business off the ground. I know this must be upsetting for you to hear, especially from Nicole. But, weirdly, it's her idea of telling you about a plan she has for the band," Drew continued. He hoped his words would help diffuse the dilemma Jerry faced.

It might be time for that drink you mentioned earlier," Jerry suggested gazing off into the distant skyline. Drew gently slapped him on his shoulder and headed inside to make them both something strong. Leaning his elbows on the railing, Jerry took a deep drag on his cigarette.

"Mom, would you please check on Nicholas. Then, I'm going to take some coffee outside to Jerry and Drew. Would you mind bringing the other carafe of coffee outside afterward?" Nicole asked pleadingly.

"Not a problem, but I think you better get out there and see what you can do. Jerry isn't taking the news about Doug very well. I told you this would happen," Kate reiterated.

"Don't worry. He hasn't heard my plans yet. I will make this right," Nicole said, pushing her chair back and standing up.

"Well, I sure hope your plans are spectacular. I hate to see Jerry this upset," Kate mentioned getting up to check on Nicholas.

Jerry was distraught, smoking like a chimney as Nicole walked outside with their hot coffee. His back was rigid, and she could see the strain on his face.

"Hey Jerry, I brought you and Drew a cup of coffee," Nicole smiled, handing him a cup. He looked down briefly before glancing up at the skyline.

"No, thanks, Sweetheart, Drew's getting me something a little stronger."

"Look, Jerry, it wasn't my idea to get you so upset. Believe me. I hadn't expected you to take the news this hard. Why don't we all sit down? Mom is checking on Nicholas, and then she's coming out with more coffee for everyone. I think you'll like what I've got to say."

"Well, Sweetheart, this better be damn good. I hate being left out of the loop. Do all the guys in the band know?" Jerry fumed, turning to look at her.

"Yes. Do you want me to wait for Mom, or go ahead and give you my thoughts?" Nicole inquired sheepishly.

"Don't see what your mom has to do with this. Think you better get on with it," Jerry seethed, taking another drag on his cigarette.

"Well," Nicole paused, trying to ensure she worded everything correctly.

"Nicole, I haven't got all day," Jerry insisted, visibly upset and frustrated.

"Okay, but for heaven's sake, calm down. You know this isn't the end of the world. It concerns Cameron," Nicole explained.

"Damn, I guess you're going to tell me he's quitting too," Jerry swore, stomping out his cigarette on the concrete with his shoe as he lit up another.

"No. Cameron doesn't have a clue about my ideas. Jerry, I want to make Cameron a solo artist. You know what a great voice he's got, and the girls love him. He has so many fans. You have to know that House of Cards has become such a huge hit in the industry because of him. Bruce worked hard to make sure the band stayed at the top, but Cameron is what's kept them there," Nicole smiled at Jerry reassuringly, reaching over to take his hand. "Listen, Jerry, I don't have to remind you that Cameron inherited Dad's talent and charisma," Nicole stated, searching Jerry's face.

"Wow, thanks, Babe. I suppose I'm just chopped liver. I never knew you thought so highly of my role in the band," Drew angrily interjected, stunned at overhearing their conversation as he walked up. Nicole turned around, slightly surprised to see Drew holding two glasses of bourbon. She had briefly forgotten he was coming back outside in her passionate discussion with Jerry.

Following behind with the carafe of hot coffee, Kate sat down, feeling the tension in the air.

"Nicholas is still sleeping. So what did I miss?" Kae asked, looking up at everyone.

"Well, Nicole has just made it pretty clear I'm not an important member of the band. So, I guess I'm definitely going to lose my job too," Drew seethed in a scornful voice giving Nicole a dirty look.

"Wow. Nicole, you're not doing very well. First, you made Jerry furious, and now it appears you've added Drew to your list," Kate remarked, looking between both men.

"Well, if everyone would just shut up and listen, maybe I could turn this around. Jerry, you know Cameron has Dad's genes. I mean, he's a carbon copy. Cameron is so talented. He's got what it takes to go solo. My idea was to take Cameron out on the road accompanied by a full orchestra. Let's revamp his career," she continued, looking at Drew. "You'll be on stage each night, and so will Harry. Cameron will need a great guitarist and drummer. Heck, I'm sure there'll be times when you'll be featured along with Cameron, possibly as a lead singer and guitarist. It's not going to be much different than it is right now. We're just going to mix things up by adding an orchestra," Nicole explained, staring intently at Jerry. "What do you think? Considering that we're losing Doug, we only need Cameron to jump onboard and Drew and Harry to agree. I think it's a great idea," Nicole smiled, squeezing Jerry's hand as she gazed into his eyes.

"Well," Jerry hesitated, stopping to light another cigarette. "I think you might be on to something," he answered reluctantly.

"Finally. I thought you would have a stroke before I could get my ideas past you," Nicole laughed.   "Drew, what do you think?" she asked, directly facing him.

"Considering that you've fired me and then hired me all in one morning, I guess it's not a bad idea. But, geez. You're not even in management yet," Drew laughed. "Jerry, I think this might work. I think this could be huge. Frankly Doll, I'm stunned. After all, you scored a home run," Drew winked, walking over to give her a quick kiss on the lips.

"Okay. You've made your point. If it's a career in management you want, you're hired," Jerry announced after a bit of hesitation. "I didn't mean to get so upset." The effects of the bourbon were beginning to calm his nerves.

"Well, I better get down to the radio station and give away a few free tickets. First, however, we'll need to finish out this tour for House of Cards. After that, I'll need to work out all the details and get things started. Okay, Sweetheart, are you ready to go to work?" Jerry finally smiled, squeezing Nicole's hand. It appeared things were going to work out after all.

"I thought you'd never ask," Nicole cried, throwing her arms around Jerry. "Mom, what are your plans for today?"

"Well, I have an appointment at the hair salon later. So I've got to get going. I'll stop by later before we leave for the concert," Kate answered, smiling at Nicole, relieved things were over and finally resolved.

Taking Jerry's hand as they walked toward the door, Kate looked up at him and smiled. "I'm so proud of you," she whispered, giving him a quick kiss.

"Okay. Doll, would you like a cigar?" Drew teased after everyone left.

CHAPTER FOUR

Taking the Plunge

Jerry had a brilliant idea after leaving Drew and Nichol's suite.

"Kate, if Nicole is serious about working in management, there's no better time than the present. I've got to go over to the radio station to do some promotional work. I think I'll ask her to tag along. What do you think?" Jerry asked, glancing at his wife.

"Oh, I think that would be awesome. I'm sure Drew could watch Nicholas," she agreed.

"Okay. I'll shower and dress. Would you call Nicole and see if she's available to join me?" Jerry asked, closing the bathroom door.

Walking back over to Nicole's room, Jerry thought it would be the perfect time to see how committed she was to her new aspirations.

Knocking at the door, Drew answered almost immediately, wearing a sleeveless tank top and jeans.

"Hey Jerry, come in. Did you forget something?" Drew asked, opening the door.

"Yes, Nicole," Jerry teased with a slight laugh.

"Hey Jerry, I'm almost ready," Nicole smiled.

"Nicole, if you're serious, we've got some promotional work to do this morning. How much longer will it take you? Drew, can you watch Nicholas for a while?"

"Yeah, man, that won't be a problem," Drew answered, glancing at Nicole.

"I'm almost ready. Give me five minutes. Why don't you have another cup of coffee," Nicole suggested running into the bathroom.

Nicholas came wobbling over on his little legs. "Up Daddy, up," he giggled, straining to stand on his tippy-toes to gain his father's attention. Drew laughed, scooping his young son up and swinging him out like an airplane while Nicholas squealed with delight.

A short while later, Nicole walked out. She looked stunning. Her hair was pulled back in a French twist, with a few tendrils flowing down her heart-shaped face. She was wearing a black pantsuit, with a white silk blouse underneath and black heels. The suit curved to her features, accenting her tiny waist. She wore a thin gold necklace that sparkled with each movement. Her matching gold hoop earrings completed her ensemble.

"How do I look?" Nicole asked, twirling around.

"Gorgeous Doll," Drew whistled, amazed at how beautiful she was. "I would be putty in your hands," he winked. Then, coming up behind her, he kissed her on the neck.

"Okay. Let's go. The limo is already downstairs," Jerry announced, hurriedly walking toward the door.

"Babe, Nicholas has bottles in the fridge. Wish me luck," Nicole mentioned giving Drew a quick kiss goodbye.

"We should only be gone a few hours," Jerry added before closing the door.

"Good luck, Sweetheart," Drew winked at Nicole as Nicholas clung to his leg, sucking his thumb.

During their ride downtown, Jerry thought he should give Nicole a quick debriefing on what to expect. He understood she was somewhat familiar with corporate meetings and negotiations through her modeling career, but everyone could use some guidance.

"Sweetheart, I know that I'm asking a lot of you to join me at the last minute without notice. However, I'm confident you can handle this. We will visit one of the largest radio stations in Singapore, MediaCorp. I'll do all the talking follow my lead. Don't panic. If you can't answer a question, I'll handle it. Mr. Chua is the station manager. I spoke with him this morning, and he's agreed to meet with us this afternoon. You'll do great. Don't worry."

As the limo parked in front of the tall building, Nicole surprisingly felt overwhelmed and nervous. However, there was no way she would ever let Jerry detect her feelings. With sweaty palms, Nicole looked inside her purse for her compact. Just one last look in her tiny mirror, a quick spray of her favorite French perfume, and she was finally ready to embark on her first official duty.

Reaching the sixteenth floor, she stepped out of the elevator behind Jerry. Looking down, she quickly surveyed her attire. Dressed eloquently, she portrayed a woman who felt confident and knowledgeable.

"Good afternoon, we have an appointment to see Mr. Chua," Jerry announced, walking in.

The luxurious waiting area held dark leather chairs and expensive art that adorned the walls. The receptionist, a young woman wearing a corporate suit, sat behind an enormous mahogany desk. She was talking on the phone while typing on the computer simultaneously.

"Have a seat. Mr. Chua will be right with you," she whispered to them while covering the mouthpiece. Then, she motioned them toward the leather chairs in the waiting area. Nicole began to feel apprehensive, taking a seat against an expansive wall of windows that exposed Singapore's immense skyline.

"Sweetheart, don't be nervous. You'll do great," Jerry smiled, squeezing her hand.

"Thanks, Jerry. I want this more than anything. Honestly, I do."

After a short time, a handsome young Asian man walked out to the reception area, where they sat patiently waiting. Nicole was a little astonished by his height. He must have been at least six feet tall with a medium build. Wearing an expensive suit that had obviously been tailored, he exuded the confidence of a man born into power. However, his appearance completely took Nicole by surprise. She had expected to meet someone much older, somebody, perhaps of Bruce's generation.

"Good afternoon, I'm Mr. Chua. Why don't we talk in my office?" he smiled, coming forward to shake Jerry's hand. Then, he gave a courtesy nod to Nicole while intently staring at her head to toe. Nicole immediately felt like his stare had just undressed her.

"Good afternoon, Mr. Chau. I spoke to you earlier. I'm Jerry Godwin. Nicole Hampton, my assistant," Jerry acknowledged, following Mr. Chua down the dark-paneled hallway. They entered through oversized double doors and into a massive, brightly lit office. The wall behind his stately wood-paneled desk was floor-to-ceiling windows exposing the vast city skyline. There were four separate dark leather chairs arranged in front of his desk. Underneath the furniture was a costly oriental carpet.

"Please, have a seat," he waved them toward one of the luxurious leather chairs. "Mr. Godwin, you're the new manager of House of Cards. They seem to have taken our city by storm," Mr. Chua smiled warmly at them both. "Typically, I would allow my staff to take care of such matters. However, I am such a fan of House of Cards I wanted to show my respect by taking this opportunity to meet you personally."

"Thank you. We're here to give away some free tickets and leave you with our publicity packets. In return, we were hoping for promotional air time on your stations. In addition, we would like to promote the concert and the band's new hit single, *Vertical High*," Jerry smiled, reaching into his briefcase. He pulled out several envelopes and placed them on the desk.

"We would be happy to give House of Cards promotional time on our stations. If it meets your approval, I'll arrange for one of our reporters to interview the band members for a promo spot. It will air tomorrow morning."

"Yes. Thank you. I'll leave you some backstage passes," Jerry smiled, reaching back inside his leather briefcase. "Is there anything else that House of Cards can do for you while we're here?" Jerry grinned.

Mr. Chua opened the envelopes and briefly skimmed through the contents. Then, pleased with what he saw, he stood up to shake hands and see them out. "This is completely satisfactory. Thank you. Do you or the band require anything further?"

"No. Thank you for your time. Nicole will be available this evening to meet with your reporter. She'll ensure he gets adequate time with the band."

Mr. Chua's gaze once more turned to Nicole. His eyes intently studied her. "Thank you and welcome to Singapore," Mr. Chua smiled, exchanging pleasantries and a firm handshake. "My secretary will show you out," he paused, staring deep into Nicole's eyes. Jerry and Nicole both stood meeting the secretary at the double doors. Nicole briefly glanced back. Again her eyes met the intensity of Mr. Chau's before the doors closed.

"Wow. That was almost too easy," Nicole remarked on their ride down in the elevator. There was no way she would comment on the rather peculiar glance he had given her before leaving. It had made her feel self-conscious and uncomfortable. Surely, she had just been too nervous and was overreacting.

"Yes. It was incredibly short. I wouldn't say today's meeting was typical regarding other meetings. Usually, the protocol is to meet with their promotional department. However, Mr. Chau is apparently a big fan of ours. I think we caught him at just the right time today. I'm sure having a beautiful young lady with me helped tremendously," Jerry winked. "Remember their time is valuable, as well as yours. Always be on time, concise, and have your promotional materials ready. There's always time to socialize later. Remember, time is money."

"Thanks, Jerry, but I'm not so sure about the beautiful young lady aspect," Nicole nervously laughed. Jerry stood back and, for the first time, looked at Nicole in the business sense, quickly assessing her strengths and potential weaknesses as a manager.

After a long moment of contemplation, he replied, "Don't be naïve or underrate your appearance. It can open a lot of doors. Just make sure they're the right ones," Jerry warned. At that moment, he felt more like her dad than a partner. He realized her beauty could either work for her or against her.

Arriving back at the hotel, she was anxious to give Drew the details of her first official duty as Jerry's assistant. Nicole was excited even though she didn't get to contribute as much as she would have liked. She felt more like a spectator at the meeting rather than an equal partner. She realized she would learn best by actively participating in future discussions and made a mental note to discuss this later with Jerry.

"See you later this evening," Jerry smiled, stepping out of the elevator. "Don't forget you will give Mr. Chua's reporter an in-depth, behind-the-scenes look at our operation and an interview with the guys. So please dress professionally," he added almost as an afterthought.

"Oh, don't worry, I'm not going to disappoint you," Nicole promised, her thoughts still on the piercing brown eyes of Mr. Chau.

"So, how did your first day go?" Drew asked, glancing at Nicole as she entered their hotel room. Nicholas began bouncing on the couch next to Jerry, seeing Nicole walk in. She was momentarily surprised to hear Drew's voice. She almost felt like she was in a trance since meeting Mr. Chau. Snapping herself out of it, she smiled, turning to the men in her life.

"It went great. It was short and to the point. We weren't in Mr. Chua's office very long," she explained. "He was a lot younger than I anticipated. I expected to meet someone much older, like Bruce. But, instead, it seemed I was just along for the ride today as Jerry did all the talking," Nicole explained, sitting in between them.

"Well, I'm sure you'll get your chance," Drew leaned over, giving her a prolonged passionate kiss.

"Oh, I almost forgot to mention, Mr. Chua is sending a reporter to interview you guys tonight. So let's try and keep our relationship out of this interview," Nicole suggested rather abruptly. She realized she didn't need anyone thinking she had used her relationship with Drew to build her career. Plus, she intuitively felt it would be best to keep her career separate from that of her family.

"Doll, that's a rather strange request, don't you think?" Drew asked, slightly perplexed.

"No. I simply want to keep our personal lives off the record. There's no need for anyone outside of the band to know. It's not as if you want your fans to know about Nicholas and me either. Think how that might hurt you. I think it's best to keep our affairs private," Nicole insisted.

Drew scratched his head. Knowing Nicole as well as he did, her request seemed somewhat peculiar. She was gorgeous, and she was the mother of his child. It would be difficult for him to have no bragging rights on or off the record, but he would play by her rules. She was right in that he had never openly advertised his family. However, now that she wanted secrecy, he almost felt rebellious. Being it was her career, and he wanted her to succeed, he would reluctantly agree. He figured this was just a short-lived phase that she would eventually outgrow.

Later that evening, during the ride downtown to the convention center, Nicole felt the excitement of finally having a real connection to the band. However, she could barely contain her nervous energy as she sipped on champagne. This evening, Nicole wore a little black dress, a red leather jacket, and strikingly tall red heels. She looked both professional and ready for a party at the same time. Her long dark hair was swept up in a loose bun using a gold clasp that matched her gold hoop earrings.

"Nicole, I've got some things to take care of when we first arrive. But don't forget the interview with the band?" Jerry said using his business voice. Nicole was still getting familiar with his business tone as he had always used his fatherly approach with her in the past.

"Not a chance. I've got it covered," Nicole assured him.

"Wow. Sweetheart, I'm so proud of you," Kate smiled reassuringly. Kate was very stylish wearing blue jeans, a loose-fitted long-sleeved black silk top, and three-inch knee-high boots. Even at her age, her mother was a sexy woman.

"Babe, please don't worry," Drew whispered into Nicole's ear. "I'm now in stealth mode, and I'll inform Nicholas." He chuckled at his joke.

"Drew, don't tease me," Nicole frowned, lightly punching him in the arm.

Arriving at the complex, the guys headed immediately to the dressing room. They had only been in the room a short time when there was a knock at the door. A young hip Asian man stood outside the door. He sported the scruffy, just out of bed hair, the current style. He appeared relaxed in blue jeans and a sleeveless shirt, which exposed his numerous tattoos. He also carried a backpack over one shoulder.

"Good evening, I'm Lee Tan. I work for MediaCorp. I'm here for our scheduled interview with House of Cards."

"Yes, please come in. We've been expecting you," Nicole answered graciously, allowing him in. "Why don't you follow me into the next room, there will be less noise, and I'll let the guys know that you're here."

"Thanks. I'll set up my recording equipment," he replied, removing the bag from his shoulder with the other hand.

Mr. Tan appeared slightly starry-eyed as the boys walked in. Fumbling with his recorder, he pushed his glasses on top of his nose. He had interviewed enough rock bands to expect the unexpected. However, being in their presence made him a little nervous. After all the introductions had been made and ensuring everyone had what they needed, Nicole closed the door to begin the interview.

Thirty minutes later, the interview was running longer than Nicole had planned. Finally, she stood up, cutting off the last question. "Okay, we have no further time for questions. I would like to take a group photo and let the guys go. I'm sorry. They only have thirty minutes before they walk on stage," Nicole interjected, extending her hand to Mr. Tan as she shook his hand with a firm grip.

"Thank you for your time this evening. Our interview will be broadcast tomorrow at 10:00 a.m. Oh, I almost forgot. Mr. Chua asked that I give you this before I leave," he smiled. Then, reaching into his backpack, he pulled out an embossed envelope.

"Thank you," Nicole replied curiously, taking it from the young man.

Later before walking back into the dressing room, Nicole's curiosity seemed to be getting the best of her. She anxiously ripped open the small envelope. As she read it, Nicole felt her heart beating faster. It was an invitation.

Please join me for dinner and an unforgettable evening.

I will show you Singapore, as only I can. I've provided a limo for you after the concert.

~ Alan Chau~

What should she do? Nicole was shaking as she put the invitation back into its envelope. She was unprepared to handle this, and there was no one she could confide in. Trying to recollect the details of her visit earlier in the day, Nicole tried to recall if she had led him on. However, all she could remember was the intensity of his stare. She had almost felt violated, as if he were undressing her with his eyes. There was no way for him to know she was in a serious relationship or even had a child, for that matter. She had no idea how this would affect the band or the remaining promotional air time required. What would happen if she didn't go? Taking the small envelope, she hid it in her purse. It was almost time for the guys to walk on stage. She would watch the concert first and deal with this situation afterward. Hopefully, the concert would erase her fears concerning the invitation and the dilemma she faced.

Momentarily forgetting her predicament, she raised her head, hearing the roar of a thousand screams from the crowd. The boys had just made their appearance on stage. Nicole looked out to them, watching as Drew picked up his guitar. She was still amazed at how excited she got each time the band made their entrance.

"Good evening, Singapore," Cameron yelled, taking his place on stage. He looked sexy wearing his ripped jeans, multi-colored tank, and converse sneakers. His tattooed muscles flexed while he held the guitar over his head. After strapping on his guitar, he ran his fingers through his shiny black Mohawk, enhanced with purple hues. The girls went crazy and almost crushed each other as he set fire to the music which thundered from his guitar.

"Singapore, we're thrilled to be here," Drew shouted, holding his guitar high. He ran up and down the stage, creating a frenzy of excitement. High-fiving and touching the girl's hands near the front of the stage, some were already swooning and falling. It was pure pandemonium, and the boys loved it.

As the colored lights crisscrossed the stage and the crowd below,

Doug yelled, "Are you ready to party Singapore?" The screams magnified louder as even those in the back needed to somehow touch the gods on stage.

Nicole listened to the band as her thoughts quickly raced back to the invitation. Nothing was working. Her mind was utterly consumed by the situation she now faced. Wow, she had to go. There was no other answer. Mr. Chua had no way of knowing about Drew or Nicholas. Subconsciously, maybe that's why she had asked Drew to keep their personal relationship quiet. What was she doing? She was happy, in love with Drew, and a mother who adored her son. Nicole felt conflicted, as though two angels were sitting on her shoulders. One whispering words of warning, don't go, and one angel whispering words of encouragement, why not? However, the bad angel spoke louder. She was going, but no one could ever know, or could they? She would need an ally, someone to cover for her. The only person who possibly could was Jerry. How would she ever be able to get up the nerve to tell him? Then it seemed the perfect moment, as she looked over and caught sight of Jerry standing next to Larry, one of the roadies.

Walking over, Nicole held her breath. She felt sick. What would he think? She had to put her career first. It didn't matter. Approaching with trepidation, she shouted to be heard over the band, "Jerry, I need to speak with you for a moment in private."

Noticing Nicole's expression, he looked at her intently. Immediately he felt concerned, "Sure, let's take a walk outside the arena."

"Thanks, Jerry," she shouted as he grasped her by her upper arm and escorted her toward the door. Stepping outside in the coolness of the evening, they sat on a half wall that encircled an abundance of lush green foliage.

Jerry pulled out his cigarettes and offered one to Nicole, who just shook her head. "Okay, Sweetheart, what's bothering you?" he mumbled while cupping his hand to block the wind from his lighter.

"Wow. Is it that easy to see?" Nicole questioned, instantly standing and starting to pace.

"Well, you look worried. Is everything alright?" Jerry questioned with genuine concern. He took a deep drag on his cigarette, not knowing if he truly wanted to hear the answer.

"Jerry, I need your help. What I'm about to ask you stays just between us. You have to promise," Nicole begged, now standing to face him.

"Okay. What is it? For heaven's sakes, Nicole, it isn't the end of the world. What's going on?" Jerry demanded.

Handing him the envelope, she thought it would be her best recourse to get his attention. With a bit of confusion, he slowly opened it. Reading it, he looked straight into her eyes.

"Oh, hell no! No. You're not!" Jerry stammered, getting more upset with every word. "Please, don't tell me you're considering it," he remarked furiously, shaking his head. "For heaven's sake, Nicole, I know how much you want to work in management, but this is playing with fire. Do you hear me? Do you understand what this man really wants?" Jerry paused, looking directly into her eyes. "Oh man, you're going, aren't you?" The air came out of his sails as he slumped on the retaining wall, still shaking his head.

"Yes," Nicole answered softly. "I don't have a choice. Do I? Think about what might happen if I should turn him down."

"Nicole, you always have a choice," Jerry vehemently demanded. "Sweetheart, I know you're young, but please don't be so naïve. Look at you. You're beautiful. Any man in their right mind would be nuts not to make a pass at you. Forget the band for a moment. Have you thought about Drew and Nicholas and how this could affect them? Drew loves you," Jerry exploded, stomping out the butt of his cigarette and quickly pulling out another.

"Damn it, Jerry, this has nothing to do with my love for either Drew or Nicholas. It's strictly public relations," Nicole answered, feeling her anger beginning to rise. How could he think she would actually sleep with another man? She never said she would have gone that far, but he immediately went there in his mind. She could feel her eyes begin to sting at the injustice of the situation. Had she been a man, they would be laughing and joking right now instead of hurling accusations at one another. It wasn't fair.

"Nicole, you'll live to regret this. Trust me, you don't want to do this," Jerry scolded, taking her by the shoulders to face him.

Nicole flung his hands off of her and continued pacing. "Jerry, I didn't ask you out here for your advice. I asked you out here for your help."

Where had he heard those famous last words? Why was he always the chosen one? The one asked to bear the secrets of those he loved. He had never signed up for this job. He knew how much Nicole wanted a career in management. But, he hadn't realized the things she might be willing to sacrifice to make it happen. He was already beginning to feel the weight of this deceit upon him. He slumped again on the wall, starting to feel his age.

"Nicole, I'm willing to help you, but just this once. Do you understand? I must be completely crazy to go along with such lunacy. But, just for the record, I'm totally against this. Do you hear me? I can't believe you would risk losing your family over someone you hardly know," Jerry fumed, crushing his cigarette butt.

Nicole finally stopped pacing and sat next to Jerry taking his hand in hers. "Thanks, Jerry, you have to trust me on this. You have to know that I'm not doing this to risk my relationship with Drew. I love him, and I love Nicholas. It's simply Public Relations. You have to remember how great Bruce was when it came to this aspect of the business. He never let others get in the way."

"Nicole, do I have to remind you once more? You're a beautiful young woman, and Bruce, on the other hand, was in a league all his own. The man was a genius. Sometimes I wondered if his commitments had cost him a chance at marriage and a family," Jerry continued looking at the ground in defeat. "I guess we'll never know. So, what is it you want me to do?" Jerry asked reluctantly. "How can I help?" he frowned, feeling defeated.

"I thought you would never ask. I need you to inform Drew that Mr. Chau invited us to a social function as his guest and that it's being held downtown at one of the hotels. Tell him you decided not to attend, but you felt I should go as your stand-in to gain experience or something like that. Heck, I don't know. Just make it sound important, a great public relations gig, in other words. He'll believe you. I'm sure of it," Nicole suggested calmly and quietly. She was already feeling exhausted and realized she had actually made her choice from the beginning. She only needed someone to play along with her. She simply had not realized how much work it would be to do so.

Early in her modeling career, Nicole had learned that wealth came in different degrees. Rock stars undoubtedly enjoyed the benefits of money which came with the territory. It allowed them more than enough luxuries to fill their days. However, multi-billionaires like Alan Chau enjoyed the extravagant benefits of buying their way through life. There was no way she could afford to turn him down. It wasn't every day you received an invitation from a billionaire, she thought. Especially tonight, when it coincided with her first day in the business.

"Okay, but here's the deal if you get in over your head tonight with Mr. Chua, you call me immediately," Jerry urged. "I can't believe I even called him by his respectful name. He's a scoundrel. I'm telling you this whole thing stinks so that you know," Jerry said, disappointed, rubbing his furrowed brow.

"Yes. Jerry, I think you've made your opinions clearly known. However, this is my decision and my career. He's sending a limo for me after the concert. I plan to sneak away before Drew even finishes his last song. I don't relish the idea of seeing him before I leave. Do you understand?" Nicole questioned, moving to stand in front of him.

"Oh, so you're telling me you have a conscience?" Jerry stared at her curiously.

"Jerry, stop it right now. I'm doing this for the band. It's simply PR," Nicole replied, moving a little closer.

"Well, I've heard it called a lot of things before, but never PR," Jerry laughed, giving her a half-hearted hug.

"Whatever. Thanks, Jerry. I'll talk to you later," she replied, giving him a gentle squeeze. Then walking away, she felt relieved it was over.

Nicole quickly realized the time and began to rush down the corridors to the dressing room to freshen up before leaving. She needed to make her escape before the concert ended. The last thing she needed was to try and explain this to Drew or anyone else.

"Hey Mom, how's Nicholas?" Nicole smiled, opening the door quietly.

Kate glanced up from her mirror. "Oh, he's fine. Is the concert over?" she inquired, stopping for a moment before she continued to examine herself in the mirror and apply powder to her nose. Nicole sat down next to her, quickly checking her hair and makeup. Sitting side by side, it would be hard for anyone to know they were mother and daughter. But, it was the benefit of being a stylist, Nicole thought, admiring her mom briefly. After finishing her touch-ups, she grabbed her purse.

"Where are you going in such a hurry," Kate quizzed her, looking confused.

"I am in a hurry. I'll explain later. Thanks for taking such good care of Nicholas," she smiled quickly, kissing them before running out. She could hear her mother snapping the compact closed and softly calling her, but she couldn't stop.

Making sure she wasn't noticed, she hurried outside to the waiting limo. As the chauffeur opened the door, she stepped inside, surprised to find no one in the car.

"Good evening, Ms. Hampton. Mr. Chua will be joining you at the airport," he said before closing the door.

Making herself comfortable, she needed a drink. Something strong, she thought. She knew she would need something to help her get through this night. Wow, she hadn't thought about what this evening might involve. The invitation had simply mentioned dinner and viewing the spectacular sights of Singapore. Opening a small bottle of vodka and adding orange juice, she gave it a quick stir. Her heart was racing as she sat back in the seat. For a brief second, she began to rethink her decision. However, everything had been put into motion, and she was determined to continue the evening as planned.

As the limo arrived at the airport, it parked next to a luxurious Sikorski Helicopter. Only a person of affluence would have such toys, she thought. Red carpeting had been rolled out onto the tarmac. Mr. Chua descended the steps of the helicopter. He walked over with the typical arrogance of a man used to getting his way.

"Good evening, Ms. Hampton. I'm glad you decided to accept my invitation," he smiled, taking her hand. "There's no better way to see our beautiful city than at night," he explained, escorting her onboard.

Once inside, he reached over and buckled her into the seat. Instantly she got a faint hint of his cologne, bergamot, and musk as it infused the air. He was more handsome than she had remembered from earlier in the day. Taking a closer look, he appeared to be in his mid-thirties. He was tall for having Asian ancestry, thin, and muscular with a hint of premature grey in his jet black hair. His tailored suit fit him like a glove making his presence even more alluring.

Popping the cork from a bottle of champagne, he quickly filled two fluted glasses as the helicopter lifted into the night sky. May I call you Nicole?" he asked, handing her a tall glass admiring the length of her slender crossed legs.

"Yes. Thank you," Nicole answered, mesmerized by his appearance and deep brown eyes. She couldn't help but feel flattered by all the attention he was giving her. What woman wouldn't want to be admired by such a man? She might as well enjoy this a little, she thought to herself. She could feel a sense of anticipation.

"Please call me Alan. There's no place for formalities tonight. Did Lee interview the members of House of Cards?" he inquired, staring at her rather seductively.

"Yes. Thank you for giving our band promotional air time tomorrow," Nicole replied, fearing she was completely in over her head. However, she was along for the ride at this point of the evening.

"It's my pleasure," he smiled. Leaning closer, he removed the gold clasp from her hair, letting it fall softly like black silk past her shoulders. Then, gently touching a few strands, he pulled her hair away from her face. "Beautiful," he whispered into her ear. His warm breath enhanced the distinct fragrance of his cologne, leaving her breathless.

Letting go, he was back to business. "We love to sponsor concerts, especially those which keep us connected with our young listeners. So please, sit back and relax. First, I'll point out the buildings my corporation built."

Nicole admired his handsome profile once again before turning her attention out the window. She was fascinated, taking in the spectacular views of the city skyline at night. Flying high enough to take in the enormous skyscrapers below was awe-inspiring. The numerous tall structures lit within appeared like beacons set against a sea of darkness as the helicopter skimmed the roofline of the towering buildings. It seemed surreal as the helicopter circled the monolithic high-rise buildings. The name of his conglomerate, Chau Corporation, and its insignia were both glowing brilliantly near the top of each building. Until tonight, this was something she had only seen in the movies.

"I own these two buildings," he enjoyed pointing out. "One is commercial, the other is residential," he stated as the helicopter hovered directly above the soaring towers. It seemed they mirrored each other in size and design. Nicole couldn't fathom the complexities it would take to design and build such massive structures. She sat buckled into her seat for almost an hour, viewing properties owned by Chua Corporation. He seemed immensely proud of his creations. Finally, the helicopter landed on a helipad atop one of the spiraling buildings.

"Awe, we're here. My chef has prepared a delicious sampling of the foods we love in Singapore. Are you hungry?" he questioned, leaning over to unbuckle her from the seat. She got goosebumps as his hands softly caressed her thighs.

"Sounds delicious," Nicole replied hoarsely, trying to clear her throat. Damn, she hadn't realized how nervous she would be. Snap out of it, Nicole, she said to herself. After all, he's just a man. But a handsome one, the little devil inside her whispered.

He took control, taking her hand in his as he led her away from the windswept rooftop. Walking over toward an elevator, Nicole finally began to feel even more overwhelmed. What was she doing? Why had she accepted his invitation? It was only her first day working with Jerry. Why had she gone off the deep end so suddenly? She desperately wanted a career in management, but she knew nothing about the business. However, Mr. Chua's motives became instantly clear once she entered his penthouse. It had nothing to do with public relations. There had been no mention of it. He simply wanted her. How foolish could she have been? Jerry was right. She was too ambitious and too naïve. Now she needed a reason to leave.

As the elevator doors opened into the penthouse, she was breathless. It was a designer's showcase. White marble floors reflected the eloquence of its modern décor. The vast skyline of Singapore was visible through a wall of glass that encased the entire living area. The panorama exposed numerous skyscrapers that twinkled like stars set against the darkness of night—the remaining wall space held expensive art lit to enhance its beauty. Alan's penthouse was sheer opulence.

He took her hand and led her over to one of the large leather sectionals. Sitting too close for comfort, she knew she needed to leave.

"Alan, please forgive me. I hate to ruin such a lovely evening, but I feel a little under the weather. I'm sure it was the helicopter ride. Could you ever forgive me if I called it a night and went back to my hotel?" she frowned impishly. To hell with PR, she needed to get out of there. It was one thing to be with such a powerful man while Jerry was present, but now she was alone with a man who evidently got his way. Her being here was not going to work.

"I'm sorry to hear that you're not feeling well," Alan asked, concerned as he removed his jacket. "Would you like to lie down for a while? I'll have my housekeeper bring you some warm towels or whatever you need?"

"Perhaps if I fixed you a drink, it would help calm you," he insisted, walking toward an exquisite lit bar.

Just like a fly in a spider's web, she had allowed herself to become potentially trapped. It felt alluring and exciting yet, at the same time, scary.

"Oh, thank you so much. That's so kind of you, but I think I should go," Nicole insisted gracefully. Then, standing up, she had to give one of her best performances. Nicole thought it might be better to help him save face. She knew pride was powerful in his culture.

"Are you sure you couldn't possibly stay?" Alan persisted. Now he seemed genuinely concerned as he walked over to her. She felt drawn to him as he stared deep into her blue eyes. She needed to hurry before she let herself impulsively surrender to his charm.

"I'm sorry. I should leave now," Nicole replied, side-stepping him and slowly walking toward the penthouse door.

"I'll have my limo take you back to your hotel," he reluctantly agreed. He couldn't hide his disappointment as he walked with her to the elevator. While waiting, he gently pressed his forehead to hers and sighed deeply. Then, inhaling her scent, he moved in and softly kissed her lips. As amazing as it was, the kiss let her know she had felt no connection to him. She simply needed to hasten her exit. As the elevator bell dinged, their time was up.

It was very evident. The night had not been work-related in any sense of the word. However, Alan was truly a gentleman. He had allowed her to escape easily tonight. She could never hold any resentment toward him or the radio stations he managed. She had simply allowed herself to become a victim of her impetuous decisions.

Many years later, she would look back and laugh, reflecting on her first day working with Jerry. Tonight had given her insight into the world of business. The experience was a great teacher. But, now more than ever, she wanted to marry the young man who waited for her back at the hotel.

CHAPTER FIVE

Meeting of the minds

Part One

Rubbing her eyes, Nicole woke the following day to the smell of coffee. She didn't relish trying to explain the details of the previous evening. But, as she lay in bed pondering the complexities of her decision and the repercussions, she could only be sure of one thing, her love for Drew and Nicholas.

"So, Boss, how was your first day at the office?" Drew teased, walking over and handing her a cup of coffee. "Jerry said he needed you to attend a spur-of-the-moment social function. After the concert, the boys and I went out for drinks, and I thought you would've been back by then. Instead, it looks like I beat you to bed last night. That's a first," he smiled, leaning back on his elbow at the end of the bed facing her. He propped his feet up by her pillow and poked her with his foot.

"Thanks for the coffee," Nicole smiled, sitting up as she placed the hot cup down on the nightstand. Then, pushing herself into a sitting position, her mind quickly scrambled for a plausible explanation.

She had things on her mind from the preceding night, and it didn't include coffee at the moment. She had finally realized the value of this remarkable man who shared her bed, her life, and even their first child. There was no way she ever wanted him to learn about her encounter last night. However, it had been a great lesson learned, leaving her to know the importance of the ones she loved.

Reaching toward him, she pulled Drew close and squeezed him tight. She loved him with every ounce of her being. Kissing him passionately, she didn't want to lose sight of him ever again. Drew grinned, pushing her back into the mattress.

Nicole whispered into his ear, kissing the nape of his neck. "Drew, let's get married."

"Doll, where is this coming from?" he questioned, looking back at her. "What took you so long?" he teased after a reflective pause. If memory serves, weren't we planning to be married in a double wedding ceremony a few years back?"

"Yes. But it didn't feel right after the accident and losing Jenna. There was too much sadness," she reminded him as she put her hands around his neck and pulled him closer.

"Sweetheart, I'll marry you today or tomorrow, you name the place. We've waited long enough," he winked.

The morning instantly became hot and passionate. Nicole was determined to put a wedding band on her finger. It would tell the world she was taken and off the market. She hadn't realized that it would be of little significance in the world of business.

Later that morning, she realized she needed to discuss the necessity of implementing her plan with Jerry and the rest of the boys in the band.

While getting dressed, Nicole glanced over at him. "Drew, I need to talk with Jerry and Cameron. I think it's time we finally clear the air and put my plan into action. You know, making Cameron a solo artist with a full orchestra behind him. What do you think? I'll change Nicholas and call mom."

"Nicole, do you know what you're saying? Jerry hasn't even made the guys aware of your ideas," Drew worried. He wasn't ready for more arguments, including the guys this time. There was no way to gauge how they might react to her plans. Jerry had been won over to her ideas after only one morning. The guys weren't used to change. They might not readily accept her redesign of a good thing, especially Cameron. He had no clue his sister would soon possibly be controlling his future. She now faced her toughest hurdle.

"I know, but it's time," Nicole said, tying the sash of her wrap dress and slipping on heels. "Mom suggested we come over to their suite. Are you ready?"

"Almost," he hesitated, wondering what had changed since last night. First, she wanted a new career, and now she wanted to get married. Was this a mid-life crisis? She wasn't even close to middle age. However, things were changing so quickly he had to wonder.

"Okay. What happened last night? It's like you're on warp speed today." He didn't relish the thought of addressing the band, knowing they wouldn't be so open to a take-over. But, on the other hand, he knew he would support Nicole no matter what. She was the love of his life, but he was beginning to feel he was simply along for the ride.

"Let's just say my eyes have been opened regarding my new career," Nicole smiled, trying to brush off the question while applying the finishing touches of her makeup.

Even though yesterday had only been her first glimpse into the world of management, she was like a horse at the starting gate, and she couldn't wait to be let out. She was about to shake things up. Jerry could've never realized the implications of her first day. The guys were about to face the force and determination of a woman who finally knew what she wanted out of life. Last night had given her insight into the world of business. She would take what Bruce had created and turn it into her creation. Nicole carried within her the strengths of her famous father. She would not stop until she reached the top.

"Hey, Sweetheart, come in," Kate smiled. Wearing her standard blue jeans and flowing print blouse, she reached out for Nicholas as she opened the door. Nicholas was fascinated by her long gold earrings. His little fingers tentatively touched the cold, smooth texture of her hoops. "Jerry is outside on the balcony having coffee," Kate smiled into the sweet face of her grandson, already dismissing Nicole and Drew.

Nicole hurried inside after handing her son off to his grandmother. "Thanks, Mom, I just fed him. He should be ready for a nap soon." Nicole immediately looked toward the balcony seeking Jerry out. She walked toward him, a woman on a mission.

"Why don't you take the carafe of coffee and extra cups out with you?" Kate called out as they moved past. There's plenty to eat outside on the table."

"Okay," Nicole replied, overlooking her mother's request. Then, feeling the cool breeze on her warm skin, she stepped outside on the balcony.

"Hey, guys, what brings you both over so early?" Jerry asked, folding the morning paper and setting it down next to his breakfast plate. Nicole noticed for the first time how tired he appeared. His dark brown hair finally reflected hints of grey at his temples, giving him a distinguished appearance.

"Well, I think I'll let Nicole explain the reason for our visit." Drew sat down across from Jerry and poured himself a cup of coffee. Then, taking a plate, he filled it with all of the assorted breakfast options the center tray had to offer.

"Okay, Sweetheart, what's on that sweet mind of yours? By the way, how did it go last night?" Jerry inquired, taking a sip of coffee. He watched her intently for any signs of a further conversation they may need to have privately later.

"Oh fine, let's just say that I'm learning the business really fast," she gave him a look which clearly implored, we'll talk about this later.

Her answer held too many implications, and Jerry was dying to know more. He had to know. However, he knew now was not the time for an honest discussion of last night's events.

"So let's get down to the point then. What brings you over?" Jerry inquired with a quizzical stare.

"Jerry, I think we need to meet with the guys. We shouldn't wait. We both know where we want to take the band. You even agreed that my ideas were great. What do you think?" Nicole questioned, pouring herself a cup of coffee.

"Well, I don't honestly see the rush. Doug isn't leaving just yet. We still have to honor our current concert dates," Jerry replied, removing his glasses as he rubbed his forehead. Once again, wondering what the hell happened to her last night. "We only have a few more months on the Pacific Rim Tour, and then we're done. So we have to honor those engagements," he reiterated, staring at her intently while putting his glasses back on.

"Well, here's the deal. I don't want to wait to discuss my plans and certain things need to be dealt with now," Nicole leaned forward, placing both elbows on the table with sheer determination.

"Okay, let's say we have this meeting. What then?"

"Honestly, Jerry, come on. Those few months will be here and gone in no time. We need to implement some of my ideas of focusing on Cameron now. Then, I can fly back to Vancouver and start interviewing musicians. Cameron is going to need a great orchestra behind him. He's going to need the best, and I can start by doing interviews at the sound studio in the Warehouse. However, suppose we don't seem to be getting the quality musicians we need in Vancouver. In that case, we'll hold auditions throughout Canada and the States if needed. We have to discuss everything with Cameron immediately and get him on board," Nicole told him passionately.

Wow. Who was this girl, Jerry thought? Where had she been? It seemed as if he'd opened Pandora's Box. But then, it hit him like a bolt of lightning. He knew. It was all too familiar. It was her father, Nicky Spade. Nicole embodied him, her looks, ambitions, drive, and most importantly, her passion. She would be a force to reckon with, he thought to himself.

"Well, when did you want to get the guys together?" Jerry asked, knowing that she had just demoted him to the back seat at this point in their conversation. He realized it was time to pass on the stress to a new generation. Sipping his coffee, he felt a weight lifted off his shoulders as he listened to the highly ambitious young woman sitting at his table.

"Jerry, I respect you for what you've been able to do with the band since Bruce died. I really do." Nicole reached out her hand and placed it on his giving him a gentle, reassuring squeeze.

"Thanks," Jerry replied, looking down and beginning to ponder his imminent retirement. It had never been a burning desire of his to take over after Bruce, but he had felt forced into taking the position. There was no one else. How could he stand by and watch everything Bruce created crash and burn. The guys depended upon him, but now it seemed things had drastically changed. Her ideas were good, damn good. He knew she was on to something. The band needed change, and Cameron could definitely take the band in a new and different direction. Once again, he knew she was right.

"All right, let's make the call. See if we can get the guys together tonight after the concert. It's our last night here. We only have a few days left before we play our next gig in Hong Kong," Jerry suggested lounging back as he lit a cigarette.

"Well, now that you're finished talking business, I have something to say," Drew announced, taking the back of Nicole's hand and briefly bringing it to his lips. His eyes were shining with love and pride at his future. "We're getting married."

Jerry almost choked as coffee spewed from his mouth. Sure, why wouldn't they? Drew was no better than himself at this point. Nicole carried within her the power and determination of a woman on a mission. Drew would always be naïvely subjected to her whims and desires, just as women had always been to Nicky's.

"Congratulations," Jerry tried to smile. He didn't know if he should feel happy or scared for the young man across from him. Not knowing what else to say, he stood and suggested they go back inside to give Kate the shocking news.

"Sure," Drew stood, assisting Nicole out of her seat.

Jerry knew he needed a strong drink, and he felt it was only right to talk to Drew. It would need to be a conversation just between the two of them. He couldn't help but think of all of the tumultuous affairs of Nicole's father. He had watched as Nicky's uncontrolled passions had caused many of his relationships to go down in flames. Jerry could clearly see these same passions in Nicole. He didn't know what happened last night, but he couldn't help but imagine the worst. He had grown close to Drew over the years and, in good conscience, felt obligated to at least give the boy some fair warning.

Kate was sitting on the floor with Nicholas playing with his toys. She looked up as they walked back into the room. "Meeting over already?"

Nicole sat down next to her mom and looked up at Drew with her blue eyes shining with excitement. "Mom, Drew, and I are officially getting married!" she exclaimed. Kate squealed with delight, wrapping her daughter in a warm hug.

"Nicholas, did you hear that? Mom and Dad are getting married! I'm so excited for you all!" Kate could barely hold it together as she grabbed Nicholas to include him in their group hug.

Slapping Drew on the back, Jerry grinned, "I think I'll take this young man downstairs for a drink."

"Babe, we won't be gone long. Do you want to hang out with your mom and Nicholas until we get back?" Drew suggested.

"Sure. I thought maybe we could all go to a celebratory dinner tonight before the concert," Nicole proposed as Nicholas got up and began racing around the room, caught up in the energy of the excitement.

"Okay. That sounds good. You guys carry on. Nicole and I have a wedding to plan," Kate smiled, standing to give Jerry a quick kiss as he walked toward the door.

"Damn, there was way too much estrogen in the air. It was so strong I couldn't breathe," Jerry laughed, stepping inside the elevator. "I had to get out." Jerry turned to Drew's reflection in the mirror and winked.

"Really, I thought you and Kate were in love?" Drew asked, a little confused by Jerry's statement.

"Oh, Drew, we are. That's not what I meant. I was referring to Nicole."

"Nicole? What's that supposed to mean?" Drew questioned.

"Let's get that drink, and I'll explain my thoughts."

Stepping out of the elevator, the lobby was just beginning to come to life as people arrived for their stay and others were possibly leaving. However, the spacious hotel bar was practically empty as they walked in.

"Wow. It looks like we're the only ones here. Do you want a table or a seat at the bar?" Jerry asked, noting all the vacant seats.

"Well, since the place is empty, let's sit at the bar."

"Sounds good."

Sitting on two barstools at the end allowed them some privacy. The bartender was finally glad to have something to do and wasted no time getting their order.

"So what can I get you, gentlemen, this afternoon?" he asked.

"Oh, I'll have Jack Daniels, straight no ice," Jerry answered, running his fingers through his thinning hair.

"I'll have a screwdriver," Drew stated. Jerry chuckled to himself inside. This young man had no idea just how screwed he might actually be.

It was only moments before the young man returned, placing their drinks on the bar.

"Wow. That was good," Jerry grinned, taking a long slow sip, after which he let out a loud sigh. "Geez. I really needed that," he added.

"Okay. What was it that you were saying about Nicole?" Drew asked, taking another sip.

"Listen, son. I'm thrilled you and Nicole are finally getting married. It's the right thing to do for Nicholas. It's long overdue, and believe me, I know you love that girl. Who wouldn't?" Jerry reflected, lighting a cigarette. "My earlier comment was just a private joke, more to do with her Dad. It's too bad that Nicky didn't live long enough to get to know Nicole, Nicholas, and yourself. Nicky and I were cousins, but more like brothers. I know you've heard all the stories from Kate. The more time I spend with Nicole, the more I see and hear her father," he paused, allowing what he had just said to sink in a bit. "Drew, she personifies him. She's no doubt his daughter in the truest sense of the word. You would've had to know Nicky like I did to see how she embodies him. Truly, she's a great girl. She'll be a wonderful wife and mother. Heck, she already is a great mother to Nicholas. However," he paused again and mentally decided to call it as he saw it. "Son, I'm not so sure you'll ever be in charge of your family," Jerry laughed, taking another swig. "She's a lot to handle, and I think you've got your work cut out for you," he forewarned while lifting his hand to the bartender to order another Jack Daniels straight.

"Well, I don't think you understand our relationship," Drew replied, trying not to be offended. Still, Drew's ego was bruised, nonetheless.

"Oh son, you're so young and naïve. Drink up," Jerry laughed, slapping him on the back and motioning the bartender to keep the drinks coming.

"I've got the feeling tonight may get a bit rough, depending on how the guys take the news. You know they're not expecting any of this. They know that Doug is leaving, but they have no idea what is about to happen. I have no idea if Cameron feels ready to become a solo artist," Jerry continued, taking a drag on his smoke. "Don't get me wrong. He's a great singer and totally capable of being upfront. I just hope that he sees his sister's vision for him."

Jerry felt resentful toward Nicky at that moment. As much as he had loved him, there was plenty not to love. Nicky had started as a passionate kid with stars in his eyes, shooting to the top, and then he ended up crashing and burning. He eventually died from a drug overdose, leaving Jerry once again to clean up his mess. Jerry wondered if there would ever come a time when his life wouldn't involve something unpleasant that Nicky had left. He wondered how he could possibly explain this to a young man with no real-life experiences.

"I need to know you are up for any battle that comes our way tonight. It will not be easy for you because you're no longer just another band member. You're Nicole's partner. Your relationship might cause you to take sides against the boys. Tempers may flare," Jerry continued looking at Drew intently with his brow furrowed. "I need to know you will have Nicole's back this evening." Though the boys were his business, Nicole was his step-daughter, and she would always come first.

Drew was a little taken back by Jerry's straightforward talk. He had been expecting a congratulatory drink. An official welcome to the family. Not an overwhelming insight into Nicole's ambitions and the consequences they might bring this evening. He had no idea waking this morning of Nicole's plan. Therefore, he had not given it much thought. Now he was forced to think about how this could impact his relationships with the other guys. He was beginning to see where

Jerry was coming from and sighed, not wanting to deal with it. "Man, I think I need a cigarette."

Jerry passed Drew a smoke and a lighter. He sat patiently waiting as Drew collected his thoughts. Drew took a few deep drags, then turned and looked at Jerry, "I hear what you're saying. I realize Nicole assumes that Cameron and the boys will just go along with whatever she wants. Nicole is not used to anyone, especially a man, telling her no. However, I have seen the relationship between Nicole and Cameron, and they both share an ambition like none I've ever seen. I don't see Cameron turning down someone as passionate about his career as he is," Drew mentioned, taking a moment and another drag on his smoke. "However, I get what you're saying about the boys. They might not be happy about being told what to do by a girl. I just want to assure you that I'll have her back. I love her, and in the end, she and Nicholas are all that truly matter to me."

Jerry looked down at his watch and realized they had been there longer than he had thought. "Think we better finish our drinks. It's getting late. We need to get ready for tonight," Jerry took his last sip. Then, reaching into his wallet, he covered the bar tab.

"Yes, I guess you're right. I don't want to show up too wasted tonight. I better save some of that for later after the concert if the crap hits the fan. Who knows, we may not even have a band after tonight," Drew frowned, starting to fear the worst.

Stumbling in, it was apparent that Jerry and Drew had too much to drink.

"Jerry, for heaven's sake, what's the matter with you? You know damn well Drew has to perform tonight," Kate demanded angrily, poking a manicured finger in his chest.

"Yes, Drew, what were you thinking? You can barely stand! How the hell do you expect to perform?" Nicole complained. It was so typical of Drew to be irresponsible, Nicole thought bitterly. It was also why she didn't feel the need to have more kids. She already had two.

"Okay, calm down," Jerry suggested slurring his words while motioning his hands downward in a calming manner.

"Nicole, call room service. Order enough coffee to hopefully sober these two idiots. I will bathe the baby. You run over and get Nicholas some clean clothes and pack his diaper bag, and you might as well bring Drew's clothes over and have him change here. We've got to revive these two, and we don't have long." Kate scooped up the baby and began carrying him toward the bathroom.

"Okay, great thinking, Mom," Nicole replied, running for the phone.

Kate's plan had worked. Jerry and Drew were stable and felt better when they walked down to the lobby to meet the guys.

The concert was a huge success. There was no doubt the guys were loved by their fans in Singapore that evening. The boys walked off stage to a standing ovation. But, unfortunately, Jerry was now more than ever indecisive about the direction in which Nicole wanted to take the band.

CHAPTER SIX

Meeting of the minds

Part two

"Okay, so what's this big meeting about?" Harry asked, stepping inside the limo.

"I'm going to wait until we get back to the hotel to give details. Then, I'll have Kate order some hoagies and beer. How does that sound to everyone?" Jerry suggested.

"Jerry, is something wrong, man?" Cameron looked at him. He was usually good at reading him, and Jerry was acting strange.

"No. Everything is fine. It was a great concert tonight. You guys have a lot of fans here," Jerry remarked, wiping sweat from his brow and glancing nervously out the window as the fans swarmed their limo. He wouldn't miss this part of being a manager, he thought. The mob of fans always made him feel claustrophobic.

Reaching the hotel, Kate decided to take Nicholas over to Nicole's room. So he would be able to sleep in his crib without being awakened if things got loud and out of control. Plus, Kate felt she was getting too old for the drama of band life.

"Sweetheart, why don't you order the hoagies and beer for the guys?

Then, I'll take Nicholas over to your room. He's already fallen asleep, and I'll stay with him. This meeting doesn't involve me anyhow."

"Okay, Mom, if you're sure. After putting Nicholas in his crib, lie down and take a nap or watch television. I'll call you later."

Hearing a knock at the door, the food and drinks had arrived. The boys were sitting around the coffee table smoking and drinking beer. It was pretty much the norm for the guys. Jerry hoped their emotions wouldn't run too high due to the alcohol. He had seen the effects of alcohol and how it could turn a simple conversation into an all-out war.

"Okay. Why don't we all enjoy our sandwiches and beers before getting started?" Jerry suggested walking over to grab another beer and pass out hoagies. He hoped the sandwiches would hamper the effects of their drinks.

"Geez, Jerry, this seems ominous. What's going on?" Cameron asked, sitting back with his left ankle resting on his right knee. His arms resting on each armrest gave him the appearance of an Italian god. There was no doubt if this were a kingdom, Cameron was the king. Sitting in a circle formation around Cameron's throne, Jerry needed to get this evening underway.

"All right, I'd like to ask Nicole to walk over. Honey, grab that chair and bring it over here next to mine," Jerry mentioned, pointing to one of the high-backed formal dining chairs. As Nicole started to walk toward the dining area, Drew stopped her.

"Wait, Babe, I'll get it for you," Drew winked. "Good luck," he whispered in her ear as he passed swiftly, kissing her on the cheek.

"In case any of you haven't been made aware, Nicole is now working as my assistant manager. She actually started working with me yesterday. It appears she's serious about her desire to work with us in management. So, I'll let her speak for herself."

Nicole waited until she knew she had everyone's attention. "Yes. Jerry is right. Managing a band has been a dream of mine. I guess you could say it all started when I heard the news of Bruce's passing. You all know how much I loved that man. He was the only father figure I had in my life growing up. Bruce was always confident I could do this job and encouraged me to go into management. However, being the wonderful man he was, Bruce never once indicated that he was disappointed it didn't happen during his lifetime. Instead, he loved me enough to let me make my own decisions," Nicole made eye contact with Cameron, who nodded his understanding. "I think you all know I had fallen in love with Drew and couldn't stand being separated from him," she said, looking at Drew with a warm smile. "That brings me to where I'm at now. I want to become involved with the band, and by that, I mean in a management position. Jerry has graciously allowed me to take over as his assistant. So you might say yesterday was my first day in the business."

"Well, Sis, that's wonderful, but what does that have to do with all of us?" Cameron inquired, raising a dark eyebrow. He wasn't sure where she was going with all of this. So he looked to Jerry for some clarification.

Nicole could sense Cameron's uncertainty. "Jerry, do you want to take it from here, or do you want me to continue?" Being new to the business, Nicole felt uncertain about explaining her ideas to the guys without conflict.

"Oh, I think you're on a roll, might as well continue," Jerry grinned and waved her on with his hand. He thought it would be best for her to take charge. After all, she needed to become more comfortable speaking in front of a group.

"Okay. Here's where it's going to affect you guys. Jerry, I'm just going to put all the cards on the table. What do you think?" she paused to ask his direction. She was starting to feel nervous. What if Cameron said no, and she couldn't get him on board? What if they laughed her out of the room? She was suddenly hit by many insecurities which weren't like her.

"You've got this. Continue," Jerry said reassuringly.

"Doug, I've been made aware that you're leaving the band at the end of the year. Is that right?" Nicole asked, glancing at him for confirmation.

"Yes. But how in the hell did you find out?" Doug furiously demanded. Confused, he looked around the room. Finally, his eyes stopped, fixated on Drew. He knew it had to have been him. "Damn, man. What the hell!" Doug stood up and threw a beer bottle at Drew's head, narrowly missing him as it hit the wall.

"Doug, calm down, for heaven's sake! It doesn't matter," Jerry yelled, standing up. He was shocked, and his temper flared as he emphasized his next words by pointing at himself, "I was the one who should've been informed! I'm the one who should be going ballistic right now! I was the one kept in the dark! Now you sit the hell down and get it together!" Jerry eyeballed Doug until he took his seat. Nicole waited until Jerry sat down and motioned for her to continue.

"Jerry, it doesn't matter at this point. It really doesn't," Nicole insisted, trying to calm him. "Listen, Doug, I know about Alondra, and I'm happy for you both. I also know that your parents are moving to Oahu, and your Dad needs your help. I think that's wonderful. We're all family here, and we're going to support each other first and foremost. So let's move past this with no hard feelings. Nicole continued trying to soothe things over. Doug, you're leaving the band. Honestly, it's only one small part of what we're here to discuss."

Harry looked over at Cameron, gesturing with his hands out. "What the hell?" he mouthed. Cameron silently shook his head and shrugged his shoulders, glancing back at Nicole. She knew then it was going to be an uphill battle as he lit a cigarette.

"What? There's more?" Doug complained, stomping over to grab another beer. "Might need something stronger than this," he muttered. Then, turning accusingly to Drew, he smirked. "Just for the record, it wasn't your place to say anything, man. It wasn't your call to talk to Nicole and Jerry behind my frigging back! My life is my responsibility, and if anyone was going to tell Jerry, it should have been me!"

"Doug, calm your ass down and bring over a few extra beers," Jerry rolled his eyes, lighting a cigarette.

"Okay. So what else is there if I'm only one small part?" Doug demanded.

Nicole stood up and glared at Doug. She could feel her face flush and her temper rising. How dare Doug attack Drew! He wasn't the one keeping secrets. She wasn't in the mood to watch a grown man throw a fit like a small child. Working to keep her voice calm, "We are keeping this meeting civil. Please refrain from finger-pointing and blaming others for your shortcomings, Doug. That's not why we are here. Everyone already knew you were leaving, and it's nobody's fault that you decided to tell everyone but Jerry. Whom you should have told first, remember what I said about us all being one big family? I expect you to act like it," she commanded. Nicole walked over to sit next to Drew, daring Doug to say anything further. "Now, here's where everyone else will be affected," she calmly continued.

"Yes, but families are known for fighting," Harry interjected like a child.

"Not here and not tonight," Nicole stared at him, communicating that she would not tolerate any more outbursts. Finally, he succumbed to her stare and slumped down farther in his seat. Cameron watching the display of power, began to laugh out loud. It amused him greatly to watch his sister terrorize the others.

Nicole realized she had finally gotten Cameron's attention. Standing up to drive home her point, she knew it was now or never. She began to pace as her passionate energy took over, and her ideas flowed freely, unstoppable. "Seriously, do you guys want to make money and sell records? Are you willing to take a few risks to make things happen? I hope you all haven't become so complacent in what you're doing now that you can't envision something bigger. House of Cards is an awesome band. I'm not here to say otherwise. There's no doubt your fans love you. Tonight was a tribute to that fact. You guys received a standing ovation as the show came to a close," turning to look directly at her brother, she was determined to get him on board. "However, I definitely want to shake things up a bit, take a risk. If, as a group, we are too scared to change things, maybe we're in the wrong business. Music changes. It always changes. What was popular ten years ago or even months ago doesn't remain in the top ten forever. Please don't misunderstand me. Music remains with us long after it's dropped off the charts. That's not what I'm saying. I'm referring to capitalizing on something new. Elvis and Madonna continuously reinvented themselves to keep it fresh. A new direction for the band," Nicole explained, hoping they understood.

"Jerry, throw me a cigarette and your lighter. I think we're about to go down in flames. Do I get popcorn with this show?" Cameron laughed, downing a huge guzzle of beer.

"I love you, Cameron. There's no doubt you are the most talented artist out there today. You have the potential to move from great artist to legendary status. House of Cards ceases to exist without you. Nobody here can dispute this," Nicole glanced around as if daring anyone to contradict her. "Everyone here loves you, and this is where it affects you," she paused for dramatic effect. Then, staring him directly in the eyes, "I want you to go solo, on your own."

A hush instantly fell over the room as everyone turned, glaring at Cameron. It was too quiet. Everyone was in a state of shock. Ignoring everyone else in the room, Nicole moved toward Cameron. She sat at the end of the coffee table, putting herself directly in front of him. "I can take you there. Nobody in this entire world would work harder or be more committed to you than me. Your legacy will be my legacy," Nicole stated, staring intently into his eyes and anticipating his response.

"You're ready. Don't you feel it?"

Cameron slowly smiled, realizing she was right. "Nicole, I love you too. But, I'll be honest, I've just been enjoying the ride so far. I haven't put much thought into the next step." Feeling the connection to the truth of her conviction, he began to feel transformed hearing his sister's passionate speech.

"Cameron, are you forgetting who our father was? It's your turn. Your time. Please trust me. Your voice is unbelievable. We all know why Bruce worked so hard to put House of Cards together. It was for you. You've got this in Spades," Nicole laughed. "Did you catch that, Spades?" she giggled.

"Cameron, she's right," Jerry finally spoke up, bringing Cameron back from the surreal moment he had just had with Nicole. "It's always been about you. I'm not saying for one minute that Harry, Drew, or even Doug aren't great vocalists and musicians. You're all fantastic. That's not why we're here. It's simply about changing directions for the band," Jerry added, pointing at each of the other band members.

"So are you saying that Drew and I are now unemployed along with Doug," Harry whined, completely confused like a lost child.

"No. Not at all. Let me make this clear right now. No one is going anywhere except Doug. Unless he changes his mind and decides to stay," Jerry frowned, glancing over in his direction. Jerry was still visibly upset with him.

Doug looked over to Jerry. A look that projected regret over the beer bottle episode and not having told him sooner of his intentions to leave the band. "Thanks, Jerry. I love Alondra, and yes, I'd give up anything to be with her, even House of Cards," he said clearly with no regrets.

"Wow, that's huge," Harry grinned, opening another bottle of beer. His pale Irish face flushed due to the amount of alcohol he had already ingested this evening. His red face almost matched the color of his red hair.

"Hey, Jerry, throw me your pack of cigarettes and lighter," Drew asked with a slightly disgruntled look. He wasn't sure how to feel about Nicole's passionate arguments for her brother. He understood what she was saying and couldn't argue that Cameron was a huge part of House of Cards, but he was her partner. She should be promoting him. He loved her passion. He was both motivated and inspired by what she had to say. However, he couldn't help but feel hurt that she didn't feel that way about him. He could feel the rumblings of jealousy beginning to stir.

"Okay. So what's the rest of this brilliant plan? I'd like to hear it, even if I'm not going to be part of it," Doug said, taking a deep drag on his cigarette.

Nicole's eyes flashed with excitement, throwing her hands up. "We go big," she stated. "We're going with a full orchestra." Pointing to Harry, who was pleased to now have a little of Nicole's positive attention by not being fired, she continued. "Harry, you will remain on drums, and Drew stays on guitar. Nothing changes, except on occasions where you'll naturally sing harmony with Cameron. Here's where it affects everyone in the band, except Doug because he's leaving. To make it fair for you guys and because it may seem like we're pulling the rug out from under you, so to speak, your pay will not change." Nicole turned full circle to make sure everyone understood. She wanted to ensure that everyone knew they would be treated fairly and with respect. "We're a family, and we're all in this together. It will be an even split among

Cameron, Harry, and Drew. The orchestra will be paid slightly above scale along with the roadies. Of course, we'll cover their transportation and lodging. So what do you guys think?" Nicole asked with enthusiasm gazing around the room at everyone.

Once again, the room fell quiet. You could've heard a pin drop. The boys were punk rock, and the idea of an orchestra was foreign territory for them.

Sensing their fear, Nicole emphasized, "What makes you afraid? Change? Are you afraid of success too?"

"Guys listen, I've given this a lot of thought," Jerry interjected. "Nicole is right. It's in her genes. Nicole is going to make one hell of a manager. That's right, everyone heard me correctly. As of tonight, I'm putting the band under her management. Now don't get me wrong, I'm not going anywhere for a while. I'll hang around, just in case she needs me. But let's face it, I'm not getting any younger, and losing Bruce has given me a reason to reflect on my life. I'm going to retire at the end of this year. I'm going to take my beautiful wife and settle down in one place. I've lived on the road for so long that it'll be like heaven to wake up in the same bed every morning. Vancouver will be the end of the road for me," Jerry announced, wiping his eyes with the back of his hand. Hearing Nicole's impassioned speech, he realized his timing was right. He no longer was needed. Without a doubt, he knew she was the only one for the job. He couldn't help but feel a little emotional seeing Nicky's family carrying the torch to a new generation. Man, was he ever beginning to feel old.

"Oh Jerry, I knew you were going to retire, but I had no idea you would put me in charge so soon," Nicole cried, embracing him in a heartfelt hug.

"Okay, someone pass out another round of beers. I think it's time for a toast," Jerry laughed, choking back his tears. "Okay, this may seem a little unorthodox, but does everyone have a beer? Raise your bottles," Jerry asked.

"Here's to the future of House of Cards. Here's to our new direction, new management, new solo artist, my retirement, Doug's wedding, but most importantly, here's to family," Jerry toasted.

CHAPTER SEVEN

A New Direction

Drew could hardly fathom the idea that his bride-to-be was now his boss. It still felt a little surreal to him. He was still mulling over his jealousy regarding Nicole's passion for Cameron's career. He understood they were family, but he couldn't help feeling disappointed in Nicole for not putting just as much faith in him. Pushing down his feeling of discontent, he turned to Nicole in bed and pulled her close.

"Wow, Babe, I guess congratulations are in order," he whispered, attempting to snuggle closer to her as he kissed her neck. "I guess I should get you a supply of Cuban cigars." Drew laughed, thinking he was going to get lucky.

"Oh, I don't think so." Nicole playfully swatted his hands away.

"So, what's on your agenda for today? Me, I hope," he laughed again, attempting to engage Nicole in a bit of fun.

"Oh, I plan on meeting with Jerry this morning. We need to synchronize our schedules and develop a plan of action regarding the remainder of the tour. I'm anxious to fly back to Vancouver and start interviewing musicians. There's so much to do."

Realizing the extent of work that needed to be done, Nicole jumped out of bed. She hurried into the bathroom to turn on the shower. As the hot water was steaming the room, she went to her closet and began throwing out possible outfits for the day. After emptying half her wardrobe on the floor, she finally found one that satisfied her. It was simple yet elegant. She decided on a grey pencil skirt with a white chiffon blouse. Walking back into the bathroom, she removed her robe. Standing under the showerhead, Nicole took a moment to enjoy the warmth of the water. It helped soothe her gnawing fears of everything she needed to accomplish. Suddenly she felt arms embracing her from behind.

"What are you doing?" she giggled.

"Conserving water, Doll," Drew said, leaning down to kiss her.

Even though it had been only twenty-four hours since Nicole embarked on her new career, she had hit the ground running. Her first day in the business had given her insight into the world of management, and she was eager to implement her ideas. Moreover, Nicole felt confident that being a woman would not be detrimental. Chau had merely been a lesson learned on her way to the top.

"I'm going to feed Nicholas. Would you mind watching him this morning?" she asked Drew as the little boy ran into their room. Lifting him to the bed, he giggled as he jumped on the mattress. His black curly hair bounced in the air each time he went higher. Nicole laughed at her blue-eyed little guy and held out her arms. "Is my little munchkin hungry?" Nicholas smiled as he flew into her arms.

Drew watched, wondering how much time Nicole would be able to spare her family now that she was taking on the management position. "Not a problem, I'll assume my new duties as a house husband," Drew grumbled loudly, wearing a frown.

"Babe, that's not fair. You know how much I want this. We're a team. We have a few down days on the calendar before we arrive in Hong Kong, and I want to take advantage of those. However, I might fly back to Vancouver tonight after talking with Jerry. It would be a quick trip. Do you want to go, or do you think you should stay here with Nicholas?" she asked, hoping he would stay. She couldn't help but feel things would go smoother if she didn't have to babysit their relationship. After all, she just wanted to focus on business in Vancouver.

"Wow, Doll, you're moving at warp speed. Well, I guess it would just depend upon your Mom. Find out if she's available to watch Nicholas." He thought maybe a few days in Vancouver would be good for them. Almost like a second honeymoon. He could feel his spirits begin to lift just thinking of it. Maybe everything might be okay after all.

"Great idea, I'll ask."

"Okay, I'm leaving now," Nicole yelled, walking toward the door. I'm meeting Jerry downstairs in the lobby. I'll find out if Mom is available to take care of Nicholas. I Love you," she answered.

"Okay, Babe, see you when you get back."

Seeing Jerry step out of the elevator, Nicole hoped he would be keen on her idea of flying back to Vancouver later that evening.

"Hey Jerry, why don't we talk in the café over lunch. Does that sound okay?" Nicole suggested giving him a quick greeting.

"Yes. I could use a cup of coffee," Jerry mentioned walking with her through the lobby and over to the Bombay Café.

Finding a small table near the back, Nicole picked up her menu.

"I think I'll have the grilled chicken salad with a glass of iced tea," she smiled, glancing up at the waiter. The waiter was obviously admiring her long slender legs. Nicole handed him the menu with a knowing smile.

"I'll have a burger with fries and coffee," Jerry stated, oblivious to the mild flirtations.

"Jerry, we're going to need an office in Vancouver. I know the band has a few down days before their next gig in Hong Kong. I want to take advantage of those and fly back to Vancouver tonight. I know Bruce has contacts there, and the sound studio in the Warehouse should be available for our use. I know it may seem sudden, but there's a lot to do. I want to put things in motion regarding hiring musicians. Also, I would like to get Cameron back in the studio as soon as possible. He'll need to start recording new music as soon as the orchestra positions are filled. I know you want to retire at the end of the year, but right now, you must be available to continue the tour with the guys. That would leave me free to shuttle back and forth to Vancouver. I know it's a lot to spring on you at lunch, but I want to leave tonight. What do you think?" Nicole asked, practically out of breath as she went non-stop through all the details.

"Wow, you're serious," Jerry was again shocked by her decisions. "Why don't you take a moment to catch your breath?" he laughed, amused at her tenacity.

"Jerry, I've never been more serious or committed to anything before. I want to stay in the penthouse at the Ritz-Carlton. I know that area of Vancouver really well. It's not far from the studio in the Warehouse. Plus, you know it's where Bruce always stayed," Nicole replied, sipping tea. She was on overdrive, anxious to implement her ideas.

"Geez, Louise, you're exactly like Nicky. Once he made his mind up to do something, there was no stopping him. I'll never forget the night our band entered a competition at the high school. Unfortunately, we didn't win, and your Dad was devastated. Nevertheless, he was determined to get out of Middleton and make a name for himself. However, what he didn't know was Bruce was in the audience. It was the beginning of his career, to make a long story short. It seemed almost unbelievable at the time, but he was on a flight out of Middleton the next morning after Bruce hired him," Jerry recollected with feelings of nostalgia.

Nicole didn't have time to hear stories from the past. She was ready to make her own stories. Wow. She thought Jerry already sounded like a retired person. She couldn't help but push through her agenda. "What do you think? Can I leave tonight?" she insisted.

"Okay. I'll call and have the plane ready. Is Drew going too?" Jerry asked while devouring his burger.

"Yes, that is if Mom can watch Nicholas. Do you think she would mind? I almost forgot to ask," Nicole implored. She knew Kate would always be available to watch Nicholas. However, she knew she should get Jerry's permission as well. After all, watching a two-year-old meant little downtime.

"Are you kidding? We both adore our little grandson," Jerry said, wiping his mouth with a napkin. "Please keep in mind that Drew will need to be in Hong Kong for the concert, so you will only have a few days," he emphasized.

"I know, but it will give me enough time to organize things. We're going to need someone in charge on the West Coast. I want to hire someone to cover our operations in Vancouver. Do you have anyone in mind that I could contact?" Nicole asked, cutting into her salad.

"Well, Bruce always spoke highly of a guy. I think his name was Lance. I can't remember his last name, but anyone working at the Warehouse would know him. Lance would be a great place to start. If he's not interested, I'm sure he probably knows someone who's qualified that might want the job. I remember Lance helped with the memorial concert for Nicky," Jerry stated almost as an afterthought.

"Thanks, Jerry. I promise you I'm committed to taking the band in a new direction and making the world take notice of Cameron. I'll do whatever it takes. I won't stop until he's reached the pinnacle of fame. Besides, I think Dad and Bruce will give me some heavenly guidance."

"Nicole, Sweetheart, I believe you. I have no doubts about your determination or abilities. I'll be here as your wingman for the rest of the overseas tour, and then I will take that sweet mom of yours back home to Vancouver and retire," Jerry winked. Nicole was like a bundle of energy. He felt tired just having this conversation with her. Yep, he was clearly ready for retirement.

"Great. I'll bring Nicholas over and leave the key to our suite if Mom needs anything for him while we're away."

"Sounds good," Jerry answered, finishing his burger.

"Okay, Babe, pack your bags. We're on our way to Vancouver tonight," Nicole yelled out while walking in. "How's Nicholas?"

"Quiet. I just put him down for a nap," Drew whispered. For some reason, it seemed to take forever to get him to sleep. The last thing he needed was Nicole waking him up.

"I'm going to pack. I think we'll only need two suitcases," Nicole said quietly.

The afternoon flew by as Nicole quickly took care of all last-minute preparations for the trip. Finally, they were on their way out to the airport. Nicole was excited. It would be her first official trip on her own. Well, almost on her own, she thought. She still had to contend with Drew.

As the limo parked next to the jet, Drew found it hard to believe Nicole was now his boss. They were getting ready to board a plane that would carry just the two of them across the Pacific to Canada. He was getting excited. Maybe they could become a globe-trotting family unit. I'm sure she could use my input now and then, he thought. They were still partners, after all.

"Hey, Babe, did you happen to call in a menu for the flight?" Drew inquired, ascending the steps to the Lear jet. He realized in his busy day taking care of their son, he had not stopped to eat, and he could feel his stomach rumble.

"Yes. How do steak and lobster sound? I also have two bottles of champagne on board. Let's celebrate my new position with the band," Nicole smiled.

As the jet lifted into the night sky, the bright city lights of Singapore quickly faded into the darkness. Reaching for a blanket to cover herself, Nicole reclined her seat for the long flight.

"Doll, are you tired?" Drew smiled, slipping his hand around her tiny waist to snuggle.

"Somewhat, it's been a long day," Nicole yawned, feeling tired.

"Well, I thought I would inquire about your mile-high club membership," Drew winked seductively. "I think it's up for renewal," he laughed, kissing her neck.

"Drew, you're funny. Wake me in about an hour, and we'll have dinner," Nicole smiled, placing a mask over her eyes. He reclined in his set feeling disappointed. If anyone were tired, it should be him. He was the one with their two-year-old all day long with no breaks. Kate was busy earlier and couldn't give him a break as she usually did. Trying to make himself comfortable, he resented Nicole's lack of attention.

It was a relatively smooth flight during the night. Finally, the following day the jet touched down on the runway in Vancouver. After the confined space in the plane, Nicole looked forward to checking into the Ritz-Carlton and sleeping in a real bed.

"Hey, Babe, I've got a meeting at the Warehouse later today," Nicole mentioned stepping inside the limo. "You'll have to fend for yourself for a while without me."

"Okay. I'll probably work out at the gym. We can meet up later for dinner this evening."

Checking into the hotel, it seemed luck was on their side. The penthouse that Bruce had always considered his home away from home was available. However, after unlocking the door, a mountain of memories came crashing in. Nicole began to feel an overwhelming sense of loss. Maybe this particular suite hadn't been the best choice.

"Geez, Babe, maybe I was wrong wanting to stay in this suite," Nicole frowned, walking inside and looking around. "I think it holds too many memories."

"Well, it was your idea. I'll arrange to have us moved into another room if you feel it's too overwhelming," Drew answered, feeling frustrated. He just wanted a place to stay. It wasn't like they would be moving in, he thought.

"Thanks. Why don't you take care of that before you work out at the gym this afternoon? I have about two hours before I have to be downtown at the Warehouse. Why don't you order room service?" Nicole remarked as she immediately began going through her clothes.

Walking over to unzip her dress, Drew kissed her softly on the nape of her neck. "Oh, I'm thinking of something much better than room service," he teased.

"Really? Drew, I feel like Bruce is watching," Nicole remarked, shrugging her shoulders uncomfortably.

"Sweetheart, I'm not bothered by an audience," he laughed, kissing her passionately as he pulled her in the direction of the bedroom. She giggled, trying to relax. I could give him a moment of my time, she thought appreciatively.

Later glancing at the clock next to the bed, she panicked, noticing the time. Then, running into the next room, she plugged in the steamer to press her pants.

"Geez. I've just enough time to take a quick shower, dress, and get down to the Warehouse," Nicole said, quickly surveying her suit for wrinkles.

The warm water felt heavenly as she jumped into the shower.

"Babe, I forgot my toiletry bag. It's got my toothbrush. Would you please bring it to me," she yelled from the bathroom.

"Yes, sir, Boss, anything else I can do for you this afternoon?" he teased.

"Yes. There's one more thing. Call downstairs and make sure the limo will be on time. I can't afford to be late." She was trying not to panic as she hurriedly got ready. Finally, moments later, she stepped outside the bedroom, giving a quick twirl. She was wearing a dark designer form-fitting pantsuit.

"Okay. How do I look?" she asked, checking her makeup in the mirror. Her dark hair was pulled back in an elegant chignon using a sapphire clip. It almost matched her eyes.

"Wow. You're stunning. I just hope the guys down at the Warehouse respect your position as the manager of House of Cards. However, Babe, I have to tell you that I certainly don't see the reflection of a manager when I look at you. Especially the manager of a punk rock band. I honestly hope this gig works out for you. I love you, and I know how much you want this. Just know I've got your back, Doll," Drew winked, giving her a quick smack on the bottom.

"Thanks, Babe," Nicole smiled, reaching for her briefcase.

Stepping inside the elevator, she caught a glimpse of herself in the mirrors. Taking a long look, she took a deep breath. There were some bits of truth in Drew's opinions. Still, she knew that her appearance did not indicate the woman of steel that existed inside. The world was yet to meet Nicole Hampton.

It was a short drive over to the sound studio in the Warehouse. She felt a tingle of excitement as she stepped out of the limo, making her way up the steps. The main lobby was slightly dark. There were only two large lights in steel frames which hung down from the tall ceilings. A musty odor that usually accompanies old buildings infused the air. Yep, without question, this looks and feels like a warehouse, Nicole thought to herself. She approached the front desk, where a young woman was busy typing away on a computer.

"Good afternoon, I'm Nicole Hampton, manager of House of Cards. I have an appointment with Lance Easton," Nicole smiled at the mousy receptionist, who looked at Nicole briefly before turning her attention back to the screen.

"Yes. Please have a seat. He'll be right out. Would you care for a drink while you wait, coffee perhaps?" the receptionist asked almost as an afterthought. Her attention was clearly on other matters.

"Oh, no, thank you," Nicole answered, brushing off the slightly dirty seat with a tissue before sitting down.

It was only moments before a tall, older gentleman walked out. He reminded her of Bruce. However, he was much thinner and completely bald. Lance had strong features and deep-set green eyes. His dark suit carried the pungent odor of cigars and cologne.

"Ms. Hampton, I believe we spoke earlier this morning. Nice to meet you. Why don't we walk back to my office," he smiled, shaking her hand.

The office was dated, emphasizing a seventies décor, reeked of cigars, and was slightly dark and dingy. Nicole couldn't help but wonder if she had the right place.

"What can I do for you?" Lance grinned, pulling out a chair for her.

"Jerry Godwin referred me to you," Nicole smiled hesitantly. Looking around, she figured if he didn't recognize the name, she would leave immediately.

"Sure, I know Jerry. I hated to hear the news about Bruce. I had just visited with him the week before he passed. He seemed to slip away so fast," Lance mentioned shaking his head with compassion.

"I know. He was like a father to me. I still can't believe he's gone. To make a long story short, Jerry has stepped down as manager of House of Cards. He plans to retire totally from the music industry at the end of this year. So I'm now the new manager of House of Cards," Nicole said confidently.

Hearing this bit of news, Lance paused for a moment. Then, sitting back in his creaky chair, he gave her a perplexed stare.

"I plan to take the band in a new direction. I'm sure Jerry may have informed you. First, I need someone in charge on the West Coast. Second, I need to bring Cameron into the Warehouse to record a new single and later an album. Third, I need to interview and hire a full orchestra. Also, I'm looking for a good songwriter. Someone who can personalize songs to fit my brother's voice," Nicole said with a serious demeanor.

"Wow, let me be very candid with you," Lance paused, puffing on his cigar.

"Please," Nicole insisted.

"At first sight, without knowing your connections, I probably wouldn't have given you two seconds of my time. I don't mean to sound crass or chauvinistic, but this industry is brutal. I'm afraid, a young woman like yourself, well, you might never be taken seriously," Lance explained, sitting further back in his chair as he took a long draw on his cigar.

"Well, I appreciate your honesty. However, I wouldn't be wasting my time sitting here if I wasn't completely serious," Nicole snapped back.

"A bit of an attitude, I see," Lance smiled. "Good. You're sure going to need it, and I like you. You've certainly walked in here with the right credentials. So what can I do for you?" Lance inquired. He truly enjoyed working with passionate and driven individuals. She fit the bill nicely.

"How about coming onboard? I need someone in Vancouver. Specifically, someone at the Warehouse to help expedite and oversee the process of hiring a group of exceptional musicians. I'm not talking mundane. I'm talking top of their game. I need a full orchestra, and I need people who can travel. You know the lifestyle, living out of a suitcase for months at a time. Also, I need a brilliant songwriter who can write songs explicitly for Cameron's voice and range. Lastly, I want to record here in the studios at the Warehouse. I would also like to interview musicians here. But if necessary, I will travel across Canada and the United States," Nicole clearly stated. "I'm looking for exceptional musicians, nothing less."

"A woman with a plan. I like that. A little aggressive, I like that too," Lance nodded. "Okay. I'm on board, but you're asking for the moon and the stars," he chuckled. "It's going to cost you. Those things don't come cheap, but I think you already know that. Okay. I'm your man. How soon do you want to get things off the ground?" he inquired, taking another long draw on his cigar.

"Today, tomorrow, but no later," Nicole smiled, relieved. "I've only got two days. Then I have to be in Hong Kong."

"Well, this must be your lucky day. I've just finished a project I was working on, and the schedule for the Warehouse is pretty much open right now," he held his hands up. "So, it looks like you've got the Warehouse, and you've got me. I have a Rolodex of musicians. It'll be a good place to start. A young friend of mine, Maxwell Kline, works on Broadway, and you need him. I want to enlist his help. He writes songs. Just the person you're looking for if you can get him. Max is in New York, and he's a busy guy. However, you might be the one person who could persuade him to join forces with us. What do you think?"

"I think he sounds fantastic. When do I leave?" Nicole answered without hesitation.

"You're serious, aren't you?" Lance laughed, relighting his cigar.

"Did you see me cringe? I have a jet waiting at the airport. I could leave tonight."

"Well, I must say, you've walked in here and blown me away with your tenacity. I love passion and ambition. You need both in this business. I'll make the call. First things first, let's see if Mr. Kline is available tomorrow. If he's free, then you might want to fly out tonight. Max is one of the best songwriters I know. You'll be fortunate to get him."

"Okay. I'm staying at the Ritz-Carlton. Call me as soon as you've talked to him. Let him know I'm available to meet with him tomorrow," Nicole mentioned getting up from her chair.

"Thank you for your time and deciding to come on board," Nicole stood. Then, reaching across his desk, they shook hands. "I'll have our attorneys draw up a contract this evening. I know there's much more to discuss, but I don't want to take up any more of your time. I'll wait for your phone call. Otherwise, if not, I'll be back in the morning around 9:00 to go over the remaining details. Again thank you for your time, and I look forward to our working relationship. Have a great evening," Nicole smiled once more as she turned around to leave.

Sitting in the limo on her way back to the hotel, Nicole contemplated what she needed to do next. Then, finally, things came into focus, realizing she needed to fly to New York. She would send Drew on his way back to Hong Kong alone. She didn't need to return with him. Jerry would be there to ensure things went according to plan. She only hoped that Drew would understand.

Nicole had only been in the business for three days, and she was already taking the world by storm. The most important part of her plan was surrounding Cameron with the right people. However, she had vastly underestimated how much time and travel would be involved as she wined and dined the most qualified candidates. Unfortunately, her career would soon impact her personal life with Drew and Nicholas.

Arriving back at the hotel, Nicole attempted to enter the room quietly without notice. She was hoping Drew was still down at the gym. She didn't relish the idea of disappointing him or, worse, hurting his feelings.

"Hey Babe, how did it go?" Drew asked, coming around the corner and kissing her on the cheek.

"Great," she paused. "I've got the Warehouse and Lance Easton to oversee things when I'm not in Vancouver. Things seem to be coming together, but I'll have to fly to New York later this evening." She didn't have to wait long in anticipation of his negative response.

"New York, Babe, we just arrived in Vancouver," Drew whined, giving her an exasperated look.

"Sorry. It needs to be done, and I've decided to go alone. So you'll have to head back for Hong Kong. Jerry made it quite clear that you need to be at the next gig on time, and I have no idea how long I might be in New York."

"Who's this person that's so important that you would leave me behind?" Drew sulked. He already wasn't liking this new Nicole. He truly felt they needed some downtime together, just the two of them.

But, instead, Nicole was all business leaving no time for him. Drew couldn't help but feel hurt.

"His name is Maxwell Kline. He comes highly recommended. He's actually working on Broadway right now, but Lance thinks I might be able to persuade him to write songs for Cameron. Awesome isn't it?" she explained, hoping Drew could share in her excitement.

"Well, not if it means I'm going to Hong Kong without you," Drew bitterly complained.

"Oh, poor baby. How did your workout go today? You look sexy in those gym shorts," Nicole giggled, walking over to sit on his lap. "Why don't you take a shower, get cleaned up, and then we'll go out to dinner," Nicole smiled, running her fingers through his wet, dark hair.

"I've got a better idea. Why don't we both jump in the shower and then go out to eat?" Drew whispered, kissing her on her ear. Just at that moment, the phone rang.

"Don't answer it," he begged.

"Drew, I have to. It could be business," she replied, reaching over Drew's arm to grab the phone.

"Nicole Hampton," she answered, sounding very professional.

"Hey Nicole, this is Lance. Well, it just continues to be your lucky day. Max is available to meet with you tomorrow for lunch at 1:00 p.m. He's staying at the Plaza Hotel. So he'll be expecting you. Good luck. I'll talk with you tomorrow."

Hearing the news, she let out a loud squeal.

"Babe, I can't believe it," she screamed, starting to do a little dance. "Regrettably, I'm out of here for the night. I'll call Jerry and have him arrange a flight back for you. I'm taking the Lear jet to New York. Mama's on a roll!"

"Geez, Doll, I was just going to tell you I was able to change our suite tomorrow, but I guess it doesn't matter now," Drew said with anguish in his voice.

"Sorry, Babe. I really am. It's just business," Nicole explained, running over to pack her suitcase. "You know, I'll probably finish out the week here in Vancouver, so I'll actually want to change suites. Can you take care of that for me?" she asked, giving him a quick kiss.

"I've got a lot to do, so I might hang back for a while and take care of things. I need to schedule further auditions for the orchestra. I also need business cards, stationary, a new briefcase, and a new business attire wardrobe."

"Doll, your new job is turning into quite the ordeal. Stop for a moment and come over here. We need to talk," Drew said, grabbing her hands as he pulled her back toward him.

"What is it? I'm in a hurry," she answered as Drew sat her on his lap.

"Nicole, remember what you said the other day about us getting married. Babe, this new job of yours, it's going to change things. It already has. Is this what you really want?" Drew asked, staring into the depths of her beautiful blue eyes. Taking his hands, he softly caressed her face. "Doll, I love you. I don't give a damn about your new job. I just want you and Nicholas. Jerry can find someone else to manage the band and Cameron's career. What do you think? Will you promise me that you'll think about it? I'm not sure I like how fast our lives seem to be spinning out of control." Drew said imploringly.

"Sure, I promise. If it ever gets to be too much, I'll quit. About us getting married, I meant what I said earlier. As soon as things slow down, we'll plan our wedding. Just take care of Nicholas until I get back. Will you?" she asked. "Now you've got me smelling like sweaty gym shorts. Thanks, Babe," she smirked, crinkling her nose.

"Well, I think I can fix that," Drew winked. Then, taking her hand, he playfully started pulling her toward the bathroom.

"Babe, this is a business trip, not our honeymoon," she giggled.

Two hours later, Nicole sat buckled into her seat as the Lear jet lifted off the runway into the dark of night. She was alone with only her thoughts. It seemed her mind kept replaying her earlier conversation with Drew. It appeared he had been serious about her quitting. She was sure of it. However, the girl he had fallen in love with was restless. She was determined more than ever to make her way to the top, and she was precisely where she wanted to be. Although, she hadn't realized how upset she would be over his comments.

"Would you like a glass of champagne?" the young flight attendant asked, temporarily pulling her away from her thoughts.

"Yes, please," Nicole replied, thinking maybe she might need something stronger. Hopefully, it would be just the remedy she needed for the long flight. After consuming two glasses and covering herself in a warm blanket, she was out for the remainder of the trip.

"Good morning Ms. Hampton. We're just about an hour out from our destination. Here's a warm towel. I thought you might want to freshen up before we land."

"Oh, thank you. Can you give me the correct time in New York?" Nicole asked, taking the towel.

"Yes. It is 9:00 a.m. Eastern Time. Can I bring you some coffee?"

"Yes, please. Thank you," Nicole smiled, stretching out her arms and standing up to stretch her legs.

"Would you like breakfast on board this morning?" the attendant asked, returning with coffee.

"No, thank you. I'll get something later after we land," Nicole said, returning to her seat.

Finishing her coffee, Nicole got up for the bathroom. It would be her last chance to freshen up before arriving downtown. Thankfully, she had brought along with her another two-piece suit. At least, it wouldn't appear she had slept in her clothes. Arriving in New York, she was anxious. Hopefully, she would recruit another vital piece to her plan.

CHAPTER EIGHT

It's complicated

Arriving downtown amid the hustle and bustle of early morning traffic, Nicole needed to make a mental outline for the remainder of the day.

First, she would grab a bite to eat from one of the local street vendors. Afterward, she would hurriedly look for a new briefcase and check on business cards. Then time permitting, she would stroll along Madison Avenue and shop for apparel. However, she couldn't afford to lose track of time. She would only be in New York for the day. Her most important goal was to leave the Empire State with Maxwell Kline in her back pocket. She needed him to agree to write music and lyrics for Cameron.

The morning had been a whirlwind of activity. Finally, glancing at her watch, Nicole noted the time. It was getting late, and she needed to hurry. Nicole's list of favorite shops seemed endless. She was also hoping to have dinner later that night with a few of her girlfriends, whom she hadn't seen in years. It appeared tonight might allow her to catch up. Finally, she wanted to brag about her new position a little.

Not too many people could claim the title of being a band manager, Nicole thought, giggling to herself.

Entering the elegant Plaza Hotel, she immediately approached the concierge at the desk to let Mr. Kline know of her arrival.

"He'll be right down. Please make yourself comfortable."

Taking a seat in the luxurious lobby, she began to feel nervous. She desperately needed him to see the importance of her visit. After talking to Lance, she was sure there was no one better. He came highly recommended.

Finally, the concierge walked over, escorting an extremely handsome young man. Appearing to be in his early thirties, he was tall with a medium build. His olive complexion and blonde hair complimented his light blue polo shirt and tan slacks. In addition, he had the most stunning blue eyes she'd ever seen.

"Ms. Hampton, I'm Maxwell Kline. Nice to make your acquaintance. Why don't we walk over to the Palm Court and have lunch?" he smiled, extending his hand. Nicole expected a handshake as she reached out. Instead, however, she was pleasantly surprised when he took her hand and briefly brought it to his lips with a kiss. It sent a shiver down her spine.

"Sure. That sounds nice," she agreed, mesmerized by his appearance.

He politely pulled out her chair, gesturing for her to sit.

"Let's order first. Then, we can discuss business while we eat. What seems tempting to you?" he asked, staring at her across the menu.

"To be honest, I'm not very hungry. However, I'd love a Mimosa," Nicole answered, placing her menu down on the table. A little something to calm her nerves, she thought.

"Well, if you're sure."

As the waiter approached their table, Max looked up. "The lady would like a Mimosa, and I'll have a glass of chardonnay, please."

"Would there be anything else?" the waiter inquired.

"No. Thank you," Max smiled, handing him both menus, his eyes never leaving Nicole.

"Lance called me last night and informed me that you're looking for a songwriter for your brother, Cameron. I believe he's the lead singer for House of Cards. He also mentioned that you've just taken over the position as his manager."

"Yes, that's correct," Nicole smiled, crossing her legs.

"Congratulations, that's quite a feat for someone so young."

The waiter returned with their drinks almost immediately. Not soon enough for Nicole, who immediately took a small sip. She was extremely nervous. She could have downed the entire glass had Max not been sitting directly across the table staring at her with his unbelievable blue eyes.

"Thank you. Now getting back to why I'm here," Nicole stated, taking another sip. "I don't know how much Lance told you last night, but I'm taking the band in a completely new direction. Lance graciously agreed to take over the West Coast operations in Vancouver while I'm overseas. I want to record some new material for Cameron at the Warehouse with a full orchestra backing. I plan to introduce him to the world as a new breakout solo artist. He's more than ready to take the stage alone. Cameron has an incredible voice. Now he just needs an incredible songwriter, you," she smiled, taking another drink.

"Did Lance tell you I'm currently working with a production company on Broadway? Unfortunately, I'm swamped these days, and I'm afraid it doesn't leave me with much free time. However, your offer does sound intriguing."

"Mr. Kline," Nicole paused, doing her best to charm him to her will.

"Let's drop the formalities. My friends call me Max," he smiled, recognizing the game she was playing.

"Well, Max, I promise you it will be a lucrative offer. I can appreciate the fact that you're a very busy person. However, your credentials are impeccable. I'm looking for someone of your caliber. The sound studio at the Warehouse is incredible, but I'm sure you're aware of that. I would only need you in Vancouver when we would be recording. I'm certainly not trying to interfere with your present partnership. Lance and I are going to be working together hiring musicians. I only want the best. That's why I'm here," Nicole reiterated while running her fingers through her long dark silky hair.

"Wow. Lance warned me about you," he laughed with a wink.

"He said you were a determined young lady. However, he never once mentioned how stunningly beautiful you were."

A feeling of warmth overwhelmed her, causing her cheeks to flush. Was Max merely flirting with her, or was this a repeat of Mr. Chau? How far would she go to ensure Cameron had the very best? Of course, it would be easier if he didn't have such ruggedly handsome looks. Unfortunately for Nicole, Max was loaded with both looks and charm.

"What are your plans for the evening? I need to make a few phone calls before giving you my decision. Maybe we could talk later this evening over dinner," Max grinned. "Have you ever been on a Broadway stage?"

"No," Nicole paused, trying not to make eye contact with him. He was starting to make her nervous. She felt uncomfortably giddy, like a teenager on a first date. What was the matter with her?

"Well, that settles it. I guess you're with me this evening," Max smiled.

Nicole instantly thought of a diplomatic solution. "Oh, I was hoping to meet with some of my girlfriends later this evening for dinner." Can't do anything with witnesses, she thought, giving herself a mental pat on the back.

"Great, invite them. The more, the merrier," Max said, amused. "Maybe they would like to take a tour of our theater as well?"

"Wow. You drive a hard bargain," Nicole laughed nervously. "Okay, I guess you've twisted my arm, but I'll need your decision before leaving New York."

Against her better judgment, she would stay over in New York. What was one day? Drew was on his way to Hong Kong. It wasn't as if anyone was waiting for her.

"All right. Thank you for the drink. Let me make a few phone calls, and I'll meet you later this evening," Nicole smiled, reaching down to pick up her briefcase.

"Wonderful. Let me walk with you back to the lobby," Max suggested, politely pulling out her chair. "May I ask where you're staying?"

"Well, I haven't decided yet."

"May I suggest here? I have lived at the Plaza for several years now, and I can vouch for their quality service."

Nicole was a little hesitant, walking up to the receptionist's desk. Certainly, there was no harm. She would be accompanied by her friends later. Even though she was still unsure what his real intentions might be, what was the worst that could happen? It didn't matter. Cameron's career as a solo artist might depend upon her decision.

"Hey John, I have a young lady who needs a suite. Could you please check the hotel availability for tonight?"

"Yes, Sir, Mr. Kline. Give me just a moment," the young man behind the marble desk replied with the quick successive sound of fingers typing on a keyboard.

"Okay, Ms. Hampton, you're all set. I have you in suite twelve on the fourth floor. Here's your room key. We sincerely hope you enjoy your stay with us."

It was done. She was in New York for the evening.

"Please allow me to show you up to your room. I'm up on the eighth floor. I've lived here for over two years. It's a great hotel and centrally located."

Taking Nicole by the arm, he escorted her over to the elevator. Reaching the fourth floor, they immediately found suite twelve. Stepping in front of Nicole, he unlocked her door.

"Okay. Why don't I meet you down in the lobby at 6:00 p.m.?" Max smiled, looking down at her staring into her sapphire blue eyes. Nicole looked up, not realizing before just how tall he was.

"That sounds wonderful. See you then," Nicole replied, almost breathless as she stepped inside. She stood with her back pressed against the door for a moment. Who was this man?

It was a good thing she had done a little shopping earlier. Finally, she would have a change of clothes. Placing her one large bag on the credenza, she took off her shoes and fell on the bed. It was time to call her old friend, Tiffany. Nicole reached for the phone on the nightstand. They had worked together as models for the same agency, and it had been a few years since she had seen her. Nicole was hoping she still lived in New York so they could catch up.

"Hey, Tiffany. It's Nicole Hampton."

"Oh my God, Nicole. It's so nice to hear your voice. It's been so long since we've talked. How are you, honey?"

"Great. I'm in New York for the evening, and I wondered what your plans were for tonight? I was hoping we could get together?"

"Sorry, I can't tonight. I have an engagement. How long are you in New York? Are you available tomorrow evening?"

"No. I'm just in town for tonight. So please, don't worry about it. I just happened to be here and thought maybe you might be available to get together."

"Well, let's chat for a minute. What have you been up to?"

"Busier than ever. I've taken over the management position of the band. I'm in New York on business."

"Wow. Congratulations. I always knew you would do great things," Tiffany exclaimed. Nicole could hear the smile in her friend's voice. "I really wished I could see you, but I've already made other plans," Tiffany continued in an excited rush. "Unfortunately, I can't get out of this meeting, and I have to go."

"As I said, I'm only in town for tonight. So it's not a problem. I'll let you know the next time I'm in the city, and we'll make plans in advance. Take care. It was nice talking to you," Nicole replied.

Next, she attempted to call Alicia, another old modeling buddy, but there was no answer. Deciding not to leave a message, she hung up the phone. There would be no point. She was sure Alicia was either working late or had plans as well.

There was only one more call to make. Calling Robin was her last resort. Please be there, she thought. Please be available for tonight. She knew she needed to have a buffer between her and Max Kline.

"Hello, is Robin there?" Nicole inquired.

"No. I'm sorry. Robin is out of town. Can I take a message or let her know who is calling?"

"Oh sure, just let her know Nicole called. I'll try to catch up with her later. Thank you."

Nicole was disappointed. There would be no one to accompany her tonight. She was on her own. She was a big girl and possibly making too much of the situation. She would be fine. For heaven's sake, she was an adult. She was the manager of a famous rock band. Deciding to set her alarm, she would take a short snooze before she needed to shower and dress for the evening. However, she only had another business suit, not knowing if the occasion would call for formal attire at dinner. Not a problem. She had been a model for too many years to let this become an issue. She would come up with something. Sliding under the warm duvet, she was out like a light bulb.

It seemed like she had only been asleep a short time when her alarm went off. Jumping out of bed, she quickly showered and dressed. Deciding to wear a prim and proper white shirt with a pair of dress pants and heels, she only needed to accessorize to pull off her ensemble. She twisted her curly black hair into a ponytail with a few loose tendrils framing her heart-shaped face. One look in the mirror told her she had managed to get it right. A quick spray of her favorite perfume, and she was finally ready. Stopping to take another glance at herself in the mirror, she panicked. What was she doing? Cameron needed Max Kline, and she needed a drink. Opening the door to the mini-fridge, she discovered a few tiny bottles of alcohol. Maybe these would do the trick and ease her anxieties, Nicole thought. Reaching for the first one, she quickly twisted the top and downed it. Perhaps one more. Just as she had finished, she remembered she hadn't eaten earlier. Hopefully, this wouldn't create a problem. However, it was too late. She could already feel the effects of the alcohol coursing through her veins. She was slightly dizzy. Hearing a knock at the door, she hesitated, almost deciding not to open it. But, that would never be an option. Cameron needed Max.

"Wow. You're gorgeous," Max complimented. "I think you might need a wrap or jacket? Our evenings can get quite cool in summer," he suggested.

"Sure. Let me grab my scarf."

Now they were out the door and on their way down to the elevator.

"Are your friends meeting us later?" Max asked.

"No. It seems they were unable to make it on such short notice."

"Well, their loss," Max smiled, stepping inside the elevator. "I've made reservations for dinner at Saville's. You'll love it. They have the best prime rib. I hope you're hungry."

"Sound delicious. Who doesn't love prime rib?"

Walking out the doors of the grand hotel and toward the waiting limo parked outside, Nicole felt dizzy. Suddenly, she slipped off the curb. The heel of her shoe caught in the steel grate of a storm drain. She panicked. Quickly, Max caught her in his arms, holding her for a brief awkward moment. He wrapped his arms securely around her waist, pulling her up against him to help steady her. His face was mere inches from hers. He was extremely handsome, looking up to thank him, and she could smell a faint hint of his cologne.

"Are you okay?" he asked, loosening his grip ever so slightly. His light touch sent shivers throughout her petite body. Then, retrieving her shoe, he gently placed it back on her foot.

"Yes. I'm fine," Nicole giggled, thankful he couldn't read her wicked thoughts.

It was only a short drive before they arrived at Saville's. It was beautifully located, near Central Park. Taking her hand, Max escorted her inside.

"Good evening, I'm Maxwell Kline. I made reservations earlier for four people. But unfortunately, not everyone could make it. Could I possibly have a smaller table for two outside in the courtyard?"

"Yes. Sir, Mr. Kline. Please follow me."

Pulling out her chair, Max seated her at one of the small wrought iron tables. Starched ivory linens stylishly covered the table draping over the sides. The glow from the candle sitting on top and the aged terracotta floors gave the courtyard an old-world ambiance. The setting was highly romantic.

"May I take the liberty of ordering for you?" Max grinned.

"Yes, of course," Nicole replied. She loved how his eyes creased around the edges when he smiled. It made him appear distinguished.

It wasn't long before the waiter came over to fill their glasses with water and take their order.

"We'll start with two house salads and two glasses of cabernet."

"Thank you. I'll be right back with your drinks."

"How was your afternoon?" he asked, staring into her eyes.

"Nothing to talk about. I took a nap."

"Sounds relaxing," he grinned.

"How about yours?" Nicole inquired.

"Oh, I spent most of the afternoon on the phone. Taking care of business," Max added.

"Speaking of business, did you happen to decide ours?"

"As a matter of fact, I've given it a lot of consideration," he paused, lounging back in his chair for a dramatic effect.

"So," Nicole smiled. "Don't leave me in suspense? What's the verdict?"

"Well, after talking with Lance again this afternoon, I've decided to accept your offer. I'm excited about the prospect of writing material for such a talented artist. Especially when he's in the process of reinventing himself."

"Thank you. You've made a wise decision. Cameron's going to be a legend. I will make sure of it, and so will you," Nicole smiled, having accomplished her mission. She raised her glass in salute.

"I know," he winked, raising his glass to meet hers.

"You talked with Lance. Did you happen to mention that I was staying over until tomorrow?" The last thing Nicole needed was word getting back to Drew about her overnight stay in the big city. It wasn't the fact she was in New York rather the reason she had chosen to stay the night. Drew could usually read her like a book. She didn't need him to read how she felt about the gentleman sitting across from her.

"Yes. I might have mentioned that fact," Max mentioned swirling the wine in his glass.

Nicole took a long slow sip. She needed to keep her buzz going. It was the only way she was going to get through the night. However, now that she had her answer wasn't she free to go? On second thought, she would see the night through. They needed to have a great working relationship. At least, this is what she told herself.

After enjoying a delectable dinner of prime rib, roasted potatoes with green peas and carrots, they decided to save dessert for later.

"Okay. I've saved the best for last. Are you ready to go?"

"Yes, of course, but wouldn't it help to know where?" Nicole asked.

"Remember, I promised to show you the theater. How does Broadway sound? The rehearsals for Good Luck Charlie, my latest production, will be over by the time we arrive, and the cast will have left for the evening. It's all ours," Max explained, checking his watch. He couldn't wait to show her his world. His name had quickly become synonymous with openings on Broadway.

Leaving the restaurant, she still felt tipsy, but she had eaten. It was only a short drive to 42nd Street and Broadway. Taking Nicole's hand, he led her in through the back entrance.

"Wasn't there a show tonight?" she asked, not remembering his earlier conversation.

"Not tonight. As I said, rehearsals are over for the evening. The show doesn't officially start until next week," Max laughed, noting her very low tolerance for alcohol.

Walking in, it was dark. Then, quickly flipping a switch, the lights came on. Nicole was amazed, noticing all the props behind the stage.

"These are the dressing rooms," Max pointed out. "Come on, let me show you the best part. Close your eyes and don't open until I tell you," he insisted.

Max took her hand as he slowly led her out to the center stage.

"Okay. Open," he instructed, watching her closely.

Opening her eyes, she found herself speechless. The view was unbelievable. It felt surreal, giving her goosebumps. Baroque details intricately encased the walls making them appear aged and worn. Nicole could visualize the long rows of red velvet seats filled with an audience each night. Pausing for a moment to soak in its ambiance, Nicole wondered what it must feel like to perform on this very stage night after night.

Before she could utter a word, Max placed his arms tightly around her slender waist. Pulling her close, he kissed her passionately. She felt weak to her knees. Being held in his arms, she was motionless, unable to stand. What had just happened? Why had she reacted with such intense feelings? It had to be the location. They were simply caught up in the excitement of the moment. Surely they had been overwhelmed by the incredible amount of passion one would have when standing center stage in such a magnificent theater. The atmosphere felt electric, awe-inspiring.

"So, what do you think?"

"Oh," she hesitated, trying to regain her thoughts as she searched for the right words. "It's spectacular. What a privilege to work in such surroundings."

Things had abruptly changed, and there was no going back. Max had definitely crossed the line of a causal relationship. She felt uncomfortable, unsure of herself.

"Well, I don't actually perform," Max smiled. "I work with the performers. The cast is very talented. I've written most of the music and lyrics for the show. I should get you back to the hotel," he added casually.

On the ride back to the hotel, it was too quiet. Nicole was confused by her sudden feelings toward him. She had accomplished her goal of obtaining the most qualified songwriter for Cameron but at what cost.

Arriving back at the hotel, Nicole was tense. She was sure he could sense her uneasiness as he took her hand carefully, helping her out of the car.

"Can I buy you a nightcap?" he smiled, staring into her eyes.

"Sure. That sounds perfect." She needed a drink, something that would hopefully numb her emotions.

Returning to the Palm Court inside the luxurious Plaza Hotel, the scenery was once again breathtaking. The maître d quickly ushered them to a table.

"Good evening," he smiled, handing them each a menu.

"I promised you dessert. They're all scrumptious," Max mentioned.

"Thanks, but I'll just stick with the drink menu. I'd like a Cosmopolitan."

"The young lady would like a Cosmopolitan, and I'd like a dry Martini."

Reaching across the table, Max took her hand.

"Please forgive me for earlier. I didn't mean to make you feel uncomfortable. It wasn't my intent. I simply got caught up in the exhilaration of the moment and overreacted. Can you ever forgive me?" Max asked sincerely.

Once again, Nicole was at a loss for words.

"I forgive you," she blushed, smiling sheepishly.

Oblivious to the late hour, Nicole and Max enjoyed one cocktail after another. Nicole no longer wished to remain sober. She highly suspected he felt the same. After what felt like hours, Max finally looked down at his watch. Surprised by the late hour, he suggested they call it an evening. Leaving more than enough money to cover their drinks and tip, it was time to go.

"Well, all good things must come to an end. I should see you to your room," Max suggested pulling back her chair.

Nicole felt hugely embarrassed. She could hardly stand. Noticing her condition, Max put his arms around her waist to offer support. His efforts at getting her to walk were futile. He would have to carry her. It appeared they were now the focus of everyone's attention. Avoiding the strange stares, Max swiftly scooped Nicole up in his arms. He carried her over to the elevator and up to his suite. Opening the door, he took her over to his bed. Gently, he laid her down, removed her heels, and placed her under the warm covers. Afterward, he grabbed a blanket and pillow. Then, being a gentleman, he slept on the couch.

Waking the following day, Nicole was alarmed to find herself in a strange bed. A raging headache and feeling nauseous soon sent her running for the bathroom. She felt like dying.

Hearing dreadful sounds resonating from his bathroom, Max came running. The door had been left ajar, revealing an amusing sight. Nicole was dealing with bouts of nausea. He couldn't remember the last time he had seen anyone so sick.

"Sweetheart, let me help you," Max said sympathetically, holding back her long hair. He retrieved a washcloth and ran it under warm water, gently wiping her face. He felt somewhat responsible for her condition. It was obvious she had had too much to drink the previous evening.

"Thanks," she attempted to smile, sitting back on her knees between episodes of sickness. But unfortunately, she still felt weak, shaky, and sick to her stomach.

"I'm so sorry. I should never have let you drink that much," Max said quietly, kneeling next to her, leaning his back against the wall. They sat quietly for a moment while Nicole pulled herself together.

Nicole's head was swimming. Had she had sex with this man last night? Her mind was a blank. She had no memory of the previous evening. Her last recollection was having drinks in the Palm Court and afterward, waking up in his bed. She could ask him about it. However, wouldn't he consider it an insult that she couldn't remember his sexual prowess? Men were so sensitive about such matters. The last thing she needed was to insult the man she needed for Cameron. She quickly decided to say nothing and wait to see if he would bring it up later.

Eventually, he stood, peeking over to ensure there would be no more bouts of sickness. Then, finding his bathrobe, he brought it to her. Once she felt like moving, he helped her back to bed.

"I'll order coffee and juice with toast," Max suggested. "Just try to sleep it off if you can. I'll be right outside in the living room if you should need me," he said, handing her two aspirin and a glass of water.

Finally, after what seemed like hours, she woke. Feeling slightly recuperated, it seemed that death had escaped her.

"Thank you. I really don't know what I would have done without you," Nicole smiled, walking into the living room. She was still embarrassed that she had allowed herself to indulge in too much alcohol.

"Sweetheart, I'm so glad you're better. I truly didn't do anything. Actually, I feel responsible for your condition," he frowned.

"Oh, I'm a big girl. I only have myself to blame for drinking too much."

"Why don't I call someone to run down to your room and bring up your luggage while you take a shower," Max suggested. "Sometimes a hot shower and a fresh change of clothes is the best pick-me-up."

"Oh, I don't want to impose."

"Trust me, it's not an imposition," he winked.

Later that evening, Max arranged for his chauffeur, Charles, to drive Nicole out to the airport. Walking her down to the lobby, he felt a connection to her. Surprised by his strong feelings, he wasn't sure how to deal with his emotions. Unaware of Max's feelings, Nicole also felt something unexpected.

"I'll see you in Vancouver. Thanks for finally saying yes," Nicole teased.

Hugging her, Max opened the car door. Watching as the car slowly drove away, Lance had been right. Nicole was extraordinary.

As the private jet lifted into the air, Nicole sat back in her seat. Finally, she had accomplished her goal. Nicole had what she came for, Maxwell Kline. However, as she thought about her past twenty-four hours in New York, there was only one word to sum it up - complicated.

CHAPTER NINE

The Warehouse

Arriving back in Vancouver, Nicole checked into the Ritz. Opening the door and walking in, it felt lonely. Drew had managed to get her suite changed before leaving for Hong Kong. Deciding to take something to help her sleep, she attempted to reset her sleep pattern. It was never easy traveling from coast to coast. Tonight she was tired. Not bothering to unpack her suitcase, she quickly changed, slipped under the covers, and instantly fell asleep. Tomorrow would come soon enough, bringing with it a hectic schedule.

Awakened by the phone in her room, she sleepily rolled over to answer it.

"Good morning, this is Lance Easton. How are you this morning?"

"Fine. Happy to be back in Vancouver. How are you?" Nicole asked.

"Great. It sounds like your trip was very productive. I'm thrilled that Max has decided to work with us. He's certainly the best at what he does. I was just calling to check what time you planned to come in this morning?"

"Well, I'm just getting up. The time change is a killer," Nicole laughed. "Give me about an hour. I haven't even had coffee yet," she mentioned rubbing her eyes as she attempted to sit up in bed.

"Okay. I just wanted to inform you that I've arranged for several musicians to come in for auditions over the next two days. I thought we should start interviewing as soon as possible. I have two guys coming in this morning at 10:00. They're both great candidates for the brass section. Do you think you could be here in time for their interviews?"

"Yes. That's awesome. Thanks, Lance, I knew I could depend on you," Nicole said, trying to wake up. She was grateful to Jerry for recommending Lance. He was everything she expected. He reminded her a lot of Bruce. He was experienced and had extensive contacts. It seemed he had stepped out of a time machine.

"No worries. I've got your back. I only have a few more calls to make. I'm trying to set up additional auditions for this afternoon. So I'll let you go and see you around 9:00."

Nicole could only hope Max hadn't spoken to Lance. She certainly owed no explanations to anyone. She needed time to sort out her feelings regarding her time in New York. She loved Drew, and she would never do anything to hurt him. Business was business. She would simply keep it as such. She felt the sooner a ring was on her finger, the better. She thought a diamond on her left hand would denote that she wasn't available, and things would begin to calm down.

Getting dressed, she was anxious to get over to the Warehouse. Hopefully, she would be on her way to Hong Kong within the next few days. So she decided to keep her wardrobe simple today. She would wear a pair of dress slacks with a silk blouse. Then, pulling her hair up in a French twist and applying her makeup, she was out the door.

Arriving at the warehouse, she looked forward to immersing herself in the process of hiring musicians. She almost couldn't contain her excitement.

"Good morning, Lance," she said, throwing him one of her smiles that can light up a room. "Thank you so much for getting the ball rolling. However, before they arrive, I'd like to get your opinion of these guys. Do you think they could readily commit to living overseas on tour? It takes more than a great musician. We're looking for unique individuals who can live out of a suitcase," she graciously reminded him.

"I know what I'm doing. Trust me. I've been doing this before you were even a gleam in your mama's eyes," he laughed, lighting a cigar. "One of the guys is divorced and has nothing tying him down. The other guy is single and unattached. It would be a waste of my time and yours to interview musicians who weren't free to travel."

After listening to their first audition with Johnathan Barnard, Nicole felt he was highly talented. Her only concern was his age. He was young, only twenty-two. Having him wait in the lobby for her answer, they discussed his resume. Lance quickly pointed out that he had recently graduated from a prestigious college majoring in music with high grades. After hearing this, it made things very clear to her. He would make a great choice.

"Okay, Lance, why don't you call him in and give him the good news. I think we've found our first musician," Nicole said, circling his name.

Next, they auditioned Jim Lansford, who was somewhat older. His resume and credentials were impeccable. The fact he was recently divorced, with no children, and looking for a change, made him a great choice. They had now found their second position.

The process was repeated over the next few days until the orchestra's brass section was filled.

Returning late to the hotel that evening, the phone rang as she unlocked the door. She dropped her briefcase by the door and threw her keys on the credenza, running to grab the phone.

"Hey, Doll. How are you? I've missed you and your cute, wicked smile, but mostly your warm body next to mine," Drew said seductively.

"Babe, I've missed you too and Nicholas. How is he?" Nicole asked, sitting down on the couch as she removed her heels with a single finger.

"Oh, he's fine. He sure misses you, though, and he asks about you. I have great news. It will make your day or evening, depending on our time differences. We'll be in Vancouver tomorrow," he stated excitedly.

"What?" Nicole squealed into the phone, sitting up straight.

"Yes. Can you believe it? Apparently, the sports dome we were scheduled to play received significant damage in a recent storm. As a result, our next venue had to reschedule. But enough talk about that. I can't wait to see you," Drew explained, barely able to contain his excitement.

"I'll come out to the airport. What time does your flight arrive?" Nicole questioned. She was mentally trying to reschedule events in her head.

"Doll, there's no reason to come. We arrive about 7:00 in the morning. We'll just see you when we get to the hotel. By the way, Cameron is anxious to get back in the studio at the Warehouse. Maxwell Kline is coming in tomorrow to work with him on some new music. He's so excited. It seems Max comes highly qualified," Drew mentioned, unaware of the implications.

"What? Did I hear you say, Max Kline?" Nicole exclaimed, feeling herself beginning to freak out.

"Yes. Sweetheart, you just hired him. Jerry says he's one of the best in the business," Drew reiterated. He was a little confused. Nicole seemed caught off guard by his news. "You did hire him, right?"

"Doll, I've got to go. I hear Nicholas crying, and I need to check on him. See you tomorrow. Love you, Babe," Drew said affectionately before hanging up.

"Love you too. Kiss Nicholas for me," she added.

She needed a drink, and the fridge was running short on mini bottles, so she called room service. She was going to need something strong and a lot of it to get through the night. She wasn't ready to see Max yet. It was too soon. Now with Drew coming to Vancouver, things were more than complicated. She needed time to sort through her feelings. More importantly, Nicole wished she could remember if anything had transpired between them. Opening a small bottle of vodka, she quickly downed it in two gulps. She needed more. Waiting for room service to arrive, she laid down on the bed. There would only be a few hours before she would see Max again. How would she handle the repercussions of her time in New York?

Hearing a knock at the door, it seemed her liquid confidence had arrived. Pouring herself another stiff drink, she sat against the bed's headboard. There was nothing she could do. Tomorrow would simply take care of itself. After two more drinks, she removed her clothes and got ready for bed. She couldn't allow herself to become inebriated. Her thoughts turned to her son. Nicholas would soon be back in her arms. It appeared the drinks had worked to calm her anxieties. She fell asleep, not waking until the next morning.

"Hey, sleepyhead. Wake up," someone softly whispered.

She could feel the warmth of his breath as it tickled her ears. Then, opening her eyes, she was ecstatic. Drew was leaning over her with Nicholas in his arms.

"Hey Babe, our flight got in earlier than expected," Drew explained, kissing her repeatedly. Nicole immediately sat up, leaning on an elbow. She reached out to the squirming Nicholas, who was anxious to be close to his mom.

"Wow. I missed you. I think this little guy missed you too," Drew smiled, putting Nicholas into her arms.

"Hey, Sweetie. Mommy has missed you so much," Nicole exclaimed. Kissing his precious little cheeks, she had never loved this little guy more than at this very moment. "Oh, Mommy missed you so very much," she smiled, kissing him repeatedly on his sweet chubby face.

"How did you get in?" Nicole asked, rubbing the sleep from her eyes.

"Oh, Nicholas and I simply stopped at the front desk. Nicholas demanded to see his Mommy, and that was that. Doll, you don't believe anyone could have stopped us, do you?" Drew laughed. "Move over. We're tired. That was a long flight," he gently pushed Nicole to the center of the bed.

Quickly removing his clothes, he slipped into bed. As he snuggled against her warm body, she was elated. Nicholas was on her right, and Drew was on her left. Having her two men so close again made her world feel complete.

"Man, I just want to hold you in my arms. It feels so nice to lay next to you again. Did you miss me?" Drew whispered, pulling her close as he kissed her on the temple.

"Of course, silly. What do you think?" Nicole giggled, turning into his kiss.

Looking over, Drew noticed Nicholas had fallen asleep.

"Wow, the little guy is out. I'm not surprised he was awake for most of the flight. He kept getting passed around by everyone on the plane. Of course, he loved every minute of it, but then I'm sure he knew he was on his way home to you. Hopefully, I can pick him up and put him to bed in the other room," Drew mentioned. Carefully, trying not to wake Nicholas, he carried him to his portable crib, conveniently packed with their luggage.

"Oh Babe, you just said *home.*"

"Doll, wherever you're at is home for Nicholas and me," Drew winked, quickly slipping back under the covers.

Hearing those words was like being hit by a bolt of lightning. She had never heard truer words. It was her defining moment. All doubts of anyone ever replacing Drew were erased. Reaching over, she put her arms around him and held him tight until he complained.

"Easy, Babe, I'm not going anywhere. Doll, I love you. Don't you know? Let me show you," Drew whispered seductively, kissing her ear.

Taking her in his arms, he kissed her passionately. Drew and Nicole spent the rest of the morning as only two people who were madly in love could, exploring the bond of intimacy which united them. Drew loved her more than he ever thought possible.

"Was it even conceivable for two people to be so in love?" Nicole wondered as she laid next to him with her long legs thrown over his.

"Doll, I'm hungry," Drew winked, rolling over to kiss her. "Let's order breakfast?" he smiled. "I'm famished."

"Drew, let's get married while everyone is here in Vancouver. It's the perfect time," Nicole mentioned with tears welling in her eyes.

"I thought you'd never ask," Drew laughed. "Wait just a minute," he smiled, jumping out of bed. Reaching into his suitcase, he retrieved a small box. Believe it or not, I've kept this with me since St. Michaels. I knew we had discussed getting married recently. I was just waiting for the perfect moment," he kneeled by the bed and placed the ring on her finger. "Okay, is it St. Michaels?" he paused.

"No," Nicole answered, wiping tears from her eyes. "St. Michaels holds too many dreadful memories," she said, admiring her left hand. "I want it to be just you, me, Nicholas, Mom, Jerry, and the guys. What do you think?" she asked, looking at him as her blue eyes sparkled with anticipation.

"Babe, whatever you want. I'd marry you anywhere. You name the place," Drew whispered lovingly.

"Okay, I'm thinking of this hotel. It was always home for Bruce. We've stayed here so much it just feels like home. What do you think?" Nicole questioned, wiping her eyes.

"The Ritz-Carlton it is," Drew replied, kissing away her tears.

"Coffee, I need coffee and food," Drew grinned, stretching back into a standing position. He reached over for the phone to call room service.

"I have to tell Mom and Jerry," Nicole sat up excitedly, throwing the covers back.

"Well, I think I would let them sleep in today. Your mom was pretty tired getting off the plane this morning. Why don't we have dinner with them later this evening?"

"Okay, I guess you're right," Nicole answered, walking into the bathroom. She needed to take a shower and get dressed.

It seemed the morning had given her the insight she so desperately needed. Her worries from the previous night no longer mattered. She was finally ready to face Max Kline.

Later that afternoon, Nicole called over to her Mom's room. It seemed she couldn't wait to give her the good news.

"Hey Mom, were you able to get some rest?"

"Yes, thanks, Sweetheart. It seems those long flights are beginning to take their toll on me. Bet you were surprised to see Drew and Nicholas this morning?" she laughed softly into the phone.

"I'll say. I really missed them a lot. What are your plans for the evening?"

"Well, it's our first night back. We haven't made any plans. Why?" Kate inquired.

"Well, I thought we could go to dinner. I haven't seen you in a while, and I have some great news," Nicole stated excitedly. She couldn't wait to tell her mother, but she had already decided that it would be in person.

"Oh, what is it?"

"I'd rather wait until tonight," Nicole explained, barely able to keep her excitement in check.

"All right, honey. Why don't you, Drew and Nicholas, come over to our room around 6:00 this evening. We'll go down to the Wharf. How does that sound?"

"Awesome, we'll be over at 6:00. See you then. Love you."

"Love you too, Sweetheart," Kate replied. She couldn't help but wonder what was up. Maybe, a new grandchild, she hoped.

Walking along the docks later that night, the water glistened as it cast back a reflection of the full moon. The Wharf had always held special occasions, and tonight would be no different. It seemed unbelievable Kate hadn't noticed the shimmering new ring she now wore on her left hand. Undoubtedly, it evidenced that her mother was still exhausted from the flight.

After being seated, ordering a round of drinks, and filling Nicholas's favorite Sippy cup, Nicole was ready to make her announcement. She couldn't contain her excitement any longer.

Looking over at Drew, Nicole smiled, taking his hand.

"The reason for bringing you both here tonight was to announce our engagement," Nicole smiled proudly, extending her left hand for everyone to see. The ring was a three-carat diamond, princess cut, set in white gold. It could practically sparkle in the dark. There would be no mistaking her status now. Again, she smugly thought to herself.

"Oh, Sweetheart," Kate cried. "I'm so happy for you both and Nicholas. I always knew you both would get married one day," Kate exclaimed, standing up to give her daughter and pending son-in-law a hug.

"So, have you set a date?" Kate inquired, returning to her seat.

"Yes. Next week," Nicole smiled, glancing at Drew. "We don't want to wait since we're all in Vancouver. Plus, we feel the timing couldn't be better."

"Wow, that's sudden. Are you getting married at St. Michaels?"

Kate asked curiously. Her mind immediately wondered if the church would be available on such short notice.

"No. I could never go back there. It holds too many painful memories," Nicole said softly, not wanting to discuss any of the details.

"Yes. I agree," Kate smiled, understanding her daughter's need to keep the mood light.

"We're getting married at the Ritz-Carlton. After all, it's our home away from home," Nicole informed them.

"Oh, Sweetheart, I think that's wonderful. How can we help?"

"Well, we've both agreed to keep things simple. We don't want an elaborate wedding. We simply want to get married."

"That's right. It could be a civil ceremony held at City Hall for all I care. I just want to marry my boss," Drew laughed, kissing Nicole.

Finally ordering dinner and a bottle of champagne, they celebrated Drew and Nicole's impending marriage.

The following day Nicole and Drew walked into the studio at the Warehouse, anxious to get the day started.

"Cameron called, and the guys have just left the hotel. Their alarm was accidentally turned off. So they overslept," Lance explained, hoping this wouldn't become a routine. However, he was old school and always expected punctuality.

"Yes. I think I've heard that excuse before," Jerry laughed, trying to lighten the mood. But, of course, being younger, he could roll with the punches better than Lance.

"Max will be arriving within the hour," Lance added. "Also, I've put us down on the schedule for a few more auditions today. It's going to be a busy day," he stated, looking over at Jerry and Nicole to ensure they were ready to get down to business.

"Just the way I like it. Maybe we can get a lot done," Nicole smiled, understanding Lance's unspoken concerns.

Finally, the boys walked in. Unfortunately, it appeared they were still half asleep.

"Wow, I need coffee," Cameron announced, casually walking toward the break room.

"Cameron, as soon as Max Kline arrives, I want you both to start working on music and lyrics. He should be here soon. After that, I will be auditioning musicians for the orchestra with Lance. Oh, one last thing, check it out," she smiled, extending her left hand. Checking out Nicole's diamond ring, Cameron was elated that his sister was finally getting married.

"Wow, Sis, congratulations," Cameron grinned. "So when's the date?"

"Hopefully next week, after we get the license. We want to get married while everyone is in Vancouver. It's going to be a simple ceremony held at the hotel. I was wondering if you would walk me down the aisle." Nicole asked her older brother with tears welling within her eyes.

"Are you kidding? I'd be honored to walk my baby sister down the aisle," Cameron answered, wrapping his arm around her shoulders while giving her a gentle squeeze.

"Thanks, Cameron. It means a lot to me. I love you."

"Ditto," he smiled, walking over to congratulate Drew. Slapping him on the back, he shook his hand and pulled him close. "Don't you dare mess this up," Cameron whispered. Cameron couldn't help but feel a little protective of his baby sister. Drew laughed it off, understanding Cameron's thoughts as an older brother.

It seemed only a short time later Max arrived. He was more excited about seeing Nicole than meeting Cameron. No matter how hard he tried, he couldn't get Nicole out of his mind. He was starting to feel like a man obsessed.

"Hey, Nicole. Max is here. He's asking for you. I think he went in the break room to get a cup of coffee," Lance informed her with a curious brow raised. Lance was no fool. He felt something was strange when Max asked for Nicole instead of Cameron.

"Thanks, Lance," Nicole answered, careful not to stare at him. It seemed he could sense what had happened back in New York. At least he had given her a heads up, and Drew was still busy talking with Cameron. But, once again, business was business. It was as simple as that. Deciding to walk over to the break room, she would see what he wanted.

Deep in thought, she almost walked straight into him. Then, finally, they were face to face. His expression was one of anticipation. Hers was one of dreaded shock.

"Oh, I've poured you some coffee," Max smiled, holding a mug. "How are you?" he smiled. Nicole was even more stunning than he remembered. As she reached for the cup, his eyes caught the diamond on her left hand. He immediately stopped dead in his tracks. Max had noticed her brilliant ring and its location.

"Wow. I must say you work awfully fast," Max exclaimed. "When did that happen?" he asked in a state of shock. He was almost speechless as he gently grasped her left hand to examine the ring more closely. He was doing his best to keep his enormous disappointment inside.

"Oh that," Nicole was also at a loss for words. She unconsciously glanced in Drew's direction. It was a good thing he was still chatting with Cameron.

"I didn't know you had a significant other? You certainly made no mention of it," Max mentioned accusingly. It was apparent he was both hurt and confused.

"Step inside. We need to talk," Nicole suggested walking in the break room as she motioned for him to follow. She closed the door behind him. Her mind was racing back to their night in New York. She still had no recollection if they had been intimate or not.

"Listen, there was no reason to discuss my private life in New York. I was simply there on business. You were the one who made things complicated."

"Complicated. Is that what you call it?" Max vented, completely perplexed.

Nicole could feel her face turning red from both shame and anger. How dare he try to make her feel guilty? He had kissed her, for crying out loud. She could barely contain her resentment as she lashed back.

"Okay. Maybe I should have told you I was already in a relationship. However, at our first meeting, I honestly didn't see the point in mentioning Drew or our two-year-old son, Nicholas. For the record, neither of us brought up our personal lives in New York," she reminded him as she pointed an accusing manicured finger at him. "Hell. You could also have a wife and kids stashed away somewhere for all I know," Nicole paused, trying to reign in her passionate indignation. After taking a shaky breath to calm down, she continued.

"I feel my personal life is simply just that, personal. As far as I'm concerned, I don't owe you any explanations. I came to New York because you're the best, and we need you. New York was just business," Nicole explained, feeling exasperated. She needed Max to understand. She couldn't afford to lose him.

Putting his hands in his pockets, he moved to stare out the dingy window. He needed a moment to process everything. He didn't know what to think, how to feel, or what to say. He didn't care that she was with another man. Hell. He didn't think he even cared she had a kid. He knew that he wanted her more than any woman he had ever wanted before. Since she had left, thoughts of her had totally consumed him.

"Please. Say something," Nicole whispered, unsure she wanted to hear his comments.

Turning to face her, he pasted a fake smile on his face. "I guess congratulations are in order. Who's the lucky guy?"

"Drew Connors, he's a guitarist with House of Cards. In fact, he's here now. I'll introduce you. However, he knows nothing of my time in New York. Except for the fact it was a business trip to hire you, and I want to keep it that way," Nicole implored, putting Max on notice.

Max was startled, surprised by Nicole's choice. He had done his research about the band before flying to Vancouver. He instantly knew the person she was referring to was Drew Connors. Max thought Drew was just another young punk in a long line of punks. The boy was a joke. He was nowhere near the caliber of someone such as Nicole Hampton. He felt his fears subsiding, so he decided to push forward. He was ready to play the part of the gentleman, for now.

"Okay. I get it. You don't have to worry. Business is business, so, when do I meet Cameron?" Max decided to put aside Nicole for the moment. He would simply get on with the reason he came.

"I'll walk you over. I need you and Cameron to go through the music and lyrics you wrote. I do appreciate the fact that you flew in this week. I'm excited to see what you have. Let's get to work," Nicole stated.

"Okay, Boss. You lead the way. Drink your coffee. It's getting cold," Max smiled, thinking this would be fun. He loved a challenge.

It seemed the morning had finally gotten off to a better start. Nicole was learning the business fast. She was organized. By the end of the day, Cameron had dropped his first single. It was phenomenal and almost guaranteed to go number one. The orchestra positions were filled, and business was good. Now it was time to do something for herself, plan her wedding.

"Drew, things are almost finished here for the day. Cameron is still going over music, but I don't need to stay. I'm going back to the hotel. I have an appointment to meet with a wedding coordinator at 7:00 tonight. I also want to check with Mom and see Nicholas. I hope she had an easy day with him. Do you want to go or hang out here with the guys for a while?" Nicole asked.

"Well, Babe, if you think you've got it all covered. After Cameron is finished, the guys and I are going down to O'Brian's for a few drinks."

"Okay. Then I will call for the car and go back to the hotel. Why don't we plan on having dinner later?"

"Sounds good. You mentioned meeting with a wedding coordinator. I thought we agreed to keep things simple?"

"Yes. That's my plan. However, we still need flowers and catering. We also need a cake and a few decorations around the pool and garden area. But, don't worry, it's nothing over the top," Nicole said, shaking her head. "It will be elegant, yet simple. Love you, Babe. See you back at the hotel," she smiled, giving him a quick kiss goodbye.

CHAPTER TEN

The Wedding

The morning sun brilliantly peeked in through the curtains immersing the room with a soft glow. Rolling over, Drew couldn't resist kissing his beautiful bride-to-be.

"Good morning, Sweetheart. Only eight hours, and you'll legally be Mrs. Drew Connors," he whispered. Using his fingers, he gently combed her long silky curls away from her face. Then, propping himself up on his elbow, he admired the beautiful woman before him.

"Oh Babe, we've waited so long for this day. It seems an eternity for us to get to this point," Nicole said softly, returning his playful advances.

"Geez, Doll," he laughed, pulling her close. "Since we're not going to have an official honeymoon, these stolen moments will have to do." Nicole giggled, catching his implications as she threw the covers over their heads.

Hearing a knock at the door, Nicole jumped out of bed. Then, securing the silk sash around her waist, she rushed over to answer it.

"Good morning. I have flowers for Ms. Hampton," the young delivery boy smiled, holding a large bouquet of red roses. The floral aroma engulfed them.

"Thank you," Nicole smiled, taking receipt of the bouquet as she quickly read the inside note. "Oh Babe, the guys have sent flowers. They're gorgeous," Nicole smiled, taking a moment to admire them and briefly inhale their lovely fragrance. "I'll order breakfast if you change Nicholas," Nicole suggested loudly from the other room. She quickly placed the vase of flowers on the credenza where all could admire them.

"Okay. After breakfast, I need to go over and check on Cameron. His fitted tuxedo was supposed to have been delivered last night."

"Mom is coming over to do my hair and makeup later. You should get dressed with the boys. Once I put on my wedding gown, you're not seeing me until Cameron walks me down the aisle," Nicole giggled.

"Doll? Haven't we already been through this before?" Drew teased.

"Yes, but this time we're actually getting married."

Only a short time later, there was another knock at the door. Drew answered it. Nicole was busy with other things. Another flower delivery. This one was a fragrant vase of pink peonies, roses, and baby's breath from Kate and Jerry. Shortly after that, another soft tap at the door announced the arrival of breakfast.

"Wow, it's beginning to feel like Grand Central Station," Drew mumbled, opening the door. He had other things to do besides answering the door all day. Nicole sensed his frustration, so she poked her head around the corner to offer a suggestion.

"I have a great idea. Things are going to get very hectic after we eat, so why don't you take Nicholas over to Jerry's? I'm sure he would love to watch him. That would leave Mom free to help me with hair and makeup while you check on the guys," Nicole proposed.

"That sounds great. It's already getting too chaotic around here," Drew answered, relieved to get away from the oncoming madness. Then, pouring himself a cup of coffee, he went to wake Nicholas.

"Babe, no complaining. It's our wedding day," Nicole smiled, attempting to calm him with a quick kiss as they passed each other in the hall.

The following six hours passed in rapid succession. Nicole and Drew, along with members of the wedding party, were busy with last-minute preparations. The wedding planner worked feverishly to finalize details. Nicole's decision to hold the small ceremony outdoors in the luxurious garden of the hotel required minimal decorations. A summer wedding at sunset under a canopy of twinkling stars provided the perfect ambiance. The soft glow radiating from numerous lit candles created a romantic atmosphere. Members of House of Cards, Lance, and Max took a seat in the empty white chairs. Since its conception, the guest list had grown to include just a few more names. It seemed worlds removed from their previous attempt at getting married at St. Michael's. Nicole had waited almost two years for this very moment.

Music played softly, signifying the time for Cameron to escort his beautiful younger sister down the aisle. Nicole looked amazing. Her stunning black curls were swept back and held in place by a shimmering veil adorned with Swarovski Crystals. She looked radiant wearing a white strapless sweetheart gown made of antique lace.

As Cameron escorted Nicole down the aisle, he desperately tried to keep his emotions in check. Thoughts of their father, Nicky, not ever having known her weighed heavily on his mind. Life wasn't fair. It just wasn't fair. It should have been Nicky standing next to Nicole, Nicky proudly escorting his beautiful daughter down the aisle.

At last, Nicole was standing face to face with Drew, the love of her life. Taking her hand, it seemed time stopped. Drew stared deep into her blue eyes. She took his breath away.

"I love you," Drew whispered, completely amazed a woman as incredible as Nicole had chosen him.

Silent tears of joy slowly made their way down Nicole's flawless cheeks. It only took a few minutes to exchange the vows that pronounced them man and wife. After a quick but passionate kiss, they turned to face those who had witnessed their vows. Kate handed a squirming Nicholas to his parents. He squealed with laughter as they kissed his sweet little face. At that point, the three of them began their way back up the aisle together. Drew and Nicole swung a giggling Nicholas into the air as they raced past the row of seats. It was time to party.

It wasn't long before everyone took a seat at the small tables beautifully decorated with flowers and candles. Arranged in small groupings, they surrounded the sparkling lit pool. It created an elegant yet informal design for everyone to gather. Before dinner, Jerry stood to offer a toast. So everyone, please raise your glass.

"Here's to Nicole and Drew. What took you so long?" Jerry laughed. "Drew, Kate, and I are happy to welcome you to the family. Congratulations."

Afterward, Cameron stood to offer his toast.

"Sis, here's to you, Drew, and Nicholas. I'm so proud to call you family. I wish you a lifetime of happiness. I love you."

Next, it was time for Harry and Doug to make their toast.

"Man, we wish you the very best. One down and one to go," Harry laughed, glancing at Doug.

The wedding party, family, and guests dined on a delicious feast of lobster, salmon, and Dungeness crab. For the non-seafood lovers, steak and potatoes were served with delectable side dishes. Champagne, wine, and beer flowed freely all night.

After everyone had enjoyed the delicious buffet, it was time for dessert. A small round table covered with a lace table cloth held an exquisite three-tiered wedding cake. The cake decorated with black musical notes and pink roses was the focus of everyone's attention. Like two kids at play, Nicole and Drew cut their cake, deliberately shoving it into each other's faces. It was hilarious as those standing nearby watched their attempts to wipe away the remains of frosting and cake.

Hotel management graciously provided music for the reception. Unfortunately, it appeared the guys had rather party than perform. However, arrangements had been made for the guys in the band to perform two songs. Cameron dedicated the songs to the loving couple. The evening turned out to be a memorable event as Drew took Nicole and Nicholas in his arms. The three danced together as Cameron and the guys finally performed their favorite songs. Kate watched lovingly with tears in her eyes. Noticing her emotions, Jerry extended his hand.

"May I have this dance, Mrs. Godwin?" Jerry smiled.

The party continued until the wee hours of the morning. Some of the guys were having too much fun and too much alcohol. Harry decided it was time for someone to take a dip in the pool. Spying Doug, he walked over and unexpectedly pushed him into the pool, fully dressed suit and shoes. It seemed to be Harry's form of entertainment for the night until Doug managed a short time later to get him back. Then suddenly, things hilariously spiraled out of control. Everyone began jumping into the pool. The guys were soaking wet as towels were brought out. It seemed an appropriate time to end the night's celebration. Photos of the saturated wet group now included Drew and Jerry. Those photos, along with the ones from the wedding ceremony, would encapsulate all the beautiful memories of their special day. Their wedding album would be incredibly hilarious.

Lance and Max walked over once again to offer their congratulations before leaving. It seemed they were the only dry men among the group. Seeing Nicole alone, Max came over first.

"Congratulations. I have to say I didn't see this one coming, but I hope you're happy," Max smiled warmly, hugging her. "I look forward to working with Cameron. You have an awesome brother."

"Yes. I know. Thank you for recognizing how spectacular he is," Nicole smiled.

Walking over to find Drew, Nicole was anxious to get this man of hers alone.

"Babe. Mom and Jerry are taking Nicholas for the night. Are you ready to leave? I think you could use some dry clothes," Nicole laughed.

"Yes, Mrs. Connors. I'm ready," Drew winked. "However, Doll, clothes won't be needed," he whispered in her ear.

"Drew, you're wicked," Nicole giggled.

They were both shocked to see a note on their door, thinking they were simply planning to spend their honeymoon night in their suite at the hotel.

"Congratulations, Mr. & Mrs. Connors. The limo is waiting to take you to the airport. The jet is ready to fly you to Maui. Enjoy your honeymoon." Love Mom & Dad PS See you next Monday.

It was the perfect ending to an unforgettable day.

CHAPTER ELEVEN

Back to Work

Even a week in Maui wasn't enough to prepare Nicole for what lay ahead. The amount of work waiting for her return was overwhelming.

"Good morning. How was the honeymoon?" Lance inquired, standing outside on the steps smoking a cigar.

"Perfect," Nicole smiled. "It was Maui. How could it not be?" she mentioned walking into the Warehouse.

"There's hot coffee in the break room. Get yourself a cup and come into my office," Lance said, turning to follow her inside.

"Okay, sounds good," she smiled.

Walking into the break room, it seemed she wasn't the only one needing a jolt of caffeine.

"Hey Cameron, what do you think of the music Max has written?" Nicole asked, giving him a huge hug. She then immediately went to the coffee maker for a cup.

"The lyrics and music are great. Max is a genius. So how was Maui?"

"Awesome, I needed that week away from work. I've got so many things that need my attention. First, lance and I have to start interviews for the remaining positions in the orchestra. Is Max still here, or did he fly back to New York?" she asked, pouring sugar into her cup and stirring it.

"Oh, Max left yesterday. He works on Broadway, did you know that?"

"How could I not know? I hired him, remember?" Nicole laughed.

"That's right. You're the boss. How could I forget?" Cameron teased.

"You may be older, but I run the show," Nicole laughed, sipping her coffee. "Talk with you later. I've got business to discuss with Lance."

Nicole walked down to Lance's office. Holding her coffee cup, she pondered what it might be regarding.

"Okay. So what's on your mind this morning?" Nicole inquired, pulling up a chair.

"Well, first, I hired three musicians. A cellist and two violinists while you were in Maui. Even though we had already filled the orchestra positions, some of them had a change of heart. Traveling isn't for everyone, and three of them decided to go with positions that kept them closer to home. I can't say that I blame them. If they're going to jump ship, at least it happened before we were overseas. Our new musicians are very talented and ready to travel. I think they'll easily meet your criteria. However, that's not the reason for my wanting to see you. I talked with Max this morning, and he brought to my attention that New York City College just graduated a class of gifted musicians. He's interviewed a few of the recent graduates for work on Broadway. Max gave me the names of two individuals. They would be perfect. I feel we should seriously consider bringing them on board also. Their young, talented, and ready to travel. He's set up interviews for you tomorrow. What do you think?" Lance questioned, lounging back in his chair.

"Really. Max set up auditions without first speaking to me?" Nicole sternly questioned. "Who does he think he is?" she demanded. She knew why he wanted her in New York. She was pretty confident it had nothing to do with interviews.

"Nicole, first hear me out. I don't think you can afford not to go. New York City College has outstanding graduates. They are some of the finest musicians in the world. I think they would be a feather in your cap if you can get them. You're looking for the best, right?" Lance explained, lighting up a cigar as he leaned back to study her. He was a little confused. Why would Nicole fight him on this? He was starting to question whether she had what it took to get the job done. Perhaps something happened in New York, he thought to himself. It wouldn't surprise him. He knew Max was a well-known ladies' man. However, she would need to learn that some men considered beautiful women weak and easy to conquer even in business.

"You're right regarding our hiring the best. Next time I expect to be informed. Do you understand? Lance, I appreciate the job you're doing here at the Warehouse. Still, no one is irreplaceable, including Max," Nicole informed him, taking a sip of coffee. "Look, I'm not trying to sound mean and unappreciative. However, I don't want to be told what to do or who to hire by some Broadway producer," Nicole remarked, attempting to get her temper in check.

She had a good idea why Max wanted her in New York but knew she would need to tread carefully around Lance. He still had no clue what had transpired between her and Max just a month ago.

"I do take your recommendations seriously. If you believe these guys are good musicians, I'll take the plane to New York this evening. You can reach me at the Plaza if you need me for anything," Nicole said, standing. She had a lot to do in a short amount of time.

"Oh, one last thing. Who said they were guys?" Lance grinned, puffing away on his cigar.

"You know Lance, you surprise me," Nicole scoffed, turning around as she opened the door. I have nothing against hiring a female. My thoughts are always what would be best for the band and logistics.

Walking down the long corridor, she saw Cameron talking with Harry. They were horsing around, pelting each other with sugar packets in the break room. Nicole poked her head in the door.

"Cameron, I'm on my way to New York. I wanted to let you guys know. I'll be back tomorrow evening. If you should need anything, ask Lance or Jerry," she smiled, walking in to hug Cameron.

"I thought you just got back?" Cameron smiled, hitting Harry between the eyes with a Sweet 'N Low packet. Then, laughing, he hugged Nicole's back, using her as a shield. "Sis, have a safe trip."

"Will do," Nicole smiled at their playful antics. She almost felt jealous of their carefree lifestyle. It must be nice to have someone taking care of you all the time, she thought.

As Nicole opened the door to their hotel suite, she could hear Nicholas laughing. "How's my little man?" she asked, reaching down to pick him up.

"Oh, he's fine. We've been playing with his fire engine. He loves anything that makes a loud noise," Drew grinned.

"That figures. He's exposed to you guys," Nicole laughed.

"You're home early this afternoon, and it's only 2:00. How's everything at the Warehouse?" Drew questioned, giving her a quick kiss.

"Well, since you asked, I'm just here to pack. I'm on my way to the airport. Max has a few auditions scheduled for tomorrow in New York."

"Babe, we just flew in from Maui last night. Nicholas hasn't seen you in over a week," Drew whined.

"That may be, but we both knew that things could get hectic when I took this job. It's going to require a lot from both of us. I love you, but I'm in a hurry. Besides, I think we've already had this discussion," Nicole explained, putting Nicholas down on the floor with his truck.

"Babe, do you want us to tag along?" Drew asked, hopeful.

"It's only an overnight trip. I think it would be best to keep Nicholas here. If I were going to be away longer, that would be great," Nicole answered, walking into the next room to grab her overnight bag. "Plus, they are going to need you in the studio. So you can't go anywhere."

Quickly removing her dress clothes from their hangers, she folded them neatly into her bag. Afterward, she grabbed her toiletry bag, which was still packed from their honeymoon.

"Drew, please let Mom and Jerry know that I'll be back tomorrow evening. I hate to leave so suddenly, but the car is waiting downstairs."

"Babe, don't you have time for dinner before you leave?" Drew pleaded.

"Sorry. Not tonight. Come over here and hug me. I love you guys.

I'll be back tomorrow," she kneeled for Nicholas and held open her arms for hugs as he ran to her. Holding him for a moment, she always felt such heartache leaving him behind.

"I will be back to tuck you in tomorrow night, baby. I promise," Nicole smiled, meaning every word of it. No sooner had she let him go, he was running to his next adventure.

Nicole was already dreading the lonely flight as she walked out to the elevator. Finally, she told herself she would no longer be Max Kline's puppet.

"Good afternoon, Mrs. Connors. Traffic looks good. It should be about twenty minutes to the airport," George, her chauffeur, announced as he opened her car door.

"Thanks, George."

Stepping inside, she made herself comfortable. Leaning her head back against the seat, she began to build a hatred for Max. She needed a drink. Reaching over, she twisted the top off a small bottle of vodka and downed it straight in only two gulps. Hopefully, this would suffice until she boarded the plane.

George was right. There was no traffic. It was only a short time before the limo parked next to the steps of the private jet.

"Have a safe flight," George smiled, opening the car door.

"Thank you. See you tomorrow evening."

"Good afternoon, Mrs. Connors. Welcome aboard," the young flight attendant smiled as Nicole ascended the plane's steps. "My name is Nina, and I'll be serving you this evening. Would you care for a drink before we get airborne?"

"That sounds wonderful. I'll have a glass of white zinfandel."

As the cockpit door opened, the pilot, Mac, walked out.

"Weather looks good. It should be a smooth flight. This evening, our flying time is estimated to be five and a half hours, and our arrival time in New York should be approximately 11:30 p.m. Eastern Time," he stated with efficiency.

"Thanks, Mac."

Nicole leaned down to open her briefcase.

"Would you like a blanket and pillow?" Nina inquired, returning with her drink.

"Oh, no thanks. I have work to do."

"All right. I'll leave you to your work. I'll be back later to inquire about dinner. Enjoy your flight."

Nicole sat back in her seat once again. Watching as the lights from Vancouver began to fade in the distance. She wasn't looking forward to her time in New York. She had just returned from the most romantic week of her life, and suddenly she was thrust back into work. Her hectic schedule had left little time to transition from honeymoon to work.

She thought it would be a great time to go over the band's expenditures, pulling documents out of her briefcase. Charles Edmond had always overseen the financial aspects of the band, but she wanted to take a quick look at the expenses for the past six months. Bruce had heavily relied on Charles. Nicole had no thoughts of replacing him now that she would be hiring musicians for an orchestra, arranging for their travel and lodging. According to Bruce, Charles was a man of few words and never sugar-coated things. Bruce had always trusted him to handle all the disbursements. Nicole was hoping to pay above scale for the new hires. It took a lot of time, effort, and expense to find the best musicians, and there was no way she wanted to lose any of them in the foreseeable future. She was determined to transform Cameron into a global icon.

It seemed she'd lost track of time as Nina came over to inquire about dinner.

"I don't mean to interrupt. You seem heavily focused on business, but I wanted to check with you on dinner. I can offer you beef bourguignon with roast potatoes, carrots, pearl onions, and mushrooms or almond-crusted salmon, wild rice, and broccoli," Nina smiled.

"Beef Bourguignon sounds delicious," Nicole replied. "Oh, I would like another glass of white zinfandel."

"I'll be right back with your wine. Your dinner should be ready in a few minutes. Is there anything else I can bring you?"

"Coffee would be nice before we arrive."

"Not a problem. I'll be right back," Nina mentioned.

The rest of the flight consisted of dinner, which was delicious, wine, work, and finally, coffee. Hopefully, the coffee would keep her awake. She desperately needed the caffeine as her body and sleep patterns were still on Hawaiian time.

"Mrs. Connors, Mac wanted me to inform you that we're only one hundred miles out from New York. Would you like a warm towel to freshen up?"

"Yes. Thank you. A warm towel would feel wonderful. I've strained my eyes looking at financial reports all night," Nicole replied, rubbing her furrowed brow.

"I'll be right back. Is there anything else I can bring you before we land?" Nina added.

"No, thank you. The warm towel sounds fantastic."

Finally, Nicole felt the wheels of the plane touch down on the runway. She was back in New York. So much had happened in less than a month. It felt as if she had entered a weird time warp. Tomorrow would be another busy day. However, tonight she needed sleep lots of sleep.

As the jet rolled to a stop, she noticed the limo waiting for her arrival. Descending the steps, the coolness of the night air felt refreshing.

"Good evening, Mrs. Connors. Welcome to New York. I believe you're staying at the Plaza Hotel," the chauffeur recounted, opening her car door.

"Yes. That's right. Thank You," Nicole answered.

Arriving at the Plaza, she was anxious to snuggle under the warm covers of a soft, luxurious duvet. She was sleep-deprived after the long flight.

After being greeted by the hotel doorman, she proceeded to the reception desk.

"Okay, Mrs. Connors, you're all set, Suite 1720. Is there anything further we can do for you this evening?" the concierge inquired.

"Yes. I almost forgot. I'd like to schedule a wake-up call for 8:00 in the morning."

"No problem. I'll be happy to arrange it. Would there be anything else?"

"No, thank you."

Receiving her room key, she felt like she had been given the keys to paradise. She walked over to the elevator. She was on the seventh floor. Finally, as the elevator stopped, she walked down to Suite 1720. Unlocking the door, she put her overnight bag on the credenza and collapsed on the bed. Slipping under the warm covers, she was out for the night.

Waking the following morning to her phone ringing, Nicole glanced at the clock. It was 8:00 a.m., the scheduled wake-up call. She had miraculously slept the entire night. A warm, refreshing shower would start the day. Afterward, she would order breakfast. After deciding which clothes she would wear, she walked into the bathroom. Standing under the warm water, it felt like heaven. Lathering her hair with shampoo, she briefly shut the water off, thinking she heard the phone ringing. Deciding she didn't care, she turned the water back on and finished up. Whoever it was would have to wait. Lingering in the shower for a few minutes more would be the only solace she would enjoy before beginning her stressful day. Drying her hair and quickly getting dressed, she felt her strength renewed. Finally, she felt confident to take on the day ahead. A jolt of caffeine was the only thing missing.

The blinking light indicated the earlier call as she reached for the phone to order breakfast. The caller had left a message. There were very few people who knew she was in New York. Only two people instantly came to mind, Drew or Max. Either way, she would need to hear the reason for their attempt to reach her. Picking up the receiver, she pushed the button to retrieve the message.

"Good morning, Nicole, Max Kline. Lance informed me last night you were staying at the Plaza. I hope I caught you before breakfast. I've taken the liberty of reserving a table for two downstairs in the Palm Court. Please join me for breakfast at 9:00. Then, we'll go over our schedule for the day. Look forward to seeing you."

Glancing over at the clock, it was 8:45. It seemed needless to order breakfast and eat alone. After all, Max was the reason for her being in New York. She knew a conversation regarding their working relationship was long overdue, and there was no way to avoid him. Picking up her briefcase, she locked the door and walked down to the elevator.

As Nicole approached the maître d, Max caught sight of her and immediately walked over. He was casually dressed, wearing tan slacks, a white button-down shirt, and a sports jacket. Max always exuded confidence and a suave demeanor. This morning would be no different. Nicole was now a married woman and would no longer be seduced by his good looks and charm. At least this was her story, and she was sticking to it. However, she braced herself upon his approach. As much as she tried, she still felt his ruggedly handsome features and blonde tasseled hair alluring.

"Good morning, Mrs. Connors. I've reserved a table for us. How was your evening?" Max asked, smiling rather seductively.

"It's Nicole," she replied as he pulled out her chair. Smoothing her flowing floral dress under her, she gracefully took her seat. Unfolding her napkin, she placed it on her lap. She looked stunning. Her dark hair fell past her shoulders, accenting her long slender neck.

"I got in about 11:30 last night. Sorry, I forgot to call. I fell asleep. Lance tells me you've scheduled two auditions today."

"Yes. That's right," Max smiled, picking up his menu. He tried not to stare at Nicole. However, he still found her completely captivating. "Let's order before we discuss business. I could use a cup of coffee," he added. Then, deciding his coffee needed a boost, he asked for a shot of Baily's to be included.

"Coffee sounds great," Nichole replied, glancing at her menu. She was feeling good. She finally felt confident and back in control.

Enjoying her cup of coffee along with a delicious fruit platter, Nicole was anxious to hear Max's plan for their day. First, however, she needed to clarify a few things with him.

"Max, before we talk business, I just want to clear the air about one thing. I appreciate that you've scheduled these appointments, but I expect to be informed in the future. Especially considering the fact you have no knowledge of my professional schedule or what appointments I've already booked," Nicole explained with a firm gaze.

"Nicole, it was never my intent not to inform you. It was simply the fact that you were unavailable and in Maui. I was fortunate enough to meet Brian and Jillian last week at the theater. They've just graduated from New York City College and are very talented musicians. I'm sure Lance told you. Brian is a pianist, and Jillian is a violinist. These kids are young, extremely gifted, and available to travel. They're exactly the artists you need to complete the orchestra. But, Nicole, time isn't something you have," Max insisted, wiping the corners of his mouth with his linen napkin and laying it on the table. He looked at Nicole with complete sincerity.

After pausing briefly, he continued stressing his words, "After their auditions today, you should get them signed to a contract. Neither of them will be available for long. Trust me. Someone will take notice of their talent. I just hope they're still available. In this town, gifted musicians don't have a problem finding work."

"You sound pretty sure of yourself. It does seem they meet my criteria. However, I've not hired any females yet. I believe it would be easier for everyone involved to have an all-male orchestra," Nicole proposed, unsure how to explain her reasoning without sounding biased or insecure.

"Wow, Mrs. Connors. You shock me," he looked at her with blatant surprise. "Surely, I don't denote a little discrimination. I certainly didn't expect to hear that from you, of all people. You strike me as a woman who would want to promote other women in this business. Since there are so few of you, I think you have enough confidence in yourself and business to hire another woman," he remarked, hoping she could overcome her nurturing nature. He figured she probably felt protective of the boys and wanted to shield them from their childish impulses. Many bands fell victim due to female drama while on the road. However, he knew you never turned away talent because of gender.

Nicole understood where Max was coming from, and she certainly had no problem hiring other women. It had more to do with Lance being old school like Bruce, and his Rolodex contained primarily male contacts. She felt utterly confident regarding hiring other females. Nicole hoped that Jillian would be her first female musician satisfying his demeaning curiosity. Max threw her a curveball as she sipped her coffee, contemplating what he had just said.

"So, Mrs. Connors, the wedding. That was fast," Max stated casually while cutting into his omelet. "As I recall, you were not wearing an engagement ring when we first met. Then almost overnight, you were engaged and married." Max questioned, looking at her inquisitively.

"Okay, first of all, stop calling me Mrs. Connors," she said a bit forcefully. "Is that supposed to be funny, sarcastic, or both? Secondly, I'm not trying to sound discriminatory. Let me meet Jillian, and I'll determine if she would be the right fit. My priorities will always be to do what's best for the band. That's my job."

Nicole was perplexed on how to address her reasons for a quick marriage. Most men wouldn't understand why a woman would need a ring to ward off unsolicited advances. So how do you explain this without sounding absurd? How do you explain this as a defense to keep men at arm's length? Men rarely had these worries. She felt quite simply a wedding ring would be her first line of defense. However, she was young and somewhat naïve. Nicole would soon learn that a band of gold on her left hand wouldn't ensure she received the respect of everyone she met. Especially in her line of business.

"What's with you? Why do you insist on calling me by my married name?" Nicole asked, highly irritated by his behavior.

"I always assumed newly married women loved their new title," Max smirked. He was pretending to be confused. It was simply an act. He was trying to understand her sensitivity regarding her married name. Maybe she wasn't as in love with Drew as she made it appear. It seemed to give him hope. "Sorry, Sweetheart. I didn't mean to upset you. Did I touch a nerve?"

"There you go again, acting like a jerk," Nicole fumed furiously.

"Okay, calm down," he said, attempting to change the mood. "I'll do my best to keep my comments about your personal life to a minimum. We don't have to discuss anything but business. So, speaking of business, have you hired an orchestra conductor? The reason I'm asking is you're going to need someone. Someone in the business who knows how to deal with individual musicians," Max inquired, sitting back in his chair sipping his coffee with Baileys.

"No. I haven't given it much thought. Lance and I are still

interviewing musicians at this point." Nicole felt herself beginning to calm down as she now turned her focus to this new task.

"Well, I'd like to apply for the position. I love my job here in New York, but I find myself getting restless. I'm totally qualified. Lance will vouch for that, and I'm already working for you. It would just be an added benefit. What do you think?" He placed his coffee cup down to look at Nicole intently.

Wow, Nicole thought, only he would be arrogant enough to make her angry and still ask for a job. The man had balls she'd give him that. "Well, you've caught me off guard. Although, practically speaking, it makes sense," she paused for a long moment hoping to make him sweat.

Max was right. He was the perfect person for the job, and she couldn't argue with that. So she decided she wouldn't let her personal feelings get in the way of a good business decision.

"All right, you're hired temporarily, at least for now. First, I need to see how you interact with the musicians. If it seems like a great fit between you and the orchestra members, then you can stay," Nicole answered, now admiring his tenacity.

"Trust me. I've worked with musicians and actors whose egos were so huge that I had to handle them with kid gloves. Hell, I've been in the industry long enough to know how to deal with all kinds of people. I could be in Vancouver later this week," Max said, obviously expecting Nicole to have given him the job. His arrogance knew no bounds.

"Okay, we've scheduled auditions for next week. If you're in Vancouver, you could become an integral part of the interviews. I'm on my way to Hong Kong the week after. After that, our overseas tour is scheduled to resume. I want to finish our commitments and introduce Cameron to his fans as a new solo artist. I want every radio station to be playing Cameron's new single by the time we return stateside," Nicole explained, unable to keep the excitement out of her voice. She loved her job, and it clearly showed.

"Wow. I love a woman with a plan. I'm excited. I can't wait to get back to Vancouver and make things happen. Since we're finished with breakfast and strategizing, I'll call for the car. I've arranged to hold the auditions at a local theater. The first one is scheduled for 10:00 and the other for 11:00. So we should be on our way," Max suggested, leaving more than enough money to cover their meal.

Only a few hours later, Nicole hired Brian and Jillian. Finally, she had her first female member of the orchestra. Max had been right. They were both gifted and ready to travel. She had accomplished her goal of signing a pianist and the remaining violinist. She had also hired Max to conduct the orchestra, something that she had simply overlooked until this morning. Unfortunately, Nicole had not thought about the repercussions of Max traveling with them everywhere.

Nicole was unaware that Maxwell Kline wasn't about to give up on winning her heart. It hadn't mattered that he had attended her wedding or that she now wore a ring on her left hand. None of the details regarding her name change to Connors meant anything to him. She had everything he was looking for in a partner. He easily recognized she had the right pedigree, connections, ambitions, and motivation. She was a challenge, and he had never met anyone with more tenacity. She mirrored his enthusiasm and fortitude. Max knew she would never stop until she had attained success, and he felt drawn to her energy. He also believed Drew was nowhere close to being her equal. It was easily reflected by the fact he had remained in Vancouver. Guys like Drew never stayed at the top. Max knew by joining forces with Nicole, they could take the music industry by storm. He would not stop until he made it happen. With Nicole's help, he planned to build an empire.

CHAPTER TWELVE

New Digs

As the plane touched the runway in Vancouver, Nicole looked down at her watch. It was only 6:00 in the evening. She had arrived earlier than expected, and Nicholas would still be awake. She couldn't wait to see her little boy and Drew.

Opening the door to their suite, she was surprised and disappointed to find the room empty. After searching the other rooms, she eventually picked up the phone and called her mother.

"Hey Mom, I just got in from the airport. By any chance, is Drew there with Nicholas?"

"Oh honey, you're back. Yes, they're here. Why don't you come over? I'll let Drew know you're back," Kate said with enthusiasm at having her daughter back.

"Mom, if it's alright, I think I'll stay put for the evening. It was a long flight, and I'm exhausted." Nicole explained, feeling the effects of the trip.

"Okay, Sweetheart, no problem. I'll let Drew know that you're back. I'm sure he'll be right over. See you tomorrow. Get some rest. I love you."

"I love you too, Mom."

Nicole could hear squeals coming from Nicholas only minutes later as Drew unlocked the door. "Mama, Mama," he called in a sweet little voice as he ran down the hall to her room. Nicholas began bouncing on the bed and into her arms for a gigantic hug. He shrieked as she began tickling him and blowing raspberries on his tummy.

"Babe, welcome home. We missed you," Drew smiled, watching Nicholas as he continued to jump on the bed. Then, after exchanging kisses with the men in her life, she leaned back on the bed.

"Mommy missed you so much. Did Daddy take good care of you?" she asked, snuggling his little body next to hers.

"How was your trip? Did you manage to finish everything?" Drew asked. He hoped they could finally have some family time since Nicole was back. It was strange having her gone so much. He couldn't help but feel she was missing quality time with their son.

Nicole decided to postpone bedtime and spend time with her boys. After playing with Nicolas on the floor with his trucks and feeding him dinner, she gave him his bath. He loved his nightly ritual. Afterward, Nicholas was out like a light bulb. Finally, asleep in his crib, it left his parents alone for the night.

"Hey Doll, would you like a glass of wine?" Drew asked, relieved that he finally had his wife to himself. He didn't want her to get too tipsy because he had plans.

"Oh, that sounds wonderful. Why don't we enjoy it outside?" Nicole suggested as Drew grabbed a bottle of wine.

The crisp evening air felt invigorating as they walked outside. Pulling up a patio chair, Nicole sat down and waited for Drew. She inhaled the night air, just enjoying being home. She hadn't realized how much she had missed them both.

"Okay, Babe, here's your glass," Drew smiled, sitting next to her. "So, how was New York?"

"Hectic as usual, I'm just glad to be back," Nicole said, giving him an appreciative glance. "Max has agreed to take the position as conductor of the orchestra and writing for Cameron. Working on Broadway for many years has given him the experience we need. I think he'll be a great asset to the band," Nicole explained.

"Well, if you say so, but there's something about him I don't trust."

He couldn't put his finger on it, but Max just gave him a bad feeling. "Promise me you'll be careful. Remember, this is your show," Drew winked, quickly finishing his drink. He didn't want to talk about other men right now or business, for that matter.

"Thanks for your support, honey. We'll be leaving for Hong Kong on Friday. Unfortunately, I had to change the venue to a different location, and it appears to be practically sold out already. So you'll be performing indoors at the Asian Art Center," Nicole mentioned pouring herself another glass of wine. The sun was beginning to set as hues of purple and pink streaked across the horizon. Nicole and Drew sat admiring the view, temporarily forgetting the world around them.

"Should be a great gig," Drew nodded to himself, bringing them back from their mental reprieve.

"Yes, should be. I have to push through more auditions starting tomorrow. I'm relieved to have Lance and Max in charge of Vancouver." Nicole didn't want to think about everything that still needed to be done.

"Wow, Babe, you've got a lot on your mind. So let's call it a night. Too much stress for such a gorgeous woman," Drew stood up and took her glass.

"I think I can help with that," he laughed. Then, reaching for Nicole's hand, Drew pulled her up from the chair. Nicole squealed as Drew scooped her into his arms and carried her inside. "God, I've missed you," he laughed, softly kissing her neck.

"Geez, Babe, maybe I should leave more often," Nicole giggled in anticipation.

The following morning after breakfast, Nicole and Drew dropped Nicholas off with Kate. She answered the door with her short curly hair held back with a gold clip. Kate was always eager to have the opportunity to be with Nicholas. He was the son she never had.

"Hey Mom, Nicholas has already eaten breakfast. Is Jerry coming down to the Warehouse this morning?" Nicole asked, placing the squirming Nicholas down. He took off like a racehorse running around looking for his toys.

"I don't know. Jerry's in the shower, let me ask him," Kate turned to ensure Nicholas was settling down before heading for her bedroom. Then, she returned a short time later with more toys.

"Jerry said he would ride down with the guys. He said not to wait that he would just meet you later," Kate put a hand on Nicole's arm, trying to keep her from running out so quickly. "Wait. You don't have to run out so fast, do you? You haven't told me about New York."

"I don't have time to discuss everything now. Maybe we can talk tonight over dinner. I love you. See you later," Nicole smiled, gently removing her Mom's hand as she went to give Nicholas a quick kiss.

Arriving at the Warehouse, it was a beehive of activity. The newly hired musicians were busy rehearsing. Musical notes blared from various instruments as she walked into the sound studio.

"Just what I like to see, a man taking care of business," Nicole laughed, poking her head into Lance's office.

"Good morning Nicole, how was New York?" Lance looked up from the mound of paperwork on his desk.

"Great. Max will be arriving later this week. I've hired him to conduct the orchestra."

"Yes, he called me, and he also informed me that you hired the two graduates. Great decision," Lance leaned back in his squeaky chair and examined her expression. "By the way, Max is an excellent choice, and it will certainly give me more time to devote to advertising. Also, I think you'll be pleased to know my Rolodex contains hundreds of well-known radio personalities," Lance nodded toward the one on his desk. His Rolodex was worth its weight in gold. Sometimes he wondered if he should keep it locked in a safe.

"Just what I wanted to hear, that's why I hired you," Nicole smiled, very pleased with how the day was starting. Drew popped up behind Nicole, putting his arm around her waist. He smiled at Lance and waved a greeting.

"Drew, what time are the guys arriving this morning?" Lance turned his focus toward him.

"I'm not sure," Drew gave a brief shrug. "However, we just left Jerry's suite. He said he would ride down with the guys."

"Okay, as soon as Harry arrives, I'd like to incorporate him into the rehearsals. Also, I'll need you on guitar," Lance said almost as an afterthought. "Nicole, I've set you up in the office near the front. I think you'll find it's to your liking. Check it out. If anything is missing, let me know. Now, if you don't mind, I need to get back to work," Lance smiled, returning his attention to mounds of paperwork sitting on his desk.

"Thanks, Lance. Drew and I will walk over and take a look," Nicole replied though she wasn't sure if Lance was even paying attention at that point.

"Doll, you have your own office," Drew grinned as he picked her up and spun her around. "Congrats, Babe." Nicole laughed, smacking his arms. She was getting dizzy and immediately motioned for him to put her down.

Walking into her new digs, it was spacious. It was more than she could've imagined. Thankfully, it was not a dingy, dated replica of Lance's office. The room was a perfect size. A mahogany desk sat in front of two tall windows, which took in the dramatic views of the city skyline. Vast amounts of sunlight filtered in, making the room bright and cozy. A stunning mahogany bookcase lined the entire length of one wall. It was lit, and Lance had already incorporated photos of the band. Looking around, she smiled, noting a blue playpen in the corner for Nicholas. Lance had thought of everything. Sitting on top of an antique credenza was a coffee pot and everything needed to get her mornings started. Finally, oversized blue pottery containing tall lush foliage sat on each end of a long sofa. It just completed the ambiance.

"Wow," Nicole smiled, spinning around in the high-back leather chair. Is this impressive or what?"

"Geez, Doll, it's unbelievable. I think Nicholas will really like it," Drew ran his fingers across the wooden details of Nicole's new desk.

"Oh, Drew, isn't this impressive. Come over here and kiss me. It's great he thought of Nicholas. I'm sure he'll like spending time here," she went around to embrace Drew, pulling him close to her.

"Hey, maybe we should think of christening this desk. Just for luck," Drew winked. Then, as he leaned down to plant a solid kiss on his woman, there was a knock at the door. Disappointed, he reluctantly walked over to answer it.

"Nicole, I just received a call from Max. He's arranged to fly in this evening," Lance grinned, poking his head in, unaware of the interruption. "So, what do you think of your new office? Does it meet with your approval?"

"Oh Lance, it's spectacular. I love it. You've thought of everything," Nicole said warmly, giving him a heartfelt hug. "Even a small play area for Nicholas."

"I'm happy you approve. I'm temporarily going to redo the corner office for Max," Lance looked around, admiring the taste of his decorators. Maybe he should think about getting his office updated. Nope, he thought. He hated change when it came to his personal stuff.

"Speaking of Max, I'm glad to hear he's decided to come over a few days earlier. It'll give us time to get things taken care of before I leave. It's going to be a busy week," Nicole thought about how much work still needed to be done. The sooner he got here, the better.

Hearing another knock, everyone glanced toward the door. It seemed the guys had finally arrived.

"Hey Jerry, come check out Nicole's new office," Drew held his arms wide, displaying the new digs.

"Wow, Sis, this is quite remarkable," Cameron grinned, walking in and plopping down in the big leather chair behind the desk. Then, leaning back, he laughed, "I need to get me one of these."

"Yes. I never had an office like this," Jerry commented, looking around with a bit of envy. "But, I'm happy for you. You deserve it."

"This is awesome," Harry added, trying to maneuver Cameron out of the high-back leather chair. Cameron got up reluctantly as Harry sat down and immediately began spinning it around. He was acting like a kid on a playground. It only took a moment for him to lose interest in the chair as he hurled himself onto the sofa. "There's even a sectional where we can hang out."

"Well, you're not hanging out here today. I think you guys have a lot to do this morning," Nicole laughed at their antics.

"Okay, boys, let me introduce you to our new musicians," Lance suggested. "Follow me, let's get out of here and let Nicole enjoy her new digs," he smiled at her knowing she would be relieved to have the room to herself for a while.

"Oh, Jerry, before you leave, don't forget we're having dinner tonight," Nicole yelled over her shoulder as she walked toward her new desk.

"All right, Sweetheart, see you later this evening," Jerry turned to Drew. "Come on, man. This includes you too."

"Babe, I'll catch up with you later," Drew smiled, giving her a quick kiss.

The guys had just closed the door on their way out when she received her first phone call.

"Good morning, Nicole Connors," she answered, loving the sound of her new name.

"Hi, Nicole, Maxwell Kline. I heard you have a new office," Max chuckled.

"Yes. It's very efficient," Nicole couldn't help but smile as she ran her fingers along her smooth desktop.

"Great. Did Lance tell you that I'm arriving this afternoon?"

"Yes. He did."

"Wonderful. I managed to tie up all my loose ends in New York faster than I originally thought. I knew you were planning to leave by the end of this week, so I wanted to come over a few days early. I'm anxious to meet the musicians which Lance and you've hired. Plus, it will give me some extra time with Cameron. I'll see you in the morning."

"Okay. I'll see you tomorrow. Have a safe flight."

"Thanks, Mrs. Connors."

Nicole could almost see his smug smile.

At last, she was alone. Spinning around in her chair, she stopped and simply enjoyed the moment. Taking a long look around the office gave her an overwhelming feeling of power. She was exactly where she wanted to be. Modeling would've never allowed her to be in control of her destiny. She would have always been signed to an agency's contract or obligated to others. It was a poignant realization. Stepping into the position as manager of House of Cards was life-changing. Indeed Bruce was looking down with a huge smile. Finally, having found the right men to assist her, she was ready to take on the world.

CHAPTER THIRTEEN

Hong Kong

Ascending the steps to the Lear jet, they were finally leaving Vancouver. Hong Kong was the next stop to finish the Pacific tour.

"Mom, do you want to keep Nicholas in the back with you and Jerry?" Nicole asked while boarding the plane. "I want to go over some paperwork before I fall asleep." Opening her briefcase, it seemed to get heavier every day.

"Sure, Sweetheart, no problem. I purchased some new books for Nicholas. I think he'll love them," Kate smiled, taking her grandson and his travel bag from his mother.

It wasn't long before everyone was on board and settled into their seats. Glancing out the window, Nicole watched the skyline of Vancouver get smaller as the plane lifted off the runway. The sun's reflection sparkled and danced on the inlets of water surrounding the city. Nicole finally felt an attachment to the beautiful city below as it began to fade in the distance. Taking one last view of Vancouver, she had a hard time focusing. So many things had transpired in such a short period. She was now leaving Vancouver as a married woman. Lost in the moment, Drew pulled her thoughts back to the present.

"Why is Nicholas in the back of the plane with your Mom?" Drew inquired as he settled into his seat.

"Oh, I wanted to go over my schedule before I got too sleepy. It's just easier to work with him in the back. Also, Mom brought along some new books," Nicole smiled, reaching into her briefcase.

"So, what's on your agenda?" Drew asked, stirring a vodka and orange juice.

"Well, after we check into the Mandarin Hotel, I want to make sure the roadies are in Hong Kong. Their flight is supposed to arrive tonight. Tomorrow, I'm going to hire a few locals to help set up the venue. After that, I have to make an appearance at the radio station. I've also decided to wait on the interview at the television station. I think it would be best not to hold interviews until we've made our announcement regarding the redirection of the band. So it appears my first day in Hong Kong will be hectic. Do you think you can take care of Nicholas? I think Mom and Jerry are planning to do a little sightseeing tomorrow," Nicole pleaded, taking a sip of coffee.

"Nicholas will be fine. I'll take him out for a walk. Oh, I think Doug and Alondra will be traveling together this time. Did you reserve an extra suite for them?"

"Yes, Doug reminded me yesterday when he called to confirm the flight plans for Hong Kong. They should arrive around the same time we do. I'm excited we get to see them again," Nicole smiled. Then, she began reminiscing about some of their past adventures and found it sad that Doug would soon be leaving.

"Yes, me too. I will miss Doug when he leaves," Drew mentioned finishing his drink.

Trying to find a comfortable position, he reclined his seat, tossing around a bit before putting a pillow behind his head.

"I'm sure Kate and Jerry will need to get some rest, so I'll try and get some sleep while they have Nicholas," Drew crossed his arms and closed his eyes.

It seemed a long and tiring flight for everyone on board.

Arriving in Hong Kong, it was raining as they descended the plane's steps. Hurrying over to the limo, Drew quickly covered Nicholas with a blanket to keep him from getting wet.

"Man, I couldn't sleep a wink on the plane. I'm exhausted," Jerry complained, stepping inside the car. Nicholas stayed awake the entire flight. He couldn't wait to turn over the rambunctious toddler to his parents.

"Geez, Jerry, you're getting old," Harry teased as Jerry gave him a dirty look.

"I agree with Jerry. Getting under the covers of a warm blanket would feel really good right about now," Cameron agreed, yawning. He always found it difficult to sleep while traveling on a plane. To Jerry's annoyance, he had fun keeping his little nephew all riled up during the flight.

"All right, guys, go get your rest. Tomorrow night is our first performance. I've given each of you the privacy of having individual suites," Nicole stated to applause from the boys as everyone climbed into the limo.

As the car drove under the brightly lit entrance of the hotel, it was still raining torrents. Jerry inquired if anyone wanted to stop briefly at the bar inside the lobby.

"Guys, in honor of Bruce, why don't you join me for a quick drink," Jerry thought they would continue Bruce's tradition of a nightcap in a new place.

"Jerry, that sounds wonderful. However, I think Nicole and I will take Nicholas up and put him down for a nap," Kate yawned. Finally, she was ready for bed.

"Mom's right, but please include me in your toast to Bruce. I'm sure he would approve," Nicole smiled, giving Jerry a quick hug.

Walking into the spacious lounge, Jerry and the guys each took a seat at the bar.

"Well, is it Jack Daniels straight, no ice for everyone in honor of Bruce?" Jerry grinned as the bartender came over.

"Yes. Absolutely," Cameron answered, slapping his hand down on the bar with a smile. Then, turning toward the bartender, "You heard the man, five tall glasses of Jack Daniels straight up."

As the waiter returned, he lined their highball glasses filled with whiskey on the bar.

"Okay, men, please raise your glasses in honor of Bruce," Jerry grinned, lifting his glass.

"Bruce, here's to you. I know you're looking down with a smile. You're the reason we're all here. Miss you, man," Jerry toasted.

Sitting here with his boys, Jerry knew he would soon miss the camaraderie of being with them when he retired. However, time marches on, and it was time for the younger generation to step up. He felt proud to know that Nicole would be in charge. She was family, but she carried Nicky's tenacity more than that. She had been right to redirect the band. Now it was Cameron's turn.

After a few more rounds, it was time to retire.

"Thanks, guys, I'll always have this as one of my fondest memories," Jerry grinned, feeling his eyes moisten. "Now, I think, we're all long overdue on some sleep," he added, covering the bar tab. "Let's go find those rooms, shall we?"

Walking in, Drew was surprised to find the room dark and quiet. Nicole had put Nicholas in his crib, and she had fallen asleep on the couch. He quietly walked over to her and leaned down to whisper in her ear.

"Hey Doll, time for bed," Drew gently picked her up. Carrying her over to the bed, he pulled back the covers and gently laid her under the soft blankets. Slipping into bed next to the love of his life, he snuggled against her warm body. It seemed the effects of the whiskey soon invaded his body with sleep.

Not waking until morning, they were all making up for lost sleep. Even Nicholas had slept soundly through the night. Finally, the brightness of the morning sun woke Drew first. He decided to ease out of bed, allowing Nicole at least another hour before he would have to wake her. After ordering coffee and breakfast, Drew walked outside to the patio for a smoke. Standing against the rail of the balcony, he took in the impressive views of Hong Kong as he lit his cigarette. Unexpectedly, thoughts of Nicky entered his mind. Even though he had never met him, he could only imagine the drive and determination it must have taken to reach the pinnacle of success as a rock icon. Drew knew without a doubt that Nicole carried within her the same motivation and strength of character. He felt extremely fortunate to know this beautiful girl was now his. Feeling someone softly touching his shoulder, Drew turned around to find his beautiful wife standing behind him with a cup of coffee. He didn't think he would ever get used to the sight of her.

"Good morning, Babe. I saw the balcony door open. Room service delivered breakfast. Are you hungry?" Nicole smiled, leaning into his chest and snuggling her head against him.

"Oh, I didn't hear the door. So I walked outside to have a cigarette," Drew leaned down, tenderly kissing the top of her head. He inhaled her scent briefly before she took a step back, handing him the coffee she had been careful not to spill. He smiled, looking over at her, "I guess I lost track of time."

"Yes. You seemed deep in thought. What was going through that sweet little head of yours?" Nicole asked, her eyes meeting his as she took a sip from the steaming mug.

"Doll, just you," he winked, giving her one of his sexy smiles. "I'm so proud of you," he grinned, giving her a more intense, passionate kiss than before.

"Thanks, but I think we better go in and have breakfast before it gets cold," she smiled, pulling back, hating to break the moment.

Walking in, it seemed someone else had finally awakened and escaped his porta-crib.

"Why don't you go ahead and start eating," Nicole laughed, trying to catch her little boy before he ducked under the table. "I'll change Nicholas. We'll be right back." She scooped him up and threw him over her shoulder as he squealed with delight.

It wasn't long before she returned with their handsome young man dressed in blue jeans and a sweatshirt which read, "House of Cards." A photo of his daddy was on the back and the rest of the band.

"I think someone else is ready to eat," Nicole smiled, trying to adjust Nicholas's baby seat. Why did they have to make these damn things so complicated, she thought? Frustration over, they finally sat down together.

After enjoying a leisurely family breakfast, the morning began to race by as Nicole looked over at the clock.

"Wow. Is it almost 9:00? I've got to shower and dress. My first appointment is at 10:30. Promise to take good care of my little man today," Nicole demanded, running for the shower.

Quickly getting dressed and grabbing her briefcase, she was ready for the day ahead. She decided to wear a standard black pantsuit with a white silk blouse. Her jacket had a single clasp currently open, and her hair was pulled back in a French twist with a diamond bobby pin holding it in place. As usual, she looked stunning. Her heels clicked against the dark marble floor as she quickly walked over to her little boy.

"All right, I'm out of here," Nicole leaned down, kissing him. "I'm not sure what time I'll be back. I have Nicholas's clothes for tonight lying next to his crib. My first stop is the radio station downtown. Then I want to check in with the guys at the venue. Stan was supposed to hire a few locals to help set up tonight. So guess, I'll see you later," Nicole stood up and kissed Drew on the cheek before walking out the door.

Turning on the television, it seemed the weather had finally cleared. Drew decided to take Nicholas outside for some fresh air. Finding their jackets, he put on a baseball cap hoping he wouldn't be recognized. Then, putting Nicholas in his stroller, they headed for the elevator. Today he would spend some quality time with his son at the park. Afterward, it would be time for lunch and a nap.

The afternoon flew by as Drew and Nicholas were out longer than expected. Exploring a toy store on the way to the park and stopping for ice cream, it seemed Drew had accidentally foregone his son's nap time. Drew began to entertain thoughts of having more children. He wanted a sibling for Nicholas. A playmate who would be close to his age. Plus, he had always wanted a little girl. He imagined how wonderful it would be to have a smaller version of Nicole to look up to him.

It appeared Nicole had easily gotten the attention of the station manager. He promised to give House of Cards promotional time for their nightly concerts and a continual play of the band's number one hits throughout each day. In return, she had left behind almost a dozen free tickets. A few of the tickets were given away randomly in a contest held by the station. The remaining tickets were for private use by those in the office.

Arriving at the Asian Center for the Arts, Nicole was anxious to get inside and talk with Stan. It was a massive complex covering an entire city block. Walking inside, she quickly found her way down to the stage. It was hectic as everyone was busily preparing for tonight's concert. Crates and equipment were everywhere. Stan came running over as he saw Nicole walking down the aisle.

"Hey, Mrs. Connors, what do you think? This place is gigantic. Eighteen thousand seats and we're sold out," Stan smiled with his arms out wide to reflect the significance of his words.

"Yes. I know," Nicole smiled, reflecting his enthusiasm. "That's fantastic, but please just call me, Nicole. How many security personnel do we have for tonight?"

"Well, I'm glad you're here. We have fifty scheduled. They routinely work the events held here at the center, but I'd like to hire additional security. I want to ensure that every part of this event is covered, from the parking lots to backstage," Stan said, quickly flipping through the pages on his clipboard.

"How much security do you think you'll need to hire?" Nicole looked down at his clipboard as if it might hold the answers.

"I would like to hire an additional fifty to beef up our crew. Would that be all right? I don't want any problems our first night. If I find they're not needed, then tomorrow night, I can cut some of them loose," he explained, hoping to get her to agree.

"Okay, do what you feel is best. It won't be a problem. Were you able to bring in a few locals to help set up for the two nights we're here?"

"Yes. Mr. Chung put out a call. He was flooded with applicants wanting the job. I think we'll have enough employees to handle everything that needs to be done for tonight easily."

"Thanks, Stan. It sounds like you've got it all under control. I'm going back to the hotel. I'll see you later tonight. If anything changes or you need me, don't hesitate to call," Nicole informed him, walking back up the aisle.

"Thanks, Mrs. C," Stan yelled with a smile.

"Okay, Mrs. C, it is," Nicole reluctantly agreed, returning his smile.

Arriving back at the hotel, Nicole was relieved to know there was more than enough time to get a quick nap, eat lunch, and change clothes.

"So, how was your day?" Nicole questioned, walking in as she tossed her briefcase by the door. She kicked off her heels and stretched out on the couch.

"Fun. How did it go at the radio station?" Drew popped his head in from the balcony, smoking a cigarette.

"Great. My day has gone extremely well. Let's just hope it continues throughout the rest of the evening. Is Nicholas taking a nap?" Nicole asked, placing her arm over her eyes.

"Yes. We were out longer than expected today. We discovered an interesting toy store, and I had to add to Nicholas's collection of fire trucks."

"Really," Nicole peeked out from her arm. "Please tell me you took the batteries out."

"Don't worry, Doll. I temporarily removed them for the evening. You should have seen his little face, though. He loved it," Drew laughed, remembering Nicholas's excitement. "Kate and Jerry visited the Peak and Giant Buddha today. You know how much your mom loves to check out all the tourist attractions. They've invited us to dinner tonight after the concert. What do you think?" he asked, taking a drag on his cigarette.

"Sounds like fun. Did they say which restaurant?" Nicole mumbled, feeling herself being pulled into the realm of the sandman.

"No. I guess we'll find out later tonight. It should be an interesting surprise knowing your mother. Jerry informed me the guys would be ready to leave for the venue around 5:30. They'll meet us in the lobby later."

"Okay. I'm going to close my eyes for a little bit. Please wake me up in an hour," Nicole rolled onto her side facing the sofa, instantly falling asleep.

"No problem. Get some rest. I'll change Nicholas when he wakes up and pack his diaper bag for tonight."

All too soon, it was time to leave. Nicole managed to rest for a while and grab something to eat during her time back at the hotel. Locking the door, Drew carried Nicholas over to the elevator for the short ride down to the lobby.

Nicole saw Doug and Alondra talking with Jerry and Kate as the elevator doors opened. Alondra looked cute in a simple black dress that stopped short just above her knees. Doug seemed extremely happy with his arm draped casually around her shoulders. Walking over, Nicole was anxious to speak with them.

"Congratulations, Doug told us about your engagement," Nicole smiled warmly. "I sure hate to lose Doug later this year, but I certainly understand. May I see your ring," Nicole looked down at Alondra's hand to admire her engagement ring. It was stunning, a three-carat diamond Marquise.

"Oh, here," Alondra extended her left hand for Nicole to get a better view. "It's funny. I never seem to get tired of looking at it. By the way, congratulations. I heard you and Drew recently got married. I'm so excited for you both. I'm sure Nicholas was thrilled to be there for his Mom and Dad's wedding. He looks a lot like Drew. He's adorable."

"Oh, thanks, everyone says he favors his grandfather, Nicky."

As the rest of the crew finally arrived in the lobby, Jerry began herding them toward the limo waiting out front.

The ride over to the venue was filled with conversation and laughter.

"Wow. Look at those lines," Alondra was shocked seeing the crowds as the limo drove around to the back entrance.

"We're sold out for both nights. It's amazing," Nicole smiled with pride.

Walking in, a long row of golf carts awaited their arrival. Everyone quickly got into a cart and followed Jerry and Kate down to the dressing rooms.

Opening the door, a floral fragrance of fresh flowers infused the air. There were colorful bouquets of roses sitting everywhere. Catering was beginning to set up for the night. Delectable aromas wafted through the air. Warming trays were being filled with a delicious assortment of Asian delicacies. Catering had arranged beef brisket noodles, egg tarts, crab claws, lobster spaghetti with Napoli tomatoes, and sticky rice. Also, a beverage service of tea, soda, and milk had been set out on a long sideboard. There was also an assortment of local beers and rice wine.

Kate had been carrying Nicholas, so she handed him to Nicole. Then, checking to ensure that she had adequate lighting above the tall ornate mirrors, Kate finally opened her makeup cases.

"All right, who wants to go first?" Kate turned to the boys sitting on the couch.

"Guess I'll volunteer," Cameron sauntered over, sitting in the vacant seat.

The following hour was spent ensuring the guys all looked spectacular. Finally, everyone enjoyed the delicious array of local delicacies and the friendly conversation of those standing nearby. House of Cards had always been a close-knit family, and tonight would be no different.

"Wow, what an assortment of local foods," Harry rubbed his hands together, walking past the sideboard holding the various assortments.

"Jerry, I've got a question. I know the venues have always offered the guys the very best of their local cuisine, but do you think they would feel offended if I mixed things up again. I'd like to request only hors d'oeuvres and non-alcoholic beverages in the dressing rooms?" Nicole questioned. "Except on special occasions," she added.

"Well, if you remember, Bruce was a food connoisseur. The man loved to eat," Jerry laughed. "He always picked local restaurants that were known for their cuisine. The guys and I always indulged him by tagging along after each concert. But you know what, Bruce was always right. I'll credit him for introducing me to some of the world's most interesting delicacies. He was an epicurean at heart. Sorry didn't mean to ramble. I miss him. Just one bit of advice, if you're serious about mixing things up before the concert, it might be best to run it past the guys. I'm not sure they would care, but best to ask their opinions first," Jerry suggested.

"Thanks, Jerry. I appreciate your advice. Soon, we're going to be traveling with an inordinate group of musicians, and I would like to offer canapés, side dishes, an assortment of finger foods, and a complement of beverages. I want to make sure all of our personnel have access to food and beverages at each concert. In addition, I want to include the roadies and security," Nicole explained.

"I think that's a wise decision," Jerry laughed. "I'm sure a well-fed group would be more productive. Look at the time. I think you better put the boys on notice. Only fifteen minutes before showtime," he yelled out to everyone in the room. "Listen, Nicole. You're doing one hell of a job. Bruce would be proud. Don't doubt your decisions, and just go with your gut. If you need me, I'm here until the end of this tour, and you know you can call me anytime," Jerry gave her a huge hug.

Alondra went over to give Doug a quick hug and kiss before he walked down to the stage with the guys.

Nicole felt like a proud parent walking her boys down the long hallway toward the stage. Even though she was younger than most of them, she had quickly earned their admiration and respect.

"Okay, guys, go out there and give your fans in Hong Kong an unforgettable concert. I'm sure Bruce, Nicky, and Jenna are watching from above. So, let's give them something to smile about," Nicole slapped Cameron on the back, giving him a knowing look.

Nicole watched her boys with purple spiked Mohawks from the back of the stage. They stood with anticipation, wearing converse sneakers, torn jeans, and T-shirts, which exposed bare arms covered in weird tattoos. They were more than ready to run on stage to the roar of their fans. It was evident Hong Kong loved House of Cards. Nicole got goosebumps.

After giving each other a high-five, Harry walked on stage, first beginning his warm-up on the drums. A few minutes later, he was followed by Doug and Drew, who held their guitars high in the air. Then, finally, Cameron walked out to the center stage, sending the girls into a frenzied screaming state of pure pandemonium. The massive coliseum resonated with the excessive movements, dancing, and screams that echoed off the walls. The atmosphere was electrifying as flames shot upward from the stage while brightly colored spotlights crisscrossed the audience and stage.

"Good evening, Hong Kong," Cameron shouted, holding his guitar high in the air.

"Hong Kong, we're thrilled to be here," Drew yelled, raising his guitar.

"Thanks for coming. Are you ready to party?" Doug screamed, fist-pumping the air.

Leading into one of their number one hits, *Backed against the Wall*, their fans were out of control, stretching forward almost as a single body trying to touch them.

Continuing to watch the monitors, Nicole caught sight of Alondra, who was dancing in the mosh pit near the front of the stage. She appeared utterly captivated by the experience of watching her fiancé perform. However, Nicole wondered how Alondra quickly got down to the front of the stage. Then suddenly, she noticed Stan leaning against the sidewall. Evidently, Doug had made arrangements for Stan to escort her. Nicole felt relieved knowing Stan was nearby. An accident in the mosh pit was the last thing she needed to happen, especially with Alondra and on their opening night.

The concert continued its energetic frenzy for an hour and a half. The fans were so enthusiastic the guys felt compelled to come back on stage and play two additional encores. It was definitely a memorable evening. Nicole seemed elated to know these were her guys, and she was now in charge. But, all too soon, the concert came to a close.

"Goodnight, Hong Kong, we love you," Cameron shouted, lifting his guitar high.

"Thanks for coming out to party with us," Drew yelled, raising his guitar.

"We love you, Hong Kong," Doug screamed with enthusiasm.

The boys walked off stage as their fans shouted out their love for Cameron and House of Cards.

"Cameron, you were awesome. You guys rocked," Nicole laughed, meeting them behind the stage. "Bruce would have been so proud of each of you."

The following evening, House of Cards completed their scheduled stop in Hong Kong. Their concerts had been very successful, and as a result, Nicole and House of Cards had become a phenomenon in the world of punk rock.

It was time to return to Vancouver as the Pacific Rim tour ended. Finally, Nicole felt confident everything was in place. It would be an easy transition for House of Cards. Lance and Max had filled the remaining positions. The dedicated efforts of the musicians who now made up the new orchestra had resulted in a cohesive unique sound. Combined with Cameron's latest singles, which were rapidly climbing to the top of the charts, there was only one thing left, take the show on the road. Nicole was like a thoroughbred at the starting gate. She couldn't wait to be let out. Finally, at last, they were on their way home to Vancouver.

CHAPTER FOURTEEN

Welcome Home and Farewell

A roar of applause echoed from the back of the plane as it touched down in Vancouver.

"Wow, Babe, we're home," Drew proclaimed, taking in the views from his window.

"Great tour, guys. Welcome home," Jerry slapped, and high-fived the band members as the private plane slowly rolled to a stop.

"Man, it's so good to be home," Cameron grinned, giving Harry a high-five.

Looking out her window, Nicole watched as the limo arrived parking at the plane's steps. She was excited to be settled once again into the luxurious Ritz Carlton. It always felt like home. Drew held Nicholas as they descended the steps of the Lear jet.

"Wow. I think there's a little bar downtown calling my name," Jerry laughed, stepping inside the limo. "You guys feel like a night at O'Brian's?"

"You don't have to ask me twice," Cameron jumped into the limo finding a seat next to the mini-bar.

"Babe, I guess this is the end of the road for us," Jerry boasted, becoming emotional. He put his arms around Kate, kissing her on the forehead.

"Congratulations, I guess I need to hire another stylist for the band. I'm sure I speak for all of us when I say how much we're going to miss you both." Nicole reached over, wrapping her arms around her mom.

"Well, it's been a fun gig, but it's time for us old people to finally retire," Jerry grinned, leaning back in his seat.

"Listen, Jerry, you might be old but don't include me in that statement," Kate insisted, giving him a half-hearted slap on his arm. "Just ask Nicholas, and he'll tell you. He has a young grandma," she laughed.

Reaching the bar, Cameron quickly filled seven shot glasses with bourbon handing each one a drink. "I think it's time for a quick toast."

"Here's to Jerry and Kate. It's been an amazing adventure. Enjoy your retirement. You've certainly earned it. You'll know where to find us if you should ever get bored. We love you," Cameron raised his glass in salute to Jerry and Kate.

"Guys, let's go to O'Brian's tonight and help these two old people celebrate. Is everyone in agreement?" Drew suggested looking around the limo.

"Here, here," Harry agreed. He was never one to turn down a party.

Parking under the brilliantly lit entrance of the Ritz, Drew exited the limo, first holding Nicholas. Everyone was anxious to receive their room keys and relax before the impromptu retirement party as they walked into the hotel.

"I've arranged for you to have your own suite," Nicole smiled, handing out keys. "We're all up on the 12th floor, except for Mom and Jerry. I've managed to reserve the penthouse for you. It's Bruce's former suite," she smiled, herding everyone in the direction of the elevator. "Mom, I guess this means you'll soon be house hunting in Vancouver."

"Yes. I know the perfect location," Kate smiled dreamily.

"Babe, I think that might be up for discussion," Jerry hinted. Kate shook her head at Nicole behind Jerry's back. Jerry might force her to settle down, but she knew she would have the final say as to where.

"Hope everyone is ready for a little fun this evening. I've arranged for the car to pick us up at 6:00 tonight," Nicole reminded them, stepping outside the elevator.

"Sounds like fun. See you later, Sweetheart," Kate smiled, kissing Nicholas on his forehead.

Opening the door to their suite, it felt like home. Noticing Nicholas was asleep, she kissed his soft chubby cheeks.

"Babe, why don't you put Nicholas to bed? I'll order dinner and a bottle of champagne. We can have dinner outside on the balcony and enjoy a glass before we leave for O'Brian's," Nicole suggested as she headed for the bedroom.

"If you say so, but I can think of better things for us to do with our time," Drew grinned seductively, attempting to follow her.

"Drew, I swear you have a one-track mind," Nicole teased, pushing him back toward their boy's room. "I'm afraid it will be dinner and champagne, at least for now," she winked.

"Okay, Boss. Whatever you say," Drew winked.

After dinner arrived, Drew popped the cork from the champagne. Filling two fluted glasses, he took their drinks outside. Grabbing her sweater, Nicole followed him outdoors. Dining on stuffed lasagna, garlic bread, and salad, they sipped champagne while taking in the dramatic views of the sunset. It cast brilliant hues of purple, pink, and orange over the vast skyline of Vancouver before finally setting behind the majestic snow-covered mountains. The panorama was breathtaking. A cool breeze swept across the balcony as Drew reached over, wrapping Nicole in her sweater.

"I love you, and I'm so proud of you. I want to make a toast to your accomplishments."

"Doll here's to our new journey. I sincerely hope the upcoming tour is everything you've ever dreamed of and more. I know Bruce will be watching you every step of the way. Babe, I love you," Drew toasted.

"Thanks, Sweetie. I love you too," she leaned over, giving him a quick kiss.

Hearing the phone, Drew went inside to grab it.

"Drew, Maxwell Kline. How are you? Is Nicole available?" he inquired.

"Yes, hold just a second," Drew answered, wondering why in the world he would attempt to intrude on their first night back.

"Nicole, Maxwell Kline is on the phone. Suppose he needs to speak with you," Drew said, clearly annoyed.

"Hello," Nicole answered curiously.

"Nicole, Max Kline. How are you?"

"Fine, just a little tired from the flight. How are you?"

"Fine, thanks for asking. Listen, I hate to impose on your first night back. Still, I just wanted to inform you I have all the musicians coming in early tomorrow morning at 8:00 for practice. I thought perhaps you might let Cameron and the guys know, so we could also run through the music with them. Will this fit into your schedule?" Max asked.

"Sure. Sounds great. Hopefully, I'll have the guys at the Warehouse before 8:00. They're planning an evening out at O'Brian's tonight. But I'll cut off their drinks earlier in the evening if need be," Nicole knew they might not like it, but this was business.

"What's the occasion, if I might ask?"

"Oh, just a spur-of-the-moment celebration for Jerry and Kate. He's retiring this week."

"Please, congratulate him for me. That's wonderful. I guess this means you're losing your co-pilot."

"Yes. Would you like to stop by and have a drink with Jerry and the guys?"

"Thanks. That sounds like fun. What time is everyone gathering at O'Brian's?"

"We're leaving the hotel around 6:00 this evening. Why don't you call Lance and let him know? I wouldn't want him to feel left out," Nicole suggested as an afterthought.

"Great idea. I look forward to seeing you tonight. I'll give Lance a call now."

"Okay. See you later this evening."

"So, what was that all about?" Drew questioned, handing her another glass of champagne.

"Oh, Max informed me he scheduled a rehearsal with the orchestra early in the morning at the Warehouse. He's anxious to get you guys together with the musicians. Max and Lance filled the remaining positions while we were on tour. I truly don't know what I would do without those two. Geez, Babe, I feel you truly despise Max," Nicole mentioned, taking another sip of champagne.

Hearing a soft knock at the door, Drew walked over to answer it.

"Drew, is Nicholas still sleeping?" Kate inquired.

"Yes, but come in," Drew smiled.

"Oh, I just wanted to stop by for a moment. I've arranged for someone to watch Nicholas tonight. If he's sleeping, you won't have to disturb him. The hotel concierge will make the necessary arrangements. Oh, please don't worry, Nicholas will be in great hands. I just wanted to let you both know. I've got to run. I'm still trying to figure out what I'm wearing tonight."

"Thanks, Mom. That was so nice of you. See you in the lobby at 6:00," Nicole smiled, giving Kate a quick kiss as she closed the door.

"I think I'll jump in the shower. By the way, what are you wearing tonight?" Nicole asked.

"Wow, Babe, let me think," Drew teased. "It isn't a formal occasion, so I don't understand why it's so important. Only you and your Mom would even give it a second thought. So what is it about women and fashion?" he teased.

Standing in the shower underneath the warm water felt like heaven after the long flight. Closing her eyes as she lathered her hair with shampoo, she felt Drew's hands. He gently pulled back her long hair as he seductively kissed the nape of her neck.

"Thought we should conserve water," Drew laughed.

The shower instantly turned into a hot and steamy rendezvous as he kissed her more intently. His romantic gestures made her laugh. They were like two kids at play and madly in love.

"Doll, it's almost 6:00. Time to go," Drew mentioned looking over at Nicole as they got dressed in the bedroom.

Hearing a knock at the door, he went to answer it.

"Mr. Connors, I'm Brianna. Tim sent me up to watch Nicholas," the young lady stated.

"Sure, please come in. My wife is almost ready. Nicholas is sleeping. I'm sure he'll probably not wake up. He's had a rather long day. His diapers and wipes are on the changing table, and he has milk and food in the fridge. If you should have any problems, the phone number where you can reach us is written down on the notepad on the table," Drew instructed.

"Thanks, I'm sure it won't be needed," Brianna smiled.

Walking out of the bathroom, Nicole took Drew's breath away. She was gorgeous, wearing a long black halter gown. It fit her like a glove, accentuating the curves of her petite frame. Her long black hair was swept back in an elegant chignon, exposing the brilliance of her diamond earrings.

"Wow, Doll, you're gorgeous," Drew winked. "I thought we discussed the fact it's not a formal occasion," he smiled, taking her by the hand as they walked over to the door.

"Oh, this," Nicole smiled, looking down at her gown. "Do you like it?"

"Like it? Doll, it's exquisite," Drew added, escorting her over to the elevator. The instant the doors closed, he took the opportunity to hold her in his arms, kissing her passionately.

"Babe careful, you'll ruin my makeup," she laughed.

All eyes were on Nicole as they exited the elevator.

"Wow, Sweetheart, you look lovely tonight," Kate complimented.

"Sis, that's quite a dress," Cameron smiled admiringly. He punched Harry hard in the arm after seeing him leering at his sister. Jerry whistled and smiled at his beautiful stepdaughter.

"Okay, everyone, the limo is waiting," Jerry turned to their small group and began maneuvering them all outside.

"So, would anyone like a drink?" Doug asked as everyone was comfortably seated inside the car to ride downtown to O'Brian's.

"Is the Pope Catholic?" Jerry teased.

Doug laughed, popping the cork on a bottle of Moet & Chandon.

Filling seven glasses with the sparkling drink, Doug handed each one a glass.

"Here's to a night of fun. Here's to Jerry and Kate," Doug toasted.

"Yes, Congratulations, Uncle Jerry," Cameron toasted.

As the limo parked in front of the small quaint bar, Nicole's legs buckled from beneath her as she stepped out. Noticing her dilemma, Drew caught her before she fell.

"Geez, Babe, I think you've already reached your quota for drinks this evening," Drew joked, trying to balance her with his arm.

"Sweetheart, are you alright?" Kate asked with concern.

"Oh, I'm fine, Mom. Drew and I had champagne earlier this evening. I guess it's the accumulative effect. Don't worry. I'll get a cup of coffee," Nicole explained, embarrassed by the incident. Drew gave her a quick kiss as they continued inside.

Entering O'Brian's, Max noticed Nicole immediately. Walking over, he hugged her, and his hand lingered ever so slightly at the small of her back. Drew scowled, watching this unorthodox display of affection.

"Wow. I must say you look ravishing," Max smiled wickedly.

"Thanks. Was Lance able to make it tonight?"

"No. However, he asked me to extend his apologies. He said he would see you at the Warehouse in the morning. It seems he had a prior engagement."

"Can I have everyone's attention," the Maître 'd announced. "We have a table reserved in the back. Follow me," he added, leading the way.

The bar was a replica of one owned previously by the proprietor in Dublin. Honed wooden beams crisscrossed the low ceilings, and aged stone covered the walls that held soft glowing lanterns. A baroque mirror enhanced the expansive dark oak bar. The European ambiance of the tavern made it feel cozy. Its unique characteristics made it very popular with locals as well as tourists.

It had seemed only momentarily before people began recognizing the guys' connection to the band. Immediately, they were inundated with requests for autographs. The guys courteously signed anything they were given as they made their way through the crowd. Straightaway fans focused on Cameron.

The evening was off to a good start as the waiter walked over to take drink orders and recommend their best appetizers, including seafood and meat pastries. Next, the guys ordered a round of Guinness while Kate and Nicole drank wine for the evening.

"Well, guys, I have an announcement to make," Doug stood, getting their attention. "I'm leaving for Oahu tomorrow evening. Alondra is meeting me at the airport in Hawaii. I can't begin to tell you how excited I am to be with her again finally. On the other hand, I'm going to miss each of you terribly. Guess you'll know where to find me after tonight. You're all welcome to come over or stop by when you're on the islands. Oh, you'll be receiving your wedding invitations as soon as we nail down the exact date. It's been a privilege being on stage with you. I'll never forget the awesome times we've all shared. Thank you for making these past two years unforgettable."

"Oh Doug, none of us had any idea you would be leaving so soon," Cameron replied, walking around the table giving him a solid hug. The other band members took turns to hug him or slap him on the back.

"Doug, I know I speak for all of us here. We're sure going to miss you. I know your family must be excited, especially Alondra," Nicole smiled warmly, raising her glass toward him.

"Doug, as soon as Kate and I get settled in a house in Vancouver, we would love to have you and Alondra come over for a visit," Jerry added. "It's been a pleasure working with you, and you'll be missed."

"Thanks, Jerry. I'm sure Alondra would love that. I'll always consider each of you as family. We've experienced some legendary moments. Thank God Bruce was an epicurean. That man sure loved to eat each night," Doug laughed. "He led me to the love of my life. Jerry, you're one hell of a good guy, and it was also my pleasure working for you. Nicole, I can only imagine the road ahead for you and the band. I'm sure Nicky, Jenna, and especially Bruce will be watching from above," Doug smiled. "Congratulations and good luck. I love you all."

"Well, since Douglas has made his announcement, I'd like to take this opportunity to express my gratitude to everyone here. You've all made my life truly rewarding. Of course, I also have Bruce to thank for bringing Kate back into my life. It seems everyone at this table has been greatly affected in one way or the other by Bruce. So let's make one last toast to Bruce, Doug's new adventure, Nicole, and, of course, my retirement," Jerry smiled, standing with a raised glass.

"Here. Here," Harry commented, slamming his fists on the table.

"Here's to our memories of Bruce, Doug's new life in Hawaii, my retirement, and my girl, Nicole. I know you're going to make quite a name for yourself in the music industry. Bruce was right. You're going to keep those seats sold out at every venue. Good luck, Sweetheart," Jerry toasted.

It was a private moment only understood by those sitting here and their connection to House of Cards. It was time to embrace a new beginning.

CHAPTER FIFTEEN

Taking Care of Business

As the morning sun peeked in through the curtains, it was time to start the day. Pushing off her alarm, it was 7:00.

"Babe, time to get up. We've got to hurry," Nicole rolled over, kissing Drew awake. "I need you to call Cameron and Harry. I have to make sure they're both awake and getting ready. Remind them the limo will be arriving to pick us up at 7:45. Then, I'll wake Nicholas and change him. After that, Mom can give him breakfast this morning," Nicole added, running for the shower. "Oh, please call Mom and remind her that we'll drop Nicholas off," Nicole yelled before closing the bathroom door.

It was a whirlwind of activity trying to get everyone ready and out of the hotel when the car arrived. Finally, after dropping off Nicholas, they were on their way downstairs.

"Whew, that was nerve-racking," Nicole sighed, taking a deep breath as they entered the elevator. "I just hope Cameron and Harry are in the lobby," she mentioned as the door opened.

This morning, luck was on her side, catching a glimpse of their sober faces. Harry was rubbing his brows, obviously still fighting off the effects of last night. Cameron looked slightly better, but he could always hold his liquor better than most.

"Wow, after last night at O'Brian's, I was afraid you guys might be running late this morning," Nicole smiled.

"Are you kidding? We wouldn't make you look bad on your first day back," Cameron grinned, stepping inside the limo.

"Well, thank God, I can depend on you," Nicole replied, sitting back. "I think Jerry and Kate are going to look at houses today. I'm excited for them," she rambled nervously.

Arriving at the Warehouse, Nicole was again anxious to see her new office. But, unfortunately, she had hardly had any time at all to use it before leaving to finish their overseas tour.

"Babe, I'm going to check out my office. Do you want to stop in for coffee before you start rehearsals?" Nicole suggested. "Cameron, why don't you and Harry come over for coffee too?"

"Thanks, Sis, but I think we'll hit the break room. I'm afraid your sofa looked too inviting last time. Wouldn't want to crash on your couch before rehearsals even start."

"Doll, think I'll join Cameron and Harry. It's almost 8:00. We don't want to be late and make the boss mad on her first day back at work," Drew winked, giving her a quick kiss and tap on the bottom.

"Okay. Suit yourselves," Nicole laughed.

Walking into her office, she discovered it was just as she had left it. Looking around, she couldn't believe it was real. Sitting down in the high back leather chair, she spun around. Life was good, unbelievably good. She had hardly had a moment to enjoy her surroundings when she heard a knock at the door.

"Please come in," Nicole answered.

"Good morning, Nicole. I brought you a Caramel Macchiato from the coffee shop on the corner. Thought it would be a nice way to welcome you back," Max smiled, handing it to her as he sat on the edge of her desk.

"Thank you. I was just discussing coffee with the guys," Nicole smiled, taking a sip. "Wow, this is a nice way to start the morning."

"Lance is in the studio with the musicians. I was just waiting for Cameron and Harry to arrive."

"Well, they should be in the studio now," Nicole mentioned.

"Nicole, after rehearsals, Lance and I would like to meet with you. We've laid out a roadmap for the next few months, but we need to go over it with you and get your input."

"Okay. Let's meet here in my office. I'll see you both after rehearsals."

"Great. See you then," Max grinned, closing the door.

Taking another sip of her Caramel Macchiato, she wondered what was on their minds. She was not going to tolerate being told what to do. Furthermore, she wouldn't accept a hint of inferiority regarding being a female in a predominantly male industry, especially her male employees. Maybe this morning would be a great time to remind them. She laughed, spinning once more in her chair.

The morning flew by all too soon as Nicole caught up with phone calls. First, she needed to contact Charles Edmond. Later, she would check on the availability of the Pacific Coliseum. It would be a great venue to introduce Cameron and House of Cards, including a full orchestra.

"Please come in," Nicole answered, hearing a knock on her door.

"Welcome back," Lance remarked, walking in with Max. "Max and I let the musicians go for lunch. We're going to resume rehearsals this afternoon. It would be a great time to introduce you to the members of the orchestra if you are available."

"Great. That would be perfect. Why don't you both pull up a chair and sit down," Nicole answered. "Max stopped by earlier and said you both wanted to discuss a few things with me."

"Yes, that's right," Lance replied. "First, let me say how nice it is to have you back at the Warehouse. We've certainly missed you. I think you'll like what we have to tell you," he added.

"Nicole, as you know, we filled the remaining positions in the orchestra," Max spoke up. "The musicians came highly recommended and ready to travel. You'll be extremely pleased once you've heard them perform this afternoon. Sorry, I didn't mean to take over the conversation," Max glanced at Lance. "Lance is a genius. I knew he had a lot of connections in his Rolodex. However, it's nothing short of a miracle what he's accomplished while you were gone. Cameron's new song, *Amazed,* is already at the top of the charts. It's receiving airtime on every major radio station in Canada and the United States. It's almost unbelievable."

"That's great. I'm thrilled about that," Nicole smiled at them both.

Lance pulled his chair closer, putting on his glasses.

"Nicole, we wanted to discuss the possibility of scheduling a tour starting on the West Coast. I believe the Pacific Coliseum would be the perfect venue to introduce Cameron and the orchestra to his fans," Lance suggested.

"Well, I'm relieved to admit that we're all on the same wavelength," Nicole smiled, sitting back in her chair. "I'll be honest, when Max came by this morning and said you both had things to discuss, I was a bit thrown off. However, I want to take this opportunity to clear the air regarding your working for me. I never want anything put on the schedule without first consulting with me. I'm referring to appointments, advertisements, or consults with other agents. I sincerely appreciate your job performance while I was away on tour. You're both great assets to our organization. Your inputs are extremely valuable, but so that you know, the buck stops here. You're both smart gentlemen."

Leaning forward, she looked at them with a serious demeanor. "Now, concerning the Pacific Coliseum, I was going to contact them this afternoon. However, since you've brought it up, Lance, contact them regarding their earliest booking. I'm in total agreement. It would be the perfect venue to introduce Cameron and his orchestra to their listening audience. If anything needs critiquing during our first concert, it's better done closer to home. Lance, I want you to interview for an additional receptionist. I need someone available out front during our daytime operations. This person will also take on the responsibilities as my assistant or secretary, at least initially. If I find that we're getting too busy, then I'll consider hiring a private secretary. She could perhaps cover all three offices, mine, Max's, and your office."

"They need to be here early to make coffee, too," she added with a small laugh raising her coffee cup. "Now, regarding setting up our upcoming tour, Lance, I'm completely okay with your making all the arrangements. However, as I mentioned before, the venues and dates have to meet with my approval before they are booked and put on the schedule. Max, I know you're in charge of the orchestra. I trust you to ensure there's never even the remotest chance of a no-show at any venue. Also, Stan has been doing a great job with the roadies that travel with us. However, now that we're going to be traveling with a full orchestra, I'm going to hire extra help. Max, I'll let you and Stan get together on that one. Just get back to me with an estimate of how many new hires we'll need as soon as possible. So please give him a call this week, don't wait. Last, Charles Edmond has always been in control of all aspects of the band's finances. He was hired by Bruce years ago and has done one hell of a job. So I'll be asking him to stay on as Chief Financial Officer. Do either of you have any further questions?" Nicole asked, walking over to pour herself a cup of coffee. "Coffee is ready if you'd like a cup," she smiled.

"No. I believe you've covered everything," Lance remarked.

"Oh marketing, I almost forgot," Nicole mentioned sipping coffee as she returned to her desk.

"Lance, I hope you're little Rolodex can also cover this. We're going to need an aggressive marketing campaign. Do you feel comfortable taking on this additional commitment, or would you prefer that I hire someone to oversee this part of our organization?" Nicole asked, setting her cup down on the desk.

"Well, to be truthfully honest, I don't have a problem with it. However, it can be time-consuming. So I'm just going to throw this out there to hear your thoughts. First, I want to suggest a team. I'm not referring to hiring many new employees to cover this. But even adding a few personnel can increase our marketing endeavors, increasing our revenues," Lance explained.

"Sounds logical to me. So consider it done," Nicole agreed. "I'll let you put that little Rolodex of yours to use again. I know you're busy, but start interviewing this week. I trust you to hire the best. Our marketing team needs to be highly qualified, skilled individuals capable of arriving in advance of each scheduled concert. Their job would consist of being first on the scene at each venue. Then, they would contact the local community, radio stations, television stations and search out the relevant marketing aspects of each city. By that, I mean they would also set appointments ahead of my arrival or that of the band for things like personal appearances," Nicole continued.

"Max, you've been quiet. Is there anything that you would like to add to our discussion?" Nicole inquired, taking another sip of coffee.

"No, Boss. You seem to have everything under control," Max teased.

"Oh, one last thing before I let you go. I'm going to schedule an appointment with Charles Edmond. He'll probably be in contact with you both before his arrival. He works with an auditor, and he might have questions. Also, our first board meeting will be later this month. Just an FYI, I'm seriously considering replacing a few of the previous board members. I think this covers it for today," Nicole smiled. "Are there any questions?"

"I think you've completely covered everything," Lance grinned, standing up to stretch his legs.

"Yes. Thanks for your time," Max replied.

"Max, let me know when the musicians get back from lunch. I'm anxious to introduce myself and get to know these talented performers," Nicole mentioned.

"No problem. I'll let you know," Max answered, making his way toward the door.

"Wow. What a woman," Max laughed after they closed the door.

"Yes. Nicole seems pretty confident. However, don't let her beauty fool you. There's a woman of steel inside that gorgeous body. You better not get on her bad side. I feel she would have no remorse in firing either of us," Lance admitted.

"Oh, you don't have to warn me. We have a lot in common," Max admitted.

Sitting back in her chair, Nicole had a huge grin. "Now that's how you take care of business," she smiled. Indeed, Bruce had been standing right behind her. The only thing missing was a Cuban cigar.

"So, Babe, how was your morning?" Drew inquired, walking in.

"Well, let's just say I took care of business," Nicole boasted with a laugh.

"Do you have time for a quick lunch?"

"Sure, I'm starved. Although, I don't have a lot of time," she replied, looking down at her watch. "We might have to order take-out from the deli down the street. I've only got an hour. I'm finally going to meet all the musicians in our orchestra this afternoon," she smiled, giving him a quick kiss.

The sun felt warm and rejuvenating as they walked along the busy street.

So how did rehearsals go this morning?" Nicole inquired.

"Great, but I think your brother already has a thing for that new violinist," Drew rolled his eyes. "It begins," he laughed as he wiggled his brows.

"What? Are you talking about Jillian Johnston?"

"Yes. There's only one female in the entire orchestra. Were you even aware of that fact?" Drew teased with a raised brow.

"Sure, silly, I hired her. So what makes you think Cameron likes her?"

"Well, for one thing, there was an awful lot of eye contact going on between those two. She also asked the most questions."

"Oh, Drew, I think you're over-analyzing the situation."

"Guess we'll see," he smiled as they walked into Sam's Deli. "So, Babe, what looks good to you?"

"I think I'll have the tuna salad and a bottle of water," Nicole answered. "Do you want to eat inside or take it back to the office?"

"Maybe we should order it to go and eat back at the office," Drew recommended.

"Sounds good."

Picking up their food, it was only a short hike back up the sidewalk to the Warehouse. Entering the front door, they immediately walked back to Nicole's office. Passing the break room, Nicole heard someone shouting her name. It was Cameron.

"Hey, Sis, I've got someone I want you to meet. Come in the break room," Cameron asked.

"Cameron, what is it? I'm starving. We just got food at the deli, and we're going to my office to eat lunch," Nicole said as her belly rumbled in agreement.

"It won't take but a minute," Cameron said, pushing her toward the break room, not caring about her needs at that moment.

"Alright, for heaven's sake, this better not take long," Nicole said with exasperation.

"Sis, I want you to meet Jillian. She's in the break room."

"I told you," Drew smirked, keeping a straight face.

"Cameron, I hired Jillian. Don't be silly. We've already met," Nicole tried hard not to roll her eyes at him.

"Sorry, Sis, I wasn't aware. I assumed she was hired while we were on tour. I guess I'm an idiot."

"Well, that's debatable," Nicole smiled, amused at her brother's silliness. Nicole didn't think she had ever seen her brother make such a fuss over a girl before. "However, since you've already made her aware that I'm your sister, I'll come inside for a moment."

"Thanks, Sis, I appreciate it. Jillian failed to mention she had already met you," Cameron freaked out, realizing his stupidity.

"Okay, calm down. You probably never gave Jillian a chance. It's possible she didn't want to embarrass you," Nicole smiled, walking inside the break room.

"Hi, I'm Nicole. I think we've met," Nicole smiled, trying to save Cameron the embarrassment. "Sorry, I guess I forgot to mention to my brother that I had hired you while in New York. So how did rehearsals go this morning?"

"Oh, great. Thank you for giving me this awesome opportunity. Yes, Cameron couldn't wait for me to meet you. There was no way I could tell him that we had already met," Jillian commented, trying to save Cameron further humiliation.

Nicole recognized her long blonde hair and green eyes. Jillian could easily have made it in the modeling profession Nicole thought to herself. She had the proper bone structure and slender figure one would need for a modeling career. So she wasn't too surprised that Cameron had found himself attracted to her beautiful features.

"That's my brother," Nicole laughed. "I'm glad to have you on board. Since we're making introductions, this is my husband, Drew Connors."

"I saw you earlier at rehearsals, but it's nice to meet you," Drew smiled.

"Okay, Cameron, if there's nothing else, I'd like to go eat now," Nicole smiled, giving him a quick hug.

"Thanks, Sis. I love you."

"Ditto," Nicole answered, closing the break room door.

"Wow, that was a bit uncomfortable," Nicole remarked, glancing at Drew as they continued down to her office.

"Yes, especially with you being her boss."

Finally, they were ready to enjoy a late lunch. The day had been so hectic neither of them had called Kate to check on Nicholas. With Jerry no longer at her side, Nicole finally felt the weight of taking on the position as manager. However, she felt confident and in charge, especially after the meeting earlier that morning with Lance and Max.

Later that afternoon, she met the musicians who now comprised the orchestra. It couldn't have gone better, and there seemed to be an instant connection among the group. She felt assured that Lance and Max had hired the right people. It seemed all the pieces of the puzzle had come together. She had everything she needed to schedule their first performance. Finally, they were ready to make their first appearance at the Pacific Coliseum.

CHAPTER SIXTEEN

House Hunting

Waking up early the following day, Kate was on a mission. The mere thoughts of finally retiring in Vancouver and hunting for a house had her excited.

"Jerry, it's time to get up," Kate smiled, kissing him awake. "Have you forgotten our appointment with Judy this morning? She arranged for us to tour some properties. I can't wait to see them," Kate smiled, jumping out of bed to get ready.

"Okay, Babe, just give me a few minutes to wake up. Have you forgotten, we're retired now," Jerry grinned, attempting to pull her back down on the bed next to him. "We're on our schedule," he remarked playfully, returning her kisses.

"Not this morning," Kate giggled, pulling the covers off him. "I'll order breakfast. It would help if you had some caffeine. Judy agreed to pick us up at 9:00, and it's almost 8:00. We'll have just enough time to eat, take a quick shower, and dress if we hurry. Now get up, sleepyhead," she demanded.

Jerry managed to pull himself out of bed. He could easily have slept in, but today there was no way he could linger in bed. Kate was desperate to find a house, and he knew she wouldn't stop until she had found the perfect home.

Finally, after consuming enough caffeine, Jerry felt ready to start the day. But, hearing a knock at the door meant Judy had arrived earlier than expected.

"Good morning. Are you both ready to check out some houses?" Judy questioned as Jerry opened the door.

"Sure. Let me get Kate. She's so excited that she had me up at dawn this morning. So please have a seat while I let her know you're here."

"Okay. Thanks."

"Babe, Judy's here. Are you ready?" Jerry asked, walking into the bedroom.

"Are you kidding? Let me grab my sweater," Kate eagerly replied.

"I've lined up three properties to show you this morning. You're not going to believe this, but the lake house is back on the market. I find it rather strange it happens to be vacant again. I know it might seem rather bizarre as it was the home Nicky had built for Jenna but do either of you want to stop by?" Judy inquired.

"Well, I'm not sure how I would feel about living there," Jerry replied. "Babe, what do you think?"

"I wouldn't mind taking another look at it. I was only there once, but I remember it being a stunning home," Kate smiled.

"All right, let's go," Judy suggested. "My car is in the valet parking lot. Please, excuse me for a moment. I'll let them know we're on our way down," she added.

"There's also another property available at Bear Lake. It's just down the street from the lake house," Judy informed them, stepping inside the elevator. The homes in this area are very exquisite, as you know. Unfortunately, they hardly ever become available. I was stunned to find those two on the market this morning as I ran your comps. The location makes it a highly sought-after community. It's close enough to downtown for people who have to work, yet it affords the luxury of being somewhat remote. The lake is perfect for boating and skiing. However, I'm sure I don't have to sell you on its amenities since Nicky and Jenna lived there," Judy explained.

"Well, Babe, what do you think? Could you see yourself living out there?" Jerry asked, opening the car door for Kate. "I know it's mountainous, and the roads are winding and steep in certain areas. What are your thoughts?"

"I haven't given it much thought," Kate replied, stepping inside the car. "I had been leaning toward a condominium downtown. I happened to love the building where Jenna lived," she answered.

"It's undoubtedly a lovely complex. I sold Jenna the penthouse, and it's beautiful. However, my only concern is that you might enjoy spending time at the lake more, especially in summer. Your grandson would love the outdoors. You could fish, have bonfires in the evening, and stargaze. It's a wholesome, healthy environment. With a penthouse, you're mainly indoors.

On the other hand, the building offers many amenities, including a pool, spa, and gym. It's in the middle of downtown and convenient for shopping and entertainment. What it comes down to is the lifestyle. How do you both see yourselves spending most of your time?" Judy inquired, driving away from the hotel.

"I love the idea of living at Bear Lake. Could we look at the lake house and the other property?" Jerry suggested. "Kate, would you at least take a look at the Bear Lake community?"

"Well, as I said before, I always saw us living downtown, but if this is something you truly want, let's check it out," Kate decided.

"Thanks, Babe. I know you'll love it. So, let's go check it out."

"Great. Why don't we start with the lake house, and afterward, we'll tour the other property," Judy recommended.

Arriving at the lake house, Judy parked under the stunning portico.

Walking in, Jerry felt overwhelmed. Memories of Nicky and Jenna instantly flooded his mind. Everything was just as he had remembered. It seemed the former owners had not made any changes. The vaulted ceilings in the living room, the expansive floor-to-ceiling windows, and the gorgeous staircase remained most impressive. Nicky had poured his heart and soul into building the lake house for Jenna, and it still captured that feeling.

"Would you like to walk outside on the deck?" Judy inquired.

"Yes. Thank you," Jerry smiled, following her outdoors. "So Babe, what do you think? Do you think you could live here?" Jerry asked, taking in the incredible views of the shimmering lake and beyond the scenic snow-capped mountains.

"Well, to be honest, the home is spectacular and offers a lot, but I feel the memories would haunt us. So we need a place to create new memories," Kate explained.

"Okay. I think you might be right. Judy, we would like to tour the other property. First, however, I would like to let Cameron know it's back on the market. He never wanted this house sold. I think he would be thrilled about the possibility of making an offer. I want to call him this evening and let him know," Jerry remarked.

"I totally agree. I'd be happy to work with Cameron," Judy replied, handing Jerry another business card. "Please give him my card. I'm usually in my office by 8:00 every morning. I wasn't sure if Jenna had made the right decision to sell at that time without his knowledge, but she needed a change. So I'll lock up, and we'll drive down and tour the other home," Judy smiled, locking the front door.

Jerry seemed rather solemn during the short drive. The emotions brought on by walking through the house had dramatically affected him. Nicky and Jenna had been a huge part of his life. Even though it had been over two years, it was never easy letting go.

"Babe, are you alright?" Kate asked, taking his hand.

"Yes. I wasn't prepared to deal with all the memories. You're right. I could never live there. However, I would love to know that Cameron had the house again," Jerry smiled.

"Okay. We're here. What do you think?" Judy asked, driving into the expansive circular entrance.

"Oh Babe, it's gorgeous," Kate gasped.

The property is known as Glen Haven Manor. It's the recreation of a Tudor Revival built-in 1950, but it's been completely renovated. I think you'll love it," Judy informed them as she parked the car. "It sets on eight acres. It also has waterfront access to the lake, a dock, and boathouse," she added.

The two-story home was magnificent with its steeply pitched roof, prominent half-timbered cross gables, two massive chimneys, and tall narrow windows. White masonry encased the exquisite home, complimenting the circular cobblestone driveway. At the same time, an oversized oak door welcomed you to the entrance.

"Wow. Jerry, this place is stunning," Kate smiled, stepping out of the car. "I think we're home," she laughed.

"Geez. How would you know? We haven't even been inside yet," Jerry teased.

The manicured lawn was impeccable—an ornate three-tiered fountain set nestled in the middle of lush shrubbery. Oval concrete benches surrounded it on both sides.

Let's take a look inside," Judy mentioned unlocking the massive door.

Walking in, Kate was breathless.

"Unbelievable," she whispered.

Vaulted ceilings enhanced with a baroque chandelier framed the foyer, and an elaborate oak staircase spiraled upwards.

An elegant great room showcased by an enormous stone fireplace was off one side of the foyer. Matching crystal lamps tastefully adorned both sides of the massive wood-burning hearth. Tall windows facing the front of the house allowed excessive sunlight to immerse the room, making it feel warm and cozy despite its size.

A masculine office was situated directly opposite the foyer. At first sight, it seemed foreboding with dark paneled walls. However, the room came alive after turning on the huge crystal chandelier hanging overhead. A large tapestry depicting a colorful Mediterranean garden graced the wall behind an enormous mahogany desk. The warm glow seemed to give radiance to the paneled walls.

"Wow," Kate replied, looking around. "This could be your room," Kate laughed.

"Follow me. I'll show you the kitchen," Judy directed.

Past the staircase, a dim, narrow hallway led to the back of the home. It opened to a large family room enclosed by French doors. The tall doors revealed a striking view of the immaculate landscape that led down to the shores of the lake.

"This way," Judy smiled.

"Wow. It's my dream kitchen," Kate exclaimed, touching the sizeable professional range.

The kitchen incorporated walls of cherry cabinetry highlighted with etched glass doors lit within to showcase a myriad of blue Dutch Delftware. Massive windows sitting in front of the aged farmhouse sink revealed breathtaking views of the lake and distant vistas of the mountainous terrain.

"So, what do you think?" Judy asked.

"I'm in love, and I haven't even seen the upstairs," Kate giggled.

"Well, I can promise you the upstairs and primary suite will not disappoint. Would you like to walk down to the dock and check out the boathouse? It offers enough room for a boat and all the water toys you could ever want."

Following behind Judy, Kate took Jerry's hand.

"Babe, what do you think?" Kate questioned.

"Well, it seems you've fallen in love with this property. If you're sure this is what you want, then we'll put in an offer," Jerry smiled.

After viewing the boathouse and taking an upstairs tour, Kate and Jerry were sold on Glen Haven Manor.

"Are you ready to put in an offer, or would you like to tour more properties?" Judy inquired as she descended the stairs.

"Yes. We want to make an offer. I don't think we feel the need to view other listings. I believe you said the sellers are asking for five million dollars. Do you think they are firm on that price? I would like to start with an offer of four million seven hundred thousand dollars. Do you think that would offend the owners?" Jerry questioned.

"No. I think that would be a great place to start. Why don't we drive back to town, and I'll write up the paperwork," Judy smiled, locking up. "Also, don't forget to inform Cameron about the lake house. I would hate to see him lose that house again if he's interested," Judy added. "Have Cameron give me a call later tonight."

The following day, it appeared Kate and Jerry had gotten very little sleep. They had finally found the home of their dreams. Kate could think of nothing else. Hopefully, the day would bring news of an accepted offer on Glen Haven Manor.

"Babe, why don't you order breakfast? I could use a hot cup of coffee. Then, I'm going to take a quick shower. I can't stand waiting, and I'm extremely nervous," Kate explained.

"Please, don't be nervous. If it's meant to be, it will be. If not, I'm sure there's another property for us," Jerry mentioned walking over to give Kate a reassuring kiss.

"Yes, but it wouldn't be down the street from the lake house. We could be Cameron's neighbors if he gets the house," Kate insinuated.

"Don't worry. I feel good about our offer," Jerry reiterated, calling room service.

Hearing a knock at the door, Jerry quickly put down the phone to answer it.

"Hey, Jerry. I had to stop over to find out if you've heard any news from Judy?" Cameron inquired, walking in. "I went down to her office last night and put an offer on the lake house. Can you even believe it? I'm so excited. I knew one day it would come back on the market."

"No. I haven't heard anything. Come in. I was just about to order breakfast. We'll eat breakfast while we wait. What sounds good to you this morning?" Jerry asked.

"I'm too nervous to eat," Cameron frowned.

"Oh, come on. You and Kate don't have any faith. You're going to get the lake house, and Kate and I will get Glen Haven Manor. You just wait. You'll see that I'm right," Jerry asserted.

"Well, I don't know what fortune teller you talked with this morning, but I certainly hope your right," Cameron scoffed.

"Hey, Cameron, are you nervous too?" Kate smiled, walking into the room.

"Are you kidding?" Cameron laughed. "I thought it might take years before that house came back on the market. What are the odds that we might be neighbors?" he grinned.

"I know," Kate smiled. "Wouldn't that be awesome?"

Hearing another knock at the door, it announced the arrival of breakfast.

"Okay, you two, let's eat breakfast. Starving isn't going to help the situation," Jerry smiled. "Help yourselves to the pancakes and sausage."

Just as Jerry was about to pour his first cup of coffee, the phone rang.

"Hello," Jerry answered.

"Hey, Jerry. It's Judy, and I've got some great news. You got the house. Are you excited?" Judy asked enthusiastically.

"You bet. Stay on the phone while I let Kate know."

"Kate, we got the house. I can buy a boat," Jerry screamed.

"Jerry, is Cameron with you? I tried calling his room, but no one answered," Judy inquired.

"Yes. As a matter of fact, Cameron is here."

"Well, can I please speak to him?" Judy asked.

"Okay, just a moment," Jerry replied, taking the phone over to Cameron. "Judy needs to speak with you."

"Hello," Cameron answered.

"Well, are you sitting down? You got the lake house!" Judy exclaimed. The sellers called me this morning. They remembered Jenna and were so sorry to hear of her passing, but they were thrilled to know that you'll be moving back. Cameron, I'm so happy for you. However, I want to set the record straight and let you know I wasn't for your Mom selling it at that time. Jenna couldn't see herself living there any longer after your Dad passed away. I hope you understand. I'm thrilled it all worked out for you. I'll put it on the rental property side of our office if you decide to rent it while you're away on tour. Again, congratulations. Can I please speak to Jerry once more before I hang up?" Judy continued.

"Yes. Just a moment," Cameron answered, handing the phone back to Jerry.

"Hey, Judy. Thanks for all your hard work."

"Oh, that's what I get paid to do," Judy laughed.

"Congratulations. Please let Kate know I'm excited for her. I'll be in my office every day this week if either of you should have any questions. Talk to you later."

The morning couldn't have brought better news. Jerry and Kate had finally found the home of their dreams. A place for family and friends to gather. Cameron's dream of once again owning the lake house had also come true. His memories of living at Bear Lake would now incorporate future memories. Hopefully, one day, it would be filled with the love and laughter of his family. At last, Nicole could take Cameron and his orchestra on tour, knowing that Jerry and Kate were finally at home in Vancouver.

CHAPTER SEVENTEEN

New Beginnings

Months later, after much hard work and preparation, opening night had finally arrived. Nicole felt a mixture of emotions. She was excited yet nervous. She knew everyone had worked hard. Yet, looking down at her watch, she panicked. It was almost time to leave for the Coliseum. Tonight would officially begin their Canadian tour. The following week would find them preparing to leave for their next venue. This tour would take them throughout Canada and the United States.

Before the concert, Kate and Jerry decided to spend the evening in a hotel close to the venue. Even though they had already moved into their new home, Glen Haven Manor, it seemed fitting for everyone to be together and close to the venue. Afterward, they would celebrate at the Wharf and later back at the lake house.

"Drew, did you find clean clothes for Nicholas? Mom is waiting for him," Nicole hurriedly dashed around Nicholas's room, sorting through his clothes. She knew Kate was waiting for her to drop him off at their suite.

"Babe, calm down. We still have an hour before the limo arrives," Drew answered. "It's a good thing your Mom and Jerry decided to stay at our hotel tonight. I'm going to miss them being across the hall. We have plenty of time to get ready."

"Well, I don't want to wait until the last minute. Drew, I'm so nervous. I'm shaking," Nicole laughed.

"Let me pour you another glass of champagne. I think you could use it," Drew reached for a glass. "Babe, listen, I love you. Everything is going to be fine, just relax. You've worked hard, and everyone is ready. I'm so proud of you," Drew smiled.

He pulled her close, giving her a quick, passionate kiss.

"Drew, please, I have to finish getting ready," Nicole laughed, trying to stop his advances.

"You look ravishing," Drew whispered. "Please, stop worrying. It's taking everything within my power not to pull you over to the bed," he winked, kissing her.

Hearing a knock at the door interrupted their special moment. Walking over, Drew wondered whose timing was so impeccable that it had brought them to their door at this very moment.

"Oh, Kate," Drew answered impishly. "Come in. We're still getting ready."

"You look flustered," Kate replied. "Didn't mean to interrupt," she laughed. "I just came by to get Nicholas. I figured it would save you both the time of bringing him over to our suite. Jerry and I will be leaving for the Coliseum a little later tonight. He hasn't gotten back yet. He found a boat for sale, so he went down to the harbor to check it out. I swear, that guy spends every second of the day shopping for a boat," Kate frowned, rolling her eyes.

"Well, I can't say that I blame him. You know how it is with men and their toys. Of course, now that Jerry has that spacious boathouse, he has to have a boat to go in it," Drew laughed.

"Mom, I think Nicholas is still sleeping. Would you please wake him and change his diaper. Drew laid his clothes on the changing table. You don't mind, do you?"

"Not at all, that's why I came over. I'll take Nicholas over to our suite. I ordered spaghetti earlier. I know it's one of his favorite foods, so I'll give him dinner. Is there anything else I can do before I leave?" Kate asked, walking over to his crib.

"No. Thanks, Mom. You're a lifesaver," Nicole called from the bathroom.

"Sweetheart, Nicholas and I are leaving. See you later tonight at the Coliseum," Kate replied loudly. "I love you. Don't worry. The concert will be phenomenal," she added, walking with Nicholas toward the door.

"Thanks, Mom. I love you too," Nicole yelled from the bathroom.

The bathroom looked like an explosion at a cosmetic factory. Opened powder containers, perfume bottles, lipsticks, eyeliners, eye shadows, and foundation were everywhere. The vanity and sink were strewn with brushes, curling iron, a hairdryer, and rollers.

"Drew, I'm in the bathroom. I need you to zip me up," Nicole yelled.

"Okay. I'll be right there."

Zipping her dress, Drew kissed her seductively on the nape of her neck.

"Doll is there anything else I can do for you?" he asked wickedly.

"Drew, get out of here. You're going to make me late."

Hearing another knock at the door, Drew moaned.

"All right. Who else needs something?" he complained.

Opening the door, Drew was surprised to find a young man holding an enormous bouquet of roses. It contained roses of every imaginable color and size. The flowers were incredible.

"I have a delivery for Mrs. Connors," he stated.

"Thanks. I'll take those," Drew replied, handing him a generous tip. "Wow, Babe, the musicians sent you a huge bouquet of roses," he shouted, sitting them on the credenza.

"Great. I'll be right out," Nicole yelled from the bathroom.

Finally, she was ready. Walking into the living room, Nicole looked stunning. She took his breath away. She was wearing a shimmering black strapless gown covered in black pearlescent sequins. The dress hugged her slim frame, enhancing her curvaceous body. The side split exposed only a decent hint of her slender legs. Nicole's long black hair was swept up in the back and held in place by a dazzling pearl hair clamp. Accessorized with pearl earrings and a pair of black satin heels, she was a vision in black.

"Wow, Doll, you're gorgeous," Drew whistled. "You sure don't fit the mold of any band manager I've ever seen. I wished Bruce could see you now," he winked, walking over to give her a quick kiss.

Drew, stop. You'll ruin my makeup," Nicole giggled.

"Okay, Mrs. Connors, are you ready to go? Are you ready for your big evening?" Drew mentioned reaching for her wrap. "Wow, you smell heavenly," he complimented, wrapping her shoulders in a silk scarf. "Wait till the guys see you," he boasted.

Locking the door, Drew took her hand as they walked over to the elevator. It was only seconds before the doors opened, revealing her exquisite gown.

"Wow, Sis," Cameron grinned, walking up to meet her. "I thought I was the main attraction for tonight," Cameron teased.

"Geez, Nicole. You're beautiful," Harry whistled.

"Oh, stop it. You guys are acting silly. I think you guys look mighty handsome in your tux," Nicole laughed. "All right, is everyone ready to go? The limo is waiting," she herded them outside to the car.

"Where's Kate, Jerry, and Nicholas?" Cameron questioned, looking around.

"They'll be coming later. Jerry is looking for a boat," Drew smiled, stepping inside the limo behind Nicole.

"Awesome. We need a boat to ski," Cameron suggested, already seeing himself having a great time on the water.

"Okay. Who wants a drink?" Harry asked. Sitting next to the bar, he began pouring drinks.

Lounging back in her seat, Nicole smiled. "I'll take a vodka and orange juice."

"That sounds good. Why don't you pour three tall glasses of Jack Daniels for us," Cameron lounged back. "I'd like to toast my gorgeous sister and all the hard work it took to make tonight possible," he smiled, raising his glass.

"Sis here's to dreams coming true. I love you. I'm so proud of your

accomplishments, but more than that, I'm glad to have you as my sister. I only wished Dad, Jenna, and Bruce could be here this evening,"

"Thanks, Cameron. Now I'd like to make a toast," Nicole sat up a little straighter in her seat.

"Here's to your first night on stage as a solo artist. I love you too. I'll never forget the night at Jenna's penthouse when I discovered you were my brother. I was thrilled to learn we were family. I'm so proud of you."

Nicole raised her glass toward her big brother, trying not to become emotional. The last thing she needed was to ruin the makeup she had applied not too long ago.

"Okay, Babe, don't get everyone started with the tears," Drew insisted, handing her a tissue just in case she needed one. "Remember, you'll ruin your makeup," he teased, giving her a quick kiss.

It appeared all of Vancouver had turned out for their opening concert. The line wrapped almost three city blocks as the limo drove into the back entrance of the Pacific Coliseum. Cameron sat mesmerized, staring at the brightly illuminated marquee that announced his name in neon lights.

"All right, guys, this is it. Let's make Bruce smile. I'm sure he'll be watching from above," Nicole beamed.

Awaiting their arrival as they walked in was the ever-familiar line of golf carts parked next to the wall.

"Drew, I'll let you drive. Meet you guys in the dressing room," Nicole smiled, picking up the hem of her gown as she stepped inside one of the electric carts.

"Okay. Last one there buys a round of drinks later tonight," Harry joked as he sped away.

Making their way down the concrete corridors, Nicole and Drew were stopped by numerous musicians. She never missed an opportunity to speak with the roadies or members of the orchestra. She always acknowledged their talent and shared her appreciation for being a team member.

Catching a glimpse of Stan in the distance, she asked Drew to catch up with him.

"Hey, Stan, did the caterers do a good job providing enough food and drinks for the roadies and security tonight?" Nicole inquired.

"Yes. Thank you. It was delicious. Catering set out a buffet of tasty food and beverages," Stan grinned.

"How's everything going so far tonight? Did you have enough personnel to help set up?" Nicole asked, visually checking out the surrounding area. "Do you have adequate security?"

"Yes. Everything is working smoothly tonight. We've not encountered any problems so far," Stan grinned. "I must say you look beautiful tonight. Don't worry about a thing."

"Thanks, Stan. I'm going down to the dressing room. If you need me, just call."

"Wow, Babe, you're truly fortunate. Your employees adore you," Drew leaned over, whispering in her ear.

Opening the door to the dressing room, it looked like a florist shop. Fresh flowers of all descriptions inundated the room. It smelled heavenly. Catering had arrived and provided an array of fresh fruits, salads, and a variety of sandwiches along with a selection of beverages.

Seeing Nicole, Lance immediately walked over.

"You look gorgeous tonight," Lance smiled. "I just wanted to let you know we're completely sold out for tonight's concert. Thankfully, all our advertising has paid off. So come with me. I want to introduce you to Pierre. He's the new stylist for the guys and the musicians," Lance grinned. "Pierre has a team of talented individuals who work for him."

"Pierre, please meet Nicole," Lance grinned, making the introductions.

"Hello, Nicole, nice to finally meet you. I've heard a lot of great things about you," Pierre smiled, extending his hand.

"It's nice to meet you too," Nicole replied, returning his smile with a handshake. "I'm looking forward to meeting your assistants."

"My team and I are excited to be working with Cameron and his orchestra. I hope we meet your expectations," Pierre mentioned.

"I'm sure I won't be disappointed. Your credentials speak for themselves," Nicole answered, reassuring him.

Moments later, Max caught sight of her and rushed over.

"Wow. I must say you look exquisite tonight," Max grinned. "Can I get you something to drink?" he offered.

"I'm fine right now. I had a drink on the way over in the limo."

"So, I guess you must be excited," Max questioned. "The orchestra was phenomenal during rehearsals. Have you seen Jillian? She was asking about Cameron earlier this evening?"

"No. I haven't, but Cameron is here somewhere. We rode over in the limo together. I'll let him know if I see him," Nicole smiled, turning around upon hearing Kate's voice.

"Hey, Mom, did Jerry find the boat he was looking for?" Nicole questioned, kissing Nicholas on his cheeks.

"Not yet. He's still looking. I think he wants a yacht," Kate laughed. "All he needs is a speed boat for Bear Lake, something with enough power to ski and pull water toys. But, Sweetheart, I must say you look stunning tonight. Your sequined gown is incredible. I might have to borrow it," Kate smiled, hugging her precious daughter. "Jerry and I are so proud of you. I don't want you to stress over anything. It's going to be a wonderful opening concert. Do you want to take Nicholas for a moment? I think I'll get something to drink and try to find Jerry. He's probably talking about boats with someone," Kate snickered.

"Sure. How's mommy's baby boy tonight?" Nicole beamed, kissing his sweet face.

It appeared everything was going just like clockwork. Nicole couldn't possibly have asked for more, at least so far. Hopefully, the fans would welcome Cameron and the addition of an orchestra. It would be her defining moment. She was beginning to get nervous as she looked up at the clock. In another hour, she would have her answer. Cameron would soon take the stage for the first time as a solo artist.

Finding Drew, she walked over.

"Babe, I need you to take Nicholas for a moment. I need to get everyone's attention. We only have about an hour before showtime," Nicole said nervously.

"Can I please have everyone's attention," Nicole announced loudly as the room quieted. You could've heard a pin drop. "I just want to take a few minutes to thank everyone. Lance just informed me we're sold out for tonight's concert. I know everyone has worked extremely hard to make tonight a huge success. It's the beginning of our tour in Canada and the United States. We're family, and I want you to know how much I appreciate you. So let's go out there and give Vancouver a night to remember."

"Mom, it's almost time for Max and the musicians to walk down to the stage. Can you watch Nicholas for a moment?" Nicole asked, handing her the little boy.

"Okay, Sweetheart, it will be a fantastic concert," Kate remarked, taking Nicholas. "Don't worry about a thing."

"All right, Max, I guess this is it. See you after the concert," Nicole smiled.

"Babe, don't worry. We've got this. I love you," Drew winked, giving her a quick kiss before he walked out the door.

"Nicole, everything will be fine," Harry grinned as he slowly joined the line of other musicians filing through the door.

"Thanks, Harry, see you afterward," Nicole smiled.

The sneakers, T-shirts, purple Mohawks, and torn faded blue jeans were gone. They had simply and elegantly been replaced. Their new attire consisted of black tuxedos, dress shoes, and refined modern haircuts. The world was finally ready to meet Cameron and his orchestra.

Now it only left Cameron and a small entourage of assistants behind.

"Cameron, are you nervous?" Nicole asked, walking up behind him as he sat in front of the mirror.

"No. Not at all. I'm excited. It's like a dream come true for me. Dad could never have envisioned a night like this for us. Somehow, I think he's up there somewhere with a huge grin on his face this evening," Cameron smiled at his little sister.

"Cameron, I'm so glad you're my brother," Nicole squeezed his shoulder.

Looking up at the clock, it seemed the past hour had flown by too quickly. It was finally time to make her last announcement. Walking over to find Kate, she informed her she would walk with Cameron down to the stage entrance.

"I'd like to have everyone's attention. Fifteen minutes till showtime," Nicole announced.

"Let's go," she smiled proudly, taking his hand.

Nicole felt elated as Cameron and his entourage of assistants filed through the door. Tonight she was living her dream with her brother beside her. Life couldn't get any better.

Nearing the stage entrance, she could hear the orchestra playing music specifically created by Maxwell Kline to announce Cameron's entrance. It gave her goosebumps.

"This is it," Nicole smiled. "Your big moment," she reiterated, giving Cameron a quick kiss on the cheek. "Go on that stage and make us all proud," she added, feeling ecstatic.

Watching from behind the scene, Nicole wiped tears from her eyes as her handsome brother walked on stage as a solo artist for the first time.

"Good evening Vancouver," Cameron smiled, walking up to the microphone. "How are you this evening? I'm so thrilled to be here. It's our first appearance, and we're so glad that you've taken time out of your busy schedule to come out and support us. Thanks for coming. We love you, Vancouver," Cameron grinned, waving to the crowd below.

The fans reacted with a standing ovation screaming out their love and support. Cameron bowed with humility before a phenomenal crowd of over fifteen thousand admirers. Their screams of approval were heartwarming.

"Thank you. Thank you so much," Cameron smiled. "I'd like to introduce you to our new orchestra. Please make them welcome with warm applause."

The response coming back from the fans was deafening. It seemed to go on forever as Cameron felt utterly captivated by their approval. He wondered if his father, Nicky Spade, had experienced these same feelings.

"Thank you, again, for your warm welcome. Later, I'll introduce you to our musicians," Cameron said as the roar subsided.

"I'd like to open our first concert by singing one of my new hits, *Amazed.* I hope you enjoy it," Cameron remarked, taking the microphone in his hand as he sat on the edge of a stool.

The orchestra began softly playing the intro. Once again, the fans gave their approval with spontaneous, thunderous applause.

Any fears that Cameron might have felt faded instantly as he began singing the words to *Amazed*. A full orchestra accompanying him gave Cameron the confidence to convey each song with feelings revealing his raw emotions. Finally, he was where he had always wanted to be center stage. He was living his dream as a solo artist. As the song ended, the vast audience began to applaud with excitement.

"Thank you. Your kindness is overwhelming," Cameron replied as a hush began to fall over the arena.

The crowd applauded with approval as he led into his next song, *Imagine Us*. Walking to the edge of the stage, Cameron shook hands with a group of fans standing near the front as he belted out the lyrics. It was mayhem as girls tried to make their way to the front of the stage, hoping to touch his hand.

There was no earthly way to describe his feelings at center stage as he poured out his love in the song. It was addictive. The energy seemed to resonate back from the fans. He had once heard it described by his father as the feeling a drug addict feels the minute heroin enters their body. The feeling was euphoric. It left you craving more. The connection shared between fans and an artist was simply indescribable.

"Thank you. I'd like to take this time to introduce you to a few musicians in our orchestra. It's impossible to name each one every night. So I'd like to start by making a few introductions tonight and continue at every concert. So I guess what I'm saying is this, if you attend all my concerts, you'll eventually know all the musicians," Cameron laughed. The audience had a sense of humor as the fans roared with delight.

"I'd like to start with Jillian Johnston. Jillian, please stand. She's one of our violinists. Jillian just graduated from New York City College with a major in music. Next, however, I think you already know and love him is Drew Connors. Drew, would you please raise your hand. Drew is our guitarist. Also, we have another familiar face, Harry Kilburn, on drums. Harry, will you please stand. Of course, you remember Harry. Drew and Harry have been with us since the beginning. At this time, I'll have the orchestra stand. Please give them a warm welcome."

The audience loudly applauded their appreciation.

"My next song, *Only You* was written by Maxwell Kline. I hope you enjoy it."

Once again, the fans seemed to connect with the song. Cameron watched from the stage as everyone sang along on the chorus. There was no doubt the fans seemed to be enjoying every second of the concert. Finally, after singing a selection of songs from a compilation he recorded, the concert was coming to a close. Cameron had been on stage for over an hour. Again, he felt such an unbelievable connection to his audience.

"I'd like to close by singing, *Because of You,* a song made famous by my father, Nicky Spade. So, dad, here's to you," Cameron smiled, looking up momentarily.

The fans stood to their feet with applause as Cameron began to sing the lyrics.

"Thank you," he briefly interrupted before finishing the song.

Afterward, he walked to the front of the stage and took a bow.

"Thank you for coming tonight. You've been the best audience," Cameron exclaimed. "Thank You. I love you, Vancouver."

As the fans continued their loud applause, Cameron bowed. Then after another long slow bow, he exited the stage. The roar from his admiring fans was deafening.

The Pacific Coliseum, Cameron's first venue, had now been played. It was history. A night to be remembered by his wonderful fans and by each person connected to the performance. Everyone had been right. Nicole's dreams had come true. On an extraordinary evening, many years previous, they had been placed in motion when she met someone special, her brother, Cameron. Now it was time to make the final preparations to take her show on the road.

CHAPTER EIGHTEEN

On The Road Again

"Geez, I'm tired," Nicole yawned, pushing off the alarm. "Time to get up," she announced, dragging herself out of bed. She was still sleepy after celebrating their successful opening concert and utterly exhausted as she walked over to draw back the floral drapes. Instantly, the room was inundated with the brightness of the morning sun. As Nicole took in the beautiful views of the lake, the water appeared to sparkle as it reflected the sun's rays. There were only a few down days before the band left for their next venue at the end of the week. However, it would provide a small respite to enjoy a few days at Glen Haven Manor with Kate and Jerry. Drew was looking forward to taking out Jerry's new boat.

Nicole looked over at Drew, who appeared to be sleeping. She knew he was only pretending. Yesterday had been hard for everyone, and he would do anything to get more sleep. Their first concert and the move into Glen Haven Manor were finally over. It had taken the better part of the past two weeks to shop for furniture. It seemed Kate hadn't been capable of making snap decisions. Finally, however, Glen Haven Manor was transformed into an interior decorator's dream. It wasn't the fact the house needed an additional wow factor but was simply Kate's idea of putting her personal touches throughout the home.

Looking around the magnificent room, Nicole smiled. Kate had insisted that she, Drew, and Nicholas move into the enormous house. The east wing upstairs seemed perfect. It had two connecting suites. Their room connected to Nicholas's nursery. Kate had spared no expense in furnishing the entire wing. She wanted the three of them to feel comfortable. So it only made sense to take her up on her offer. Living out of hotel rooms was getting hard with Nicholas, and he loved his new room. Kate had purchased a tall stuffed giraffe to sit in the corner. It seemed to complete the jungle theme, which now encompassed his room.

Taking another look at the time, Nicole had to wake her sleeping prince. She knew the magic words that would open his eyes.

"Drew, Jerry's already down at the boathouse. He's ready to take a spin around the lake. Are you going?" Nicole whispered in his ear.

Instantly, Drew shot upward from the bed.

"Jerry didn't leave without me? Did he?" Drew freaked, reaching for his clothes.

"I knew that would get you up," Nicole laughed.

"No. But we should go downstairs. I know you're tired. Heck, we're all exhausted. Yesterday was grueling. I have to be at the Warehouse before 10:00 this morning," Nicole frowned. "Don't enjoy your time on the lake too much. On Thursday, we leave for Quebec," she reminded him with a quick kiss.

"Wow. Can't we just stay forever," Drew pleaded hurriedly, buttoning his shirt.

"I'm afraid not. I've got a band to manage," Nicole giggled.

Walking into the kitchen, Drew was amazed to find Jerry awake. He was sitting in the breakfast nook with Kate. They were enjoying their morning coffee.

"Are you ready to take the boat out?" Jerry laughed, seeing Drew.

"Are you kidding? Yesterday was rough," Drew grimaced. "I'm ready for some fun in the sun," he laughed, pouring himself a cup of coffee.

"Nicole, I thought you might help me interview nannies and a cook today," Kate mentioned pulling out a chair for Nicole. "The agency is sending out a maid to help with the care of the house later this evening."

"Wow, Mom. You're sure living a pampered life now," Nicole teased. "I'd love to help, but I have to be at the Warehouse before 10:00. We leave on Thursday, and I have a lot to do."

"Oh, I completely forgot about the upcoming concert in Quebec. I've been so wrapped up in moving," Kate mentioned walking over to refill the carafe with hot coffee. "Don't worry. The agency is sending over several highly qualified applicants this afternoon. However, since you're both here, I wanted to discuss something. Why don't you leave Nicholas with Jerry and me while taking the band on tour? He's all settled in his gorgeous nursery, and hopefully, I'll have hired the perfect nanny for him before Thursday. What do you think?" Kate questioned, filling their cups with coffee.

"Well, to be honest, I've never given it any thought. But, Babe, what do you think? I know Mom and Jerry will take great care of him," Nicole replied. "Our only other option is hiring a nanny to travel with us. However, he'll be left totally in their care when we're away at the venues. But, at least with Mom and Jerry, they'll be here to guarantee the nanny takes great care of him."

Kate was acting silly as she crossed both fingers with a huge smile.

"I guess you're right. I know Kate and Jerry will probably spoil him rotten," Drew laughed. "Have you seen that kid's room? It's a jungle."

"Oh Drew, what are grandparents for, if not to spoil their grandkids?" Kate laughed. "Believe me. He'll have a nanny. I'll have a cook plus a maid, so I'll be free to play with Nicholas. Jerry will be taking his boat out almost every day, leaving me free."

"Speaking of boats, are you ready to go?" Jerry grinned, glancing at Drew.

"Aren't you guys going to eat breakfast first," Kate suggested waving a hand over all of the food still on the table.

"Really, Kate?" Jerry teased. "Let's go."

The guys ran out the back door like two kids on Christmas morning.

"Neither took sunscreen nor grabbed a hat," Kate shook her head in disbelief.

"Oh Mom, I think you've got your hands full with Jerry," Nicole laughed. "Who knew retirement could be such fun. Although I'm not worried about Nicholas getting into trouble, I think you'll need a nanny for Jerry," Nicole laughed hysterically.

"Yes, you might be right," Kate smiled, picking up the empty cups.

"I think Nicholas is still sleeping, so I'm going upstairs to get a shower and dress for work. Thanks for the coffee," Nicole smiled, giving Kate a big hug and kiss. "Mom, you know what? You certainly made the right decision when you purchased this home."

"Yes. Awesome, isn't it? I can't wait for the holidays. It will be spectacular."

"Yes. It'll be amazing," Nicole agreed, placing her cup in the sink.

Later that evening, Jerry and Drew walked into the kitchen. They were starved. Taking one look at them, Kate roared with laughter.

"Wow. I've never seen two guys so sunburned in my entire life. You both look redder than cooked lobsters."

"Have you started dinner? We're starving?" Jerry asked.

"You look like you are dinner. Your face is completely cooked," Kate exclaimed, touching Jerry's burned cheeks.

"Ouch. Stop it. That hurts," Jerry yelled playfully, slapping her hands away.

"I told you to use sunscreen and get a hat to cover your face. Remember?" Kate smirked. "Honestly, Jerry, you're a big boy. You should've known better."

"All right. I guess we've learned our lesson this afternoon. I'll keep extra sunscreen and hats down at the boathouse so I won't forget," Jerry agreed, gently touching his tender face.

"You two go clean up and put aloe vera on your burns. Then, I'll make a couple of homemade pizzas. Unfortunately, the agency called and informed me that Gloria, our new cook, won't be in until tomorrow morning."

Living at Glen Haven Manor was wonderful. But, as they say, all good things must come to an end. It was Thursday morning, and the limo was scheduled to arrive at 10:00. Nicole and Drew would soon be on their way to Quebec.

"Drew, have you finished packing?" Nicole yelled from the bathroom.

"Yes. Are your bags packed?" Drew asked loudly.

"Yes. The suitcases are sitting by the bedroom door. Why don't you go ahead and take them downstairs? The limo will be here any minute."

Kate watched from the windows in the great room as the limo slowly drove up to the entrance. Then hearing Drew as he descended the stairs with his hands full of luggage and his squirming son, she offered to help.

"Drew, why don't you let me hold Nicholas while you go upstairs and let Nicole know the car is out front," Kate smiled, taking her grandson.

"Nicole. The car is here," Drew yelled, bounding up the stairs.

"Okay. Okay. I'm coming," Nicole shouted from the bedroom.

Holding Nicholas at the bottom of the stairs, Kate felt her eyes moisten. She had vowed not to let her emotions get the best of her this morning. She now had Nicholas to take care of, and she was determined to be strong for him. It was hard seeing them leave so soon. The past few days had been incredible. She loved having her family all under one roof. Nonetheless, Kate had to face reality. After a lot of hard work, Nicole finally lived out her dreams. She had become prominently known in the music industry.

"Okay, Mom. I guess this is it," Nicole walked over to hug them. "Please take good care of my little man," she said, wiping her eyes.

"Oh, Sweetheart. Please don't cry. You're going to make me cry, and I promised myself not to become emotional this morning," Kate frowned, wiping tears from her face.

"Mom, where's Jerry? I wanted to say goodbye."

"He's working on the boat. He said to tell you both goodbye. I think it's his way of dealing with everything this morning. Do you know how many years he devoted himself to the band? I think it's hard for him to let go. He loves you both."

"Okay. No more tears. We have to go," Drew grinned, kissing his young son.

"I'll talk with you this evening," Nicole waved, stepping inside the car.

"Thanks, Kate. We'll call you tonight when we arrive at the hotel," Drew reiterated as the chauffeur closed their door.

Waving as the limo slowly drove away, Kate tightly hugged Nicholas kissing his sweet little face.

"Okay, Nicholas. Let's go inside and see what Gloria has cooked this morning," she smiled, wiping her moist face.

Arriving at the airport, Nicole could see Cameron and Harry standing on the tarmac next to the Lear jet.

"Is everyone already on board," Nicole questioned, stepping out of the limo.

"Yes. Lance and Max arrived earlier. We're just stretching our legs before the flight," Cameron said, lighting his last cigarette for a while.

"Okay. Let's get this plane in the air," Nicole insisted, carrying her briefcase with her as she ascended the steps to the jet. "We've got a long day ahead."

"Good morning, Mrs. Connors. Welcome aboard," Nina smiled.

"Good morning."

"Good morning," Max smiled, walking to the back of the aircraft.

"Oh, good morning, Max," Nicole replied hurriedly, sitting next to Drew. "After we're airborne, I need to speak with Max and Lance," she mentioned buckling her seat belt.

"Would you like something to drink before takeoff?" Nina inquired.

"Yes. Thank you. Orange juice would be wonderful," Nicole answered.

"I'll take a cup of coffee," Drew spoke up.

"Okay. I'll be right back with those," Nina smiled.

"Doesn't it seem strange to be leaving our little guy behind?" Drew frowned. It was harder than he realized not to have easy access to his boy.

"Yes. But I thought we agreed to that?"

"Oh. We did. But, I already miss him," Drew sighed.

"Babe, don't worry. Mom and Jerry will take excellent care of him,"

Nicole assured him. She didn't have the same reservations about leaving their boy behind, knowing her mother would be taking care of him.

"Mrs. Connors, Mac wanted me to inform you the weather looks good over to Quebec this morning. Our flying time should be approximately five hours, arriving around 6:00 tonight," Nina informed as she handed her a glass of orange juice. "Sir, would you like any cream or sugar for your coffee?" Nina inquired.

"Oh. No, thank you," Drew replied, putting his magazine down.

As the jet lifted into the air, Nicole glanced out her window. She would never allow Drew to know she felt sick in the pit of her stomach. Of course, it bothered her to leave her baby behind. But she knew without a doubt, he was in the best hands possible. However, it wasn't hers. Quickly finishing her orange juice, she reached for her briefcase. She had work to do.

"Babe, I'm going to the back of the plane to discuss the concert with Lance and Max. It shouldn't take long," Nicole informed him, getting up from her seat.

"Okay. I'll be right here. I'm not going anywhere," Drew teased.

"Hey guys," Nicole smiled, sitting her briefcase on the small table. "Have you heard from our marketing team?"

"Yes. It appears they're doing a great job. Brad has contacted the major radio stations, giving us premium air time. So we're getting extensive coverage with the new singles, but two of the stations are also running promotional campaigns. They're giving away tickets and T-shirts. Would you mind if I had a cigar?" Lance asked, already taking a cigar from his pocket.

"I guess not. You've been working hard. I wouldn't want to deprive you."

"The roadies and musicians arrived yesterday. I booked them into the Westin Hotel. Yesterday, rehearsals were phenomenal. But I've got one more scheduled for tomorrow morning with Cameron and the orchestra. It's our last run-through before the concert. Things are going right according to plan," Max grinned, running his fingers through his disheveled blonde hair.

"Great. It sounds like you both have things under control."

"Oh, Brad will be contacting you in the morning. He's arranged a radio interview with you and Cameron for tomorrow. I'm not sure of the exact time or station, but he'll give you all the details," Lance added. "By the way, I've booked two suites and the penthouse at the Hilton. Max and I will share a suite. Cameron and Harry will share the other. Then, of course, I booked the penthouse for you and Drew. I'm sure you'll love it," Lance smiled.

"Great. Just what I wanted to hear. How are ticket sales going?" Nicole asked, glancing at Lance.

"Oh, I'm glad you reminded me," Lance grinned, taking a draw on his cigar. "Extremely well, we're almost sold out. I'm positive we'll sell out before tomorrow afternoon."

"Awesome. I couldn't ask for more. Do you know if Stan has enough security for tomorrow night?"

"Yes, as a matter of fact, I talked with him before we left this morning. Stan said he had more than enough personnel to cover the venue," Lance continued. "The Sports Dome has twelve thousand seats, not counting the upper boxed seats."

"What about our food vendors? What time do you have them setting up tomorrow night?" Nicole asked, taking notes.

"Well, I've contracted with local vendors. They assured me they'd arrive no later than 5:00 in the afternoon. They will offer us a hot and cold menu and provide beverage service. They came highly recommended," Lance added. "Oh, Pierre and his crew arrived yesterday. I talked with him this morning. He seems to be excited that he's part of our organization. I've also booked them into the Westin Hotel."

"We're fortunate to have Pierre and his crew. I'm totally in love with him," Nicole smiled. "He's doing one hell of a great job. The guys really like him."

"He came highly recommended," Lance smiled. "He's a great guy."

"I heard he formerly worked on Broadway before we hired him."

"That's right. Pierre has worked on Broadway for years. So yes, you were extremely fortunate to get him," Max agreed.

"Excuse me. I didn't mean to interrupt your meeting. I came over to get your menu preference for dinner. I can offer you spinach chicken parmesan with a side dish of roasted potatoes and garlic bread or steak teriyaki served with a side of white rice, steamed vegetables, and rolls. Which would you prefer?" Nina inquired.

"Wow, it all seems delicious. I'll have the spinach chicken parmesan with a glass of red wine. So that you know, I'll be returning to my seat to eat with my husband," Nicole replied.

"I'll make this easy for you," Lance smiled, putting down his cigar. "I'll have the same, including the glass of red wine."

"I'll have the steak teriyaki," Max said with a wink. "However, I'd like a cup of coffee with my meal."

"Thank you. I'll be serving dinner within the next hour," Nina informed them as she wrote down their requests.

"Well, if there are no further questions, I think I'll return to my seat and keep my husband company for the remainder of the flight," Nicole smiled.

"No. I think that about covers everything for now," Lance mentioned. "Oh, one last thing. Are you planning to stop by the Sports Dome later tonight after arriving at the hotel?"

"No. I think I'll stay in for the evening. I've got a lot of phone calls to make," Nicole answered.

"All right. I think Max and I are going down to the venue to check things out. If we run into any problems, we'll give you a call. Don't worry. I'm not expecting any," Lance laughed. "Enjoy your dinner."

"Thanks. Talk with you both later," Nicole grinned, closing her briefcase.

"Hey Babe, did you miss me?" Nicole teased, returning to her seat. "What did you order for dinner?" Nicole asked, trying to make herself comfortable.

"Oh, I requested the steak teriyaki. What did you order?" Drew asked.

"I'm having the spinach chicken parmesan with a glass of red wine."

"Geez, Babe, do you think she would bring us the entire bottle?" Drew laughed.

"Maybe, if you ask her nicely," Nicole smiled.

It was almost dark as the plane began its descent into Quebec.

"Would you like a warm towel?" Nina inquired.

"Yes. That sounds wonderful. Might as well give me two," Nicole answered, looking over at Drew, who was still sleeping."

"Babe, wake up. We're almost there," Nicole whispered in his ear.

Drew didn't budge. Taking one of the warm towels, Nicole gently wiped his face.

"Oh, that feels nice. Where are we?" Drew teased.

"Funny, Babe, we're still in the air. We'll be on the ground soon. Please remind me to give Mom a call as soon as we get checked into our room," Nicole insisted.

"Don't you mean penthouse? I believe you told me Lance reserved the penthouse for us."

"Yes. Don't be ridiculous."

Finally, the wheels of the jet touched the runway in Quebec.

"Wow. I'm so glad we're here. I feel completely exhausted," Nicole yawned, resting her head on Drew's shoulder.

"Well, the past two weeks have been hectic. Getting Kate and Jerry moved into their new house wasn't exactly easy," Drew commented.

As the plane rolled to a stop, Nicole reached for her briefcase.

"Let me take that for you," Drew insisted.

Descending the steps of the private jet, Nicole was anxious to be on her way to the hotel.

"Good evening, Mrs. Connors. I believe it's the Hilton Hotel," the chauffeur inquired as he opened the car door.

"Yes. Thank you," Nicole smiled.

Arriving downtown at the Hilton, Lance immediately checked each person into the hotel. Then, receiving room keys, he quickly passed them out as everyone made their way to the elevator.

"Well, this is our stop," Lance announced as the elevator reached the sixth floor. "Cameron, you're both right across the hall in room number 615. I'll see you tomorrow. I'll give you a call if anything important comes up tonight," Lance stated. "Nicole, you look exhausted. Drew, please make sure our young lady gets some rest. See you tomorrow," Lance mentioned as the guys stepped out of the elevator.

"Wow, Babe, you look tired," Drew frowned, closing the elevator door.

"Maybe it was the wine," Nicole suggested with a yawn.

Drew knew she was tired. Unlocking the door to the penthouse, they were both too sleepy even to take notice of their surroundings. Immediately, they fell onto the bed. Drew put Nicole under the warm blankets and slipped into bed next to her. Within minutes, they were out for the night.

Later the next morning, Drew was awakened by the phone sitting next to their bed. Quickly turning over, he panicked, noting the time and the fact they had forgotten to set the alarm the night before.

"Hello, is Nicole Connors there?" the young man asked.

"I'm afraid she just stepped out for a moment," Drew quickly answered. "Can I take a message for her?" He had to improvise for Nicole.

"Yes. Would you please let Nicole know Brad called? I'm staying at the Westin Hotel in room 1280. She can reach me through the hotel operator at that extension. Please have her return my call as soon as possible. Thank you."

"Okay. I'll let her know," Drew replied.

Drew freaked out. It was 10:30, and the morning was half over. Nicole was still asleep. He had to wake her. Undoubtedly, she would be upset when she realized the time and the missed phone call.

"Babe, you have to wake up," Drew gently nudged her. "Babe, we're in Quebec, and it's getting late. I hate to tell you, but it's 10:30."

Somewhere in her unconscious state, she had heard him.

"What?" she screamed, instantly sitting up. "Drew, please don't tell me it's 10:30?" Nicole exclaimed, wiping the sleep from her eyes.

"Yes, Babe, I'm afraid it is."

"Did anyone call for me?" she asked, running for the bathroom.

"Yes. But don't worry, I covered for you. I told them you had stepped out for a moment."

"Drew, who was it? Did they leave a message?" Nicole yelled from the bathroom.

"Yes. It was someone named Brad. He's staying over at the Westin Hotel," Drew answered loudly.

"Oh no," Nicole screamed. I think I might have missed an interview," she yelled.

"Babe, calm down. He left his room number at the hotel. Just call him back," Drew suggested. "I'll call room service and order breakfast with extra coffee," Drew added.

Nicole came running out of the bathroom and grabbed the phone. She took a deep breath, needing to calm herself before picking up the receiver.

"What was his room number?"

"It was 1280. He's in the Westin Hotel."

"Thanks, Babe. I knew he was staying at the Westin."

Her hands were shaking as she made the call. What if she had missed her first interview? How could she ever have allowed anything like this to happen? She had always prided herself on her professionalism. It wasn't good.

"Hello. May I please have room 1280?" Nicole asked.

"Yes. Please hold for a moment," the operator replied.

"Hello, this is Brad," the voice on the other end answered.

"Brad, this is Nicole Connors. My husband said you called earlier while I was out."

"Yes. How are you?" Brad asked.

"I'm fine. How are you?" Nicole said hurriedly, exchanging pleasantries.

"Great. I called earlier to let you know that I scheduled an interview downtown for you and Cameron at the radio station, 95.1 QFM. It's at 2:30 this afternoon. Will you both be able to make it? I hope it's not too late in the day for you?" Brad questioned.

"Not at all. Thank you. We'll be there," Nicole replied, greatly relieved.

"If it's alright, I've asked Lance to accompany you and Cameron. He's an old friend of Mr. Wallingford, the General Manager," Brad suggested.

"Yes. That's fine. Thank you. See you later this evening," Nicole said, hanging up the phone.

She wondered why Lance had made no mention that he knew the manager personally. Oh well, it wasn't important, she thought.

"Wow, Babe, someone must be looking out for me today. The interview is later this afternoon," Nicole smiled. "Oh no," she screamed.

"For heaven's sakes, what is it now?" Drew freaked.

"Babe, we forgot to call Mom last night," Nicole yelled.

"It's okay. Get a grip on yourself. You need coffee. I'll call Kate."

Walking over to the phone, Drew made the call explicitly explaining all the details to Kate, who completely understood. She was relieved to know they were fine, even though she had gone to bed worried the night before. It seemed everyone back home was great, especially Nicholas. According to Kate, he was a very happy baby. He was now the center of attention of his nanny, Kate, Jerry, and even Gloria, who already knew which foods he loved.

"Babe, everyone back home is fine. It seems Nicholas loves his new nanny. Kate also mentioned the fact that Gloria is so in love with him that she's specifically cooking things he likes to eat. So, you panicked for nothing."

Hearing a knock at the door, Drew raced over. He had never been more relieved to know that breakfast, especially coffee, had arrived.

"Awesome. We finally have caffeine," Drew laughed, quickly pouring two cups of coffee.

At last, Nicole was beginning to calm down. After consuming lots of coffee, eating breakfast, and getting a warm shower, she felt much better.

"Why don't we just stay in bed today?" Drew suggested taking his coffee and newspaper outside on the balcony. "Wow, this place is nice. Nicole, come out here. We have a spa," Drew laughed.

Later that afternoon, after Cameron and Nicole had left for their interview, Harry stopped by to check out the penthouse. Harry quickly noticed another door in the hallway near the patio door. It was a private screening room for movies, and it contained a popcorn machine.

"Geez. Man, you two must have been tired last night. You're not going to believe it. Come in here and check this out," Harry insisted. "You have a small private theater in here. Do you want to watch a movie?" Harry asked, looking through the DVD selection.

"No. But you're welcome to watch whatever you want. I think I'll take a quick nap on the couch while Nicole and Cameron are gone."

"Okay. I'll be in here," Harry grinned, lost in movie-land.

Drew must have been asleep for over an hour when he heard Nicole and Cameron walk in.

"Wow. So that's what you do when I'm not here?" Nicole laughed. "Did Harry leave?"

"No. But you're not going to believe this? We have a movie theater down the hall. Harry is watching movies."

"Really? Where?" he questioned, excitedly looking around to figure out which door. Drew pointed down the hallway and motioned as to which door.

"You should join him," Drew suggested. "So, Doll, how did the interview go?"

"Great. Cameron has a lot of fans in Quebec," Nicole mentioned sitting down on the sofa next to Drew, removing her shoes. Everyone was extremely excited about the concert. Lance has turned out to be a vital asset to the band. He knows everybody. You should see his Rolodex," Nicole laughed. "Oh, by the way, we're sold out tonight. Can you believe it?" she grinned.

"Well, Babe, if you ask me, I think you're fast becoming a VIP in the music industry. You're a force to reckon with, and if I were another manager, I'd sure hate to confront you. Especially when it comes to booking venues," Drew smiled, putting his arm around her.

"Oh, Drew, I'm as meek as a little lamb," Nicole smirked impishly.

"You can sell that line to someone who doesn't know you," Drew laughed, letting her hair out of its clip as he leaned over to give her an appreciative kiss.

The next few hours passed quickly as Cameron and Harry watched movies until Nicole chased them out, demanding they get ready for the concert.

"Drew, you only have thirty minutes before the limo arrives. Did you remember to have your tuxedo pressed?" Nicole inquired.

"Yes. Does that surprise you?" Drew teased, wiggling his brows.

"Of course, but thank you for remembering. Now go get dressed."

"Yes, sir, Boss," Drew snapped back, finally getting up from the sofa.

Walking out of the bathroom, Drew looked handsome.

"Wow. I must say, I love your new attire," Nicole winked. "Come over here and let me straighten your tie," she mentioned. "Babe, you look incredible."

"Let's go make Momma some money," Nicole laughed, brushing a few pieces of lint from his tuxedo.

"Sweetheart, shouldn't that be, make Momma some music?" Drew laughed.

"Music is money," Nicole laughed, giving him a quick kiss. "Have you forgotten what business I'm in?"

"Let's get out of here," Drew grinned, taking her hand.

Entering the elevator, Nicole kissed him passionately.

"Doll, where did that come from?" Drew smiled, taking advantage of the moment.

For a brief second, he almost considered hitting the stop button.

"Babe, you're frisky tonight. Sleeping late must have energized you. Maybe, I should turn off the alarm again tonight," Drew suggested.

"Don't you dare?" Nicole giggled, punching him in his upper arm.

"Ouch," Drew laughed, pulling her close.

Quickly, Nicole had to check her makeup in the mirrored walls of the elevator before the door opened.

Walking into the lobby, Cameron and Harry were waiting for them.

"Hey guys, ready to go," Nicole smiled, walking over to meet them.

Stepping inside the limo behind Nicole, Drew couldn't stop snickering.

"What's so funny?" Cameron asked.

"Oh, it's just your crazy sister. She's gone off the deep end tonight," Drew smirked.

"It's nothing, just a private joke," Nicole mentioned, discreetly pinching Drew in his backside.

"Stop it," Drew laughed.

"Okay, kids, we're almost there. Calm down," Cameron insisted. "Sis, I have something I want to tell you before we arrive."

"What is it, Cameron?" Nicole asked seriously.

"Did you know the Sports Dome was where I met Dad for the first time?" Cameron looked over at Nicole, a little misty-eyed.

"Oh, Cameron, I had no idea. Are you going to be alright? Why didn't you tell me?" Nicole sympathized. "Cameron, I would have changed this venue if I had only known," she stated in shock.

"Don't worry. I'm fine. You had no way to know. Mom was born and raised in Quebec. She came back here when Dad left for London, England. Grandpa's job transferred him back to the plant here in Quebec after a short time in Middleton. Do you know what's so weird? I was a huge fan of Black Tie Affair, and I had no way to know Dad was their lead singer. Mom told me only a few days before the concert. Jerry knows the story. He arranged for us to be in Dad's dressing room immediately after the concert. Sis, you'll never know how much that night meant to Mom and me," Cameron reminisced. "Dad even dedicated a song to Mom that night without knowing we were both in the arena. Someday we'll sit down, and I'll tell you more about my life before I met Dad."

"Cameron, I can't believe this. Are you going to be able to perform on the same stage as Dad with those memories?" Nicole questioned, scooting next to him. "I love you," Nicole smiled, putting her arms around him. "I wish I had known before now. I would never have asked you to perform at the Sports Dome if I had known."

"It's all right. I'm going to be fine. Trust me. I've got this," Cameron remarked. "Actually, I'm proud to be standing on stage tonight where Dad performed his last concert. Who would have ever known that one day I would be her?" Cameron smiled.

"Wow, Dude, that's heavy," Harry commented, handing Cameron a tissue. Cameron took the tissue and threw it back at Harry.

"Cameron, we're here. Do you need a few minutes before we go in," Nicole asked.

"No. I'm fine. I have you. Thank God you're here," Cameron smiled, putting his arm around her shoulders giving them a gentle squeeze.

"Cameron, I'm so proud of you. Dad will be standing beside you tonight. I feel it in my spirit. Just know you're not going to be alone on the stage. You're tough. Remember you have Dad's DNA pulsing through your veins."

"I know. Let's go," Cameron agreed.

Walking in at the back entrance of the Sports Dome, Nicole was still trying to process her talk with Cameron. Taking Drew's arm, she held on tightly, following him inside.

"Geez, Babe, there are no carts. Guess we'll have to hoof it down to the dressing room," Drew remarked, looking down at her heels.

"You're right. That's not acceptable," Nicole complained. "Wait till I see Stan. Okay, guys, you're on your own. I'll catch up with you later in the dressing room."

Continuing their slow pace down the maze of concrete corridors, Nicole looked up at Drew.

"Babe, I've got goosebumps. I'm walking in my Dad's footsteps tonight. Just think, he was here. He performed on this stage, and he used the same dressing room we'll be in. Wow. I feel so honored to be here. His last performance was here on this very stage," Nicole said in wonder.

"Sweetheart, please don't let your emotions consume you. It isn't the time or the place. People are counting on you tonight to be their strong, confident captain. Stop and look at me for a moment," Drew smiled, staring into the depths of her gorgeous blue eyes. "Doll, you can do this," he encouraged, wiping her moist cheeks. "I love you," Drew whispered lovingly into her ear.

"Babe, what would I do without you?" she smiled. "I only hope Cameron finds a partner in life as wonderful as you."

"Oh, I think he possibly already has," Drew winked. "Jillian."

"Really, you think he likes her?"

"Sure, have you seen how those two look at each other? Guys have a way of detecting these things in other guys," he winked.

"Drew, girls are the ones who pick up on those sensations, not guys." Nicole laughed and slapped him on the butt.

"Whatever, Babe. Now, let's get down to the dressing room. I want to see what tasty things you have for us tonight. I'm starved."

They continued their walk for a short distance when Nicole caught sight of Stan.

"Hey, Stan. Where were the golf carts tonight?" Nicole asked, realizing her feet were ever so slightly beginning to ache.

"Oh, they weren't by the wall when you came in tonight?" Stan stretched his neck in the direction of where the vehicles were supposed to be parked as if he could magically summon them.

"No. Not a single one."

"I'm sorry. Trust me. It won't happen again. You know, I saw Pierre and his group using them earlier. I'll talk with them. You'll probably find the carts down by the dressing room door. I told them repeatedly to make sure they returned them to the back entrance. I guess someone didn't take me seriously. It won't happen again," Stan reassured her.

"Okay. Thanks," Nicole replied. "I'll hold you to that, so make sure it doesn't happen again."

The carts were clearly visible as they approached the dressing room corridor. They were lined up against the wall next to the door, just as Stan had suspected.

"Doll, I guess those are your missing golf carts," Drew laughed.

"Stan was right. It was Pierre and his guys. I'm not going to come down too hard on them. My legs aren't broken, and I could use the exercise. However, I'm going to make sure if they plan to use the carts, Pierre and his guys better make sure they're returned to the back entrance before we arrive," Nicole retorted.

"Okay, Boss, whatever you say," Drew smiled.

Walking into the dressing room, it was chaotic. Pierre and his crew laughed boisterously up to nonsense as they styled hair and makeup for some of the musicians.

"Wow. There must be a party going on in here. It appears I finally found the golf carts," Nicole hinted sternly.

At once, Pierre laid down his comb and walked over.

"Oh, Mrs. Connors. I wasn't aware you would be here so early. It won't happen again. I assure you," Pierre apologized.

"Thanks. Please make sure your guys know if they use the carts before we arrive, to please return them to the back entrance. The golf carts are available for everyone to use. But just make sure to return them. That applies to each venue. Got it?" Nicole smiled.

"No problem. I hear you. I'll let my guys know. Don't worry," Pierre replied, walking back to his station.

"Boss, I'm hungry. I think I'll see what we have to eat," Drew said, heading toward the table, which held an assortment of delicious goodies.

Nicole smiled as she noticed Cameron sitting on the long sectional beside Jillian. Evidently, Drew was right. They appeared immersed in their conversation. Hopefully, Jillian would be just the person to distract Cameron from focusing too much on his memories. She contemplated walking over but quickly decided against it. Cameron seemed happy. Walking over to the buffet, she found Drew stuffing his face.

"Wow," Nicole commented, looking down at his plate.

Drew had filled it with fruit, egg salad, corn chips, and a giant sub sandwich.

"Could you possibly get anything else on your plate?" Nicole teased in disbelief.

"Babe, would you please grab me one of those cold drinks?"

"Really, Drew. I thought you just referred to me as your boss a few minutes ago."

"Doll, I live with you, remember. I think I recognize that ring on your left hand," Drew mentioned giving her a quick kiss.

"Okay. What do you want to drink?" Nicole hesitated, glaring at him through narrowed eyes.

It appeared everyone was having a great time. Looking around the room, Nicole felt rewarded, noting all the smiling faces. She was no longer bothered by memories. The following hour seemed to race by quickly. Finally, it was almost time to walk Cameron down to the stage. Nicole always ensured that orchestra members were cleared out of the dressing room at least fifteen minutes before showtime. Bruce had always allowed the guys to linger behind, giving them a fifteen-minute warning. Now, Cameron remained behind with a small entourage of assistants.

"Cameron, fifteen minutes till showtime," Nicole announced, feeling butterflies in her stomach. It didn't matter that she wasn't the one on stage. She didn't know if she would ever outgrow her nervousness for the band before they walked out.

"How are you holding up? Are you going to be okay out there tonight?" Nicole asked, praying for a miracle Cameron would pull it off.

"Sis, I'm fine. Don't worry. Everything is going to be okay. You'll see," Cameron assured her with a wink and a smile.

"Go out there, and make Dad smile."

Nicole felt proud and exhilarated as she walked alongside Cameron and his entourage through the dimly lit concrete corridors. She could only imagine that other band managers felt the same. Squeezing Cameron's hand, Nicole quickly kissed him on the cheek.

"You've got this," Nicole grinned, watching him ascend the steps leading up to the stage.

Cameron nodded in agreement with his head high as he quickly turned around from the top step.

The roar from the fans in the arena was almost deafening as Nicole stood watching behind the scene. Before Cameron walked on stage each evening, Max always directed the orchestra into a crescendo of music he had written, especially for Cameron's entrance. She was instantly covered in goosebumps once again as she heard the brilliant musical score. Maxwell Kline was a genius.

Walking out to center stage as fans in the vast arena yelled out his name, Cameron took the microphone in his hand. Then, standing to their feet, they welcomed him with thunderous applause. It was earth-shattering.

"Good evening, Quebec. How are you? I'm thrilled to be home. I was born and raised in Quebec for those who don't know. What an amazing place to call home," Cameron grinned as pandemonium ensued among his fans. They roared their delight upon hearing this amazing fact.

"Thank you for your warm welcome. I'd like to open tonight with a song written by Mr. Maxwell Kline titled, *Amazed.* Taking his mic, Cameron walked to the edge of the stage and began softly singing the lyrics. It seemed he was starting new traditions. He always quickly grabbed the hands of those standing near the front and closest to the stage. It appeared his fans loved that he was so personal with the audience. Security had to diligently guard the girls nearest the stage as it was not unheard of for some of the girls to push and shove their way up to the front.

"Thank you. My next selection is entitled, *Imagine Us.* I hope you like it," Cameron remarked, turning around briefly to face the orchestra. Max made sure the musicians followed his queue. This particular song was one of his slower numbers. Cameron felt ecstatic to hear everyone singing along on the chorus. He felt entranced while singing. He could only wonder if his father had felt the same.

"Thank you," Cameron humbly took a bow. "I'm sure many of you remember my father, Nicky Spade," he announced. The arena resonated with thunderous applause at the mere mention of his name. The noise level from the applause could have registered on the Richter scale. My father performed his last farewell concert here on this very stage. I'd like to honor him tonight by singing one of his most famous songs, *Because of You*, Cameron stated. Once again, it was pure pandemonium as the crowd stood to their feet.

"Dad, here's to you," Cameron proclaimed, holding his mic high. Then, pausing momentarily, he looked up. "I love you."

A hush instantly fell over the entire arena. It seemed Cameron had made a soul to soul connection with his audience. Some artists can perform a lifetime and never experience such an encounter with their fans.

Taking his mic, Cameron quietly began singing the lyrics, A Capella, as he slowly walked to the front of the stage. The fans were captivated. Turning around to face the orchestra, it was always Max's queue to bring in the musicians. Cameron's rendition of the song was magical, and everyone loved it. Cameron was a natural at reading his audience and giving them what they wanted.

The fans stood to their feet again and vigorously applauded as Cameron brought the song to a close.

"Thank you so much," Cameron smiled, placing his hand over his heart as a gesture of gratitude.

Once more, he surprised his fans as he looked up and whispered. "Thanks, Dad."

"All right, Max, let's give them something to sing about," Cameron suggested looking back at the orchestra. The musicians instantly led into his next song, *Nobody like You*. Its contemporary tempo had the fans swaying with the music.

"Thank you," Cameron grinned, expressing his appreciation.

Cameron delivered one hit song after another, leaving his audience spellbound. Finally, his hour and a half performance had come to an end. It seemed over way too soon.

"I'd like to thank everyone for coming out tonight. I've loved being with you this evening. I want to end by singing one of my favorite songs, *Stranger in Paradise,* written by Mr. Robert Wright and Mr. George Forrest. It goes something like this," Cameron smiled, turning around to queue Max and the orchestra.

Standing center stage, Cameron's song delivery was nothing short of perfection. As he finished the song, he quickly walked along the edge of the stage, trying to touch hands with as many of his fans as he possibly could within that short period. His fans adored him with outstretched hands.

"Thank you, Quebec. I love you," Cameron smiled, waving his hand high in the air as he left the stage.

"Wow. Cameron, you were brilliant," Nicole yelled, catching sight of him backstage. "You knocked it out of the park."

Noticing Cameron as he descended the steps leading down from the stage, Lance came running over.

"Man. You were phenomenal," Lance shook Cameron's hand. "That was incredible," he added, quickly embracing him.

Making his way back to the dressing room alone, Cameron began removing his tie and unbuttoning the top buttons on his white dress shirt. Needing to decompress, Cameron immediately poured himself a glass of bourbon upon entering the dressing room. He took a quick sip, walked over to the long sectional, sat down, and lit a cigarette. All performers build up energy after being on stage. Cameron was no exception as he poured his heart into his performance. Quebec was special. It always would be. It was simply home, and he wanted to leave nothing on the stage. He now craved a few minutes alone with his bourbon. However, it wasn't to be. A group of reporters rushed into the dressing room to congratulate him and learn more about his connection to Nicky and Black Tie Affair. By the time Nicole and Lance reached him, he was bombarded by news media.

Upon seeing the chaos in Cameron's dressing room, Lance was shocked. He turned to Nicole, visibly upset, expressing his horror, "What the hell?" It was a major miscommunication between Nicole and security to risk the chance of this happening to any artist. Security should have been posted outside the dressing room to prevent such disturbances.

"You've got to get him out of there," Lance yelled. "Now, Nicole," he demanded sternly.

Pushing and shoving her way through the mob, Nicole finally grasped Cameron's hand, pulling him through the crowd and out of the dressing room. Leaving Lance behind to deal with the news reporters.

"Cameron, I'm sorry," Nicole repeated. "I had no idea you were alone. I never expected that to happen. But, I promise you, it won't ever happen again."

"Sis, it's okay. Honestly, it wasn't your fault. You're new to this business too," Cameron laughed. "Do you know where Jillian is?"

"No. But here's my plan. I'll discreetly get you safely inside the limo parked at the back entrance. Stay in the car, and I'll find Jillian. Then you can have the driver take you back to the Hilton, at least for now. Later tonight, we'll devise a strategy if you want to go elsewhere," she suggested.

Making their way down the corridor, Cameron saw Jillian walking toward them. She hadn't noticed him or Nicole as she rushed past them evidently on her way down to the dressing room.

"Jillian, stop," Cameron demanded, sprinting after her.

Nicole panicked, feeling completely ill-equipped to handle the situation. She felt overwhelmed. Finally, she felt someone grab her hand. Turning around, it was Cameron. He had Jillian with him.

"Sis, there's an empty golf cart up ahead. It's got a back seat. Let's take it," Cameron suggested. "Can you drive? Jillian and I will hop in the back. Drive it to the back entrance. I'll somehow squat down so no one will hopefully recognize me. It has a horn. Use it if you need to clear the corridor," Cameron laughed.

Holding onto Jillian, Cameron crouched down behind the front seat as best he could in such a tiny space. Clearly, luck was on their side. As Nicole took the first corner, she ran straight into Drew and Harry.

"What the hell, Nicole?" Drew yelled.

"Quick, both of you, get in," Nicole commanded. "I can't talk now. But, Drew, please help me navigate through the crowd of people ahead."

"Babe, for heaven's sakes, scoot over. Let me drive," Drew demanded.

Quickly taking control of the golf cart, Drew used the horn to part their way through the crowds. Hearing Cameron snickering, Harry looked behind his seat.

"Geez, Louise," Harry roared with laughter. "Cameron, why the hell are you squatting behind the seat like a duck?"

"Quiet," I'll tell you in a few minutes," Cameron replied, trying to control his laughter.

Finally, Drew got them through the masses and to the back entrance.

"Quick, everyone inside the limo. Hurry," Nicole demanded.

"Whew," Nicole sighed, taking a deep breath as the limo drove away with everyone safely inside.

"What the hell just happened back there?" Drew inquired as everyone in the car began laughing hysterically.

"Wow. I guess I was a little unprepared. Sorry about that," Nicole giggled.

"I'll say," Cameron agreed.

"Will someone please just tell me what happened?" Drew insisted, looking around.

"Yes, please," Harry spoke up, lighting a cigarette. "I've got to hear this."

"Well, it goes something like this," Cameron snickered. "I had just walked off the stage after briefly encountering Lance and seeing Nicole. So I continued down to the dressing room. I walked in, poured myself a bourbon, and relaxed on the long sectional to smoke a cigarette. Then, suddenly out of nowhere, I was bombarded by a mob. News media and fans descended upon me like ants," Cameron laughed. "I'm sure they meant no harm but wanted to congratulate me on a great concert," Cameron explained. "Kind of scary," he continued.

"Nicole, Cameron had no security. So where the hell were they?" Drew questioned, completely embarrassed for her. "Babe, where was Lance?" Drew continued.

"Oh, he was back near the stage," Cameron interjected.

"Are you telling me that no one in this organization thought or planned for Cameron's security after leaving the stage?" Drew interrogated.

"Guess not?" Cameron laughed. "Apparently, I'm expendable."

At that point, the whole car roared with laughter. Harry could hardly catch his breath. He was laughing so hard.

"Unbelievable," Drew responded, utterly perplexed.

However, after looking over at Harry, who had totally lost it by now, Drew started laughing. The more Drew seriously gave thought to what had just transpired, he had to laugh. It was, after all, hilarious. Something you hopefully only saw at the movies, never expecting to experience in real life.

"So, Babe, what kept this from happening back in Vancouver at the Coliseum?" Drew grilled Nicole.

"Oh, I don't know. Stan must have been on top of security better."

At that point, everyone was overtaken with laughter. The more you tried to rationalize the dilemma, the funnier it got.

"Who needs a drink?" Cameron asked, grabbing a bottle of champagne.

"Just bring out all the bottles and keep pouring," Drew laughed.

"Jillian, you're quiet?" Harry questioned. "I hope we didn't scare you too much."

"Oh, not at all," she smiled, snuggling closer to Cameron.

"Well, Babe, I guess you just managed to blow your professional image to smithereens in front of Jillian," Drew teased.

"Really, Babe. Thanks a lot," Nicole retorted.

"Oh, Mrs. Connors, I completely understand how that could've happened," Jillian replied, unsure of responding to Drew's statement.

"Jillian, please call me Nicole. You'll soon get used to the crazy antics of these boys," she added.

Cameron passed drinks to everyone. At this point of the evening, they were certainly needed. It seemed the night had truly been remarkable in more ways than one.

Nicole was beginning to become well known in the music industry after their performances in Vancouver and Quebec. Her reputation for booking venues and having them sell out preceded her. The venues were sold out before she even arrived at the location in most instances. Nicole worked hard. She had built a network of competent individuals who never failed to have her back in any given situation. She had surrounded herself with the best.

For the remainder of the year, Cameron and his orchestra completed their Canadian and the United States tour. Then, taking a few down days in-between venues, Nicole and Drew always raced home to see Nicholas. He was growing up too fast. Finally, celebrating his third birthday, Nicholas was ready for preschool. After enrolling Nicholas, Nicole finally felt comfortable extending their tour to Europe.

The following spring, after performing in London, Dublin, and Amsterdam, Cameron and his orchestra were scheduled to perform in Paris. Kate loved Paris. She had anxiously waited for Cameron and the band to perform in her favorite city. Kate had spent every summer in France as her father's business always necessitated them spending their summers in Europe. Kate had many special memories of Paris. However, her time spent with Nicky in Paris was by far her fondest. With eager anticipation, Kate and Jerry decided to come over with Nicholas unannounced. Kate wanted to surprise her daughter. Nicole had not been home in over six months.

It was late in the evening when their plane lifted off the runway. Kate looked out her window. Watching the brilliantly lit skyline of Vancouver begin to fade slowly in the distance, she looked down at her watch. She would soon welcome the following day in the City of Lights.

CHAPTER NINETEEN

Paris

"Wow, Babe. Can you believe it? We're in Paris," Nicole smiled, taking Drew's hand as they walked over to the elevator. "We have the entire day to explore. Where do you want to go first?"

"Well, we might as well start with that big tower," Drew teased as the elevator door opened.

"You're funny. Mom says the best way to see Paris is by moped. Do you think you could manage the city traffic?"

"Doll, are you doubting my abilities?" Drew smirked. "I wasn't the one who wrecked the moped while we were on tour in Bangkok. It was Harry. Of course, that happened before we met," Drew grinned, giving her a quick kiss.

Taking a side street, Drew held Nicole's hand as they walked along a narrow cobblestone path that separated their hotel from a nearby park. A sea of yellow daffodils covered the grounds, and a fragrant bouquet of floral scents vigorously infused the air. Window boxes overflowing with bright red geraniums gave color to the aged stone buildings that faced the common area. It was by far the best time to see Paris. It was spring.

"No wonder Mom loves Paris. It's gorgeous," Nicole smiled, walking past the park. "Hey, over there. I see the moped rental," Nicole eagerly pointed out.

"Geez, Nicole. Calm down. We've got all day," Drew laughed.

Grasping her hand, Drew hurriedly led Nicole across the busy street. It was only a few minutes before they were given the moped of their choice. After helping Nicole with her helmet, Drew strapped on his helmet as she jumped on behind him. Within moments, they sped away down the busy, narrow streets.

"Hey, Babe. Please be careful," Nicole yelled hysterically as Drew dodged his way through the traffic.

Noting the Eiffel Tower in the distance, Drew managed to weave in and around the smaller European autos as Nicole held tightly to Drew with her arms securely wrapped around his waist. Then, narrowly missing one of the smaller compact cars, Nicole screamed.

"Drew, for heaven's sakes, you're going to get us both killed."

Shouting out directions, she didn't stop until they had finally arrived at their destination. Drew was frustrated. After finding a suitable spot to park, he took a deep breath.

"Nicole, you could have got us killed," he scolded.

"Babe, you were driving," she snapped back, removing her helmet.

Suddenly, they burst out with laughter from the mere thoughts of having survived the ordeal.

"I think we should take a taxi tomorrow," Nicole suggested, giving Drew a quick kiss.

"Why don't we get something to eat? Let's buy a bottle of wine, some cheese, and a couple of sandwiches."

"Sounds good. We should have come better prepared with a picnic basket," Nicole said, taking notice of the locals. Both young and old were relaxing on the green grassy knolls taking in the incredible views of the Eiffel Tower, which loomed overhead.

After purchasing all the necessary items, they found an open spot. Spreading out their blanket, they lounged back, relaxing as Drew uncorked the bottle of wine and poured them each a glass.

"Doll, is this the life or what?" he smiled, laying down on the blanket.

Taking Nicole's glass, Drew pulled her down next to him.

"I wonder what Cameron and Jillian did today?" Nicole asked.

"Oh, I'm not sure. It doesn't matter. Nothing could be better than being here with you," Drew winked, giving her a quick kiss.

"You're so romantic," she laughed.

For the next hour, Drew and Nicole soaked up the sun's warmth while taking in the ambiance of the City of Lights. Then, enjoying the cheese and bread, it wasn't long before the entire bottle of wine had been consumed.

"Why don't we go pay a visit to your tower," Drew teased.

"I thought you would never ask."

Reaching the top of the Eiffel Tower, Nicole and Drew walked over to the railing. Feeling the warm breeze as it gently swept across her face, Nicole felt like she was standing on top of the world. With wind-swept hair, she stood with her arms locked tightly around Drew, observing the incredible vistas below.

"Wow, Babe, this is truly unbelievable," she smiled, giving him a quick, passionate kiss. "I can see why Mom loves Paris," she smiled, staring at him.

After remaining at the top of the Eiffel Tower for over twenty minutes, taking in its amazing views, Drew was ready to call it a day.

"Doll, as great as today has been, I think we should probably go back to the hotel," Drew suggested, giving her one last kiss.

Nicole had no idea the surprise that awaited her.

Arriving back at the exquisite Regency Hotel, Drew desperately needed to relax. After their perilous drive back, he had to unwind. Unlocking the door, Drew immediately walked over to the mini-fridge to get a bottle of beer.

"Why don't we stay in for the evening and order dinner. Is that okay?" Drew asked, walking outside on the patio to light a cigarette.

"Sounds perfect. I have some phone calls to make. I need to talk with Lance and Max about the concert tomorrow night," Nicole replied, taking off her shoes. "I'll pour myself a glass of wine and join you on the balcony."

Hearing a knock at the door, Nicole walked over to answer it.

"Surprise!" Kate laughed. "I've got a little boy who's anxious to see his mommy."

"Oh, Mom, this is the best surprise ever," Nicole exclaimed. "I had no idea you, Jerry, and Nicholas were coming over," she answered excitedly. "I'm so happy to see you," Nicole grinned, taking Nicholas. "Hey Jerry, it's great to see you too. Come in. Drew is outside on the balcony drinking a beer," Nicole smiled, giving him a huge hug.

"I wanted to surprise you. I've just been waiting until Cameron performs in Paris. You know how much this city means to me," Kate smiled.

"She's been counting down the days," Jerry interjected.

"Mom, you didn't have to wait until Paris. You're welcome to come over at any time," Nicole laughed, kissing Nicholas on his chubby cheeks. "How's my little man?" Nicole smiled, putting him down. Nicholas ran straight back to the patio door.

"Mom, why don't you open the balcony door and let him surprise Drew," Nicole suggested.

"Great idea," Kate giggled quietly, opening the door.

"Daddy," Nicholas squealed upon seeing Drew.

"Where did you come from?" Drew exclaimed with excitement, scooping Nicholas into his arms.

"Look what I found?" Drew laughed enthusiastically, carrying Nicholas back inside. "Hey Jerry, we didn't have any idea you guys were coming over. Grab a beer from the fridge."

"Oh, I know, Kate wouldn't let me say a word. She wanted to surprise Nicole," Jerry smiled. "So, how are things?"

"Oh great, the concerts have been sold out. Everything has been going just like clockwork, and Nicole is building quite a reputation for herself over here. So we took today off and did the tourist thing. We rented mopeds and went to the Eiffel Tower. I don't know which was worse, the terrifying traffic or Nicole freaking out," Drew laughed.

"Sounds like fun. Don't let Kate hear you?" Jerry teased. "You know how she loves to sightsee. I swear, she should have been a tourist guide," Jerry snickered.

"So, how's that boat of yours?"

"She's running like a champ. Too bad you're not there to take her out."

"How's retirement? Do you miss traveling with the band?" Drew asked, handing Jerry a beer.

"Well, not as much as I thought. Kate tries to keep me too busy. She's constantly trying to find things for me to do. So I stay down at the boathouse out of sight. I try to stay out of her way," he laughed.

"What was that, Jerry Godwin?" Kate frowned, overhearing their conversation as she sat down next to Jerry.

"Babe, I just meant there's always something to do back home."

"That's better," Kate gave him a quick kiss. "Have you guys had dinner?"

"No. We were going to order in tonight," Nicole explained, sitting on the couch. Nicholas was bouncing next to her.

"You're kidding, right? We're in Paris. I know the best French restaurant, it's located downtown on the left bank of the Seine. Why don't we go?" Kate suggested, excited about revisiting her old stomping grounds.

"Great. Let's invite Cameron and Harry," Nicole recommended trying to get Nicholas to stop jumping on the furniture.

"Babe, why don't you give the guys a call? I almost forgot you should ask Cameron to bring Jillian," Drew proposed as he stood up to get him and Jerry another beer.

"Okay, that sounds like fun," Nicole stood, picking up Nicholas and swinging him off the couch. Together they went into the next room to call Cameron.

"Cameron said they would meet us down in the lobby at 6:00 tonight. Jillian is staying in Cameron's room. Can you believe it?" Nicole snickered. "He's going to call Harry, so I'll make arrangements for the car."

"Nicole, he's your older brother. You knew they were together. Remember Bruce's policy was to stay out of our personal relationships unless it became a problem with the band. Jerry grab a beer. Let's sit outside and have a cigarette. The girls can talk inside," Drew said as he stepped out onto the patio.

Later that evening, the La Mirabelle Restaurant was just as Kate remembered. Its old-world charm was stunning. It had detailed ornate trim that outlined its architectural features. Walking inside, the large windows along the back of the restaurant offered spectacular views of the Seine. Tourists in long glass-covered boats slowly drifted past on the river. Nicole reserved a large table near the back of the restaurant, which allowed them privacy. After being seated, the maître 'd handed out menus and quickly returned to take their orders. The evening was getting off to a great start. Nicholas enjoyed the French version of mac-n-cheese, while Kate, Nicole, and Jillian ordered Ratatouille, eggplant casserole with tomatoes, zucchini, and onions. Jerry, Drew, Cameron, and Harry ordered Boeuf Bourguignon beef stew. Later that evening, after dinner had been served, Kate began to fill Nicole and Cameron in on her past. Kate shared many exciting experiences with Nicky and Black Tie Affair.

"This restaurant brings back such happy memories. Nicky and I came here for dinner one evening after his concert. We spent an incredible weekend in Paris. I took him to all my favorite haunts. After Paris, the band was scheduled to perform in Frankfurt. Randy, Alex, and their girlfriends left immediately afterward for Rome. Unfortunately, their plane never made it," Kate frowned somberly. She had to pull herself out of her dark memories. She needed to focus on the present, which was filled with joy and laughter.

Jerry could sense Kate momentarily going back to some of the band's darker days. He needed to bring her back to the moment.

"It was during this time I came on board with Black Tie Affair," Jerry interjected. "It's been a family affair from the beginning. I'm so thankful that both Nicole and Cameron will carry on the traditions that Bruce started."

Later that night, after enjoying the ambiance of the quaint La Mirabelle Restaurant, their superb French cuisine, and conversations recollecting memories of Paris, it was time to call it an evening.

Arriving back at the hotel, Nicole and Drew were ready to put Nicholas to bed and retire. It had been a long day.

"Doll, why don't I pour us a glass of wine before calling it a night?

Then, we can sit outside on the balcony," Drew said, picking up two wine glasses and heading towards the patio.

"Sounds great. Let me put Nicholas in his porta-crib. He's asleep already," Nicole smiled as she carried a sleeping little boy into their room.

Sitting outside under the brilliance of the evening sky, life was good. Nicole was thrilled that Kate and Jerry had decided to surprise them by bringing Nicholas to Paris. Finally, Nicole had her son back. Her world was complete.

"Hey, Babe. I have a brilliant idea. Why don't we keep Nicholas with us? He's older now and easier to manage. So Nicholas could finish out the European tour with us. What do you think?" Nicole questioned.

"Well, sweetheart, to be perfectly honest, I think it would be better for Nicholas to return to Vancouver with Kate and Jerry. He's starting preschool next week. It's a vital time in his life, and we're not set up to handle preschool or any school on the road. I love him with all my heart, but school is important. So don't you want him to get the best possible start in life?" Drew questioned, snuggling up closer.

"I do want what's best for him, but I could teach him."

"Doll, I love you. But there's not enough time in your day to teach preschool. So today was our first day off in months," he stated, sipping his wine. "We need to do what's best for him," Drew insisted with no reservations.

"Drew, I'm not sure that is what's best for Nicholas. You're not a mother, and you don't have the same feelings. But, if he's with me, I can make sure he's safe. We can ensure he has everything he needs," Nicole continued. She was fighting off feelings of overwhelming guilt being away from her baby.

"Are you trying to tell me that you don't think your mom or Jerry is capable of caring for Nicholas? Really, she's your mother. She raised you, and I think she did a wonderful job," he grinned, pouring himself another glass of wine. "Listen, Babe. We've had an incredible day. Let's not argue about who or what is best for Nicholas. He's sleeping peacefully right now. I think it's time to turn in for the evening."

Taking Nicole's hand, he led her back inside.

"Babe. I'm sure after you've given this more thought, you'll see

I was right in deciding to have Kate and Jerry take Nicholas back to Vancouver," he reaffirmed, squeezing her hand.

"Well, I'm still not sure. But if you think it's the right choice for us to make, I'll go along with your decision. You just better hope nothing ever happens to my baby," Nicole demanded.

"Stop that nonsense," Drew teased, giving her a quick kiss. "Speaking of babies, do you remember our conversation during the flight from Honolulu? I made you aware that I wanted more children, what do you think? Nicholas is three now, and I think it's the perfect time to be thinking about a little sister or brother for him?" Drew winked with a grin.

"Oh, Babe. You're right. I couldn't agree with you more," Nicole smiled, putting her arms tightly around him. "I love you," she giggled, stopping to kiss him passionately.

"Okay, Mrs. Connors, follow me. I believe I know how to end this perfect evening," he laughed, pulling her into the bedroom.

Sunlight streamed in through the opened curtains, waking Drew. Today was their first concert in the City of Lights.

"Doll, it's almost 8:00. " Drew grinned, kissing her awake. It's time to start the day.

"You're right. I've got so much to do today," Nicole replied, jumping out of bed. "I'm taking a shower. Why don't you order breakfast and check on Nicholas? Cameron and I have a radio interview at 1:00. Then, I need to stop at the Seine Auditorium later this afternoon. I want to make sure Stan has enough security for tonight's concert," she smiled, giving him a quick kiss. "Oh, one last thing," she quickly returned. "Last night was magical," she whispered in his ear.

"Thanks, Babe. I'm glad you approved. Now go take your shower," Drew laughed.

Later that morning, Drew dressed Nicholas and took him over to Kate and Jerry's suite. Nicole was on her way to meet Cameron and Jillian.

Knocking at their door, Cameron answered.

"Hey, Sis. Come in. Would you like coffee?"

"No. It's almost noon. We better hurry. Do you know if Lance is planning to be at the interview?" Nicole inquired.

"Oh, he called earlier this morning. He said he would meet us there. So I guess we're ready to go," Cameron mentioned locking the door.

"Jillian, you look nice," Nicole remarked, admiring her attire.

"Thanks. Cameron picked out my dress," Jillian smiled.

"Geez, Cameron, I didn't know you were a fashionista. I thought I was the only one in the family who loved clothes.

Wearing a floral sundress that stopped just above her knees, Jillian was stunning. A short white sweater, sandals, and beautiful blonde hair in a ponytail completed her cute ensemble.

Arriving at the radio station, Lance waited for them in the lobby.

"I'm glad everyone arrived a few minutes early," Lanced smiled. "Jillian, you're welcome to go in with us if you'd like."

"Thanks. I would love to," she smiled.

After a short time, they were called into the manager's office.

"Good afternoon, welcome to Paris. Please have a seat," Mr. Blain smiled. "I must say, Cameron, you seem to have a lot of fans in our beautiful city. How can I be of help?"

"Thank you," Cameron replied confidently. "Let me introduce my manager and sister, Nicole Connor." Then, turning to the stunning blonde sitting next to him, Cameron squeezed Jillian's hand. "This is Jillian Johnston, one of our extremely talented violinists, and this is my assistant, Mr. Lance Easton," he acknowledged.

"You look familiar," Mr. Blain spoke up, staring at Lance.

"Oh, I knew the former manager, Paul-Henri Fontenot. We worked together on promotional campaigns in the past," Lance smiled.

"Great. So what can I do for you?"

"First, I'd like to give you ten free tickets for tonight's performance. Perhaps you could offer your callers a chance to win those. Also, I would like to get extra air time for the band over the next two days. We want to ensure our fans in Paris know of our arrival and the upcoming concerts at the Seine Auditorium this evening and tomorrow night. I would also love to offer you and your family boxed seating for tonight's performance if you're available," Nicole smiled, handing him a pack of tickets.

"Thank you. I do appreciate the tickets. I'm sure my daughters, Renee and Chantel, will be excited to attend tonight's performance," Mr. Blain reciprocated.

"If your daughters would like, I'm sure Nicole could arrange a quick meet and greet along with a photo session this evening before the concert," Cameron spoke up.

"Yes. I'd be happy to make those arrangements," Nicole added. "Lance has arranged an on-air interview with your staff and Cameron for tomorrow. I'm genuinely grateful for your cooperation. It gives us the exposure we need to ensure our fans stay connected while we're in Paris. I'll leave one of our promotional bundles. I think you'll find it helpful if you should decide to incorporate a free giveaway with the tickets. It includes autographed T-shirts, among other things. I appreciate your valuable time today," Nicole smiled.

"Thank you for your time. I look forward to meeting you and your family later this evening," Nicole smiled as she stood, extending her hand.

"Mrs. Connors, it's been my pleasure. Nice to meet you," Mr. Blain grinned, shaking hands with Nicole, Lance, Cameron, and Jillian. "You can count on my continued support," he smiled, showing them to the door.

Leaving the building, Nicole felt the meeting was very successful.

"Lance, I swear you know everyone," Nicole laughed.

"Well, that's why you hired my Rolodex and me, isn't it?" Lance chuckled.

Their two-night performance in Paris was exceptional. It was evident by the sold out status of each concert. The surprise visit by Jerry, Kate, and Nicholas made this venue even more special. Paris had given them time to reconnect with the past and the present.

Cameron and his orchestra were next scheduled to perform in Frankfurt, Germany. It was apparent Nicky was with them in spirit as they continued their European tour, walking in his footsteps.

CHAPTER TWENTY

Frankfurt

As their private jet circled Frankfurt on its approach into the International Airport, Nicole hurriedly closed her briefcase. She had spent the last hour going over expenditures. Taking care of business meant staying abreast of the numerous financial aspects of the band, and traveling with a full orchestra, accrued a lot of overhead expenditures. In addition, Nicole had the additional worries of the added costs and logistics. Until everyone was accounted for at each venue, she could never relax. However, she had surrounded herself with the best team possible, which helped tremendously. Lance Easton and Maxwell Kline appeared to be worth their weight in gold to her organization. With Jerry no longer onboard, they filled the gap resulting from his retirement.

"Babe, aren't you tired?" Drew asked sympathetically, watching Nicole rub her eyes. "You've been working nonstop since we left Paris."

"Yes, but taking advantage of our flights lets me focus completely on business," Nicole yawned.

As the plane rolled to a stop, Nicole looked forward to a nice warm bed and hopefully a good night's sleep. However, this was not to be the case.

Nicole received an urgent message while checking everyone into the Hyatt Regency in downtown Frankfurt. It had awaited her arrival.

"Mrs. Connors, I have a message for you," the concierges stated. "I'm afraid it's marked urgent. It's from Mr. Jerry Godwin. Would you like to use our phone at the desk?" he inquired.

"No, thank you. I'll make the call from my room," Nicole answered, looking perplexed. "Oh Drew, you don't think it's Nicholas?" she asked in a state of panic.

"Babe, whatever makes you think that. No. It's probably nothing at all," Drew replied, somewhat worried but not wanting Nicole to worry further due to his concern.

Quickly ensuring everyone had their assigned rooms and keys, Nicole ran for the elevator.

"Nicole, take a breath. Please, try to calm down," Drew yelled, trying to catch up with her before the door to the elevator closed.

Hurriedly, she unlocked their door. Then, racing over, she quickly picked up the phone sitting next to the bed. Her hands trembled as she dialed the number.

Hearing Jerry's voice, Nicole felt weak.

"Jerry, I just got your message. What's wrong?"

"Sweetheart, are you alone? Is Drew there with you?"

"Yes, Jerry, what is it? I'm a nervous wreck."

"Why don't you give the phone to Drew?"

"Jerry, you tell me what's going on. Do you hear?" she screamed, demanding an answer.

"Nicole, there's been an awful accident," Jerry paused.

"What kind of accident? Give me details."

"An automobile accident," Jerry reluctantly stated.

"Oh Nicole, I don't even know how to say this. Nicholas is in critical condition. The doctors aren't giving me much hope, and Kate is in serious but stable condition. After arriving home yesterday evening, Kate decided to take Nicholas back into the city to buy some school supplies. Nicholas was supposed to start preschool tomorrow. But, Sweetheart, it was raining, and the roads were wet and slippery. I advised her not to go, but Kate didn't listen," Jerry cried.

"Jerry, why did you let Mom leave the house? How could you? Are you telling me school supplies were more important than my baby," Nicole screamed.

"Sweetheart, you need to come home as soon as possible. They're both in the Presbyterian Hospital. How soon can you get here?"

"Oh my God. I'm leaving right now. It's almost midnight, but I'm on my way. You do whatever it takes to ensure Nicholas hangs on. Do you understand?" Nicole yelled, hanging up the phone. She knew it. She knew something terrible was going to happen. She just couldn't put her finger on it. Why had she let Drew talk her into giving up her son? She turned toward Drew, her anger and grief consuming her.

"Drew, it's Nicholas. He was in a car accident with Mom. He might not make it. I hate you! Do you hear me?" Nicole screamed. "I hate you! I hate you," she repeated. "I had a premonition. I felt he should stay with us," Nicole screamed, falling to the floor. Unable to handle the tragic news, Nicole fainted.

Running for warm towels, Drew was shaking. His heart was racing, and a million thoughts ran through his mind. If she'd had a premonition regarding Nicholas, why hadn't she told him? He was angry with her, with God, with himself. He wanted to die. Why would God take Nicholas? He was young and innocent. It should have been him, he thought. Quickly trying to revive Nicole, he picked up the phone to call Cameron. Thankfully, Cameron answered after the first ring.

"Cameron, I need you to get over to our suite as fast as possible. There's been a terrible auto accident back home. Nicholas might not make it, and Kate is in serious condition," Drew frantically explained.

"I'm coming right now," Cameron panicked, hanging up the phone.

He was unsure of what he had just heard. "Jillian, there's been an accident. It involves Nicholas and Kate. Drew needs me. Nicole has fainted, so I'm going over to their suite. Do you want to go?" Cameron asked.

"Yes. Maybe I can help. Let's go," Jillian urged.

Running for the elevator, Cameron was devastated. Nicole was his only sibling, and Nicholas was his nephew. He felt sick. He had lost too many family members over the past three years. He wasn't ready to go through this again.

Hearing a knock at the door, Drew instantly ran over.

"Cameron, I'm going to need your help. First, call the front desk and ask if a doctor can be sent up immediately. Second, I want to ensure Nicole is well enough to get on a flight. Also, I'm going to need you to call Lance and Max. Finally, Nicole would want the concerts to continue as scheduled. That's very important," Drew explained, fighting back the tears. "Nothing changes, do you understand. I know you're upset and hurt over the news, but Nicole will need you to be strong. You've got to pull this off for her. Can you promise me?" Drew pleaded.

"Sure, just take care of Nicole. I'll ensure nothing changes regarding the scheduled concerts," Cameron suggested. "Try not to worry."

It seemed Nicole was beginning to gain consciousness. She began lashing out at Drew. He physically had to restrain her.

"Sis, please hang on. A doctor is on his way," Cameron begged.

"Doll, please, there was no way to know this would happen," Drew cried, trying to keep her hands from hitting him. "I love him. He's my son too," Drew cried out.

Hearing a knock at the door, Cameron quickly raced over.

"I'm Doctor Stewart. How is she?"

"Not very well, please come in. She's lying on the couch," Cameron replied, giving details.

"I'm Drew Connors, and this is my wife, Nicole. We were given some devastating news. Our three-year-old son, Nicholas, was in a serious automobile accident back home in Vancouver. Unfortunately, he might not make it. My wife was the first to hear the news. Afterward, she passed out. I revived her with some warm towels, but she seems to be lashing out at me," Drew explained, still holding Nicole's arms.

"Mrs. Connors, I'm Doctor Stewart. I'm here to help you. How are you feeling?" Doctor Stewart asked while checking her vital signs.

"My baby, it's my baby. I can't lose him," Nicole repeatedly screamed.

"Her vital signs are good. Her blood pressure and pulse are elevated, but that's expected. So what are your immediate plans?" Doctor Stewart asked.

"I need to know if she's stable enough to take a flight back to Vancouver tonight," Drew questioned. "She'll be flown by private plane, but we'll need to leave immediately."

"Yes. There's no medical reason she shouldn't physically be fine. However, emotionally I realize she's going to be under a lot of stress. I can give her an injection that will keep her calm. I'll give her some medication to take with her. It should help to sedate her until she gets back home. Hopefully, she'll be able to cope a little better considering the situation," Doctor Stewart explained.

"Thank you," Drew answered.

The doctor pulled out a syringe and a small glass vial from his medical bag. Then, swabbing her arm with alcohol, he withdrew the substance and administered the sedative.

"Okay. I've just given your wife the injection. She's going to be sleepy. Will you be able to manage?" Doctor Stewart inquired.

"Yes. Thank you for coming so quickly. I really appreciate it," Drew mentioned walking Doctor Stewart to the door.

"Wait about four hours before giving her the extra medication. I'm giving you some of the same substances but in pill form. Please only use as prescribed on the bottle. I'm so sorry about your son. I hope he makes a full recovery," Doctor Steward replied sympathetically.

Walking back over to check on Nicole, it seemed she was already asleep.

"Drew, I just talked with Lance and Max. They've got everything covered. Lance has the jet waiting at the airport. He said to tell you that he's praying for Nicholas, Kate, and Nicole. He also said not to worry about a thing back here. They've completely got it all covered. In fact, he's sending a car. It should be downstairs momentarily," Cameron stated nervously, glancing at his sister.

"Cameron, I know she's your sister, and I know it will be hard to remain behind in Frankfurt, but as Bruce would always say, the show must go on. So besides praying, the best thing you can do for her is to get on that stage tomorrow night and give Frankfurt one hell of a concert. Nicole has worked so hard. You have to do this. It's her dream, and you're a huge part of it. She's already making a name for herself.

I'm sure Max will find a temporary guitarist. So have you got this covered?" Drew anxiously repeated.

"Yes. Don't worry. You need to get going. Nicholas needs you both," Cameron acknowledged, wiping tears from his eyes. "Call me as soon as you get to the hospital," Cameron added, reaching for the door. Seeing Lance and Max walking up, he stopped.

"Hey, Cameron. We had to come. Where's Nicole?" Lance asked.

"What can we do?" Max asked impatiently, walking inside.

"Well, Nicole is out cold. A doctor came by earlier and gave her an injection. But, of course, she was utterly freaked out, as any mother would be hearing such devastating news," Cameron replied.

"Thanks for coming. Our bags are still packed. I just need to carry Nicole down to the car. Maybe you could grab those. No time to call for a bellhop," Drew instructed.

"Sure thing," Lance replied, picking up two of the bags.

"Don't worry, I've got the others," Max answered.

"Cameron, if you can get the door, I'll pick up Nicole."

Quickly carrying her to the elevator, Max, Lance, Cameron, and Jillian followed.

"Lance, I just spoke with Cameron concerning the scheduled performances here in Frankfurt. He's agreed to go on stage each night despite the tragic news," Drew explained.

"Drew is right. I've got this," Cameron spoke up, entering the elevator.

"Say no more, Max and I have everything covered. Unfortunately, I've been through this scenario a few times. So don't worry, and make sure Nicole doesn't worry about the concerts. They will go forward exactly as planned. No one in our organization is going to let her down. I promise you," Lance assured everyone setting the bags on the curb.

As the chauffeur opened the car door, Cameron helped Drew place Nicole inside.

"Oh, we should have taken one of the blankets off the bed to cover her," Jillian mentioned.

"I'll get her one as soon as we're on board. Thanks, everyone.

Cameron, I'll call you as soon as we arrive at the hospital," Drew stated, closing the car door.

Standing on the curb, Jillian put her arms around Cameron as they watched the limo drive away.

"Cameron, if you should need me tonight, you know where to reach me," Lance informed him with a light touch to his shoulder.

"Cameron, please don't worry about a thing. Lance and I are here for you. So hang in there, Buddy. Everything's going to be all right. I'll call you in the morning," Max reiterated, walking back inside.

"Cameron, do you want to stop in the lounge for a drink before going up to our room? It might help you relax," Jillian suggested compassionately.

"No. I want to go back upstairs. I'm so worried about Nicholas and Kate. After losing my parents and Bruce, I don't think I could go through this again," Cameron answered softly, wiping his eyes.

"Cameron, everything is going to be fine. I'm here for you, Sweetheart. Let's go back inside," Jillian answered, reaching for his hand.

As the limo parked next to the steps of the jet, their chauffeur, James, helped Drew carry Nicole onboard.

"Mr. Connors. I'm truly sorry. I hope everything is all right when you arrive in Vancouver," James tried to smile reassuringly, leaving the aircraft.

"Thanks, James. I appreciate your help," Drew replied, trying to make Nicole comfortable for the long flight.

"Mr. Connors. I'm so sorry about Nicholas," Nina stated. "What can I bring you to make the trip more relaxing?"

"I think a blanket would help tremendously. I'm afraid Nicole will be out for most of the flight. The doctor gave her a sedative. Also, a few extra pillows would be nice," he added.

Quickly returning with the blanket and pillows, Nina smiled as Drew attempted to make Nicole comfortable.

"Mac wanted me to inform you that our flying time into Vancouver tonight is estimated to be eleven hours, weather permitting. Would you like a cup of coffee?" she asked with sympathy in her eyes.

"Sure, coffee sounds good," Drew smiled, trying to be as cordial as possible, considering the circumstances.

As the plane lifted off the runway, Drew watched out his window as the city lights of Frankfurt became a distant blur. How could things have changed so drastically in such a short time? They had hardly arrived when given the shocking news of the accident. He couldn't lose Nicholas. No parent could ever be prepared to lose their child, he thought. He couldn't lose his little boy.

Looking over at his beautiful wife, she appeared lifeless. Only a few days ago, they had stood atop the Eiffel Tower? She had held him so tight while they took in the incredible views. Their world seemed perfect. If it were only possible to return to that day and prevent the tragedy, he swore he would do anything to keep it from happening, anything to take away her grief.

"Would you like cream or sugar?" Nina asked.

"Neither, thanks."

"Would you like a blanket after you finish your coffee?" she offered.

"Yes. Thank you."

His mind was racing as he took a sip of coffee, contemplating their devastating situation.

Handing him the blanket and extra pillow, Nina quickly returned to the front of the aircraft.

He covered himself with the blanket and tucked the extra pillows behind his head. How could he sleep? There was no possible way to drift off until he knew that his son would make it.

However, it appeared sleep quickly invaded his body without him being aware of its presence. He must have been out for a few hours when he was awakened by someone calling his name.

"Where am I?" Nicole softly whispered, unaware of her surroundings.

How could he possibly give her the dreadful news once more? How could he even begin to tell her? It wasn't fair that she would have to hear the horrible details of the accident once again. He felt as if he was going insane.

"Babe, how are you feeling?" Drew asked, brushing back her long black curls with his fingers.

"I feel exhausted. What happened? Where are we?" Nicole was insistent.

Looking down at his watch, he noted the time. It had definitely been longer than four hours. Then, buzzing for Nina, he asked for a glass of water. Perhaps giving her more of the medication would keep her calm. At the same time, he contemplated a way to give her the news as painlessly as he possibly could.

"Babe, please take this," Drew instructed as Nina quickly handed him a glass of water.

"What is it?" Nicole asked.

"Oh, it's just a little something to make you feel better," Drew smiled, attempting to keep his emotions from consuming him.

Taking the pill, Nicole looked up.

"It's Nicholas, isn't it?" she cried as Drew held her in his arms.

"Yes, Babe. We're on our way home," he attempted to console her, wiping her face with his hands. "I love you, Doll. I wish it were me," Drew answered, hardly able to speak as his voice quivered. "We'll be home soon. Just try to sleep. The medication should help," he whispered, tucking the blanket around her petite frame.

Watching as she softly cried herself back to sleep, Drew felt helpless. How could this have happened? He was just holding his precious son only two days ago in Paris. Life wasn't fair. It just wasn't fair, he thought, wiping his eyes.

The rest of the flight passed in a dizzy unrealistic blur as he drank tons of coffee and tried desperately to make sense of everything. Thankfully, Nicole had not awakened during the remainder of the flight. But now, he was faced with the problem of trying to revive her. She would need to be fully conscious to walk into the hospital. Once again, he buzzed Nina for more coffee and a warm towel. Maybe he could wake her long enough to get caffeine inside her. As Nina returned with the hot coffee and towel, he had to try.

"Babe. Please wake up. We're almost home," Drew whispered, wiping her face. Lifting her upright, he gave her a sip of coffee. "Nicole, I need you to stay awake. I have coffee for you. Babe, please take another sip," Drew repeated as he wiped her face.

After a few minutes, Nicole slowly began to open her eyes. Finally, hopefully, his attempts were starting to work.

"Doll. Can you hear me?" Drew asked, continually wiping her face. "Babe, please wake up.

Thinking they might be needed, Nina began to warm more towels.

"Here's another towel. Maybe it will help," Nina tried to remain unaffected by the mere sight of the sadness which enveloped Nicole's body.

"Thanks," Drew once more wiped her face encouraging her to wake up.

At last, she opened her eyes.

"Are we there?" Nicole questioned, barely audible.

"Almost, Babe. I need you to stay awake. I have coffee for you. So please drink this. It will help. Take a few sips," Drew begged affectionately.

"Okay. I'll try," Nicole answered, taking a few sips.

Thank God. Maybe his attempts were finally beginning to work.

"Mrs. Connors, is there anything I can bring you before we land?" Nina asked.

"Maybe some orange juice," Nicole whispered.

"Okay. I'll be right back with your juice."

After drinking the orange juice, Nicole was finally becoming coherent.

"Mac wanted me to inform you that we're only one hundred miles out from Vancouver. So we should be on the ground soon. Is there anything I can do for either of you before we land?" Nina inquired.

"No. But thank you for asking," Drew said, handing Nina the glass.

"Babe, we're almost home. The car will take us immediately to the hospital. Do you feel strong enough to walk down to the car?" Drew lovingly asked.

"Yes. I feel a little better," Nicole whispered, squeezing his hand.

As the wheels of the jet touched the runway, Drew panicked. What news was waiting for them, Drew wondered? It seemed like a never-ending nightmare. Glancing at Nicole, she appeared to have aged years in only a few hours. She seemed entirely consumed by stress. Hopefully, the news would be good. But, he wasn't sure if either of them could survive hearing anything worse.

He noticed the black limo waiting for their arrival as he looked out the window. It looked ominous and foreboding. What was wrong with him? He felt as if he were in a trance. Everything around him seemed to move in slow motion.

"Can I be of any help getting either of you inside the limo?" Nina offered thoughtfully.

"No thanks. I believe we're able to make it," Drew answered, snapping back into reality.

"I sincerely hope you find your son in good health," Mac stated sympathetically, opening the cockpit door. Nina and I will keep him in our prayers," he added with sincerity.

"I'm sure everything will be fine," Nina smiled, putting on a brave face.

The limo sped away in only a few short minutes, taking them downtown to the Presbyterian Hospital. It was already late afternoon, the middle of rush hour, and the freeway was congested with bumper-to-bumper traffic. Drew began sweating profusely. How was it possible to fly for eleven hours to find themselves stuck on the freeway? Looking over at Nicole, Drew noticed she was becoming emotionally unglued. Watching as she tightly clenched her hands, tears rolled down his face. Quickly wiping his eyes, they were almost there. He had to remain stoic. Nicole would need him now more than ever.

Finally arriving at the hospital, the chauffeur made arrangements to take their luggage to the manor house at Bear Lake. Running inside to the front desk, Drew immediately inquired about Nicholas and Kate. He felt a panic attack coming on as they were instructed to have a seat and wait for the doctor. After what seemed like an eternity, Drew caught sight of Jerry and an older doctor walking toward them. Jerry's appearance didn't bode well. Glancing over at Nicole, Drew braced himself for the worst.

"How's my baby?" Nicole begged tearfully.

"Mr. and Mrs. Connors, I'm Doctor Gregory. Why don't you both follow me?" he asked caringly. Taking them over to a quiet room, he closed the door. "I'm sorry to inform you that Nicholas didn't make it. He sustained tremendous injuries from the accident. I want you both to know that he fought hard once he arrived at our hospital, but I'm afraid the odds were heavily stacked against him. I'm truly sorry," Doctor Gregory said compassionately, putting his arms around Nicole. "It never gets any easier giving a parent this news, especially when it's someone as young as Nicholas. Do either of you have any questions?" he asked. "Someone on my staff will be in momentarily. Again, my deepest sympathy," Doctor Gregory repeated, stepping out of the room.

Nicole sat motionless as if she had not heard a word spoken. Then, suddenly, she began screaming fiercely. "Not Nicholas, not my baby. He's not dead. I want to see him right now," Nicole demanded hysterically.

Jerry walked over and held onto her. Trying to console her was futile. Nicole was more than distraught. Looking up, Jerry noticed Drew was no longer in the room.

"God, help me," Jerry said repeatedly.

All at once, Drew walked in with a nurse.

"I'm Bethany, a Registered Nurse in the Emergency Room. How can I help you?"

"My wife, Nicole, is going to need assistance. We were just informed that we had lost our three-year-old son. Can you please do something for her?" Drew begged.

As Bethany walked over, Nicole appeared unstable. Looking up at Drew, Nicole attempted to stand. Suddenly, she went limp as a rag. Before she hit the floor, Drew managed to catch her in his arms.

"Hold her while I get a wheelchair. Then, I'll take her down to the Emergency Department. Someone will evaluate her in just a few minutes," Bethany explained.

Quickly coming back with a wheelchair, Nicole was still unconscious. Carefully placing Nicole in the chair, Bethany pushed her down the long hallway towards the ER.

"Please, follow me," she instructed.

Once Nicole arrived at the Emergency Room, she was transferred to a hospital bed. Drew stood nearby and watched as the intern thoroughly examined Nicole. Again, drew felt out of reality leaning against the hospital bed. It seemed everything around him was spinning out of control. Quickly noticing his condition, Jerry ran over and brought him a chair.

"It seems her blood pressure is high. So we'll be keeping her until she is conscious and stable enough to go home," the intern informed him.

"Drew, are you all right? Can you hear me?" Jerry questioned, fearing that Drew might possibly faint.

"I'm okay. I just wish it had been me instead of Nicholas," Drew cried as he buried his head in his hands.

"Drew. I'm sorry. I can't even imagine how you must be feeling right now. What can I do?" Jerry insisted.

"There's nothing you can do. Nothing anybody can ever do," Drew sobbed.

Gaining control of his emotions momentarily, Drew inquired about Kate.

"How's Kate?" Drew asked, glancing up at Jerry.

"Not very good, I'm afraid. Kate was admitted with internal bleeding and several broken bones. She came through surgery last night, but she's still unconscious. The doctors had to put two pins in her legs. She's upstairs in intensive care. She's in serious but stable condition," Jerry explained.

"Why don't you go back up to Kate? I'm not leaving Nicole's side," Drew suggested looking distraught.

"Oh, I'm not leaving either of you. Kate is receiving great care in the ICU. She's in the best hands possible," Jerry answered.

Suddenly, Nicole tried to get up from the bed. She had regained consciousness.

"Babe, you're in the hospital," Drew explained, gently grasping her hand. "Sweetheart, Nicholas didn't make it," Drew whispered as he leaned over her bed, holding back a myriad of tears.

"I know," Nicole answered, closing her eyes. "I know."

"Nicole. I'm so sorry. Is there anything I can do?" Jerry asked sympathetically, walking up to her bed. "Is there anything I can get you?"

"No. My precious baby is gone," she cried softly with her head buried in the pillow.

One of the nurses walked in, noticing Nicole was conscious.

"Mrs. Connors, how are you feeling? My name is Emily. I'm a Registered Nurse in the Emergency Department. You fainted a few minutes ago, so you were brought to the ER. All your vital signs look much better now. I'm so sorry about your loss. We'll be letting you go home in about an hour if nothing changes. Would you like something to drink?" she asked compassionately.

"No. I don't want anything. I just want to see my son," Nicole cried.

"Well, I believe arrangements can be made to take you down to the morgue. Sometimes, we ask parents to give us time to prepare their loved ones before they see them. We don't want your last memories to be anything except what you would normally expect. I'll be back in a few minutes to check on you," Emily stated, leaving the room.

"Nicole, I'm not sure that's a good idea. Wouldn't you prefer to remember Nicholas as we last saw him, a very happy three-year-old little boy?" Drew strongly suggested wiping his eyes.

"Drew, I don't give a damn what you say or think. I will see my son. Do you understand?" Nicole demanded bitterly.

"Sweetheart, I was thinking of you. I can't stand to see you hurt anymore?" Drew replied empathetically.

"I don't give a damn. Do you hear?" Nicole repeated angrily.

"Drew, listen. Don't agitate her. She's been through a lot today, and so have you," Jerry whispered.

"Jerry, I just want what's best for her," Drew reiterated.

"I know," Jerry agreed, understanding Drew's dilemma. "This is going to be hard for everyone. I dread having to tell Kate. She's going to be devastated," Jerry frowned.

It appeared Nicole was beginning to fall asleep as the nurse walked in.

"Doctor Rutherford has filled out your discharge paperwork. He's giving you a prescription for Xanax. Take it only as needed. The directions will be on the bottle. If you're not feeling better within a few days, he suggests that you check in with your family physician," she explained, handing her the paperwork. "You're free to go," she stated, giving Nicole the prescription.

"I want to see my son. You told me you would make arrangements," Nicole vehemently reminded her.

"I'm sorry. Let me check on that for you, and I'll be right back."

A few minutes later, an intern walked in, pushing a wheelchair.

"Mrs. Connors, my name is Albert. I'm an intern in the ER. Emily informed me that you wanted to be taken down to view your son's body," he continued.

"Yes," Nicole answered.

"Okay. I'll need you to have a seat in the wheelchair. I'll take you down."

"I'm Mr. Connors, Nicholas's father. I'm coming with my wife," Drew demanded. "Jerry, do you want to go, or do you prefer to stay here until we get back?"

"I think I should stay here. I'll just go up and check on Kate," Jerry suggested. "I'll be back in a few minutes."

"That's fine. I'm sure we won't be long," Drew mentioned.

Walking close behind Nicole's wheelchair, Drew followed them down the long dim hallway and over to an elevator. Taking it to the basement level, Drew felt uneasy. He wasn't sure he was prepared to see his young son's body. How could anyone ever be prepared for such a task? Then, suddenly, the elevator stopped taking Drew's heart with it.

"Okay. We're here. It's just a short walk down this hallway," Albert informed them.

Approaching two large double doors, Drew felt the hairs on his arm stand up. Finally, Albert pushed a buzzer next to the door, a voice answered.

"Can I help you?"

"I've brought Mr. and Mrs. Connors down to view their son's body," Albert announced. At that instant, the doors opened.

Drew felt nauseous and cold as he followed Albert inside.

"Come this way," the young man instructed.

Following behind Nicole's wheelchair, Drew and Nicole suddenly faced the cold metal lockers in the morgue. Drew began shivering from the cold and his nerves. Watching as the young man reached for the bottom locker and opened the door, Drew had to brace himself. Slowly, their son's lifeless body was pulled outward from the dark compartment. Drew gasped, unable to breathe, as the stark white sheet which covered Nicholas's body was removed, exposing his son's sweet innocent face. His eyes became fixated on the small tiny body lying motionless before them in full view. They were face to face with mortality. Drew could hardly stand. He felt his knees buckle. Their son appeared merely asleep, resting peacefully. There were no outward signs of his injuries.

With tears in his eyes, he watched as Nicole reached over to touch their precious child. Drew had to grab the wheelchair to keep from collapsing.

"Nicholas, Mommy loves you. I'll always love you. Rest peacefully, my sweet baby," Nicole cried. Pausing, she looked up as tears streamed down her face. "Dad, he's yours now. Please watch over my beautiful little boy," Nicole bitterly sobbed. Then, without hesitation, she leaned over, kissing him for the last time.

Witnessing Nicole express her eternal love for their son, Drew felt paralyzed, unable to move or speak. Then somehow miraculously, barely audible, he said goodbye to his son.

Gently taking his son's tiny hand, he held it briefly, kissing him for the last time.

"Nicholas, Daddy loves you. I'll always love you forever," Drew whispered.

"Please take me out of here," Nicole urgently requested.

Albert immediately pushed Nicole out of the morgue and back into the hallway.

"Mrs. Connors, how are you holding up? Are you okay?" Albert questioned.

"I'm okay. I just want to get out of this hospital," Nicole sobbed bitterly.

"Not a problem. I completely understand. I believe Doctor Rutherford has already signed your release paperwork," Albert mentioned pushing her wheelchair into the elevator.

Once upstairs, Drew asked that Nicole be taken back to the waiting room outside the ER. Jerry rushed over immediately, seeing Nicole brought in through the double doors.

"Honey, are you alright?"

"Jerry, do you have your car here? Nicole is ready to leave," Drew asked.

"Yes. But I'll call for a car. It would be easier. You can take Nicole out to the house?" Jerry suggested.

"Nicole, do you want to go to the lake house tonight, or would you rather stay at the Ritz Carlton, considering Nicholas's nursery is next to our room?" Drew inquired.

"I want to stay at the Ritz. It feels more like home right now. Honestly, I couldn't bear to see my precious baby's belongings," Nicole sobbed.

"Okay, we'll keep in touch," Jerry mentioned. "I'm not leaving the hospital until Kate regains consciousness. She's in room 120 in the ICU upstairs. Don't hesitate to call if you need anything," Jerry reminded them.

Walking over to use the phone, Jerry called for a car.

"The car should arrive in about ten minutes. I'm going back upstairs to stay with Kate. Sweetheart, I love you," Jerry smiled, giving Nicole a quick kiss. "Listen, Nicole, please try to get some sleep. Don't worry about your Mom. She's going to be fine. I love you. Drew, you take good care of our girl," Jerry laid a gentle, reassuring arm on his shoulder as they walked toward the elevator.

Albert pushed Nicole outside and helped her into the limo. "Take care."

During their short ride, no words were spoken. The Ritz was only about twenty minutes away.

Arriving at the Ritz, Drew held tightly to Nicole's hand as they walked over to the reception desk.

"Good evening, Mr. and Mrs. Connors. It's a pleasure to have you back. If available, will you be checking into your usual suite?" the young man asked.

"Yes, please," Drew said somberly.

"Okay. Here's your room key. Do you have any luggage?" the concierge questioned.

"No. Our luggage was taken out to Bear Lake. However, I'll be making arrangements for it to be brought over. Would you please ring our room when it arrives?" Drew informed the young man.

"Yes. Is there anything else I can help you with this evening?"

"No. Thank you," Drew replied, walking with Nicole over to the elevator.

As the elevator reached the sixth floor, Drew attempted to pick Nicole up. His intentions were simply to carry her down the hall and into their suite.

"Please, leave me alone. I'm completely capable of walking. Don't touch me," Nicole cringed, pulling away from him.

"Babe, what's wrong? I love you. I just want to help," Drew replied empathetically.

"I want a divorce," Nicole said defiantly, facing the elevator wall.

"Doll, you can't possibly," Drew reacted in shock.

"Look at me," Drew pleaded, trying to turn her to face him. But, instead, she pulled away with such revulsion that it made Drew cringe.

"I can't look at you. Drew, this is your fault. All your fault," she cried, trying to keep her clichéd fists at her sides.

"Doll, you don't know what you're saying," Drew pleaded.

"Trust me. I know exactly what I'm saying. I'll stay here tonight. Tomorrow, I'm getting another room until I leave for Europe," Nicole insisted.

At a loss for words, Drew unlocked their door. Immediately walking over to the mini-fridge, he grabbed a bottle of beer and walked outside to the balcony. Standing against the rail, he lit a cigarette. It was a good thing Jerry had offered him a pack of cigarettes back at the hospital. He undoubtedly would need them. Staring out at the night skyline, he was perplexed. Surely Nicole was suffering from mental exhaustion. There was no way she wanted a divorce. It was utter nonsense. Twisting the bottle cap from his beer, he took a long sip deciding to remain on the balcony. Hopefully, he wanted to give Nicole enough time to be asleep when he came in. Pulling another cigarette from the pack, he sat down with his beer. His world was crumbling around him. Taking another huge gulp of beer and lighting his cigarette, Drew was worried. How was it even possible for anyone's life to change so dramatically overnight? He couldn't bear the thought of losing both Nicholas and Nicole. It would be the death of him. Why was she saying such vile things? He never meant any harm to anyone, especially his young son, when he suggested Nicholas return to Vancouver with Kate and Jerry. If she'd had a premonition, why hadn't she told him? He wasn't an evil, uncaring person. He loved Nicholas.

All of a sudden, he remembered to call Cameron. Finishing one last cigarette, he finally walked inside. Nicole was asleep. Thank God. He wasn't sure he could've dealt with more unkind words from her tonight. But, even he had his limits, especially on a day such as this. Picking up the phone, he walked back outside to make the call. He was taking no chances at waking her.

After only two rings, Cameron answered.

"Cameron, I'm so sorry I have to give you such news, but we lost our precious son earlier today. Nicholas passed before we could even see him," Drew broke down. His emotions finally overwhelmed him. Sobbing so hard, he could hardly speak, "Sorry, I didn't mean to let my emotions consume me like that," Drew cried.

"Drew, I completely understand. I'm devastated. Jerry called with the news earlier today. You were still in the air on your way home when I received the call," Cameron was at a loss for words. What do you say to someone who just lost their child?

"Cameron, are you going to be able to perform this evening?" Drew questioned, not even caring at this point.

"Drew, our first performance ended a few hours ago. I'm sure you're not aware of the time difference, and with everything you're dealing with, it's not surprising that you wouldn't remember. It went amazingly well. It was completely sold out. All I can say is that Dad, Jenna, and Bruce must have surely been my strength earlier this evening. Our fans loved us. I walked off stage to a standing ovation. Please let Nicole know," Cameron insisted.

"Yes, I will. Well, this will be short for now. I'm both mentally and physically exhausted. I think it's time to see if I can sleep," Drew replied. "We love you. Thanks for a great performance. Talk with you tomorrow."

"Thanks. Drew, take good care of my sister. Please let her know how much I love her," Cameron asked, hanging up the phone.

As the early morning sun crept in through the curtains, it brought sadness and emotional discontent as well as physical. It simply contained grief. Heartache and misery had regrettably spilled into the days that followed.

Arrangements were made to have Nicholas cremated and his remains interred in a Mausoleum. Nicole and Drew had decided against an elaborate celebration of life or a funeral. It didn't matter to them if the world or those around them knew of the loss of their son. It was insignificant. Drew prepared for a small private service to be held the following morning at the Mausoleum. It would be attended only by Drew, Nicole, and Jerry.

It seemed after talking for hours that Nicole was adamant about her pursuing a divorce. She blamed him for Nicholas's death. It hadn't mattered the words he had said or the numerous tears he had shed. She was relentless. After much thought, Drew had reluctantly agreed to her crazy whim. He loved her unconditionally. He knew deep in his heart it was only grief and anguish that were controlling her emotions and actions. Nicole just needed time. He had nothing left at this point in his life but time. He would wait forever.

Drew handed in his resignation to Jerry, who had become their middle man. He hadn't bothered to wait until Nicole asked. There was no way he could see her day in and day out without touching her, holding her, or feeling the warmth of her body as she lay beside him. Drew's world had utterly ended as he knew it. He would remain behind in Vancouver. It was home. It was where his precious son's remains were. He moved into the stately manor house after much insistence from Jerry and Kate. His solace would simply be boating on the lake with Jerry. He could only wait and pray for a miracle that someday she might return.

Kate slowly recovered from her injuries. However, she had been left with a slight limp in her left leg. It was a constant reminder of her loss. Dealing with the death of Nicholas had destroyed her spirit. It appeared Nicole's decision to leave not only Drew but also her had been the catalyst that turned her world upside down. Kate simply wandered aimlessly through the days ahead, feeling as if her soul had been ripped from her chest. The degree of hurt was overwhelming. If there was any truth in the saying, misery loves company, it simplistically defined her existence.

Nicole left the day after Nicholas's interment. She had been in Europe for almost two months, and her name was becoming known worldwide in the music industry. Nicole was effortlessly making her way to the top. However, as she chased her dreams, someone close to her relentlessly pursued her.

CHAPTER TWENTY ONE

Rome

As the Lear jet circled Rome two months later, Nicole sat next to the window fixated on the famous landmarks below. Seated next to Max, he had easily replaced Drew, managing to become a vital part of her life, sharing her days and nights. Watching as the Roman Coliseum and the Pantheon came into view, Nicole tingled with excitement.

"Would either of you like something to drink before we land?" Nina smiled.

"Yes. Thank you. I'll have a gin and tonic," Max laid down his score chart. "Sweetheart, would you like a glass of chardonnay?" he inquired, trying to get Nicole's attention for a quick second.

"No, thanks. My stomach has been queasy. I think I'll pass," Nicole smiled weakly.

The plane gently rolled to a stop as Nicole reached for her briefcase. It seemed everyone was excited to be in Rome.

"Wow. I can't believe we're here," Cameron smiled, walking past Nicole's seat. Then, quickly stopping for a brief moment, he turned around. "Sis, do you need any help?"

"Oh, no thanks. I've only got my briefcase."

Entering the limo, it appeared everyone was talking at once. The excitement of being in the Eternal City felt overwhelming, almost energizing.

"So, where are you and Jillian going first?" Nicole inquired, looking over at Cameron.

"Oh, I'm not sure. It seems Jillian has a list of places," Cameron laughed, rolling his eyes.

"Cameron, stop. You also put several tourist attractions on that list," Jillian interjected, gently slapping his arm.

Arriving at the Villa Roma Hotel, it was truly spectacular. The limo stopped underneath a tiled entrance which was brilliantly lit. The vaulted stone arches were breathtaking as they stepped out of the car. Giant terracotta pots sitting on each side of the door held massive bouquets of blooming red geraniums.

"Wow, Sis. I'm impressed," Cameron mentioned as he admired the spacious and ornate lobby.

"Well, I'm glad you approve," Nicole smiled at Cameron's childlike curiosity.

The polished white marble floors mirrored the reflection of the crystal chandeliers hanging above. The sound of trickling water bubbled from a three-tiered fountain that sat in the middle of the massive foyer. The lobby was elegantly furnished with red velvet chairs and ottomans. Walking to the back of the expansive room, Cameron discovered it was open to the outside, revealing a sparkling Olympic-sized pool with a continual overspray of water streaming from its sides. There was no end to the hotel's descriptive details. It truly felt like paradise at its best.

"Geez, Nicole, can we afford such luxury," Harry laughed, crashing on one of the elegant ottomans.

"Harry, what kind of statement is that?" Nicole asked with a raised brow. "I think the mere fact that you're standing here should answer that."

After checking everyone in, she passed out room keys.

"Okay. Tonight is free time. You're on your own. Just please stay out of trouble. The only publicity I want is outstanding coverage of tomorrow's performance," Nicole stated as everyone entered the elevator.

"Don't forget, I scheduled rehearsals early in the morning. So don't be late," Max advised as everyone exited the elevator.

Unlocking their door, Nicole sat down on the luxurious duvet, removing her shoes. "Wow. This feels much better," she sighed, massaging her feet.

Their suite was luxuriously furnished with oversized European décor. A floral tapestry hung above an ornate credenza. Sitting on top was an alabaster bowl overflowing with every fruit imaginable. Tall French doors opened onto the balcony, encased with natural stone balustrades.

"I've ordered a bottle of champagne and canapés. How does that sound?" Max questioned, drawing back the heavy brocade drapes.

"Great. However, I'm not hungry."

"Come check this out," Max suggested taking in the incredible view. "You're not going to believe this one," he laughed, totally astonished by his field of vision.

A cool breeze blew in from the treeless terrain as Max opened the French doors.

Walking outside to the balcony in her bare feet, Nicole felt the coolness of the marble floors against her tired aching feet. It felt invigorating.

"Wow. You're right. That's incredible," Nicole smiled, gazing at the spectacular view. Rows of orchestrated vines covered with purple grapes extended beyond her field of vision. They traversed the rolling hills like a tapestry.

"Geez, that's amazing. We don't have to worry about a wine shortage," Nicole laughed.

Hearing a knock at the door meant room service had arrived.

Max rushed over to answer it, giving a generous tip to the young man.

Popping the cork from the champagne, he immediately filled two fluted glasses with the sparkling beverage and walked outside to the balcony.

"Let's toast our first night in Rome," Max grinned devilishly.

"Here's to my beautiful girl, Nicole. Hopefully, our first night will only be the beginning of many adventures we'll share in the future. Here's to our time in Rome, The Eternal City," Max raised his glass in salute. Then he lounged back in the wrought iron chaise, unbuttoning the top buttons of his dress shirt, exposing his smooth chest. Max could pass for one of the Italian gods as his messy blonde hair glistened in the sun.

"Thanks, that was nice," Nicole smiled, sipping champagne and admiring the view.

Nicole wasn't exactly sure of her feelings for Maxwell Kline. Still, he made it evident that he was more than attracted to her.

Walking back inside, the evening breeze had given her a slight chill. She reached inside the closet for a sweater.

"Would you like to have dinner in one of the local restaurants this evening or order from the hotel?" Max asked as he followed her inside.

"It doesn't matter. I'm still not hungry. I still feel a bit queasy," Nicole unconsciously placed a hand on her stomach.

"Okay. It's not a problem. We'll see how you feel about dinner later this evening. Would you like another glass of champagne?" Max smiled as he precariously held two wine glasses in a single hand.

"Maybe, but not a full glass," Nicole replied, getting into bed with a magazine as she rested her head against the dark mahogany headboard.

Within a few short minutes, she had fallen asleep. Max came over to put away her magazine and put her under the warm covers. Somehow miraculously, she had slept through the entire night without waking.

The morning sun warmed their room as it streamed through the French doors. Rolling over, she rubbed her eyes. Almost as if by instinct, she expected to find Drew still sleeping peacefully beside her.

"Good morning, Sunshine," Max smiled, giving her a quick kiss. "I think we should get up and order breakfast. We have rehearsals at 9:00 this morning," he reminded with a kiss to the forehead. "You sure fell asleep early last night," he smiled, reaching for the phone to call room service.

"Yes. I felt extra tired for some reason. There's nothing like a good night's sleep to get the day started," Nicole mentioned stretching out her arms. "I think I'll get a quick shower before breakfast arrives."

"Great. I'll bring you a cup of coffee when it arrives."

"Oh, don't bother, I'll just get a cup after I get dressed," Nicole replied, tossing back the covers as she got up.

Later that morning, after breakfast, it was time to leave for the amphitheater. Waiting for the elevator, Cameron and Jillian walked up.

Max looked handsome, wearing tan slacks and a button-down dress shirt. He thought there was no time like the present to discuss tonight's business.

"Cameron, I was going to speak with you later at rehearsals, but it seems we have a few minutes while we wait for the elevator. I wanted to go over your performance tonight. An amphitheater will feel a whole lot different from performing inside an auditorium. Have you given it any thought?"

"No, but I expected this much even though I've never performed in an outdoor arena before," Cameron stated. He could easily pass as one of the locals with his natural Italian heritage. His short black hair and striking blue eyes were a perfect complement against his olive complexion. Today he wore a tourist's ensemble of blue jeans and a T-shirt with sandals.

"Well, we will go over everything this morning at rehearsal. I don't want you to worry. You'll quickly get a feel for it after a few songs. By the way, Lance called earlier this morning and informed me the entire amphitheater is sold out. Every seat, can you imagine. I believe it holds over twenty thousand people. It's incredible, isn't it," Max stated, holding the elevator door open for everyone.

"Where's Harry this morning? Isn't he coming?" Nicole questioned.

"Oh, he left earlier this morning. Some of the guys from the orchestra came over to his room, so he went out with them," Cameron smiled, putting his arm around Jillian. She looked beautiful in blue jeans, a floral blouse, and white sandals.

It was apparent that Cameron was in love, and Nicole felt happy. Cameron had waited a long time to find that special person to share his life with, and she couldn't have been more thrilled for them.

"Sis, how are you feeling today?" Cameron asked, somewhat concerned.

"Oh, I'm fine. Just feeling a little extra tired lately, that's all," Nicole smiled, stepping outside the elevator. Nicole had decided to dress casually for the day in a simple halter dress and sandals.

Walking over to the limo, everyone quickly stepped inside, making themselves comfortable.

"Would anyone like a drink?" Max asked, raising an empty glass.

"I'll have a small glass of Jack Daniels," Cameron spoke up. "Bruce always swore that kept him alive. So I'll have one in honor of Bruce," he laughed.

"What about you girls?" Max inquired.

"I'll just have a glass of orange juice," Nicole answered as she pulled out her briefcase and flipped through some papers.

"Sure, orange juice sounds good," Jillian smiled, staring out the window. She couldn't wait to see the famous tourist attractions Rome offered.

"Great, two glasses of orange juice coming up," Max smiled.

"Cameron, I forgot to ask, did Judy rent the lake house?" Nicole inquired.

"Yes. She rented it to a nice young family, the Daltons. They came highly recommended. They have three children and only needed a one-year lease. It worked out perfect," Cameron smiled, amused at how taken Jillian was with Rome.

"Awesome. I was just curious," Nicole smiled, focused on her work.

Arriving at the amphitheater, it seemed everyone was already there.

"Wow. I think we're the last ones to arrive," Max laughed. He couldn't wait to hear his musical arrangements in one of the world's most famous theaters. It was centuries old and appeared to have been there since the beginning of time.

Cameron, as well as the musicians, rehearsed for over three hours. They were finally ready to give their first open-air concert later that evening. It hadn't been as hard as Max had expected to transition Cameron and the band to the familiarity of an outdoor arena. Max was confident they were ready, and he was ecstatic. It was their first outdoor performance in Rome.

Finally, the limo arrived to take them back to the hotel.

"What does everyone have planned for this afternoon?" Max inquired. "Well, whatever your plans involve, please keep a close watch on the time. I expect everyone to arrive early tonight."

Sitting back in her seat, Nicole noticed a disturbing pattern with Max. It was one she didn't like or appreciate, even though she would give him the benefit of the doubt for now. It seemed he was taking over every aspect of her job. Maybe it was his way of protecting her, giving her a little space to revive after living through such a nightmare. She couldn't be sure. Only time would give her the answers she needed.

"Sis, Jillian, and I are going to have dinner at Giuseppe's tonight after the concert. Would you like to come?" Cameron asked.

"Oh, we'd love to," Max instantly replied. "Wouldn't we?" he questioned, glancing at Nicole as he reached for her hand.

"Max, you're welcome to come, but I was actually inviting Nicole." Cameron awkwardly explained. He was tired of Max hanging around his sister like an obnoxious pet. He still held hopes of Drew and Nicole reconciling in the future. Max just rubbed him the wrong way most of the time.

"Oh, I'm sorry. I guess I spoke out of turn," Max replied with a slightly hurt voice. "Sure, I understand. It's not a problem."

"It's all right. Max and I would love to come," Nicole finally interjected. It was her attempt at helping him save face.

Returning to the hotel, Nicole immediately went up to her suite. Officially, it was her suite, even though she was allowing Max the privilege of staying with her. It was her desperate attempt at not being alone.

Unlocking the door, she immediately removed her shoes and got into bed.

"Is everything okay?" Max asked, sitting next to her on the lofty duvet.

"Sure, as I said before, I'm a little nauseated and extremely tired," Nicole complained, wanting him to go away.

"Sweetheart, I think you should check in with a doctor. It seems you've not been feeling well a lot lately," Max leaned down to place the back of his hand against her forehead. She felt a little warm to the touch. Nicole gently pushed his hand away from her face. She didn't need him to mother her right now.

"I'm fine. The past two months have been difficult," Nicole grimaced, not wanting to remember any of the past events. It was too hard.

"Okay, Sweetheart, you rest. Don't worry about a thing. I'll wake you in time to get ready," Max smiled reassuringly, kissing her on the forehead. "I'm going downstairs to the lounge and have a drink. Get some rest."

Nicole fell asleep the minute her head hit the pillow.

Unlocking the door upon his return, Max was shocked to find Nicole still sleeping.

"Sweetheart, you have to wake up. We only have an hour until the car arrives," he stated, gently nudging her. "Please, you have to wake up now," he repeated, brushing her long black curls away from her face.

"What time is it?" Nicole whispered groggily.

"It's almost 4:00, and the limo will be here within the hour. I think you should jump in the shower. Maybe, it'll help wake you up. Then, I'll call room service and order coffee," Max suggested. He was beginning to become concerned.

Pulling herself up from the bed, Nicole walked into the shower. The warm water appeared to be working its magic to resurrect her tired body. However, she still had to dress, style her hair, and apply makeup. When did the normal process of getting dressed ever turn into such an ordeal? Suddenly, it hit her like a bolt of lightning. She knew. She remembered. It was just after she found out she was pregnant with Nicholas. She was pregnant, and every ounce of her being confirmed it. She was carrying Drew's child. Nothing else made sense. Standing in front of the bathroom mirror, she gently rubbed her belly. Tears welled within her eyes, then gently rolled down her delicate cheeks. She remembered the night with Drew. It was only a few days later their lives had been shattered. The early hours, before their world tragically fell apart. They had discussed having a baby. Drew desperately wanted a little sister or brother for Nicholas. The night they had shared afterward was magical. She even remembered quoting those exact words to Drew the following day. A faint smile emerged from her face, taking one last look in the mirror. Once again, gently laying her hand over her abdomen, Nicole smiled. She had just lost the most precious thing on earth—someone she could never replace. However, looking down at her body, she carried a new life, a new beginning within her. She could tell no one. This secret stayed with her, at least for now. Gathering the strength to dress, she was finally ready to go. Walking out of the bathroom, she smiled.

"Are you ready to go?" Max asked. "It seemed you were in there forever. Are you sure you're okay," he insisted, handing her a hot cup of coffee.

"Yes. I couldn't be better," Nicole replied. "I'll pass on the coffee. I'm feeling much better. Thank you."

"All right, I think we should go," Max said, grabbing his briefcase. "I need to be there early. I don't want any mishaps tonight. It's a big night for us," he grinned. "It's the largest crowd we've ever had the privilege of entertaining."

Opening the door, he held it for her.

"You look radiant tonight," Max complimented. Maybe she was feeling better, he thought to himself.

"Oh, thanks. The sleep I got this afternoon revived me," Nicole smiled, knowing the real reason.

They were finally ready to leave for the amphitheater, meeting Cameron, Jillian, and Harry downstairs in the lobby.

Stepping inside the limo, Max put his arm around Nicole.

"Doesn't your sister look radiant tonight?" Max smiled, glancing at Cameron. "Why, she's practically glowing." Max figured Nicole must finally be back on track. Their goals would now be one, he thought to himself. Together they would build an empire. This night would just be the first of many unforgettable moments for them.

"Nicole, as a matter of fact, you look stunning," Cameron smiled, examining his sister a little closer.

"Stop it. You're both going to make me blush."

Arriving at the theater, it was the perfect night for an outdoor concert. Stepping out of the limo, Nicole briefly looked up. Stars twinkled brightly overhead. It seemed surreal. Somehow, she knew everything was going to be okay after tonight. She didn't know how or the direction her life might take her. She just simply knew without a doubt everything was going to be fine.

Watching from the back of the stage, Cameron gave the performance of his life. She had no way of knowing Nicky Spade, their father, had performed on this same stage on a night very much like this.

As Cameron sang his last song of the evening, the crowd thundered with applause. His remarkable fans stood to their feet, screaming their approval during his performance. It seemed to reverberate into the night sky. Nicole looked up. Indeed everyone heard it above Nicky, Jenna, Bruce, and her sweet baby boy. Wiping a tear from her face, Nicole was finally at peace.

"Okay, let's go eat," Cameron yelled, stepping down from the back of the stage. "Was that incredible or what," he shouted as he unbuttoned the top button of his crisp white shirt and removed his tie. Tonight, Nicole had doubled Cameron's security. Personal bodyguards surrounded him as he left the stage. Walking back to his dressing room, he had established a routine. It consisted of a bottle of Jack Daniels and a pack of cigarettes, all vices. They seemed to work together in unison to help him unwind. Decompression was vitally important after being energized for over an hour and a half on stage.

Finally catching up with Cameron in his dressing room, Nicole walked over, giving him a huge hug.

"Cameron, you killed it out there tonight. I'm so proud of you," she smiled, kissing his cheeks until he pleaded with her to stop.

"Sis, you're not exactly helping my image here," Cameron laughed, holding his hands up.

At last, Jillian, Max, Lance, and Harry walked in.

"Wow, that was amazing," Max shouted, his face beaming with pride.

"Yes. Great performance. It was unbelievable," Lance agreed, touching Cameron's shoulder as he walked past. "Completely brilliant," he added.

"Cameron, that was incredible," Jillian smiled, giving him a quick kiss. "Do you even realize how many people you performed in front of tonight?" she asked with wonder.

"A lot," Cameron laughed, taking a drink of Jack Daniels.

"Is everyone hungry? I think tonight calls for a celebration," Max announced, looking around the room. "Cameron mentioned eating at Giuseppe's earlier today, so I called this afternoon and made reservations for the six of us at Giuseppe's tonight. Let's celebrate! Are we ready to go? The limo is waiting," Max grinned, herding everyone out the door and down a short hallway that led outside.

It seemed everyone was in a festive mood. The limo was filled with laughter. A bottle of Jack Daniels and a pack of cigarettes made their rounds among everyone seated in the back. All except Nicole, who passed discreetly when given the bottle.

Arriving at Giuseppe's, the limo scarcely fit through the narrow cobblestone side street. Parking at the entrance, Giuseppe's was a small Italian restaurant inconspicuously hidden from view near the Piazza di Santa Maria. A warm glow radiated from two large wrought-iron lanterns framing the entry.

Walking in, everyone was still reeling with excitement from their performance at the amphitheater. Greeted by the maître 'd, he quickly ushered everyone to a long table in the back near the kitchen. His recommendation for the evening was Saltimbocca Alla Romana, a savory dish of veal medallions dressed in prosciutto and sage. Having noticed the impressive wooden wine rack near the entry showcasing over two hundred bottles of wine, Max immediately asked to see their wine list. The night was filled with merriment and great food complemented by an overwhelming variety of local wines.

Having just completed their appearance in Rome, the next stop on their tour was Athens. Without knowing, Nicole continued to follow a path that had ultimately made her father, Nicky Spade, a world-renowned rock icon with Black Tie Affair.

The next morning Cameron and his orchestra boarded a plane to Athens, one of the oldest cities in the world.

CHAPTER TWENTY TWO

Athens

Descending the steps of the plane, Nicole had arrived in Athens, Greece. She had slept most of the way. Traveling, even by private plane, was becoming an exhausting ordeal. Max, at this point, continued to be helpful, but she wasn't sure how much longer she could depend upon him and continue her secrecy.

Arriving at the gorgeous Athena Hotel, Nicole was anxious to check everyone in and pass out room keys. The Athena was a Five Star Hotel. The best Athens had to offer, and it came with more than enough amenities to keep everyone happy. Passing out room keys, she remembered Bruce. As manager of Black Tie Affair, Bruce always took great care of his boys. The stories surrounding him were legendary, and Nicole hoped she would continue to meet his impressive benchmarks as a manager. Then, recalling how Bruce had succumbed early in life to the viciousness of Alzheimer's, she felt depressed. She missed him terribly.

"Nicole, Nicole," Max repeated. "What room are we in?" he laughed. Everyone has already gone up to their rooms, and I wasn't sure what floor we were on."

"Oh, I'm sorry. I suddenly had memories of Bruce as I looked around the hotel. It reminded me of him," Nicole smiled. "We're up on the twelfth floor. Did you ever meet him?"

"No. I never had the pleasure. However, I know his reputation in the music industry kept him at the top of his game. Lance knew him personally. He said Bruce was one hell of a good manager. Was Bruce Weber the reason you chose the management side of the music industry?" Max inquired, pushing the button to the twelfth floor.

"Yes. As a matter of fact, it was Bruce."

"Sweetheart, you're doing a terrific job as Cameron's manager and working with the orchestra. Everyone loves you. But I'm sure you already know," Max teased, leaning his head down closer to hers.

Reaching their floor, Max held the elevator door for her. They were in suite 1225 at the end of the hall.

Walking inside, it didn't disappoint.

"Wow. Undoubtedly, you're a chip off the old block," Max smiled, looking around the room quickly. "Lance always talked about Bruce. He said Bruce always ensured his guys experienced nothing less than the best each city had to offer regarding hotels, amenities, restaurants, and local attractions. But, Sweetheart, I must say, I think you've exceeded his reputation. Just look at this place. It's incredible," Max grinned, opening the double French doors to the balcony.

"Thanks. Perhaps I'm doing an okay job after all," Nicole replied, hanging up her clothes.

"Nicole, what's wrong? You seem distant," Max questioned. "Are you still feeling under the weather? I'll call room service and order dinner. Maybe we should stay in for the night," he suggested as he walked over to put his arm around her.

"No. I'm fine. Ordering in sounds like a great idea. But, I think I'm a little jet-lagged," Nicole answered, pulling herself free from his arms.

"So, what sounds appetizing to you?" Max asked. "I was thinking seafood. What do you think?"

"Actually, that sounds delicious. I trust you. Just order for both of us. I'm going to change into something more relaxing," Nicole yelled from the bathroom.

Hearing a knock at the door, Max answered.

"Hey Max, do you and Nicole have dinner plans this evening?" Cameron asked. "Jillian, Harry, and I have decided to have dinner at the Heliopolis later. Would you both like to join us?" Cameron inquired, quickly surveying the room behind Max for his sister.

"Oh, I'm afraid not. It seems Nicole is somewhat tired from the flight. We've decided to stay in and order seafood, but thanks for stopping by and inviting us. Maybe tomorrow night after the concert, we can all go to dinner. How does that sound?" Max suggested.

"Awesome, I'll let everyone know. Please tell Nicole I hope she gets rested up from the flight. See you tomorrow," Cameron smiled, turning to leave.

"Who was at the door?" Nicole yelled again from the bathroom.

"It was Cameron. It seems they're all going to eat at the Heliopolis tonight. I told him you were a little tired and that we had decided to order in this evening. Hope you didn't mind?"

"No. That's fine," Nicole replied, walking out of the bathroom in her robe.

"Geez. Sweetheart, are you ready for bed this early?" Max laughed. "Not that I'm complaining."

"Please, don't tease me. It feels comfy," Nicole mentioned pulling her long curly hair into a ponytail.

"Well, you look ravishing, even if you're in a bathrobe," Max remarked. "I'll order dinner. Then, we can sit outside on the balcony and enjoy a glass of wine while we wait."

"Great, sounds nice," Nicole replied, picking up a magazine. "I think I'll walk out to the balcony. Come outside and join me after you call room service."

"Okay. Be there in a few minutes. I'll bring out a bottle of wine and glasses."

"Thanks," Nicole smiled, walking outside.

A few minutes later, Max joined her on the balcony with two glasses of wine.

"Dinner will be up soon. I ordered lobster, baked potatoes, corn on the cob, and cucumber salad. Does that meet with your approval?" Max gave her a sexy grin as he handed her a glass of red wine.

"Yes. However, I'd much prefer a glass of water to wine this evening. But dinner sounds delicious. I'm starving," Nicole mentioned.

"Do you feel up to talking business, or would you rather wait until tomorrow?"

"That's fine. What's on your mind?" Nicole smiled, putting down her magazine.

"Lance just called. Can you believe we're completely sold out for tomorrow and the following evening? He's got a radio interview scheduled for Cameron tomorrow morning. He knows that you've been feeling a little under the weather, so he's agreed to go with Cameron. He wanted me to tell you it's not a problem. It's weird, but Lance has been on this circuit of venues before. He knows a lot of people. In fact, I believe he knows someone at the station here in Athens. Isn't that unbelievable?" Max commented, taking a drink.

"Oh, I'm sure. Lance knows everybody. That's why I hired him," Nicole smiled knowingly.

"Nicole, I'm going to throw an idea past you. I've given it a lot of thought and consideration. You've made quite a name for yourself in the music industry in a relatively short period. Someone with your connections in the music business is rare. You're truly one in a million. Your father was a global icon, and to have connections to Bruce Weber, boggles my mind. So no wonder you're a genius. It's in your blood. I love your tenacity and style. I know a lot of people who would love to join forces with you. Have you given any thoughts to putting another band under your management and the umbrella of your organization?" He was entertaining thoughts of a global enterprise. Nicole had everything he needed to ensure he easily reached the pinnacle of success in the music industry. Max sipped his wine, carefully watching her reaction.

"Wow, that's pretty heavy. But, truthfully, I've not given it a single thought," Nicole answered, somewhat perplexed.

She was utterly shocked that he would even suggest such an idea. However, she knew it was best not to reveal her thoughts to anyone, especially him. Knowing Maxwell Kline, he was driven, much like herself, so she should have expected this at some point. However, that's where the similarities ended. It seemed he would stop at nothing to get what he wanted. Nicole would not allow herself to be used as the steps on a ladder as Maxwell climbed his way to the top. Bruce had warned her to be careful of anyone she allowed in her inner circle. Maybe it was time for him to go. It would definitely give her food for thought.

"Frankly speaking, I'm quite happy with my success so far. I've got Cameron in a real sweet spot as a solo artist. Also, I love being a hands-on manager. I'm not looking for anything more now, but thanks for throwing that past me. Interesting idea," Nicole added.

Hearing a knock at the door, it seemed dinner had arrived.

"I'll be right back," Max said, setting his glass down.

"Dinner has arrived, and I must say, it looks delicious. Do you want to eat inside?" Max asked, quickly returning to get his glass.

"It's getting a little cool on the balcony. Eating inside would be wonderful," Nicole replied, picking up her glass and magazine.

Dinner was totally sumptuous. Nicole thought she had never tasted a more succulent lobster. As she dipped the meat in the warm butter, it was heavenly. She ravenously cleaned her plate, enjoying the corn, baked potato, and cucumber salad.

"Wow. I don't think I've ever seen someone clear a plate so fast," Max laughed.

After enjoying their unforgettable meal, Nicole jumped on the bed with her magazine. She'd had enough conversation with Max for the evening. However, it wasn't to be. Instead, it seemed he was in the mood to carry on a lengthy discussion.

"You were sleeping as our plane circled Athens today on our approach into the airport. The waters of the Aegean Sea were the bluest I've ever seen, somewhere between sapphire and azure. I almost thought of waking you as the Acropolis and Parthenon came into view. But I looked over, and you were sleeping so peacefully," Max continued without noticing she wasn't listening. "We have two days in Athens. I'm not sure we'll be able to visit all the historical landmarks, but I think we should give it our best shot. If Lance covers for you tomorrow, we might be able to sneak away for a few hours before the concert. What do you think?" Max asked, finally looking over at Nicole. It seemed he had been talking to himself, as she had fallen asleep again.

Putting her under the warm covers, Max decided to head downstairs to the bar. He wasn't ready to call it an evening. Instead, he needed another drink and a cigarette, and not wanting to smoke in the room, it seemed like the perfect idea.

Walking into the small lounge, he was shocked to find Lance sitting at the bar.

"What are you doing down here this time of night?" Lance questioned as Max took the stool next to him.

"Well, I suppose I could ask you the same thing," Max laughed. "Nicole fell asleep after dinner. So I needed a drink and a cigarette. It just made sense. Oh, I'll have a gin and tonic," Max stated to the bartender as he lit a cigarette. Would you care for one?" he asked, offering the pack to Lance.

"No, thanks. Cuban cigars are my vice. So how's our girl doing? Seems like she's been under the weather a lot lately?" Lance inquired while sipping his drink.

"It does. But sadly, I'm sure it must be due to the trauma she experienced. Losing a child can't be easy," Max surmised. Although, he couldn't help but feel it freed her up to do great things with her life.

"Yes. I'm sure you're right. Can you believe we're sold out for tomorrow's concert and the following night?" Lance stated.

"Great. Speaking of business, are you still going with Cameron to the interview tomorrow?"

"Yes. Why?"

"Well, I just thought if you were going to cover for Nicole, we might do the tourist thing and check out a few landmarks. Athens is an amazing city. It's the first time I've been here," Max remarked, taking a drink.

"No problem. I've been through here a couple of times over the years. You might want to get started early. There's a lot to see. Make sure you take your camera. Athens offers a lot of amazing photo opportunities," Lance suggested taking a sip of bourbon. "Have you seen Cameron this afternoon?"

"Yes. He came by earlier and invited us to dinner at the Heliopolis."

"That's a great little place. You should go before you leave Athens and have the ouzo," Lance laughed. "Maybe we should visit that place tomorrow night after the concert. What do you think?" Lance grinned.

"Great. It's a date. I would never turn down the chance for an authentic Greek meal and a little ouzo," Max agreed as he lit another cigarette.

"Nicole was talking about Bruce Weber earlier this afternoon. That girl sure comes with an impressive pedigree," Max laughed, ordering another drink.

"Yes. She reminds me of Bruce. I really admired that man. He made her father, Nicky Spade, a rock icon, and Nicole will do the same for Cameron. Her name is already the buzz of the music industry. She's smart. You better watch yourself. She'll have you out of here in a New York minute if you cross her," Lance laughed, enjoying a sip of bourbon.

"Oh, is that supposed to be funny? You know I'm from New York," Max laughed, taking a drink. "What's that supposed to mean?" he added.

"Read into however you like. Nicole is tough as nails. I have a lot of respect for that girl," Lance mentioned.

"Well, I guess it's time to go back upstairs and find out what the boss is doing. She was out like a lightbulb when I left earlier," Max stated, extinguishing his cigarette in an ashtray.

"Okay. See you tomorrow," Lance grinned, ordering another bourbon.

Quietly unlocking the door to their suite, it seemed Nicole hadn't moved at all. She was still asleep. Silently, he removed his clothes and slipped into bed next to her. Maybe it was better she was still sleeping. He reeked of cigarettes and alcohol.

CHAPTER TWENTY THREE

Wake Up Call

Max woke the following morning, finding Nicole sick in the bathroom. It was a disturbing pattern. He instantly remembered the last time in his hotel suite in the Plaza Hotel in New York, Nicole had become nauseous. Then, he had discovered her fiercely sick in his bathroom. It had been due to consuming too much alcohol the previous night. However, last night she had no alcohol. Nicole's bouts with sickness were beginning to paint a picture. Max contemplated the possibilities.

"Sweetheart, what's going on? How can I help?" Max asked compassionately. He gently pulled her long hair away from her face with his hand. "Let me wet a washcloth for you," he suggested. Then, quickly grabbing a cloth, he warmed it under the sink and wiped her face.

"Thanks. Sorry, I didn't mean to wake you so early," Nicole replied, sitting on the cold marble. Finally feeling strong enough to stand, Nicole, walked back to the bed and sat down.

"Would you like some cold soda or something to settle your stomach? How about crackers? Isn't that what you're supposed to do?"

Max questioned, sweating profusely. "Sweetheart, I'm losing it right now. Look, my hands are shaking," he stated, barely able to speak as he sat down on the bed next to her. "Is there something you need to tell me?" Max blurted out, not believing his own words.

"It's not yours. So calm down," Nicole laughed. "Don't worry. You're off the hook."

"Oh my God," Max sighed, standing up as he rubbed his forehead. "Are you sure? You're positive," he repeated, pacing the floor. "I need a strong drink and a cigarette."

"You're acting silly. Sit down. I suppose we should talk."

"I'll say we need to talk," Max exclaimed. "Nicole, you almost gave me a heart attack. I mean, I was beginning to freak out for a minute. But, Sweetheart, I'm just not ready for kids. Honestly, I've never wanted kids," he turned to look at her earnestly.

"Max, come here and sit down. You're overreacting," Nicole patted the bed.

"Okay," he replied, wiping his forehead with the warm cloth he had gotten for her.

"Listen, I wasn't going to tell you. I never planned on you knowing, at least not now. It's Drew's baby. Trust me. You're probably as surprised as I am. No one knows yet. You're the first person I've told. I had no idea when I left Vancouver after losing Nicholas that I was pregnant. All I can say is this baby is a miracle. No one could understand what this baby means to me. He or she is a new beginning for me and Drew. Unlike you, I adore children. Drew and I wanted more children," Nicole paused to wipe her eyes.

"Sweetheart, aren't you and Drew getting a divorce?" Max questioned, staring intently at Nicole. Had he missed something? He was more confused than ever at this point. He thought they would build a life together, an empire perhaps.

"Yes. I guess the right word here would be *were*. I've decided to go back to Vancouver today. I'm getting Drew and our marriage back on track. Max, I like you a lot. However, I was never in love with you, nor were you in love with me. I think you'd agree if we're truly honest. You've always treated me with kindness. But, on the other hand, I've always suspected an ulterior motive. Maxwell Kline, you know what, you and I are alike. You're driven. I can respect that. So am I, but there's a huge difference. Here's where our similarities end. I don't want to build an empire at this point. I just want my family back. I don't have to reach the pinnacle of success by sacrificing people," Nicole looked back at Max with the emotion of a woman who's being given a second chance. "Drew means the world to me, and it took this new child of ours to realize it. I really screwed up. I need to make Drew's transition back into my life as easy as possible. Maxwell Kline, you're fired."

"Sweetheart, you've got this all wrong. Trust me. I had planned to help you grow this organization into a much larger one. I have plans for us," Max insisted relentlessly. Surely he couldn't be hearing her correctly. What person would turn down the opportunity to build something bigger than themselves?

"Oh, I'm sure you thought so. However, those plans will never materialize, at least not with me. You've been a huge lesson learned for me. Max, I like you as a person. We just disagree on business. I don't need you to become successful in the music industry, and I won't allow you to use me so that you become successful. Got it? I'll get you back to New York. Oh, I hope you remember how to use a ticket because it will be a commercial flight for you today. I'm taking the jet back to Vancouver.

Max quickly grabbed his things and slammed the door on his way out. It was the last Nicole ever saw of Maxwell Kline.

Calling Cameron and Lance up to her suite, Nicole needed to speak with them. After that, she was going home to get her husband back.

Hearing a knock at the door, Nicole walked over.

"Hey, guys, come in. Have a seat. I know this isn't an office, but it'll have to do since we're on tour. We don't have much time, so I'll try to hurry. I just fired Maxwell Kline," Nicole said, watching their expressions for any signs of concern or stress.

"I knew it," Lance grinned. "I had the feeling he was on his way out."

"Sis, what's going on?" Cameron inquired, utterly shocked.

"Well," Nicole smiled. "I'm pregnant."

"What?" Cameron gasped.

"Wow," Lance remarked, scratching his head. "I think we all knew you weren't feeling your best."

"I took a pregnancy test last night while Max was downstairs in the lounge. It was positive," she smiled.

"Sis, please don't tell me it's Max's baby," Cameron demanded. He couldn't fathom the idea of this man becoming a permanent addition to his life.

"Calm down. It's Drew's baby. I had no way to know I was pregnant in Vancouver. I was so devastated when we lost Nicholas," Nicole explained.

"Oh, Sis, I can't believe this. I'm so happy for you," Cameron smiled, jumping up to put his arms around Nicole.

"Congratulations, Nicole. I couldn't be happier for you," Lance smiled warmly.

"Thank you. I can't even begin to tell you how excited and happy I am. There's no need to get into the reasons why I fired Max. It's a long story. Let's just get on with business. I think I knew that he wasn't right for our organization from the beginning. Let's just leave it for now and save the discussion for later. We're short on time this morning. I know you both have a meeting scheduled at the radio station later today. Here are my thoughts. I'm going to take the jet back to Vancouver today. I'm going to get my husband back," Nicole smiled radiantly.

"Really, today?" Cameron questioned, looking at Lance for confirmation of this.

"Yes. I don't want to wait a minute longer," Nicole laughed.

"Nicole, don't worry about a thing. Go with our blessings. We've got everything covered. The musicians are in sync with Cameron and the songs he performs on stage until there's almost no need for an orchestra conductor. However, our pianist, Brian Newman, can also queue the musicians regarding song selections. I'm trying to say simply that it's not going to be a problem with Max gone. When you're ready to hire his replacement, we'll simply go back to my trusty old Rolodex," Lance laughed, shrugging his shoulders.

"Thanks, Lance. I plan on leaving within the next two hours or as soon as the jet is fueled. Hopefully, if everything goes according to plan, I should be back before you leave for Istanbul. I'll see you both when I get back. Cameron, stay out of trouble, and good luck with your performance tonight. I know you've got this," Nicole smiled, giving him a huge hug and kiss.

"Well, I think we should let you start packing. Have a safe flight. I'll see you when you return," Lance added.

"Please give my love to Jerry and Kate," Cameron smiled.

"I will."

Boarding the plane felt surreal. Nicole was once again on her way back to Vancouver.

"Welcome aboard, Mrs. Connors. How are you this morning?" Nina inquired.

"Great. I can't wait to get home."

"We should be in the air soon. Can I bring you a beverage or something to eat before we're airborne?" Nina asked.

"Maybe ginger ale and saltine crackers," Nicole laughed, placing her hand across her tummy.

"Okay, I'll be right back with those," Nina answered, oblivious to the reference from Nicole.

"Mac said to inform you that our weather looks good into Vancouver. So we should be there in approximately eleven hours," she smiled, handing her the drink and crackers.

"Great. Thanks, Nina," Nicole smiled, attempting to get comfortable in her seat.

Looking out her window, Nicole saw the Parthenon and the Acropolis as their jet circled Athens. It was as stunning as Max had mentioned. However, she would tour those later with the love of her life. Right now, there was only one view she longed to see. It was the skyline of Vancouver.

Nicole managed to sleep during most of the flight. She hadn't planned on getting any work done during this time. Nicole had other things on her mind which were more important. Finally, after grueling hours spent in the air, she was close to home.

"Mrs. Connors, we are only one hundred miles out from Vancouver.

I wanted to let you know. Would you like a warm towel and a cup of coffee," Nina inquired.

"Yes. That sounds wonderful," Nicole smiled.

After refreshing herself with the warm towels and enjoying a cup of coffee, she took a quick peek out her window. She began to see the most precious sight of all coming into view, the gorgeous skyline of Vancouver.

As the private jet touched down on the runway, she was *home*. The implication of this one single word was everything to her. As the plane slowly stopped, she noticed the limo waiting for her arrival. Her journey was almost over. Only a short drive out to Glen Haven Manor stood between her and the love of her life.

Nicole's heart raced as the car slowly wound its way down the steep mountainous roads toward the lake. Hopefully, Drew was there. But she had no way to know for sure. She hadn't bothered to call. Then, finally, the manor house came into view. Slowly, the car entered the driveway stopping at the front door. Jumping out of the car without closing the door, Nicole ran up to the front door and rang the doorbell. Quickly, the door opened.

"Oh, Mom, it's so good to see you," Nicole smiled as tears ran down her face.

"Sweetheart, you're home," Kate cried, taking Nicole in her arms. "I've missed you terribly. I love you. I'm so sorry. Can you ever forgive me?" Kate wept.

"Mom, it wasn't your fault. It was an unfortunate accident. Is Drew here?" Nicole asked, anxiously searching for a glimpse of Drew.

"Oh, Sweetheart, he's down at the boathouse with Jerry. None of us knew you were coming home today. Do you want me to go down and get him?" Kate asked.

"No. Thanks, Mom. I want to surprise him."

Nicole sprinted through the house, almost tripping on a throw rug. Then, opening the massive French doors that faced the lake, she caught sight of Drew in the distance.

"Babe, I'm home," she yelled, running toward him.

As Drew looked up, the expression on his face, even from a short distance, was priceless. He ran to meet her with open arms.

"Doll, you're home. You're home," Drew repeated, scooping her into his arms. "What took you so long? Babe, I've missed you so much. I knew you would come back. I would have waited forever. Thank God you didn't make me wait that long," Drew smiled, kissing her repeatedly.

"Babe, we need to talk," Nicole smiled, reaching for his hand. "Let's take a walk along the shore," she suggested.

"Jerry and I built a bench last month. We dedicated it to Nicholas. It has his name carved on it. Why don't we walk over and we can sit there? Is everything all right?" Drew worried.

Reaching the bench, they sat down.

"Doll, it feels so good to hold you, touch you," Drew smiled, continually touching her face.

Taking both his hands, Nicole gently placed them over her stomach. Tears slowly began rolling down Drew's face.

He knew.

The following day on their way to the airport, Nicole asked the chauffeur to make one last stop before leaving Vancouver. As the limo parked at the entrance of the Mausoleum, Nicole took Drew's hand walking inside. Nicole and Drew had to say goodbye to their sweet little boy.

"Sweetheart, Mommy, and Daddy love you. God let us have you for three short years, but you'll always be with us. Nicholas, you're going to be a big brother. Somehow, I think you already know. Rest in peace.

EPILOGUE

Seven months later, while on tour in Quebec, Canada, Nicole went into labor. Racing to the hospital, they made it just in time for Drew to scrub and put on the necessary items that allowed him to be present in the delivery room.

"Nicole, one more strong push," the doctor urged. "Just one more," he insisted. Within moments, the cries of a newborn filled the room.

"It's a girl," the doctor announced.

"Babe, we have a daughter," Drew screamed. "She has curly black hair," he smiled. "She looks a lot like Nicholas," he cried.

As the nurse gently laid the tiny infant in Nicole's arms, she quickly counted little fingers and toes.

"She's perfect," Nicole smiled.

The arrival of Nikki Katrina Connors had blessed their world.

After years of being in management, Nicole finally reached the status of an icon in the music industry. Her name was world renown. She had finally reached the pinnacle of success. Nicole had suffered scrapes and bruises on her journey to the top but not once had she stepped on others to achieve her dreams.

Looking back over her long career, she had finally found the answer to the one question that had consumed her in the beginning, "Was their room at the top for a female?"

The answer was a resounding, *"Yes."*